THE CORNISH SERJEANT

The Cornish Serjeant

A Novel

SHEILA REDDICLIFFE

WILLIAM KIMBER · LONDON

First published in 1984 by
WILLIAM KIMBER AND CO LIMITED
100 Jermyn Street, London SW1Y 6EE

© Sheila Reddicliffe, 1984
ISBN 0−7183−0538−8

Typeset by Scarborough Typesetting Services
and printed in Great Britain by
Biddles Limited, Guildford and King's Lynn

Contents

A map of part of mediaeval Cornwall
and Devon appears on pages 48–9,
drawn by Mr R. D. Penhallurick of
the County Museum, Truro, Cornwall

Author's Note on Place Names

The spelling of mediaeval place names was largely a question of phonetics and the clerk's interpretation; some places would be spelt differently in the same document. The spellings used in this book have been selected from the Register of Patent Rolls and other documents of the period as being the nearest phonetically to our twentieth-century pronunciation.

TO THE W.I.

for its educational opportunities
and the encouragement to stretch our talents
beyond the kitchen sink

PART ONE

Visions of Youth

1

Little did John realise, when he set off to ride over to his uncle's farm at Pengelly, that a chance encounter he would make that bright spring day in 1417 was to change his whole life.

Full of excitement, and a little nervous — for this was the first time he had made a long day's journey on his own, and there had been tales, even here in Cornwall, of foot-loose soldiers from the French wars turned highway robbers and murderers — he waved goodbye to his two small sisters and rode his pony up the lane and on to the moor.

A stonechat eyed him cautiously from the tip of a distant furze bush, and as he headed north-eastward along the escarpment track a flock of meadow pipits flitted away over the heather, piping excitedly to each other, dipping and clustering where one had found breakfast, then scattering towards other feeding grounds on the higher moor. Below, to his right, the valleys awoke to a still morning of dew drenched sunshine, with shreds of fleecy white mist still hovering along the line of the several river courses where the sun's warmth had not yet penetrated. Beyond them the tors of Dartmoor formed the distant backdrop, soft browns and greens emerging from the lower shadows as the sun reached them. Alone, in the middle distance, one solitary hill raised its craggy summit above the valley mists; John stopped for a moment, searching the lower slopes of that hill for his uncle's farm, and fancied that he found it, a huddle of thatch at the head of a wood, just beyond a small town.

He continued on his way, letting the pony amble at its leisure as he sniffed the sharp moorland air and gazed at the emerging world below as a prince might survey his kingdom. He had quite forgotten his fear of strangers, of robbers and unknown dangers; in the beauty of the morning he was lord of the land. Half closing his eyes he imagined himself a knight errant who had just rescued a damsel in distress and was now proceeding in triumph to her father's castle.

The pony's hoof rang against a stone. John almost fell from its back in startled surprise as two buzzards scrambled clumsily into the air with a frantic flapping of huge wings, from almost under his feet. Recovering his seat he pulled the pony to a halt and watched the birds in fascination as the air cushioned their great bulk and they glided away with grace and ease. Soaring, gliding and mewing the while they went, away to the south-east where a strange flat-topped hill seemed an inviting landing place. Cadsonbury! The hill of mystery; some said Merlin had once lived there and even that it was the ancient Camelot, and John had always longed to explore it.

Thoughts of his mission evaporated as the sun climbed higher and a boy's romantic imagination waxed stronger. He would find Camelot this very day!

As he pulled his pony round and urged it down a steep path leading from the moorland pastures to a hamlet nestled at the foot of the escarpment, John excused himself with the thought that the southern highway was more direct, and only entailed fording the river Lynher instead of crossing it by the stone bridge at Rillaton further north. Conveniently he forgot that his mother had advised the northern route as being less frequented by strangers and therefore safer.

He came out on a bridleway where the going was easy and the pony broke into a happy canter. But the main highway, when they reached it, was another matter; deeply rutted by the wheels of wagons and wains, there were places where huge muddy pools stretched from one hedgebank to the other. The pony picked its way with care, as John strained to see the flat hilltop reappear through the trees ahead.

Had he gone the wrong way? It seemed hours since he had left the moors and started winding his way among fields and woods. Perhaps it really was a magic hill and had just vanished. His heart sank, and disappointment blurred his eyes.

The road straightened and flattened, and there, suddenly, over the hedgebank packed with primroses, and across a stretch of surprisingly flat land, stood Cadsonbury.

It was a beautiful round, with the top seemingly sliced off and a great ditch and bank clearly visible round its perimeter. Behind it dense woods made a sharp contrast to the bareness of the hill under the cloudless blue sky.

I must get up there, thought John. He set the pony to a canter along the flat road until they came to a gap in the hedgebank where a track led across a rough meadow, past a thatched mud hovel in a yard swarming with children and pigs — who all stopped screaming and squealing to stare at John as he rode past. The track passed close to the foot of the steep slope of the fortress hill, before dropping away down a narrow valley, and there John tethered his pony to a tree and, taking the saddlebag in which his mother had packed food and a flask of ale, scrambled up to a gap in the massive barricading bank. Breathless, he emerged into a vast upland island, smooth, green and inviting. The surrounding bank sheltered it from the breeze, and right by him bees were humming among early spring flowers. There was, however, no sign of Merlin's cave or the ancient city of Camelot.

Disappointed, he sauntered across the smooth green sward, startling four sheep which scuttled away to stand in an anxious cluster watching him from a safe distance. It was past noon and he was hot and hungry, but still inquisitive. He dropped his bag in the shelter of the far bank and climbed to the top — and found the world at his feet.

Far below him the river wound past meadows and marshland, its further bank a precipitous slope densely covered with oak and ash trees just bursting into leaf, amongst them magnificent beeches still pearly grey and leafless. Downstream the woods stretched right down to the river's edge on the near side too, and he could see over the tree tops to the widening valley where the river took yet another twisting turn towards the sea.

What a stronghold! If this wasn't Camelot it was certainly made by people as a fortress. Who were they? Bemused by his own thoughts he jumped back into the encampment, where the huddle of sheep still stood motionless, alert to his every movement. But John was not concerned with sheepfarming now, his thoughts were on wars and tournaments, the marching of armies and the flight of arrows. He settled himself against the bank and munched his way absentmindedly through bread and cheese. It was probably the ale which was his undoing, for in the warmth of the afternoon sun he was soon fast asleep.

His dream of tournaments was not a happy one. He did not win the lady's favour, and then found himself unhorsed and lying on the ground with his adversary standing over him, sword upraised. The menace was so real that he awoke from his dream, only to find a real life adversary standing over him, silhouetted menacingly against the setting sun.

'To your feet, varmint!' growled the stranger. John blinked, rubbed his eyes and hurriedly scrambled to his feet. As he stood up he realised to his great relief that the stranger was no warrior in chain mail but a boy, only slightly taller than himself, and the weapon threatening him only a willow stake. Courage seeped back into his sun-warmed body, he shook off the remnants of sleep, squared his shoulders and faced the stranger.

'I do no wrong. I only rested awhile before continuing my journey.'

There was a note of defiance in his voice, which made the other boy scowl. For a moment the two stood facing each other, tensed, measuring up and preparing for battle — well, for a scrap rather than a tournament jousting. Then the moment of tension eased, the stranger relaxed, lowered his weapon to rest on the ground and looked enquiringly at John.

'Why did you climb to the top of Cadsonbury for your rest?' he asked in a more friendly tone of voice. 'This is my castle, and I allow none to enter here without my permission.'

Without waiting for John's reply he indicated with a sweep of his arm the whole expanse of the enclosed hilltop and launched into a detailed description of the guard posts, the barracks, the king's palace and the pleasure gardens with which his imagination had supplied it. John listened with rapt attention, believing every word because this was just what his own boyhood dreams had expected to find here. He glanced shyly at the dramatic figure beside him, sensing a regal confidence in the dark aquiline features and the slim straight figure. The boy's homespun tunic was similar to John's, but under it he wore a fine linen shirt, and it was held neatly to his hips by a girdle of finely embossed leather which also carried a leather purse. John had no belt or purse, and the message which he was carrying to his uncle was in his head — and now temporarily forgotten. Hardly daring to breathe, he whispered: 'Are you King Arthur?'

The question startled the other boy and broke the make-believe. He laughed, and sat down on the grassy bank amongst the violets and primroses, picking up a weather-beaten old beaver hat which he slapped on the back of his head.

'No, I am not King Arthur. Would that I were! I am Nicholas Ayssheton, and my home is over the river beyond Calyngton town. Who are you?'

'I am John of Fursdon in St Cleer parish. I go to visit my uncle, Henry Hicks of Pengelly, with a message from my mother.'

He paused. A peacock feather attached to the beaver hat danced a little dance as the other boy nodded slightly, his deep brown eyes still watching John attentively. John cleared his throat and continued, his eyes riveted on the peacock feather still nodding from the beaver hat.

'My father died two years ago, of a coughing sickness in the late winter. Since the days of the Black Death in my grand-father's time we have had no bondmen to work the land, and my father was mainly rearing sheep. Now he has gone, and the flock has increased to more than two hundred ewes and lambs, and we will need help with the shearing, come the summer.'

He hung his head in shame as he went on to explain that he had been too small to learn the skill before his father died, so now he was to beg the help of his uncle and cousins until he was practised enough to do all the shearing himself.

'Two hundred fleeces? That would be a mighty task, even for a grown man,' said the other boy, drawing in his breath in an appreciative whistle. The peacock feather danced again, and John's heart thumped with excitement at the compliment from so grand a person. Who was he? Surely a person of great import-ance?

Again the day-dream was shattered, as Nicholas Ayssheton

explained that he lived at Theupath, a neighbouring farm to that of Henry Hicks. In spite of his natural swagger and self-assurance he seemed to be only a farmer's son like John, and like any local boy he knew shortcuts and offered to guide John over the ford and up through the woods. John accepted with enthusiasm, and a few minutes later the two were running full tilt down the steep hillside to where both had left their mounts tethered under the trees.

They rode back together to the highway and turned towards the river, John on his shaggy moorland pony following behind the well-groomed glossy black stallion on which Nicholas rode as one born to the saddle. The animals picked their way with care down gullies left by the winter rains as the highway dropped sharply into the river valley. They came out on the river bank in front of a smithy, but the forge was not working and they found the blacksmith down by the ford, standing barefoot in the shallow water as he washed the day's grime off his body and clothes.

'Good day to you, Master Nicholas.'

'Good day to you, Robert, I will be down tomorrow with my father's horse. He goes to Exeter to attend the lord bishop's court.'

As they splashed across the river John heard the boy ahead of him add, almost as an afterthought to himself: 'And one day I shall go with him.' John wondered why anyone should want to go to Exeter, it seemed to him as far away as the moon. From what he had been told it was peopled by grand lords and ladies who even spoke in a language no Cornishman could understand, and anyone travelling the difficult road over the moor ran the risk of being robbed and murdered. His uncle's farm at Calyngton was as far as John ever wished to venture away from home.

They left the river behind them and climbed out of the valley through the woods, up a deeply gouged and rutted track even more precipitous than the one they had descended. Dusk was falling as they reached the open heathland and the road levelled out. An engraved waystone in the hedgebank marked the track branching off to the north to Calyngton market gate, but Nicholas ignored it and trotted on eastward on a bridleway between enclosed fields and open common land.

'No need to go through the town,' he explained to John. 'This way is shorter. I will leave you where the Pengelly farm track runs down to into the grove. Theupath lies further ahead, but perhaps you may ride over and see it before you return to Fursdon.'

'I must go home tomorrow, my mother needs my help.'

John spoke sadly, for he longed to see more of his new-found friend. The easy air of command and the masterly self-confidence, so foreign to John's own nature, attracted in him a hero-worship he had never before experienced in his short life. Here was someone he could follow to the ends of the earth. But the practical side of his nature told him clearly that this was no time for daydreams; as the man of the family he was needed at home. He sighed, audibly, and the object of his thoughts shifted uneasily in his saddle, sensing an emotional situation. They trotted on together in silence, rather slowly, as if to make the last part of the journey take as long as possible.

Suddenly, round the corner of the Cornish hedge which they were following appeared a trotting donkey, the bell on its neck tinkling agitatedly, and its passenger bumping up and down like a load of hay on a rough road. It drew up alongside, and the load of hay revealed itself to be a corpulent friar.

'Young masters! Take care!' panted the friar, clinging to the donkey's ears as he struggled to straighten his robe and recover his dignity. 'There are footpads ahead, just over the brow of the common, where the hedge ends. They tore my sandal from my foot, and would have had my saddlebag too, had it not been securely fastened and the ass fleet of foot!'

John's courage drained away and his legs turned to jelly. This was just what his mother had feared. Fleetingly he thought to himself that if he had gone by the Rillaton bridge as instructed he would by now have safely reached his uncle's farm by the other route.

Nicholas's decision was instant. 'Then we must go down through the town,' he declared, turning his horse in its tracks. 'Come, good friar, you are safe with us,' and he trotted back a few yards, then set his horse at the bank and cleared it with just the lightest touch.

Desperate not to be left behind, John did the same with his pony, which scrambled over in less dashing fashion, followed by the friar virtually wrapped around his donkey. They cantered across a field in the gathering dusk, over another hedge, and found themselves in a narrow path between cultivated strips of beans and corn. Ahead of them some lights flared, and suddenly they emerged between two buildings into a lighted market square.

It was the end of the day. Teams of oxen stood patiently in the shafts as baskets and bundles were loaded on to the wagons. A drover shouted for passage as he steered his wain, piled high with fleeces, through the crowd towards the western gate. As the three riders crossed the market place the stench of blood, bones and entrails from the shambles was overpowering, but Nicholas seemed unaffected, and pressed on past the old stone monument in the market centre. He pulled up on the far side by the lighted doorway of a small chapel, and turned to the friar.

'May Saint Nicholas go with you, good friar,' he said, in a tone of polite dismissal. 'Here in this chapel you may find rest and shelter.'

The friar began a long paean of praise, but Nicholas cantered off down the street and John hastened after him. At the bottom of the hill where a small flat bridge spanned the stream, Nicholas reined in his horse and waited for John to catch up with him.

'I had to leave him there,' he said, answering John's unspoken question; 'he would not have been a welcome guest at Theupath. I doubt whether he will go into the church; I can picture him already in the hostelry on the other side of the street, earning himself a free night's lodging with his tale of footpads.'

'Was it not then a true story?' asked John in puzzlement.

'Likely it was, but well-embroidered to make a good tale in the telling. Come, let us press on. Now we have come this way I can deliver you to your destination.'

They crossed the bridge and immediately turned off the main highway into a narrow lane running eastward through a wooded valley. By now the full moon had risen and they were able to pick their way up the track, emerging among open fields with the shadow of farm buildings a short distance ahead. As they drew rein at the farm entrance dogs barked and a figure appeared in the doorway of a lighted shippon.

Nicholas spoke quietly, almost under his breath, to John. 'I will come down tomorrow morning.' Then he was gone. John slid down from his pony and led it into the farmyard to meet his uncle.

The arrangements for sending help to Fursdon were soon made, and before he settled to sleep that night in the big feather bed which he shared with his cousins, Henry and Thomas Hicks, John had also learned something of the history of Nicholas Ayssheton.

Aunt Christian had pursued her lips in silent disapproval when John related his meeting with Nicholas, and so he did not dare to tell her that a visit was to be expected the following morning. But he was secretly delighted when his uncle suggested that John should stay a few days with the family at Pengelly.

As they sat quietly by the dying embers of the peat fire in Pengelly kitchen, John eventually summoned all his courage to put the question hovering in his mind.

'Aunt Christian,' he asked apologetically, 'who *is* Nicholas Ayssheton? He has the air of someone other than a farmer's son.'

There was a long pregnant pause. John wished he had not spoken. Then his aunt murmured softly, almost to herself – 'Aye, he is a farmer's son. One that loves to give himself airs. His father grazes a thousand sheep on Hingston Down and keeps a goodly herd of cows in the home pastures, but never do you see Master Nicholas herding the flock or pitching the hay. The only farm work he ever does is tending the horses.'

'He is good with horses – he has a fine seat and rides well.' This came from Uncle Henry, who was still studying the dying fire, stirring the mound of ashes with his boot.

'He has ambition, that one,' continued Aunt Christian. 'I doubt we shall see him overlong at Calyngton once he has finished his schooling at Tavistok Abbey.'

'He is training for the church?' John asked in some astonishment.

'Bless you no, not him! His grandmother ended her days there at the convent, and she left provision for his education by the monks – education for a gentleman.'

The trace of jealousy in her voice so surprised John, who knew his aunt for a warm, kind-hearted soul, that he gawped at her, amazed. She saw the look on his face and hastened to correct herself. 'Not that he is a bad lad really, but different. He has a will of his own, and grand ideas — ideas which do not fit in with our way of life.' Christian paused, gazing into the dying fire, then turned to John with an air of resolution:

'You are young for the ways of the world, nephew,' she said, 'but perhaps you should know the story of the Aysshetons. Nicholas's father, Reginald, is a bastard, the son of old Hubert of Aiston and the Lady Catherine Arundell. They say that the old man was something of a handsome galant in his youth. She was only fifteen, and with her father at Peverell for the bishop's visitation when they met. Hubert swept her off her feet and seduced her; the poor child in her innocence had no defence against a man of experience. Months later when her condition became apparent, she was sent to the nuns at Tavistok by her outraged parents. There Reginald was born — and there his lovely young mother stayed to the end of her days.'

Her voice trailed into silence. John prompted her eagerly: 'What happened to Reginald?'

She seemed unaware that he had spoken.

'I remember the Lady Catherine as a benign and gracious old lady,' she continued, 'She was much revered by the good folk of Tavistok as a giver of alms to the poor and as a comforter of any young woman in distress. She never knew her son. The newborn babe was put to a wet nurse and his mother never allowed the joy of suckling him or even cradling him in her arms. Prayers of penitence became her lot in life — and she a fresh young girl barely sixteen years of age.'

'But what became of the boy?'

Henry took up the story: 'Hubert had him brought to Aiston and forced his wife to accept the child as one of the family. I remember him as a belligerent little demon, doing battle with his elder brothers, and constantly being scolded by the girls for errors which were none of his doing. They all resented him in every way, and even more so when he grew into his father's favourite. From time to time he would disappear, when it was said in Calyngton that he was summoned by his grandfather to give account of himself. When he returned from these visits, he was always more pugnacious than before, and would fight any of us local lads who crossed his purpose. So of course we did not care for him either, and his reputation has stuck to his son. The family feud might have simmered down if he had not flaunted his own parentage by building a chapel on his land in memory of the mother he had never met. The legitimate family bitterly resented this, and the whole town has disliked him ever since. His marriage to Will Crabbe's daughter Susannah did nothing to improve his popularity, for the Crabbes are too much in the pocket of Squire Champernowne, John, to be popular with tenants of the manor. Their son Nicholas seems much of the same mould as his father. No one likes his air of superiority in our small community, and there are many, like your aunt, who say that he will soon shake the dust of Calyngton from his feet and make his name in the wider world.'

'But I did not find him at all superior, as you call it,' protested John hotly. 'A leader, yes, a captain, but also a friend. At no time did he behave to me as if I were a person of no account.'

'And why should he indeed?' declared his aunt indignantly, 'and you a Fursdon, as well born as any Ayssheton!'

'We are only poor farmers, aunt,' murmured John.

'Ah, but of good stock and your family has held Fursdon since Saxon times. One day you will prosper again as your family did before the terrible time of the Black Death.'

She rose from her stool to go to bed, bringing the discussion to an abrupt end.

2

The following day was one of such happiness for John that he remembered it always, with pure pleasure, even through the vicissitudes of later years. He had slept late in the airless dusk of the garret under the thatch at Pengelly, and did not hear either of his cousins get up. A call from his aunt below eventually roused him, and he tumbled out of bed and down the ladder to find Nicholas Ayssheton being hospitably entertained by Christian to a breakfast of buttermilk and fresh crusty bread.

His cousin Henry had been bringing in the cows for milking

when Nicholas rode up to the farm gate, and he later recounted
to John how the unwelcome visitor had so charmed his mother
by his deferential courtesy that she had put down her milking
stool and offered him refreshment. The pair were chatting
amiably when John appeared, making him wonder if the previous night's conversation had been merely a dream. He ran out
to the well to douse his head in the bucket and clear the cobwebs
of sleep from his eyes and brain, and then joined them at the
table.

Nicholas explained to Christian that he wished to take John to
the fair and show him the town in daylight. She was so charmed
by his manner that she quite forgot her wholesale disapproval of
his family and readily gave permission.

But when the boys rode out of the farm, Nicholas did not turn
down the lane towards the town but continued over the common and down through the lush pastures of Theupath on the
upper slopes of the Tamar valley, to his home. There, with
pride, he showed John a farmstead so different from the straw-
thatched huggermugger of byres and shippons at Pengelly, that
John was lost in wonder. Solid buildings of square cut moorstone, roofed with the blue slate from Delabole, stood on three
sides of a square, their arched doorways and mullioned windows
giving them a palatial appearance. The house facing them was
taller, and sported a cluster of chimneys. To the left of a massive
oak door the largest window John had ever seen glowed with
coloured glass between its granite mullions. Smaller windows
high up on the right showed that here was a home with lighted
bedrooms, and moreover there was a glint of glass in all the
windows. John resolved at once that Fursdon too must have its
windows glazed so that his mother and sisters could enjoy sunshine and light even on windy days instead of clapping to the
shutters.

'Do you like it?' asked Nicholas simply. John nodded.

'My father designed it himself,' continued Nicholas. 'He is
very talented in the art. He has ridden over to Exeter today at
the behest of my lord bishop to advise on his lordship's new
summer residence. Come, I will show you the work which is his
pride and joy.'

He led the way down a lane which brought them to a small
grove of trees on the slope of the valley. Framed in front of the

trees stood a tiny chapel, with a stream trickling from an opening in its eastern wall. Everything about the building was in miniature, even to the bellcote in which a small pealing bell hung. But the most surprising feature was the roof, which was neither slated nor thatched, but roofed entirely in long slabs of moorstone, which fitted together exactly in spite of their rough texture.

Nicholas lifted the door latch and led the way in. The only embellishment inside the chapel was an altar of highly polished pink and yellow stone which Nicholas described as Crenbeare marble. On it stood a tiny triptych in gold and sapphire blue depicting the Crucifixion on the centre panel, the Virgin Mary at prayer on one side panel and St Catherine kneeling by her martyr's wheel on the other side.

'My father painted that himself,' the boy told his friend proudly. 'He dedicated the chapel to St Catherine to honour his mother. Some folk disapprove of it, suggesting he sought to canonise his mother. They are too simple, they do not understand — although, indeed, my grandmother did deserve a martyr's crown, she was cruelly used by both families. He did right to remember her thus. He never did know her in person.'

Pointing to a shallow basin in the floor before the altar, where spring water bubbled gently up and ran away in a channel, Nicholas went on; 'I was baptised here, but there were no more after me as my mother died soon afterwards. One day my children will all be baptised here. My mother caught the coughing sickness from a travelling friar — that is why my father will welcome none of them at Theupath. Local people imagine that my baptism saved me from the sickness and they attribute healing powers to the waters of this spring. Any child with croup will be brought here and dipped — even on the rawest day in November or amid the snows of January! Much good it does them!' Both boys laughed at the credulity of the ignorant.

Outside the chapel they saw the several paths which led to the spring from all directions, and Nicholas pointed out the one which his father had ridden that morning to take him over Hingston Down to the river crossing into Devon. Then they walked back to the farm where the smell of new-baked bread persuaded them they were hungry once more, and they enjoyed a second breakfast in the huge stone-flagged kitchen where Ellin the cook was having a bake-day.

It was high noon when the two boys eventually rode down into Calyngton in the bright spring sunshine, with a cool wind from the sea blowing in their faces. Ahead of them, inland from the coast, the craggy western outcrops of Foyemoor showed clear and crisp. John shielded the sun from his eyes and tried to find his home in the fields below Carnedon, but while he knew where it should be, he could not make out the farm or its trees.

Ahead of them several ox carts trundled over the common, market-bound, and as they came within sight of the town a bustle of movement at the gates identified itself as a flock of sheep leaving the market. There was the tinkling of a bell, and a small brown shape at the head of the flock.

'Ah, that will be Erasmus,' said Nicholas, reining in his horse at the side of the track to await the flock's passing. 'Erasmus always accompanies Brother James, and leads the animals, whether they are milch cows, oxen or sheep. If Brother James should fall asleep on his mule one hot day, I swear Erasmus would take the animals safely home to Tavistok, not even losing one at the river.'

The donkey trotted sedately up the track, his bell tinkling a welcome. With a twitch of his long ears and a swish of his tail by way of greeting he continued past the boys, his woolly followers pressing behind him in a tight agitated pack. There were some two dozen ewes and a sprinkling of young lambs, and behind the concourse another brown shape. This one however was human, and Nicholas hailed him.

'Good day to you, Brother James. Have you done good marketing today?'

'Indeed, yes, Master Nicholas — and a good day to you. I found a good price for four oxen from Master Ferrers. Brother Hugh will be pleased with my work this day, for beside these fine creatures I have bought three rolls of good broadcloth and one of linen — fine quality linen, only recently received from Ireland by Humfrey the draper. And even then I have five marks of silver for Brother Hugh to lock away in the treasury.' He shook the leather purse at his girdle to indicate the wealth within, then hurried after his flock, pulling behind him a young donkey laden with his purchases.

'He's always early to market, and strikes the best bargains,' commented the knowledgeable Nicholas as he looked after the

retreating monk. Yet again John puzzled to himself why his
friend should be so unpopular with the townsfolk, when he
appeared to be always so amiable, so well informed and so ready
to talk sociably with anyone he met. But then he remembered
the scant courtesy meted out to the friar the previous evening,
and concluded that Nicholas reserved his charm for those whom
he knew and admired or liked. If so, did Aunt Christian realise
her great success this morning? He laughed aloud. Nicholas
asked somewhat indignantly the reason for his amusement, and
receiving no reply from the giggling John, set his horse at a
canter down the hill. John raced after him.

They tethered their horses behind a barn on the outskirts of
the town, and squeezed their way on foot along the crowded
main street. It was the second day of the annual three-day
charter fair. Yesterday, Nicholas explained, assuming once
more his role of guide, was mostly for the sale of fleeces and
leathers, even some shoes and garments. The cordwainers and
drapers did good business the first day of the fair, and many
bright new spring gowns and fancy shoes were paraded in the
town by the last day. This second day was 'on the hoof', and
tomorrow it would be the turn of the farm wives and dairy maids
with their eggs and poultry, round juicy cheeses and freshly
churned butter.

John did not fancy 'on the hoof' day. Farm boy though he
was, he still preferred an orderly farmyard with the midden
tucked away where its smell was least obtrusive. Calyngton Fore
Street seemed to him to be one vast midden, with the added
stench of many animals pressed together in the narrow street.
The two boys threaded their way between cows and horses and
the little knots of men discussing and examining the animals. At
last the street widened out into a central market area where
John recognised the weather-worn lantern cross which they had
passed in the dusk of the previous evening.

The doorway to a big timber-framed house they were passing
was adorned with a bundle of cloth, faded and torn and tied
together with faded ribbons. This was Humfrey the draper's
establishment, but without money on his person, John would
not dare to enter even just to admire the fine Irish linen. Next
to it a tumbledown building with a tattered thatch sprouting
weeds and dandelions sported a creaking signboard on which

the picture of a bull was just discernible. John nodded absent-mindedly to himself — 'at the sign of the Bull', yes, he had heard tales of that tavern, it was a place of ill-repute.

At that moment the door swung open and two men fell out backwards into the mire of the street. After them a dozen others surged, swinging their fists.

'Come away,' whispered Nicholas, turning back quickly. They pushed their way back to the narrow end of the street, where Nicholas turned in through an archway. There, in the middle of a cool, cobbled close, stood the town's well.

'Our Lady's well,' explained Nicholas, scooping up some of the water and making the sign of the cross before drinking. John followed his example, then they walked down the hill to the northern entrance of the town where on an open space all the fun of the fair was now gathered. They spent a happy hour watching the tumblers and fire-eaters, and a magician who produced a snow-white dove from Nicholas's tunic. Fortunately John had no money and Nicholas could only muster two groats from his fine leather purse, so they were not tempted to accept the challenge of the swordsman nor wrestle with the Stannaries champion, and neither had the taste for taking a look, for one groat each, at the bearded fat woman who bellowed continuously and with enormous venom from inside her tent.

Finally, as the sun sank towards the conical top of Carnedon, they retrieved their horses from the barn in the back lane and trotted slowly back to Pengelly, discussing the pleasures of the day and making plans to go to the fair again the next day.

However when the morning came it was obvious that Christian too proposed going to the fair, for when John rose from his bed bright and early he found his aunt dressed in her hooded cloak, and four large baskets covered with damp homespun cloths lying ready at the dairy door.

'I shall need help with these, nephew,' she said firmly, and handed him one of the baskets.

At that moment Nicholas rode into the yard. John stood, shamefaced, feeling more than a little foolish after their talks of knights and tournaments, to be found with a woman's basket in his hand.

Nicholas took in the situation at a glance. To John's surprise he did not laugh but took his horse into the stable, as if to walk into Calyngton was exactly what he had expected that morning. When he came out he picked up two of the farm baskets and stood alongside John ready to set off.

Christian had frowned with disapproval when he appeared at the gate, but now she positively purred. After a final scurry back into the kitchen, she picked up the remaining basket and with a beam of pleasure at Nicholas she led the way down the lane to the north gate of the town. The two boys walked in single file behind her.

As they crossed the little bridge near the crowded fairground and started up the hill to the market place a volley of whistles and catcalls followed their progress. John would have dropped his aunt's basket and run, but the sight of Nicholas ahead of him swinging nonchalantly along enabled him to keep his shame, and his fear, under control.

Suddenly a half-dried lump of horse dung landed squarely on Nicholas's face and fell away leaving his left eye and cheek covered with dirt. The crowd roared with delight and then a voice called, 'That'll smarten 'ee up, little squire.'

John pushed up behind Nicholas and took one of the baskets from him, and there were further shouts of derision as Nicholas drew out a white silk handkerchief with his free hand and wiped his face, his nonchalance now replaced by a look of smouldering anger.

Serenely unaware of the assault going on behind her, Christian advanced up the street towards the market. Something wet and smelly hit John on the back of his neck, and traces of dung fell on the basket cloth.

At that moment there was a yell of anguish from the crowd following behind them, and somewhere ahead a voice called out: 'Advance, ye varmints, at your peril!'

'Richard!' called Nicholas in obvious relief, and quickened his step.

On the raised entrance to a large but dilapidated house just below the chapel stood a miniature warrior behind a long-bow several feet taller than himself. He was only able to operate the bow by standing its base two steps below him, but his broad shoulders and strong arms revealed at once the natural bowman. He kept his fearsome weapon trained on the crowd, which quickly melted away like the snow in summer.

The boys pressed on up the hill and deposited Christian's baskets where she was to set up her stall for the day. Still unaware that anything untoward had occurred, she thanked them and asked them to return at sundown.

Freed of duty they sped away like two arrows from Richard's bow, and in no time at all they had joined him and were fingering and admiring the magnificent weapon.

Richard Chyket's father had fought as a bowman to the king at the great battle of Agincourt. He could no longer fight, a chest wound having left him wheezy and breathless. He now traded in wool, somewhat haphazardly when his health permitted, and at other times sat in the solar pensively gazing at his orchards and pasture and the distant moor hills beyond.

Today he had gone up to the market and the boys had the rambling old homestead to themselves. Richard led them to a quiet corner by the linhay where he had built a practice butt. Here he demonstrated what he had learned from his father on the use of the long bow, and here for most of the day the boys played at archery.

Richard and Nicholas were quite at home together, chaffing each other mercilessly over poor shots with the bow, and reinforcing arguments with a playful punch or two of fisticuffs. John stood aside, a little overcome at this sudden wealth of friendship after his lonely childhood on the farm. In fact, he felt a small pang of jealousy as he watched the two together and sensed that his wonderful friend Nicholas must be shared with this tow-haired, stubby Richard, who in spite of his small stature and shabby attire seemed to consider himself the superior of the slim and elegant Nicholas. And Nicholas, John could see, greatly admired his little friend.

Nicholas turned to him, his sharp perception immediately aware that something was amiss. He held out the long bow to him.

'Brother John, show us what a true yeoman can achieve.'

The word 'brother' restored John to his euphoria, and he joined in with enthusiasm at the archery.

After they tired of their attempts they walked through the tangled herb garden, which had been the pride and joy of Richard's mother before she died, and stretching themselves out on the grass in a sunny corner of the orchard, they talked of their ambitions for the future.

Richard was already determined to enlist for the French wars, as a bowman like his father.

'But you are too small for a soldier,' protested John.

Richard looked at him with disdain. 'I can prove my strength and my skill,' he said. 'The front rank bowmen must be shorter so that the men behind can shoot over them. I shall go. You'll see.'

John's protest turned to admiration as he thought of the vulnerability of the front rank.

Nicholas also had a driving ambition to be a soldier, and he confided to his friends that his great uncle had promised him a place in his entourage when he reached his fifteenth birthday.

'I have first to improve my grasp of Latin,' he said, admitting ruefully that he had not until recently devoted himself with any seriousness to his studies with Brother Luke at Tavistok. But, he added cheerfully, his sword play was superb, and he jumped up to demonstrate his skill with a piece of broken apple bough lying in the grass. The others rolled away for safety, laughing.

Nicholas thrust the point of his 'sword' towards John. 'And you, brother John, what will you do with life?'

'I must stay home and work for my mother,' John admitted reluctantly. 'Mary is only six and Elizabeth at three scarce tall enough to sit at table. And Mother has baby William to care for as well as the rest of us. We have no hired hands nowadays, I am the only man on the farm.'

The others murmured their sympathy at this unexciting prospect, and then promptly forgot it. Nicholas sat down against the trunk of an apple tree and gazed over at the little chapel just visible beyond the hedge.

'One day I shall build a fine new church for our town,' he said dreamily. 'I shall build it with a high tower pointing to the heavens and visible from all the countryside around. It will have big light windows and room inside so that no townsfolk will be shut out in the rain when mass is being said. It will even have a fine Delabole slate roof, such as my father put on the Theupath buildings.' He paused, then a fresh inspiration came to him. 'Yes, we will ask my father to design this church. Perhaps then people will forgive him for Theupath.'

It was to be twenty years before that dream was fulfilled, long after Reginald Ayssheton had died. But he left his son a folio of sketches and designs for the church, with full details of where the stone was to be obtained and where the most suitable oak timbers were grown. The townspeople did not forgive him, for they had long since forgotten him.

3

John did not see Nicholas or Richard again for several years. He went home to Fursdon the day after the fair, and work at the farm left him no time for going visiting again. Months later he heard talk at Liskerret market of young Richard Chyket of Calyngton having run away from home the day a recruiting band went through the town. From time to time his aunt dropped word in her messages that Nicholas Ayssheton had called to visit Pengelly when home from his studies, and John wondered longingly why Nicholas never rode over to Fursdon as well. It did not cross his mind that an invitation might be expected, and as he could neither read nor write no written message was ever sent.

Then suddenly, in the autumn of 1420, came word from Christian that Nicholas had gone to the French war as squire to Sir John Arundell.

John Fursdon, now a brawny farmer with broad chest and huge fists which ill-fitted his shy, quiet face, his blue eyes and silky fine hair, was so shaken by the finality of the news that he rode over immediately to Calyngton. There at Pengelly he found Christian in a distressed state, as though there had been a family bereavement. She told him how Sir John had ridden into Calyngton with his retinue, augmented his troops with thirty men from the parish and marched them south to embark for overseas at Landulph quay.

'And there was young Master Nicholas, close behind Sir John,' she sighed sadly, but proudly, as if describing the death of a loved one. 'Mounted on his fine black stallion, with silver spurs to his feet and a fine sword at his side.' She dabbed her eyes with the corner of her apron, and sighed. 'I can see them now, disappearing over the brow of Balston Down, and the pipes playing. Such a loss to Calyngton! He had great plans for it . . . a new church . . . a town school . . . an association of free-men to build up our commerce and prosperity . . . such a loss!'

'It was you who forecast that he would not stay long in Calyngton once he had finished his schooling,' John reminded her gently.

She nodded. 'Aye, I did, but I never thought to send him to his death!'

On his way home to Fursdon, John climbed once more to the summit of Cadsonbury. This time he did not go to sleep. He stood on the grass parapet with the wind-blown rain beating on his back and the leaves flying from the trees on the far river bank, and he gazed at the flood waters flowing out towards France.

He thought and he prayed.

PART TWO

All's Fair in Love

1

It was a very different Nicholas Ayssheton who returned to Cornwall some two years later. The gaunt and frowning man standing in the shelter of the *Esmeralda*'s poop as she moved slowly up river with reefed topsails, was generations away from the laughing, lively youth who had sailed down that water with the king's Cornish troops.

Absorbed in apparently gloomy thoughts, he gazed blankly at the wooded slopes slipping slowly by, showing not a flicker of interest as familiar landmarks came into view.

The ship's master muttered something under his breath to the helmsman, for the fourth time, and moved forward to accost his difficult passenger.

He tapped Nicholas on the shoulder, none too politely, and bowed slightly in an insolent manner.

'My lord?' Nicholas did not seem to hear him.

'My lord, we have reached the haven. I have brought you safely through all the storms of the English sea and successfully evaded the pirates of Prawle. Think you not I have earned the remainder of your passage-money? Shortly we will be off the quay at Halton Manor. They do not like me there and I fear to tie up alongside, lest they rob me of my ship and merchandise. If I am to risk my fortune doing so for your sake, I need the feel of those silver marks in my hand to give me courage.'

Still Nicholas did not move. Without any change of expression in his face he said flatly, 'You will have your money when I land. I will see you leave again in safety.'

The sailor swore softly to himself, indignant not only at his passenger's refusal to pay but even more at his arrogant attitude.

His anger might well have given way to violence against this haughty stranger but at that instant there was a violent lurch as the helmsman swung the tiller to port and with a creaking of yard-arms and a flapping of sails, the barque rounded the last bend in the river within sight of the quay at Halton.

In a flash bargaining was forgotten and the master sprang back to the duty of ensuring his ship's safety. It was a tricky moment, for as the *Esmeralda* left the shelter of the Devon bank, the full force of a south-easterly gale caught her on the beam and she heeled over, shooting Nicholas feet first into the scuppers.

As he picked himself up he realised how near to home he was, and clinging to the shrouds he searched ahead through the driving rain, keenly interested at last in the world about him.

He could just make out the grey bulk of Halton Manor and its huddled 'town' of workshops, cottages and barns, on the higher ground behind the water meadows. Straining his eyes he saw at last, past the meadows, the firm straight line of the quay with its lime-kilns and cottages, and the tiny chapel perched high on the quayside at the water's edge.

A few moments more and he could distinguish a small group of figures standing in the shelter of the chapel steps, watching the ship approach.

One of them he knew, would be Polder Hutchins, the manor reeve, who would be looking for landing dues or a charge for the storage of goods in the warehouse behind his cottage.

Then he recalled the captain's professed fear of the people at Halton, and for the first time he wondered whether he had been wise to come home in a strange ship.

However, here he was, home at last. With no baggage to encumber him he stood quietly by the bulwarks until the *Esmeralda* bobbed gently against the quay. Without waiting for her to be made fast he leapt ashore, then turned and flung a small leather purse back on to the deck where, only a short while before, the captain had been demanding payment.

Before the watchers by the chapel realised what was happening, a sharp order from the captain had converted *Esmeralda*'s landfall into a departure. She slipped past the quay, swung out into the river and was soon disappearing downstream with the ebbing tide, the crew shouting obscenities at Polder Hutchins as he shook his fists at them in frustrated anger.

The rest of the bystanders turned their attention to the newly arrived traveller, studying him in grave silence as he scanned their faces, looking in vain for a familiar or friendly face.

At last Nicholas broke the silence.

'Is there none willing to hire me a horse to take me home?' he demanded. A ripple of interest ran through the group, then from the back a voice called out bravely — 'And where's home?'

'Where would you suppose?' Nicholas retorted scornfully. 'Theupath, of course, where I have lived all my life. I trust that my home has not disappeared while I have been away on the king's business?'

'Why of course, it's Master Nicholas back from the wars!' It was Robert Clay of Southill who recognised the young man from Calyngton and hobbled forward to greet him. Taking both hands in his own and peering short-sightedly at the grey face, he declared tactlessly — 'How you have changed, young master!'

Receiving no reply or sign of recognition he hurried on: 'Wait you here while I go with Polder to the manor house and find you a good riding horse. Unhappily I have nought here but my wain loaded with lime for the fields.'

In a few moments he and the reeve were rattling away from the quay on a low-slung two-wheeled cart.

The crowd dispersed, and Nicholas sat down wearily on the quayside bollard to await their return.

The south-easterly blowing in from the river chilled his back with rods of hard, cold rain. The lime-kiln and cottage walls glistened with wet, and behind them the leafless trees and bushes waved strands of 'Old Man's Beard' disconsolately, as if saying goodbye for ever.

Nicholas looked grimly about him, finding nothing in the November landscape to welcome him home. He closed his eyes and let memory take him back to the higher summer of France.

Unhappily memory was unkind to him. Figures danced before him in scorching sunshine — but their feet never touched the ground as they swung at the end of the gallows' rope. Behind the long execution line, castle walls shimmered in the heat, and in the silence as the fifty bodies became still and limp he heard the peaceful plop of a frog diving into the green waters of the moat.

Then pandemonium broke loose. Before him hundreds of men, women and children, most of them ragged and barefoot, came running from the castle, screaming as they fell like nine-pins, caught by the deadly accuracy of the king's archers. He put his hands to his ears as if to shut out those remembered screams of terror, but he could not shut out from his mind's eye the spectacle of the wounded clinging desperately to the legs of the soldiers before being pushed into that peaceful green moat to drown.

Then he was with Lisette, in the refuge of his tent. But while the remembrance of her warm person pressed close to him brought an upsurge of warmth through his chilled, wet body, he could no longer see her at all. He sighed, wishing he could feel more romantic about that first experience.

'Good morrow, young sir.' Something brushed past him, and he opened his eyes to see a priest smiling at him from the foot of the steps leading up to the chapel. It was a chance reminder to Nicholas of his first duty on returning home safely. He stood up, shaking off at the same time his introspection and the rainwater collected in his hat brim, and followed the priest into the chapel.

As he knelt to pray, his thoughts turned to the king whom he had attended on similar occasions, to give thanks to the Almighty after a successful battle. Thinking of the body of Henry V now lying in state at Westminster, his first prayer was for the soul of his monarch, a man of inspiration and leadership who had known only warfare and killing since the days of his boyhood.

Robert Clay was waiting with a saddled horse when Nicholas emerged from the chapel, and he was soon riding away from the river, over the downs towards his home.

He had given the news of the king's death to the priest, and paid for a mass to be said the following day. They had wondered together at the future of their country with the nine-month-old Henry VI as its monarch, a baby who was also heir to the throne of France.

'This will surely bring more war,' the priest commented sadly, 'The people are worn out with wars and taxes, we need peace and a strong law to rescue us from the brigandage, the pillage and piracy which are now rampant in these parts.'

'Piracy, here, on our river?' asked Nicholas in surprise. Cornish pirates sailed from coastal harbours, and he had never associated them with inland areas.

'Even so,' replied the priest. 'The master of the ship which brought you here, did he seem an honest man to you?'

'A rough fellow, with a rough crew, but he did his work well. Had he been less skilled we might well have foundered on the Mewstone.'

'Perhaps he would respect the contract he had with you. But at other times he has respect for no man. He raids the river quays from time to time, when the weather out at sea is not to his liking. He robs hard-working Cornishmen of their wool and tin awaiting shipment, stealing in by night when the tide is right. I'm told he sells it at a handsome price at Winchelsea or Dover.'

'I took passage from Dover.'

'So, he was coming home. With this storm blowing in from the sea, we must expect a visit from him soon. Would that you were a law man, Master Ayssheton, not a military. It is a powerful law presence that is sorely needed here.'

As Nicholas rode away from Halton, half his mind was not on the anticipation of reaching home but on the words of the priest — 'Would that you were a law man.'

Well, he was certainly finished with soldiering, with its vicious brutality and its heartless disregard for the rights of innocent bystanders. The ragged, starving crowds that followed the army begging for bread, and the sight of whole villages burning, would, he felt sure, haunt him for the rest of his life.

Could service in the law be a happier path to fame and fortune?

He came to the junction where the bridleway curved away to the west to Calyngton town and distant Foyemoor. Neither was visible today in the driving rain sweeping across the landscape in the arms of the south-easterly gale.

Only a mile along the pack-horse road going north lay the shelter of his own home at Theupath, where Ellin would have a roaring fire in the big hearth and some good beef turning on the spit. The thought of Ellin brought him to a sudden halt, wondering what his welcome home would be.

Very probably she would be alone. If his father happened to be home on one of his very rare visits, the talk would be only of architectural progress at Exeter; accounts of war and pestilence in Normandy and Anjou would pass over his head like birds of passage unobserved.

And Ellin, poor simple soul, hardly knew the time of day. She lived only for cooking and cleaning, and humming profane tunes. How could she understand what he had been through, when her comprehending world ended at the farm gates?

A lump formed in Nicholas's throat, and hot tears of self-pity moistened his eyes. For the first time in his life he felt a desperate loneliness, accentuated by the pressing need for sympathy and comfort to ease the misery of his heart.

A sympathetic listener? Christian Hicks, why, of course! She who had listened to him patiently, even with interest, when he talked for hours about his plans and ambitions — she would soothe his battered soul. He turned the horse from the main roadway and splashed along the bridleway towards the town.

An hour later he was sitting in warm contentment at the hearthside at Pengelly, warmed both by the fire and the tankard of mulled ale in his hands, and also by the attentions of Mistress Hicks. She had produced a dry homespun shirt and braies for him to wear while his own soaked attire steamed before the fire, and then insisted that he eat half a loaf of bread spread thickly with her best butter and covered with sweet honey.

He sat there glowing, while Christian settled herself back at her spinning wheel. Her gentle voice matched the soothing action of the wheel as her fingers deftly produced fine thread from the wool heaped in a basket at her feet.

Lolling just inside the door stood Thomas and Henry, dripping pools of rainwater on to the slate floor from their mud-stained clothes. They had slipped in from their work, ostensibly on account of the storm, but really to get first-hand news of the war and the outside world from the returning warrior. Christian gave them short shrift, forbidding them to come near the fire or to remove any of their soaking garments, and Nicholas was aware of their glowering disapproval.

But he also knew why they had come in, and from time to time, as he supped his ale in the drying warmth of the fireside, he tossed — as crumbs to the poor — odd bits of news of the campaign in France.

He quite enjoyed telling them of the march south into Anjou when the Cornishmen were put under the command of the Duke of Clarence. He remembered the green spring countryside and the fields of Easter lilies nodding in the sunshine near towering castle walls, and he described for his male audience the triumphal march and capture of several magnificent castles.

But then the reality silenced him as he recalled the disastrous battle at Bauge. His audience waited. He sighed, took a deep breath, and started again.

'The duke, our commander, was struck down in battle and killed. I was only a few feet away when I saw him clubbed down by a huge ferocious creature in Scottish dress who shrieked and yelled the while, in a manner fit to curdle the blood.' He took a quick reassuring sip of his ale.

'It was the first time I had ever seen a man killed. Within a minute of urging us on to do battle with the enemy our leader lay smashed — literally — a lifeless mound of armour, blood and bits of skin.'

The spinning wheel had stopped. Christian shook her head slowly, in horror. Thomas and Henry merely shuffled their feet. Then Thomas demanded: 'Did you kill anyone yourself?'

'Ay, I did. I ran my sword through one young Frenchman, and sent another screaming from the field, with his arm hanging loose at the elbow. But those Scots! Ah, they were a different matter. To see a hundred of them tearing down the hill at you, swinging their clubs around their heads and shrieking in their weird tongue like a thousand devils — well, few men could withstand such an onslaught.

'Most of our troops turned and ran . . . my Lord Salisbury took command of the rest of us and we made a more orderly retreat, carrying the body of our commander the duke with us.'

'So you, the English, were defeated?' The question from Thomas was an accusation.

'Yes, we were defeated. But it was a battle fought, even if lost. I would sooner fight ten more such than endure one more siege like Rougemont or Meaux, even though we were the victors there.'

Only Christian noticed the bitterness in his voice.

Thomas protested angrily: 'But our lord the king never loses battles! I would have had you all hanged!'

'I understand that he was equally displeased at the defeat and distressed at the death of his brother the duke,' replied Nicholas, flatly. He gazed unseeing into the heart of the fire, and added slowly, 'He too is dead.'

'The king is dead? Lord bless us!' exclaimed Christian, shocked. Nicholas nodded, without lifting his head. Christian quickly recovered her composure and murmured a prayer for her dead monarch, and crossed herself. 'May he rest in peace.'

The door slammed. Nicholas looked up, and noted with some bitter amusement that the brothers had rushed out, keen to be the first to spread the sad news in the town.

Christian tossed her head at the unmannerly departure of her two sons, then picked up her stool and came to sit beside Nicholas.

'Tell me how it all happened,' she murmured softly, laying one arm round the boy's shoulders.

For the next hour Nicholas unburdened his memory of all the excitement, the disillusion and horror of his years at war. Then he told Christian how the king had sent for him during the campaign at Rougemont.

'He had heard my name and fancied I must be a cousin to his battle commander, Sir John Ashton, now the bailli of Cotentin on behalf of the king. When I admitted belonging to a bastard branch of an obscure Cornish family, he studied me carefully for several moments and then said: "I like your spirit in not claiming to be better than you are. Such honesty, allied with a fine appearance, deserves to go far." From that day I was attached to his personal entourage as one of his squires.'

'That was a fair reward,' murmured Christian, giving his shoulder a gentle squeeze.

'It had grave disadvantages.'

He slid down off his stool and settled himself on the floor with his arms resting on Christian's lap and his chin on the back of his hand.

'He was a noble and gracious king, and a supreme fighter.

But in the justice of his cause he lost touch with chivalry and justice for others. I excuse him now because I know that he was ill and in pain, and the more ill he became, the more bitter he grew and the more wanton in his killings. Murders, they were; pointless, savage and vindictive. There at Rougemont, when the castle fell into our hands he had the entire garrison of 500 — archers, pikemen, pages, esquires, even the knights — hanged on special gallows which he had had erected on the bank of the castle moat. This was after they had surrendered according to the accepted mode of warfare. And there they were hanged, fifty at a time, while the castle burned before their eyes and our bowmen shot down the camp followers as they tried to escape across the moat.'

His voice tailed off as the memory of that horrible day hit him again, and he buried his head in his arms.

Christian stroked the dark curly head on her lap without saying a word. Presently he emerged and gave his head a vigorous shake. 'I did save one life, quite by chance,' he continued. 'A young French girl — I took her with me and hid her in my tent until the morning when the pursuit was over and she was able to slip away. I suppose she went home. We could not talk as she knew no Latin or English and I speak no French. Now I cannot even recall her face.'

'But she did you good. You comforted each other, and that was good.'

Nicholas looked up at Christian in surprise, then nodded. Then he described to her how the English army sat in the mud outside the city of Meaux throughout a long hard winter, cursed alike by the starving townsfolk and the country people whose food stocks the soldiers commandeered.

The king's illness became worse and more apparent to all, and water sickness among the troops brought added misery and many desertions. 'Men who were too ill to fight were hanged because they went looking for a warm shelter in which to lie down and die.'

'War is like that. It is the way of men!'

'Ah, but need not be. Even the king imagined at times that he could have won his cause more magnificently and more nobly. After one of his bouts of pain, when he was lying on his couch — recovering in warmth and comfort, unlike his unfortunate soldiers — he asked me, quite suddenly, if I considered his war just. Of course I said yes, for his claim to the throne of France is recognised, and it is right that a man should seek his inheritance. But then, to my surprise, he sighed heavily and said, "The battle may be won, or the town taken by siege warfare, but the war goes on until all are weary and most are dead. I have been at war all my life, from the day when, younger than you, I first went into battle against Glendower in Wales. That war is not finished and neither is this one. Take my advice, young Nicholas, fight your battles with words, and tangle not with swords and sling-shot."

'The following day he ordered the hanging of twenty men who had deserted to look for food. Four months later he had grown as haggard and wasted as the most ill-nourished of his soldiers, unable to sit his horse and having to be carried in a litter. I was there when he died on the last night of August.'

'And the funeral?' prompted Christian.

'All pomp and politics,' was the surprising reply. 'Two months we were in bringing him home from St Denis, with masses and grand orations at Rouen, Caen and Calais. Those who cursed him flocked to bend the knee to his funeral carriage. When we landed at Dover and the same obsequies were put on for the journey to Westminster I felt I could stand it no longer and I slipped away by a boat coming down to Tamar. War is not for me, I have sheathed my sword for good.'

Again Christian stroked his hair gently. 'But we need soldiers to defend us from invaders,' she pleaded softly: ''Tis not so many years since the Bretons came to Plymouth, and what would have become of us, even here in Cornwall, had there been no soldiers at the castle to protect the town? We women need the strength of your arm to defend us.'

The pleading in her voice made Nicholas turn to look at her. What he saw — the blue limpid eyes and the trembling lips — awoke in him a tenderness he had never known before in his motherless childhood. He rose to his knees and, gathering Christian in his arms kissed her gently on the mouth. Her response was immediate and the embrace grew more passionate.

There was an angry noise at the door, and they pulled apart. Henry and Thomas had come in again at that moment, and they had brought with them an older, broadly built man of swarthy complexion, who stood in the doorway, a riding whip gripped fiercely in his hand.

'So, this is what the young pup of my bastard brother gets up to when he comes home from the war? Think you all the tender matrons will fall into your bed because you have tales to tell of fancy valour abroad? You shall have a good thrashing!' He brandished his whip in the drifting fire smoke, but before he could take two steps, Nicholas was on his feet with his sword in his hand. The boy's demeanour had changed instantly and he was now the self-confident and experienced warrior.

'Come, Philip, dear uncle!' he challenged with something of a sneer on his lips, 'throw away that bully's weapon, you cannot beat me with that any longer! Where's your gentleman's sword? Rusting in the cowshed, I shouldn't wonder!' He gave a playful lunge towards his uncle, flicking the whip from his hand with an adroit wrist action. Philip stepped back hurriedly, stared a moment, then beat a hasty retreat to the door, threatening and cursing as he went out.

Nicholas turned to Christian, ignoring completely her two sons, and taking up her hand kissed it flamboyantly over a deep bow.

'Thank you kindly, Mistress Hicks, for your understanding and sympathy. If you will permit, I will now assume my own garments and continue to my home.'

In an ostentatiously leisurely manner he resumed his own travelling clothes. Christian sat, still as a board on her stool, only her eyes darting in fright at the three men as if she were not sure whether they were about to fight each other or to molest her for her lapse from proper behaviour. Nicholas sheathed his sword, strode past the brothers as if they did not exist, and with a final salute from the door, went out. The three members of the Hicks family remained still, like three statues, as the sound of his horse's hooves faded away.

2

Nicholas had been wrong to think that he would receive no welcome when he arrived home at Theupath. Reginald was in residence, and news of his son's return had already reached him, through his reeve's daughter, Mattie Jewell, who had rushed home with the news after meeting Thomas in the town. Delighted at the prospect of seeing his son again, Reginald had drawn a flagon of his best malmsey wine and instructed Ellin to prepare the brace of pheasant hanging in the larder. When Nicholas rode into the yard he found his father awaiting him at the house door, and Dan Jewell standing by to take care of the horse. Nicholas gave him instructions to have it returned to Halton as soon as the storm had abated, before splashing over the cobbles to the house.

Reginald took no notice of the drained and weary appearance of his young son, but seized him by the shoulder and ushered him without ceremony through the great hall and into the glowing warmth of his own chamber, where wine stood ready on the table amid a pile of parchments and drawing instruments.

The visit to Christian Hicks had released from Nicholas all the pent-up emotions which he had brought back with him from the war, and he chatted freely to his father about his experiences in France and on the way home. Reginald quickly scotched his son's expressions of concern for the starving and homeless French peasants, seen as innocent victims of the war for kingship.

'There is need for the culling of the peasant population from time to time,' declared Reginald, with the authority of a teacher. 'All those of use would long since have left the settlements to serve in their lord's household or army. The burning of villages is like the cauterising of a wound, it cleans the spot and enables a new start to be made with better stock. Without occasional wars, pestilence and famine we would soon be over-run by a useless swarm of idiots, thieves and scoundrels. They do not think, or learn, or use their minds at all; merely to eat, sleep and breed is their life. Waste not your time and thoughts on the protection of such cattle.'

Nicholas saw at once the force and reasoning of his father's argument, and was happy to wipe all memories of maimed bodies and crying children from his mind. Nonetheless, sub-consciously there lurked a remembrance of Lisette, the under-standing in her eyes and the comfort of her embrace, and the realisation that one French peasant, at least, could not be dismissed as 'cattle'.

The thought of Lisette took his mind to the less happy experience at Pengelly, and he confessed the whole tortuous episode to his father, who roared with laughter at the account of his half-brother's discomfiture. Nicholas was not at all afraid of his uncle, whom he knew as a cowardly bully, but remembering the scowling faces of the Hicks men, he asked Reginald just a little anxiously:

'Will Thomas Hicks take issue against me, think you, father?'

Reginald laughed again. 'Nay lad, he will let the matter lie. He comes here to work after his marriage to Mattie Jewell at Eastertide. He will not wish to risk his future with complaints about the master's son making advances to his mother. Mistress Hicks, poor soul, has been a little soft and weepy this past year, since old Henry died last winter in an accident when felling an oak tree. She must have thought you were the knight of her dreams, with your sad face and tales of war!'

'She was like a mother to me,' said Nicholas thoughtfully — 'until I kissed her. Oh dear! What a chameleon change can be wrought by a touch!'

Both men laughed together in companionship, and put the fate and feelings of Christian Hicks out of their minds as they fell to discussing Nicholas's future. Reginald approved his son's idea to train for the law and undertook to ask advice of the bishop.

'It may take some months to arrange,' he said. 'In the mean-time you would be well advised to consider accepting election to the king's parliament for one of the Cornish boroughs. It is difficult to find willing burgesses because of the expense and length of travel involved and the reluctance of the voters to approve adequate recompense, but on the other hand it would be for you an invaluable experience and introduce you to many of the ruling class.'

'That also would surely take months to arrange,' demurred Nicholas doubtfully.

'At this point, no,' replied Reginald. 'I heard only yesterday that a parliament is being summoned to attend at Leicester in March and that one of the members for Liskerret borough is unwilling to go because it will be lambing time for his flock. So there will have to be an election, and the manor steward has been enquiring around anxiously for anyone willing to stand.'

'But I am not a resident of Liskerret.'

'If they can find no willing burgess among themselves they will be happy to give you a fictitious local residence so that you will be eligible. Come now, I think this is an excellent idea, let us proceed with it.'

Nicholas needed no further persuasion and was happy to leave all arrangements to his father.

It had grown dark while they sat together before the fire in the big hearth, and the dancing flames were reflected on the small glass panes of the window against the blackness of the night outside. Presently Ellin came into the room bearing two platters of whole roast pheasant, a small loaf apiece, a huge fruit pie and a bowl of cream. In silence they consumed it all, wiping the platters clean with the last hunks of bread and washing the whole delicious repast down with more wine. Then as they finished, Reginald went to his table and rummaged among the rolls of parchment. He lit a candle to aid his search, and produced a new and tidy roll, bound with dark blue ribbon.

'Come, see, this is my gift for you,' he said, and as Nicholas unrolled it on the table he held the candle aloft for him to see better.

'It is my design for the new church you have talked about for years.'

In the flickering candlelight Nicholas could see a tall buttressed tower standing guard over a long grey church framing beautifully coloured windows. He unrolled the parchment further and found details of a barrel vaulted roof upheld by clustered granite pillars. He looked up in delight at Reginald, then drew in his breath audibly in amazement as his gaze lighted on the drawing at the foot of the sheet. It was a rood screen, a delicate tracery of carved oak surmounted by a minstrel's gallery. Above the gallery the painted figures of the Great Rood looked appealingly realistic, and the trumpeting angels among the silver stars on the tympanum backing the rood looked just as Nicholas imagined Heaven to be.

He beamed at Reginald. 'May the Lord bless you, father. This is superb, and we will have it done.'

Reginald laughed dryly. 'Maybe the Lord will bless me,' he said 'but the good people of Calyngton will never do so. It will be up to you, my son, to prove to them that the name of Ayssheton is a worthy one.'

3

Richard Chyket also came home from the war. He slipped off a cart carrying the travelling toothpuller and his family on its annual tour of the south-west, and disappeared into the market-day crowd before the toothpuller could recover his breath and demand payment for the ride. Like Nicholas, Richard looked gaunt and grey, but although his left sleeve was tucked empty into his belt, he still walked with his old accustomed jauntiness — the defiant self-confidence of the small man pitting his strength and wits against all comers. Soon he was surrounded by friends welcoming him home, and borne into the tavern for celebrations. It was only the following morning that he extricated himself from the pile of slumbering revellers and staggered down the street to his home. None of his friends had thought to tell him that his father was dying, and Richard arrived home barely in time for a smile and a mumbled blessing as the old man breathed his last.

However the friends rallied round when two days later the coffin had to be carried over the common and down through Manaton fields to the mother church of St Sampson for burial in the churchyard. With heads down against a northerly gale, they trudged and slithered along a muddy bridleway, and were all glad when a closed gate leading into Manaton mill pasture gave them a chance to lower their heavy burden on the hedge-top and ease their aching shoulders. For Richard the task was not only wearisome but unnerving, for he found his left shoulder reacting as though the arm left behind in France were still attached to it, raising itself as if to assist the right arm and shoulder weighed down under the coffin. They stopped again at the footbridge below the mill, and here they were joined by the miller, who took Richard's place for the steep hill up to the church. Richard followed gratefully behind.

The graveside ceremony was brief and the six men were soon heading homewards. Without their load they walked the three miles back to Calyngton in record time, and at the sign of the Bull were soon reviving their spirits with Mistress Bullen's best ale. Then the usual post-funeral argument developed its noisy theme, with Warne Pengelly leading those who claimed the need for Calyngton to have its own burial ground.

''Tis not right,' said he, 'for citizens of this town to be carried out into the country for burial. They should rest here in our midst.'

''Twould do no good to the ale trade,' countered Nat Bullen. 'With a burial party across the street there, we would be forced to close our doors.'

His comment was the signal for everyone to demand the filling of their tankards, and there the matter rested, until the next occasion.

Within a few weeks Richard had wearied of his drinking companions at the tavern and began looking for other, livelier company. It was not until then that he discovered Nicholas Ayssheton had returned before him but had gone away again, having been summoned to Exeter by the bishop, said the tavern gossips, 'to be made a lawman'. The news unsettled him, not only through disappointment at missing his friend, but also because of an unaccustomed feeling of envy — envy that the favoured Nicholas was forging ahead toward fame and fortune while he, the best archer in the king's army at Beaugency, was already discarded from the career of his lifetime. He spent the next two days with his drinking friends at the tavern, but finding this merely made him fuddled and ill without bringing any solace, he mounted his horse one sunny morning and rode westward towards the moor.

It was only January, but one of those rare days, which only Cornwall knows, when the rain-washed air is so clear and bright as to be almost tangible, while in the shelter of the south-facing cliffs the warm sunshine encourages the primroses to bloom months before their due time.

Richard was not in the mood to admire primroses, or any other adventurous spring flower, but as he rode along the sun on his back and the cool breeze on his brow soon swept away all dejection, and with sudden confidence in his single-handed control he urged his horse into a canter. He had no aim for the morning, other than to escape from all thoughts of the future.

Perhaps the horse knew better, for without guidance from his rider he turned south at the moor's edge and trotted down the lane to Fursdon, where he halted at the manor gate as if by invitation. A few yards away in the nearest meadow stood John Fursdon, a small sister at each hand and two hounds at heel. The dogs bounded forward towards the horse, and John, about to call them off, suddenly recognised the friend of years ago and ran towards the gate in delight.

'Why, Richard Chyket, as I live and breathe! How is it with you?'

Richard took the empty sleeve in his right hand and waved it as though it was a scarf, in silent explanation. John said nothing, but came close and gripped the hand in friendly understanding. Richard dismounted, and the two young men walked down to the farmhouse together, filling in for each other the events of the past six years, while the girls peeped shyly at Richard from a safe distance, then ran ahead to tell their mother about the visitor.

This chance visit to Fursdon extended to a stay of two weeks. Richard's war wound and obvious low spirits aroused all the motherly instincts of John's mother Mary, who cosseted and pampered him in a way which warmed his lonely heart and quickly revived his natural cheerfulness. Within a few days he was in demand with the children, teaching the girls to ride, and being himself the horse for little William as they dashed around the orchard with the hounds snapping playfully at his heels.

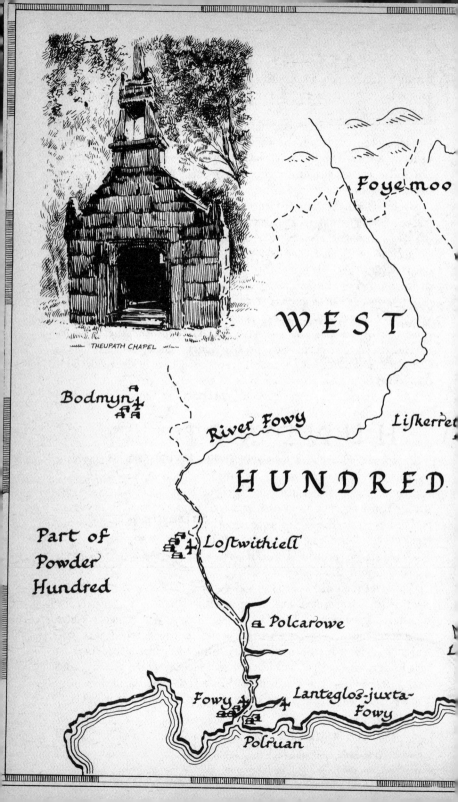

THEUPATH CHAPEL

Foye moo

WEST

Bodmyn

River Fowy

Liskerret

HUNDRED

Part of
Powder
Hundred

Lostwithiell

Polcarowe

Fowy

Lanteglos-juxta-
Fowy

Polruan

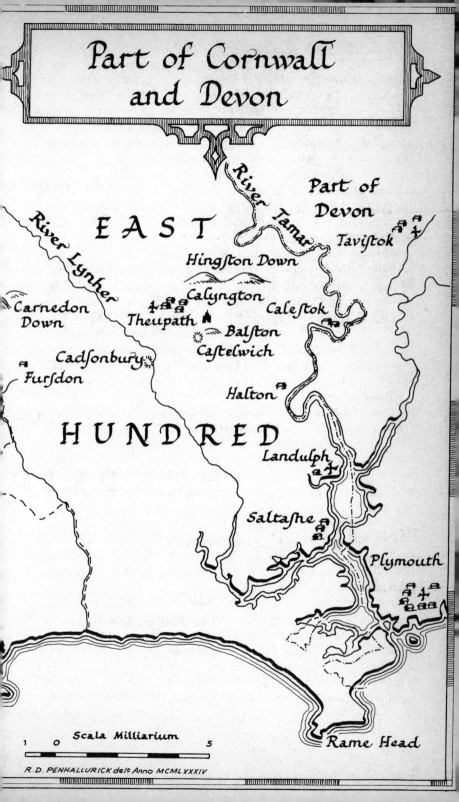

Part of Cornwall and Devon

River Tamar

Part of Devon

EAST

River Lynher

Hingston Down

Tavistok

Calyngton

Calestok

Carnedon Down

Theupath

Balston

Castelwich

Cadsonbury

Fursdon

Halton

HUNDRED

Landulph

Saltashe

Plymouth

Rame Head

John's steady devotion to his farm duties amazed the feckless Richard, but gradually he too felt drawn into the more serious side of country life and took on some of the lighter farmyard duties. He found he quite enjoyed getting up with the dawn and spending the morning cleaning out the shippon after the milking was done. John made no comment on his one-handed inefficiency, an attitude which brought out all Richard's determination to do better, so that in a short while he was able to feed the pigs and fork hay down from the loft, returning to the house for dinner in a warm glow of deep satisfaction at the work he had accomplished.

Always he was attended by his faithful clutch of young admirers. Eight-year-old Elizabeth fetched buckets and shovels for him, followed him up the ladder to the hay loft, all the time chattering and laughing, and disregarding completely the farmyard dirt collecting on her skirt. Her elder sister Mary was a much quieter spectator; at eleven years of age she felt responsible for keeping William out of mischief, and endeavoured most of the time to hold him firmly by the hand. Together they made an admiring audience for the two workers.

In the afternoons, while the children were indoors with their mother, the girls at their needlework and William making painstaking efforts to form letters on his slate, Richard walked with John up to the commonland to check the sheep. Day after day the bright clear sunshine painted the hillside in rich browns and subtle greens under an arch of pure blue which contained neither frost nor mist, and from the higher slopes they could see the huddle of small thatched buildings which made up the town of Calyngton at the foot of Hingston Down. In the clear air a dozen fine columns of smoke spiralled upwards. The only reminders of winter to the gentle and peaceful scene were several white touches of snow to the very tips of the Dartmoor hills in the background.

But at last the weather broke. The wind swung round to the east and flurries of snow warned Richard that he should not delay any longer his return home. Having announced his departure for the following morning he sat very quietly that evening by the fireside, watching Mary and her family, and storing in his memory some of the delights he had found in their company.

How could he leave them? To be alone again, without aim or ambition, and no one to care how he fared? This was what he needed − a family, of his own. The thought brought him to the sudden realisation of how this could be achieved, and he looked searchingly at the two little girls, now bowed at their mother's knee for their bedtime blessing.

The following morning, after Richard had bid the whole family a very fond farewell and ridden off under the grey, snow-laden January sky, John told his mother that Richard had asked for the hand of little Mary for his bride.

'He intends to establish himself as a wool merchant, as his father before him,' said John. 'He has promised to replenish his house, or build anew, and bring proof of his worth when returning to complete the bond.'

'He is a fine young man, and I am well pleased for Meg,' replied Mary Fursdon, with a deep sigh of maternal satisfaction.

4

The Liskerret election was held in the guildhall on the last day of February, and Nicholas found himself duly elected to serve the borough at the coming parliament. The portreeve saluted him warmly, and pressed a rolled parchment into his hands.

'I trust you will put every effort into pressing the need for a reduction in taxation of our people. We have here a petition stating our case, and we beg you to present it at the parliament, and to speak on our behalf.'

'I will do my best,' Nicholas assured him.

The portreeve prattled on. 'Master Fursdon went last year for us, but said nothing at all, and returned home to his farm without making any report on the proceedings to the court leet. Now he declines the duty, saying he be too much occupied in lambing his large flock to take the time to travel to the council.'

'Who did you say he was?' asked Nicholas, his memory stirring.

'Why, John Fursdon of Fursdon in St Cleer. Did you not know?'

'Indeed no, I did not know. But I was acquainted with John Fursdon some years ago in our youth. I beg you to remember me to him.'

'Aye, good sir, that I will,' said the portreeve as he bustled off on his other duties.

Riding home to Calyngton, Nicholas cast his mind back to his meeting on Cadsonbury with the fair-haired boy on the diminutive pony. They had spent two days together, he remembered, like old friends, but had not met again since then. He pictured John as a stocky farmer, stolid and steadfast in his devotion to his family and the rural life, supported by a dutiful wife and a quiverful of children growing up to help him expand his thriving estate.

And now he, Nicholas Ayssheton, was following the shy country lad as a burgess in the parliament.

He rode into Theupath to tell his father of his success in the election, and all thoughts of John Fursdon slipped from his mind.

A few days later Nicholas set off for Leicester where the king's regent, the Duke of Gloucester, had called the parliament. At Dunheved he met up with the other Liskerret burgess, Richard Tredevy, and they travelled on together in easy stages so as not to tire their horses. The wages promised by the Liskerret court leet were barely sufficient to provide them with bed and board during the journey, with nothing to spare for the provision of fresh horses. Nor did they know how long they would be required to remain at Leicester and what sort of expense that would entail.

''Tis all very well,' grumbled Tredevy, as they clattered through Oakhampton determined to press on to Crediton before looking for lodgings, 'these miserable folk at Liskerret demand our services to cut their taxes but expect us to do their bidding for a mere pittance.'

Nicholas had money in his pouch from his father and was not too concerned about the cost of his parliamentary duty, which, as his father had said, could be counted as useful experience. But he agreed with Tredevy that the success of their mission was not encouraged by their treatment.

They reached Leicester safely, having lost their way only once when they took the wrong road out of Gloucester and had to ride into Worcester before finding the right road again. On the last day's journey they were joined by other burgesses, some from Devon and Somerset and some from Gloucestershire, so that when they reached the gates of Leicester, they resembled a small army — an army of grumbling, reluctant representatives of the king's parliament, whose only arms were the petitions most carried in their saddlebags.

The grumbling grew as the days passed and everyone waited for the parliament to be convened. Nicholas and Tredevy found the rest of the Cornish contingent established in a sunny corner of the castle courtyard. Lengthy discussions on the petitions from Cornwall led to noisy arguments and some brawls, for the men from the far west were particularly belligerent. But when two weeks later the duke arrived and took up residence, convening the council for the following day, a plan of campaign had been agreed by the Cornishmen and John Arundell chosen as their spokesman.

It seemed to Nicholas that all was in vain. Only two of the burgesses were allowed to speak and they had been picked by the chancellor because it was known they would support the duke's demand for an increase in funds for the king's education and for the rebuilding of the army. Some of the petitions were waved pathetically by their holders from the back benches, but the chancellor declined to accept more than a handful, and put these aside to be perused in private by the duke. However he could not continue to ignore the growing rumble of hostile discontent among the burgesses and at the end of the day he closed the proceedings with a warning.

'My lord duke, the regent of England, will attend the council tomorrow and address you. He has important news for you from his brother the regent of France. All the members of the council must be in attendance in this hall by eight in the forenoon, under pain of a hundred pounds.'

The threat of so high a fine was sufficient to prevent any malcontents abandoning their duty and returning home before the parliament was dissolved. Nicholas and Tredevy left their lodgings early the next morning soon after daybreak, and even so found the meeting hall already buzzing with activity and talk.

There was an air of expectancy among the representatives, and many rumours flying round as to the content of the message from the Duke of Bedford in France.

At last the trumpet sounded, cutting off the chatter like a knife. As its echo died away in the high rafters, the delegates sat still and silent, then rose as one man when the great oak door leading to the private chambers of the castle swung open. The chancellor entered, then turned and bowed low to the Duke of Gloucester who swept past him followed by his retinue.

The party strode up to the dais, where the duke took his seat in the canopied chair bearing his coat of arms, and sat scowling at the throng before him, strumming his fingers the while on the arm of his chair.

'Good Duke Humphrey' was popular with the people, although there was some criticism of his method of governing the country for his nephew the king. Nicholas studied him with interest from his position at the back of the hall in the Cornish delegation. Under an ermine-trimmed houppeland he wore a black silk padded doublet studded with rubies and emeralds. A heavy chain encrusted with diamonds glittered on his chest, and his regent's coronet lay straight across his brow complementing the severity of the scowling face beneath.

His audience waited, standing, and not even daring to shuffle their feet or clear their throats. At last he spoke, his bejewelled fingers still tapping lightly on the arm of his chair.

'Good master burgesses, we bring you greetings from your sovereign lord the king, who is presently at Berkamstead castle with his tutor my Lord of Warwick. You have heard our request' — he spat out the word with quiet scorn — 'for further funds to make provision for his education to a standard worthy of a king. I now have to tell you that he has approved the plans for him brought from my Lord of Bedford in France.'

He paused and scanned the crowd, a wintry smile touching his lips.

'His Majesty has approved that he be crowned king of France, not only at Westminster before his lords and you, his commoners, but also in Paris. This will ensure, so my Lord of Bedford opines, that his French subjects will at last acknowledge him as their rightful sovereign, as his father before him.'

A ripple of excitement ran through the crowd. The duke rose

to his feet. 'This will surely bring a cessation to the fighting and a reduction in the cost of maintaining our garrisons in France. Meanwhile we must ensure sufficient funds are available for a coronation worthy of an English king, as well as the proper maintenance of his households.'

He swept out of the hall without pausing to see the effect of his words. He did not need to see, for he knew these Englishmen would vote for any project against the French, whatever the cost.

By early afternoon it was all over. Funds for the king's education, coronation and the maintenance of his households had been approved by a large majority, and the burgesses had agreed to carry back to their boroughs the demands for the taxes required. Hurriedly they dispersed to their lodgings, and took to the road on their homeward journey in large droves, the Cornishmen in a band of their own well to the fore.

In the event Nicholas did not reach home until the eve of May Day, having spent the whole month of April in Devon. On the first night of their homeward journey he had met up with John Copleston, another aspirant to the Court of Common Pleas, who, like himself was filling in time as a parliamentarian.

'We have good hunting in the woods and up on the moors,' said John, 'massively strong boars, good runners all, and stags too. Come to Copleston, I will lend you a steed for the hunting, and you may care to stay with us until after Easter.'

Nicholas did care, and enjoyed himself hugely both in the days spent riding the Devon hills and valleys in pursuit of the boar and in the relaxed pleasures to be found in the home of a rich Devon squire. It was not until John received instructions to travel to London that Nicholas took leave of his friend and returned to Cornwall.

No similar instruction awaited him, however, and his father was away from home. Having rehearsed a detailed and lively report for Reginald of his experiences attending the parliament, Nicholas felt sadly deflated. Rather grudgingly he rode over to Liskerret to complete his duty there, knowing full well that he would be held personally responsible for the tidings he bore for further taxation. The portreeve insisted on convening the court leet, and he was submitted to a long and gruelling inquisition, finally suffering the indignity of having his wages cut by half, 'as a contribution,' in the words of the portreeve, 'towards this further onerous and iniquitous tax.'

No wonder, thought Nicholas, as he rode slowly homeward, no wonder they have such difficulty in finding willing volunteers for the parliament.

At home at Theupath he found a messenger in the bishop's livery striding up and down in the great hall with some impatience. Nicholas greeted him and the messenger bowed in return with a grandiose flourish.

'My lord bishop sends you greetings. He has news for you and asks that you accompany me to Exeter where he will instruct you.'

Eagerly Nicholas enquired: 'Would the news be for the acceptance of my apprenticeship in London?'

'I am not instructed further in this matter,' replied the messenger woodenly. 'If it please you we should set off at first light tomorrow, so that we may reach the bishop's palace before the *cena*.' Then relaxing his official stance just a little, he smiled at the young man and added: 'The news, I am sure, must be good news.'

Nicholas had to be content. Dutifully he made arrangements for their departure the next morning, and after a light meal they both retired early.

The news at Exeter was good, and in addition Nicholas found his father in attendance at the bishop's court. Together they waited on the bishop after compline.

Bishop Lacy was a man of energy and enthusiasm, coupled with a keen sense of charity and compassion, which his attendance on the late king at the battle of Agincourt had done nothing to diminish. It was through his encouragement that Reginald Ayssheton had achieved his reputation as a designer of fine modern buildings. In the full knowledge that Reginald was not a truly devout man in the terms of the age, he had even sent him to Rome so that he could study the fine architecture of the period.

Now he smiled warmly at both men, and especially at the familiar figure of the older man, carelessly dressed in well-worn clothes and with his iron grey hair lying untidily at the nape of his neck.

How like his father the young man is, he mused to himself, and already half an inch taller. He nodded silent approval at the careful spruceness of Nicholas's clothes, his well-fitting doublet matching exactly the deep blue hose and the silk lining of his houppeland, in its turn a precise match to his soft leather pointed shoes. Dark curls clung tightly to his head, cut severely short and shaved at the nape in the military style.

Father and son bowed low to the bishop, and awaited his pleasure.

The smile on the face of the bishop broadened. 'My friends,' he said, laying emphasis on the plural, 'I have good news for you, as you may have surmised. I have had word from Master John Fortescue that he is prepared to accept two assistants at midsummer, subject, of course, to his own personal approval of them after a proper examination.'

He paused, then continued.

'There is one small problem here. I can well picture you, Master Nicholas, presiding in Westminster hall in the habit of a serjeant-at-law, and I know from your father that you have the aptitude for this important calling. But I must tell you that no fewer than three other young men have begged my assistance for the same purpose. I am therefore advising Master Fortescue that he must choose his two new assistants from the four whom I send to him.' He looked seriously at Nicholas, 'This will demand exclusive application to the matter of your examination.'

Nicholas replied eagerly: 'My lord bishop, have no fear, I will convince the serjeant that a man of Cornwall is the best possible assistant he could have.' He straightened his back and threw up his head with arrogant confidence.

'That may well be, Master Nicholas, I commend you for your confidence. But I repeat, take care. I like what I hear from brother Reginald that you wish to bring the rule of law back to your native province. This is a worthy ambition, and one which I shall remember and hope to make use of one day when those unruly Cornishmen are troubling me.' He caught Reginald's eye, and the two men smiled together at the youth's impetuous ambition.

'But now, Master Nicholas,' continued the bishop, 'tell us both what you achieved in the king's parliament.'

For the next half hour Nicholas gave a detailed account of his journey to Leicester and what had happened at the parliament, and the two older men considered the implications of his news.

'What think you, brother Reginald?'

'Sir, it is plain to see that there will be much disquiet, and perhaps rioting when the tax-gatherers appear, especially in the remoter districts — such as Cornwall. I would not gainsay the right of the Duke of Bedford to have the king crowned in Paris; after all his French subjects need such a manifestation, and may then accept his authority more readily. But his English subjects have already been squeezed of more than they can afford to contribute, and will desire, very rightly, that the expense of this French coronation should be borne by the French.'

'I agree, it presages trouble,' said the bishop.

There came a tap at the door and he stood up to close the interview. The two Aysshetons knelt and bowed their heads for his blessing and dismissal. As they turned to go, Bishop Lacy called to Nicholas. 'The man waiting outside to see me now is Master Walter Moyle, another aspiring law man. You are to return here within a week after Whitsuntide to meet up with him and Masters Peter and Paul Tillman, so that you may journey to London in company. They are both Devon men, so you need have no fear,' he added with a chuckle, then more seriously, 'but look to your laurels.'

5

The four travellers reined in their horses at the top of Tyburn Hill for their first view of London Town. It had been an exhausting ride through the hot June day, from the dew-damp early morning, through the scorching mid-day of high summer to the blessed relief of evening and a cooling breeze. The horses drank long and noisily from a spring at the roadside, while their riders drained their flasks and feasted their eyes on the great town spread out before them.

A soft haze hung over the winding river, but the evening sun glowed pink on the great square white tower on its bank at the further edge of the town. Before it a wide sweep of grey walls and battlemented gate towers encircled a huddle of buildings from which a multitude of delicate spires and chunky towers reached towards the sky.

'Why, there are more churches there even than at Oxford!' declared Walter Moyle.

Nicholas Ayssheton laughed at him. 'And if you plan to attend compline at every one of them we must needs leave you here till Martinmas!'

As they stood by their horses, relaxed and laughing together as they admired the view, the sound of church bells came wafting on the evening breeze — only two at first, but within a few moments taken up by dozens more until the air rang in a crescendo of joyful pealing.

Walter dropped on one knee and bowed his head. The other young men followed suit. Then, brushing the dust off their white summer hose, they clambered back into their saddles and pulled their horses back on the road, Walter leading the way.

'There will be no compline this St John's day if we fail to reach the new gate by sundown,' he called, as he set off down the hill at a brisk trot.

The twins Peter and Paul Tillman followed after him, but Nicholas hesitated briefly, his eye caught by the breathtaking sight.

Following the line of the river he had discovered, beyond the riverside mansions in the open country, the royal city of Westminster. He gazed entranced at the grandeur of towers and turrets, cloisters and courtyards, their outlines etched in evening shadow and their many windows twinkling like diamonds in the light of the setting sun. Somewhere there was the great palace where the law courts were held. At the prospect of taking part in such grand occasions he felt strangely elated, as if he were coming home to a place where he belonged. Excitement surged through him, he dug spurs and galloped recklessly down the hill after his companions, his loose white shirt billowing behind him and his flat cap riding up on the back of his head.

With Walter in the lead and Nicholas bringing up the rear, the little party trotted in through the gate under the forbidding prison walls just before nightfall. They were soon caught up in a great tide of townsfolk, all running or walking briskly in the same direction towards St Paul's, talking and laughing as they went, and apparently bent on some communal festivity. It was with difficulty that Nicholas and his friends disentangled themselves from the surging crowd as it swept past the cathedral and on into the wide thoroughfare beyond, where even greater crowds were already gathered. At the Mitre Inn they stabled their horses and bespoke beds for the night.

''Tis little sleep you will be having this night,' grumbled the innkeeper, pleased though he was to have four unexpected lodgers. 'The Midsummer Marching Watch is now preparing, and goes on for most of the night. I will be up all night myself, serving food and drink to the revellers.'

Walter was not interested in any revelries but hurried off across the churchyard to attend compline at the cathedral. In a more worldly frame of mind, Nicholas and the twins decided to join the festivities, and rejoined the crowds pressing into the Chepe.

'It is, after all, in honour of our blessed saint, John the Baptist,' declared Paul in self-justification, 'that great white and shining light! Let us all celebrate together!'

They were pushed and jostled until, in the gathering dusk, they came close to a towering memorial in the middle of the street. The crowd parted like water round a rock and swept on so fast that Nicholas caught only a glimpse of the Madonna and Child and above it a great gilded cross. He then found that he had become separated from Peter and Paul when the crowd split. With a great effort, and some judicious use of his elbows and shoulders, he managed to cross the streaming crowd and cling to an iron railing at the end of the monument. The crowd swirled on, and Nicholas climbed on the base to see if he could find his friends.

The twins had disappeared completely, but Nicholas had accidentally found for himself an ideal viewing point for the midsummer festivities. Chepe, the widest street in London, stretched for some distance in either direction, from St Paul's on the hill down to Cornhill and the Leaden Hall Market. The shops and houses lining the street were all hung with arras and velvets, and even some with rich silk embroidered in gold thread. Over every door hung a garland of leaves and white flowers, mostly lilies and St John's wort cradled in delicate green birch sprays. Apprentices were running from the houses and shops with lighted tapers, lighting up the oil lamps set in the greenery, and as dusk deepened to nightfall, a myriad lights twinkled in the darkness in all directions.

Most of the houses were timber-framed, interspersed with one or two newer stone buildings. Only a few yards from where Nicholas had perched himself on a narrow ledge, with his back against the alcove sheltering the Madonna and Child, stood a wide stone building which had the unusual feature of a projecting balcony fronting a line of arched doorways which now stood open, revealing glimpses of a crowded and gaily decorated hall within. Beneath the balcony a wide carriage entrance was guarded by four pikemen in the royal livery, and in the flare of their cressets Nicholas could just make out the royal arms carved in stone over the archway.

So this was Crown Seld. Nicholas strained his eyes, trying to make out which of the royal dukes was feasting this midsummer at the Marching Watch. The little king, he knew, would be out in the country at Wallingford, too young to be aware of his destiny.

There was a great roll of drums from the direction of the market. The crowd hushed, and heads craned to see the March approach. The revellers in the Crown Seld flowed out on to their balcony and seated themselves sedately behind the richly embroidered cloth of gold which covered the balcony front. Nicholas could not identify either of the royal dukes whom he had seen in France, but he surmised that the central figure in the party was either the Duchess of Bedford or the Lady Gloucester. She was short, plump and undistinguished, relying for regality on an exceptionally tall horned head-dress flashing with diamonds and rubies and supporting the flimsiest of wimples. Suddenly his attention was riveted on her attendant, who stood up and leaned over the balcony to look along the street. The cressets below lit up long tresses of rich auburn hair, generous well-shaped lips now parted in smiling and eager interest, a dainty chin and sensuously curving throat and shoulders over a low-cut gown of rich blue silk.

Nicholas held his breath as if stunned, then felt his heart start to thump madly as if out of control. In his excitement he almost fell from the ledge, but was grabbed in time by a young apprentice who had squeezed in with him on his perch.

'Steady now,' said the lad, ''twould be an unpleasant death to be impaled on those iron spikes below. But see, here comes the March.'

The noise of drums had grown louder, and was now joined by the higher pitch of fifes, cymbals and trumpets. Looking down towards Cornhill, they saw a river of lighted cressets swaying and bobbing up the street towards them. The head of the procession drew abreast of the Cross and paused to salute the Crown Seld audience. Then the drums beat again, and led by the mayor's serjeant-at-arms and common crier the whole procession moved on along the Chepe to the accompaniment of the cheers of the delighted Londoners.

Troop after troop of veteran soldiers marched past bearing their arms with great pride and yielding nothing in disciplined drill to the younger serving soldiers who had joined in. The trumpets and fifes played on vigorously, and several parties of morris dancers clattered by, followed by a band of sword players resplendent in blue and gold tunics, several conjurors and even a dancing bear led on a golden chain. In the light of thousands of lamps the whole scene became as clear as day, and Nicholas found his attention divided between the ever-changing chaos passing below him and the beautiful young lady who still stood watching the scene in great excitement, pointing and laughing and clapping her hands.

Who could she be? he wondered. His heart thumped again, urgently, several times and he resolved then and there to find out her name and parentage, so that he could trace her.

The apprentice next to him grabbed his arm again, and pointed. 'Here come the rich men!' he shouted over the cacophony of cheering and trumpeting. Along the street, behind the last team of morris dancers, rode the mayor surrounded and protected by his entourage of esquires and sword bearer. His scarlet houppeland, trimmed with ermine, hung down over the contrasting blue and gold of the caparison of his horse. Behind came the aldermen, equally sedate and only a degree less richly gorgeous in their outfits, followed by two sheriffs, whose retinue glowered threateningly at the cheering spectators as if challenging them to dare to be involved in law-breaking this festive night.

As the procession dwindled away up the hill and out of sight, the crowds in Chepe broke up, some running after the procession to follow it round the town, others starting up their own little processions and street parties.

Nicholas saw the auburn-haired beauty withdraw from the balcony into the hall behind. He climbed down from his perch and slipped through the crowd to the carriage entrance across the street. There he waited patiently, ignored by the guards who were passing round a flask of brandy and enjoying their own party.

At length he heard the clatter of horses' hooves in the cobbled court-yard. Walking boldly through the entrance past the guards, he found himself almost immediately holding the bridle of a chestnut mare as its rider was lifted to her sidesaddle. The lovely face which he had been watching from across the street looked down at him in surprise.

'Who are you?' she asked. Nicholas whipped off his cap and was about to declare himself when the servant intervened.

'My lady, we must go,' he urged, seizing the bridle from Nicholas. As he pulled the horse away, its rider turned again towards Nicholas, and their eyes met.

The mysteries of all the world seemed at that instant to pass between them. A gentle smile warmed her eyes as Nicholas poured his whole soul into his gaze. His legs turned to water and his hand trembled as he raised his cap in a feeble salutation. For a moment he felt unable to move, and when he did recover his normal senses and ran out into the street, the horse, its rider and the footman had all disappeared. He stood, in the middle of Chepe, a dejected young man who had lost the love of his life — for he still did not know who she was.

After a night of celebrations, London awoke next morning to another scorching hot urban day, unrelieved by breeze or dew. As Nicholas and his companions walked down to Ludgate on their way to the inns of court, the stench of rotting garbage and uncollected night soil caught their breath. The twins, who had spent the night drinking in rowdy company, had difficulty in restraining their heaving stomachs in the foul air. Nicholas tucked his mouth and nose inside the collar of his houppeland, but his eyes continued to scan the faces of the passers-by in the

forlorn hope of finding there some clue to the identity of the
lady with the auburn hair. Like the twins he had had no sleep,
having spent the night tossing on his straw pallet as he relived,
over and over again, the events of the evening, and imagined
more pleasant and successful results of the encounter. Now, in
the stifling heat of the city morning, he felt listless and confused, his usual drive and determination completely evaporated.

Only Walter seemed unaffected either by the events of the
previous night or by the unwholesome smells of the morning.
Indeed, he described with considerable relish the frightening
frieze of the 'Dance of Death' which he had discovered on the
cloister walls at St Paul's, but receiving no response from his
audience, he strode ahead and was soon lost to sight in the
crowd pressing through Ludgate. Collecting their befuddled
wits the other three hurried after him towards the inns of court.

They found the Serjeants' Inn and walked in through the
archway beside a tailor's shop into the courtyard. There they
halted uncertainly, wondering at which house they would find
Serjeant John Fortescue. On their left were two tall houses, each
with many windows and two entrances; on the right stood a
smaller house, with stables and outhouses leading down to a
garden which lay across the foot of the courtyard.

A voice hailed them, and the four men, startled, turned
round to find a man standing in the doorway of the archway
building behind them. He was dressed in a full-length gown of
taffeta-lined velvet, particoloured blue and green, with a cape
of the same, so that at first glance he looked like two persons,
one blue and one green. Above this strange garment his
chubby, well-fed face sat like a round ball in a neat border of
white lawn — the serjeant's coif, which fitted snugly round his
head and fastened under his chin.

'Your business here at Serjeants' Inn?' he demanded
brusquely. Walter stepped forward and explained their
mission, and the serjeant's manner immediately softened when
he realised the four young men were there on legitimate business.

'The Serjeant Fortescue is not presently here,' he said, 'He
spends much of his time at Chichester Inn, where he still main-
tains his former chamber. You will find him there.'

Walter looked bewildered and spread his hands enquiringly, whereupon the serjeant undertook to show them the way. They trooped after him up the Chancellor's lane to Chichester Inn, where their guide left them in the care of the gate porter. By then Walter had recovered his buoyancy and self-confidence, but his three companions felt as jaded as ever.

It was only the beginning of a long and exhausting day. One by one the four men were taken to the chamber where Serjeant John Fortescue conducted a long and gruelling examination in Latin, extracting full details of their family histories, their lives and ambitions, and the extent of their knowledge of the king's law and the conduct of the courts. Then they returned to the porter's stuffy lodge where in the stifling heat of the afternoon they sat and awaited the result, struggling to keep awake. Even Walter found himself yawning, and at last the others fell asleep.

Nicholas dreamed of a princess in blue and gold, who wrapped her long auburn tresses round his body and took him prisoner, dragging him helpless past a line of white-coifed serjeants-at-law, all of them with the stern and disapproving face of John Fortescue. Walter ran after him, calling to him to free himself, and grabbed his shoulder. He awoke to find Walter was indeed shaking his shoulder and calling him to wake up as they were all summoned to the serjeant's presence.

The little chamber had a window looking north over the rough ground of the rabbitry, and as the four candidates filed in the serjeant was standing by it, the shutters flung back and a gentle breeze ruffling the fur on his hood. They stood neatly in line and waited anxiously. The serjeant took a deep breath from the open window and turned back into the chamber to take his seat at his document-strewn table. Out of the corner of his eye Nicholas observed that the covers on the alcove bed had been disarranged since he was formerly in the room, and he guessed that the serjeant also had required some rest after the exhaustive examinations. The thought brought back a little courage to his dejected spirit, and he stood more erect.

Serjeant Fortescue came straight to the point. 'Two of you may stay here at this inn as mootmen. I have reserved a chamber, which you will share — until such time as one or other of you progresses to the rank of apprentice at the bar. I would warn you that the exercises required of you in your training, as well as the duties you will perform as my assistants, will leave you little time for dalliance over many years.'

Nicholas shifted his stance uneasily. The serjeant looked keenly at him. 'Master Nicholas, your Latin speech and understanding is excellent, and your experience in the parliament and in the late king's retinue fits you well for the legal life. But I had the impression this morning that your thoughts were not exclusively with me.'

Nicholas hung his head. How could he have let admiration for a woman's physical attributes ruin his chance of a successful legal career? Cursing himself — and the witch with the auburn hair, who still smiled into his very soul if he so much as closed his eyes — he vowed that never again would any woman come between him and his work.

Serjeant Fortescue turned to Walter. 'Master Walter, you have done well.' Walter beamed. The serjeant continued: 'I fear that your godliness has kept you remote from the troubles of the worldly. In the Court of Common Pleas we deal with disputes over property and inheritances, many of them squabbles of a petty nature between persons whose selfishness we have to understand — and identify with, if we are to plead their case in court. I find myself doubting your capacity to reach such an understanding of ordinary mortals.'

Walter sagged visibly, his ego deflated and his self-confidence sapped quite away. The serjeant turned smiling to the Tillman twins. 'And here we have two honest men from Devon, who also wish to become lawmen.' The twins nodded eagerly. 'Go back to your tutors and start again. You could serve the bishop of Exeter well in your own county — but I fear that the gentleness of your upbringing has not fitted you for the cut and thrust of the courts of the palace of Westminster. Good day to you, sirs.'

They all stood rooted to the spot. Who then? Or none of them? The serjeant stood up and extended his hand to the Tillmans, shaking hands with each dejected twin before he turned to Nicholas and Walter.

'The porter will take you to your chamber. Report to me on the morrow, after matins.'

6

It was five years before Richard felt able to claim his bride. He had flung himself into the merchandising of wool with the same determination and devotion which he had previously given to his archery, and had soon built up the old connections which his father had allowed to lapse. He bought and sold at market, and became a well-known figure at St Ive and Menheniott fairs. The farmers soon discovered that a better bargain could be struck by taking their best quality wool to Mr Chyket's warehouse in Calyngton than by trusting to the vagaries of the market, so that any day of the week would see mule-drawn wains in the yard at the back of the house, the animals standing patiently in rain or sunshine while in the store the standard of the fleeces was discussed and a price agreed on.

From his success as a buyer it was only a small step to establish himself as a respected merchant selling top-grade wool to the Devon serge makers, some of whom came regularly to the town to inspect the combed wool awaiting sale in Richard's warehouse.

It should be said that other merchants also found a revival of trade at this time. The little town enjoyed a wave of prosperity as it became known in the area as a recognised wool market. Several more substantial homes appeared, their granite walls and Delabole roofs so solid they seemed likely to squeeze out of existence the dung walls and thatched roofs of the older cottages between them.

These more grandiose houses aroused Richard to the need to apply himself to providing a home worthy of his affianced Mary. He was happy and comfortable in the old house, where he was looked after, in a rough and ready fashion, by his father's cousin Margery Allin and her husband Diggory. When it rained too heavily through the cracked walls they simply moved to a drier part of the house. For some years — indeed, since Richard's childhood — the top storey had remained empty and unused except by mice and bats, whose squeaking would be drowned on wet nights by the sound of rainwater dripping through the ragged thatch.

But while none of these signs of decay bothered Richard, so long as his warehouse remained weatherproof, vivid recollection of the tidy cosiness of an evening at Fursdon convinced him that great changes must be made at Chyket. Mary would not be content, as he was, to sit of an evening by the great fire in the kitchen in company with Diggory and Margery, for Margery chattered incessantly while Diggory snored from the depth of a settle, exuding at the same time a rich odour of warm wet fustian and baking dung. No, his wife would need her own boudoir for the winter evenings, as well as a prettier solar than the ramshackle room where his father had spent his last days. He grew quite excited, picturing Mary presiding in a gracious hall at a banquet given by the leading wool merchant of the town to a visiting justice, or perhaps the lord bishop himself!

He set to work roughing out the sort of house he would like to have.

Within a week Diggory had put up a new cottage for himself and Margery at the side of the stables. Margery had set up her kitchen there, Richard had moved his mattress and his few possessions into the wool store and the ramshackle old house had been knocked down and burned to the ground.

It was not long before news of the rebuilding work going ahead at Chyket reached Reginald Ayssheton, on one of his rare visits home. The harbinger was Mattie, his reeve's daughter, now married to Thomas Hicks and sharing with Ellin the domestic duties at Theupath. Her graphic account of great teams of giants throwing up a magnificent stone palace aroused Reginald's curiosity, and he rode into town to see for himself.

Mattie's sense of hyperbole was a godsend for Richard Chyket, in that it brought him the free services of an expert architect. His masons were in fact in no way giants, merely some of his drinking companions from the tavern pressed into service. He had planned to build the lower storey of the new house in quarried moorstone, but was so disheartened at the ragged appearance of the first four feet of wall erected that he had just decided to revert to a frame and plaster building when he saw his friend's father at the gate, stroking his chin thoughtfully as he studied the work from his horse's back.

Richard hurried over to greet him, but was cut short by Reginald declaring curtly, as he slid down from his saddle: 'Those walls cannot survive a twelvemonth.'

He strode over to the wall, seized the tool from Diggory's hand and briskly knocked away the stone which had just been laid. Diggory gazed at him open-mouthed as Reginald demolished his end of the wall — work which he had been labouring on for three days.

'There!' said the master craftsman. 'Clean up those blocks and then I will show you how to build a good wall.'

And so it happened. Those eight unskilled men had their first instruction in stone-masonry and unwittingly embarked on the career of their lives. They were shown how to lay a true face, how to break the joints between the courses, and above all, how to build from the corners to obtain an upright, sturdy building.

Reginald stayed all day at Chyket, watching and correcting with patient explanations. Little did he realise that these same men would one day be building the church which he had designed.

Only when dusk was falling, and the men had gone off down the street to their homes, did Reginald relax from his professionalism. With a smile of satisfaction he turned from his final inspection and sat down with Richard on the bench outside the Allins' new cottage. He accepted a tankard of ale from the bustling Margery, and the two men fell to discussing the general design details of the house. Richard produced his roughly drawn plans, which the older man scrutinised at length and in complete silence.

At last he spoke with the plans still on his knee.

'This is indeed a sumptuous house and a fine family home.' Richard blushed with pleasure.

'It deserves to be built entirely of stone, for an outward dignity to match the spaciousness and luxury you plan within.'

'I fear we are not skilled enough for such a mammoth undertaking,' replied Richard, shaking his head regretfully.

'Young man,' said Reginald, with all the authority of the senior generation, 'you are a prosperous citizen of this town, with an important future before you. If you will allow me to guide your plans and oversee the workers, I will produce for you a house that will be the pride of your family for generations to come. How say you?'

Richard could say nothing. Overcome by emotion, he merely offered his hand to Reginald, beaming at him with the excitement of a boy, his eyes sparkling with enthusiasm.

Margery brought out more ale. They drank to the success of their joint project, and sat on in the dusk until night had quite fallen and the new moon dangled a rosary of stars over their heads.

As Reginald stood up to leave, Richard at last put his house to the back of his mind, and enquired for Nicholas. Reginald sat down again. 'I understand he is well, but he does not come home and seldom writes. He now represents Helston in the parliament, and he is also an assistant to Serjeant Fortescue in the court of Common Pleas. I am pleased that his career is now well-established at the heart of affairs in the capital. But I miss him.'

Richard nodded silently in sympathy, fully understanding the other man's loneliness.

'I had seen too little of him during his boyhood,' he continued, 'I am not of the nursemaid type. But a man came home from the war — I expect it was the same with you,' he added apologetically, glancing down at the empty sleeve. 'We were friends, companions. There was fun and excitement in our companionship, but it was cut short too soon when he went away. I find myself wondering why he no longer visits his old father — and sometimes fear I will never see him again.'

'I hope he comes back to Calyngton one day,' said Richard, as he led Reginald's horse out of the stable.

'Why should he? Calyngton is a small, unimportant place,' replied Reginald. He sprang into the saddle, gathered the reins, and with a brief wave was gone into the night.

The house was nearly finished, and already the envy of all the merchants in the neighbourhood, when the plague made one of its periodic visits. It was not a severe epidemic, and of the dozen who fell ill, only two died. One of these was Reginald Ayssheton who caught the infection from one of the men building the new Chyket house.

7

News of his father's death reached Nicholas two months later, by a messenger bringing instructions to the serjeant-at-law, John Fortescue.

Stricken with remorse that he had for so long neglected to visit his father, or even send him word on his progress and activities, Nicholas sought leave of absence from Master Fortescue to go home and see to his father's affairs.

The serjeant nodded acquiescence, without looking up from the document he was studying. Then as Nicholas turned to leave, he raised his hand to stay him and said, his eyes still on his work, 'There is work for you here, Master Nicholas, which you can deal with whilst you are in the west country. Bishop Lacy of Exeter requires our assistance in settling a dispute which has long been brewing between the religious houses at Plympton and Tavistok, touching the chapel at Plymstok. The bishop is rightly concerned that such an unholy squabble between two religious houses should not be left to ferment any longer. He asks for arbitrators to be sent down. I think you could well fulfil this office.'

Nicholas bowed, his eyes alight with pleasure. This would be his first independent assignment and in his excitement the sad occasion for his visit slipped from his mind.

'Who would you like to go with you?' asked the serjeant thoughtfully. 'It must be someone with whom you can work amicably, although you will each be representing the opposing factions in the dispute.'

'May it please you, Master Serjeant, Master John Copleston and I have done much work together this past year. We understand each other's methods of pleading and we have mutual interests and pleasures. He is a Devon man and would be much at home, as I am, with the monks of Tavistok and Plympton.'

'So be it.' The serjeant was well satisfied that a problem had been so easily solved. 'You may travel to Exeter as soon as you have made all proper arrangements here for handing on your work to another apprentice. Report to the bishop; I will give you my written reply to take with you, and then you may proceed to your home for the settlement of your father's estate while the bishop makes arrangements for the arbitration. Master Copleston will go with you as the other arbitrator.'

He looked for the first time at Nicholas, gave him a brief wintry smile, and returned to his study of the parchment on his table. Nicholas bowed and withdrew from the room, well-accustomed to such cursory treatment by his legal seniors.

Two days later the two lawmen rode together out of London, and headed west on the long journey to Exeter.

Bishop Edmund Lacy was deeply upset at the tragic death of his talented architect Reginald Ayssheton, but in his charity he also thought with concern of Reginald's son, whom he had assisted with his appointment to the establishment of John Fortescue. He expected the young man to hasten home, in all likelihood angered that so much time had elapsed before he had received the news, and so he was more than a little taken aback when Nicholas presented himself at the bishop's palace with John Copleston, apparently more interested in legal affairs than in his family duty. However, he was pleased for his own episcopal affairs to proceed and spent a whole day discussing the thorny problem of Plymstok chapel with the two young lawmen.

'This is a perennial dispute between my lord and prior of Plympton and his brother-in-God the abbot of Tavistok,' he said, shaking his head in mild remonstrance at the unneighbourliness of the two religious houses. 'It is time the whole question of ownership and income were finally settled and both parties bound by arbitration. I will send word to them to choose their representatives, among whom must be—' he hesitated and looked quizzically at Nicholas and then at John — 'Yes, I think the prior of Plympton must have Master Nicholas and Master John will be chosen for Tavistok. Thank you, kind sirs, I will now proceed with all arrangements, and will be pleased to have you meet with me at Tavistok in two months' time.'

As the young men made to take their leave, the bishop stood up and spoke directly to Nicholas. 'Rest assured, our brother

Reginald, your father, is ever in our thoughts and we pray for him. We shall always remember him by his beautiful halls and palaces. He needs no other memorial.'

He spoke simply and without any hint of reproach to this young man who had up to now made no reference to his bereavement. The sincerity of his tribute both warmed Nicholas to the memory of his father and brought him at last to the reality of his loss. He dropped to his knees in penitence. The bishop laid his hands on the bowed shoulders.

'May the Lord go with you in your endeavours to build your life to His praise and glory, as your father did before you.'

He knew the exact spot from where he would obtain his first glimpse of Theupath – and there it was, nestling on the slope of the river valley above its little grove of trees and the chapel. This was his home, and now also his responsibility. As he trotted on down the hill, Nicholas found himself quite looking forward to meeting this new challenge.

He was, he discovered, very well served by his father's retainers, all of whom had continued without pause in their duties, even when there was no longer a master to guide and pay them. Dan Jewell gave his new master a full report on all that had been done on the land and to the buildings; the harvest had begun, and the new barn built last year was already half full of good quality corn. A new hedge ordered by the master last spring had been completed, with the use of stone from Balston quarry. Four pigs should be taken to market next week, he recommended, and his daughter Mattie – now living in a new cottage beside the stable with her husband Thomas Hicks – was established as the poultry keeper, and had six fine geese fattening for Christmas.

Nicholas nodded approval to every item, then cut in at last. 'Where is my father's grave?'

Dan looked down at his clogs, then at last, sweeping his eyes over to the trees behind the chapel, said simply: 'Because of the plague no one would carry him to the burial ground at Southill, so we laid him to rest there, behind his own chapel.'

He paused, then rushed on: 'The rector was sore cross with us, for there 'tis not holy ground, he say. But then, as I see it, the ground where he built a beautiful chapel to the glory of

God must be holy — for him leastways. His spirit will be happy there.'

'Thank you, Dan,' said Nicholas deeply moved. Within minutes he was kneeling by the new, fresh grave close to the south wall of the chapel, praying for the soul of his father.

Later that evening Mattie told him how his father had caught the plague from a carpenter who had walked in from Calestok on hearing that Mr Chyket was building a new house. The two men had worked together on some fine linenfold panelling for the banqueting hall. It was now all closed up, said Mattie with a long face; no one liked to go in there, even though so many sulphur candles had been lit that the patrons in the tavern up the street complained of the smell. The young master was living in the kitchen wing, and they said in the town that there was no hope now of his intended marriage going forward.

'Who was he to marry?' enquired Nicholas politely.

'Why, a maiden from over Liskerret way, daughter to Widow Fursdon. So sad indeed!'

Mattie did not notice Nicholas's increased interest at the mention of the name Fursdon; she was too busily occupied dabbing her eyes with her apron in a matronly way which somehow reminded Nicholas of her mother-in-law, Christian Hicks. ''Tis a fine palace, such as Calyngton has never seen before. And there is a young man who sorely needs a wife, living the life of a churl in one small part of it. We were hoping to see processions and festival banquets!'

Remembering the words of Bishop Lacy that his father would always be remembered by his buildings, Nicholas resolved to go into the town and see this new palace. But first he was mindful to inquire of Mattie concerning her mother-in-law's health. Mattie looked at him meaningfully.

'She was wed to a widow-man who works for Squire Trelawny,' she announced solemnly, as if pronouncing sentence. 'She lives now at Coldrennick, and Henry has the farm at Pengelly. She is contented there, and says she will never return to Calyngton.'

Much to Mattie's amazement, her master seized her by the shoulders and danced her round the chanber and down the stairs, much as they had done when playing together as children. There was no doubt about it, he was very happy and not in any way crestfallen at her news. She went off home to her cottage a mite disappointed that there would be no romantic developments to report to her friends in town.

8

Nicholas spent the following two weeks learning all that he could from Dan about the running of the estate. Alone in the evenings he shut himself in his father's chamber and went through all the documents and architectural designs packed in three chests and meticulously labelled. His father's design for the Calyngton church he put carefully aside, excited at the realisation that this was the means for him to build to the glory of God and further his father's work. His father's testament he also found and put aside; there were bequests there which must be attended to. There was also an inventory to be made, no one having dared to come into the house to carry out this duty because of the fear of infection. Ellin helped her new master in this task: she could not write, but she was happy to tell him how many feather beds the household contained, to give him a full description of her kitchen equipment and the contents of the pantry, the buttery, the cheese house, the bakehouse and the salthouse. When the inventory was made out, Nicholas felt amazed that he was now the owner of so much domestic equipment.

Eventually, all the paraphernalia of the new owner taking over his inheritance was completed and on a sparkling autumn morning he rode out from the farm and down the hill to the town. From force of habit he tethered his horse in the old barn in the back lane, although it was not market day and indeed few people were to be seen in the fore street. The small group passing the time of day before the draper's establishment, gave only a passing glance at the tall young man in riding clothes who strode past them with purposeful air.

He found the tavern looking even more dilapidated than he

remembered it, and the little Norman chapel across the street shabby and sad. Then as he turned the corner he stopped, amazed at the contrast of the new building just below the chapel.

He had expected to find a half-built house, and hurried down the street to look more closely, for at first glance the fine oak door and large leaded windows gave the appearance of a completed and lived-in home. Then he noticed that while the main roof glistened with new grey-blue Delabole slates, immediately behind a wing had been roofed in thatch, while closer inspection of the windows showed that some had no glass in them and had been boarded up behind with painted timbers.

In spite of such signs of hasty unskilled completion of the work, Nicholas gazed in appreciative admiration at the overall effect of elegance in the design. He recognised his father's influence in the way the moorstone had been cut and laid in almost geometrical courses so that the granite posts of the windows and doors became focal points of an overall design.

His excited gaze passed from one carved granite lintel to another; somewhere a craftsman had been found who was more than a mere carver in stone, but an artist and observer of the countryside. Over the upper windows he had carved in the granite lintels buzzards and hawks, curlews, snipe, larks and linnets, and even a tiny wren. Animals were depicted on the lower windows, from rabbits and snakes to a fine horned ox. Nicholas was deeply engrossed in studying the carving over the main door — a complicated design in a border of grapes and acanthus leaves — when he was disturbed by the noise of horses trotting up from the north gate. He turned just in time to see a young man ride in through the entrance at the side of the house, a diminutive lady perched on the pillion behind him, and followed by a second rider whose horse also carried a wooden chest and a large rolled bundle.

Richard had brought his bride home.

The following morning Nicholas sent Mattie to call on the new Mistress Chyket with an invitation to dine at Theupath. Richard was touched by what he saw as an olive branch from a man whose father had died through his work for Richard's new house. The invitation was accepted and a day agreed.

In the event it turned into a happy party. The formal greetings were a trifle strained, as was to be expected, but the ice was immediately broken by Nicholas, who stooped down rather exaggeratedly to salute Mary, and then slapped his friend on the back and declared:

'You rogue! That was clever of you, to find yourself a bride so small that even you can stand tall as a big man! And she has beauty too!'

Mary blushed shyly, not quite sure whether to be pleased at the compliment or offended at the way it was put by this tall rather arrogant stranger. Richard took her hand and said proudly: 'Go find your own beauty! This is my pearl, my Mary Fursdon and the mother of the Chykets of Calyngton.'

He looked up at his old friend with an air of confident defiance, and Nicholas realised that, in spite of the lost arm, Richard had lost none of his old ebullience. Restraining the urge to pick him up by the scruff of his neck to prove his own superior size and strength, he went instead to stand behind them, and taking Mary's hand from Richard he ushered her with gentle courtesy to the table, where he seated her in the best chair.

Over the meal the two men exchanged news of their lives over the years since they parted as boys, and discussed in considerable detail the battle campaigns in which they had taken part in France. It was a shock to Nicholas to learn that Richard had been at the siege of Rougemont. Remembering the archers shooting down the refugees, he looked questioningly at Richard.

Richard immediately understood his thoughts and said simply: 'No. Thank the good Lord, I was not involved in that. In fact, I knew nothing of that day, for I was in the hospital tent with my arm poisoned by an arrow wound obtained at Beaugency. The surgeon took it off that same evening. I was mad with fever a full sennight – indeed lucky to have survived.'

He was pensive for a moment, then stretched out his arm across the table to Mary.

'Now I have one arm, and one wife. I am one fortunate fellow!'

'Amen to that' said Nicholas, pushing back in his thoughts a momentary recollection of his auburn-haired goddess of the Chepe. He went on to describe to his guests his life in London and some of the festivals such as the Midsummer Marching Watch. With a little harmless embroidery to his narrative he soon had Mary gazing at him in wrapt attention, her modest shyness quite forgotten in this revelation of the world and its grandeur. Even Richard was visibly impressed, and his eyes glittered with professional interest when Nicholas described the rich clothes of the aldermen and the ornate hangings on the buildings lining the streets. He asked a number of questions about the colour of the cloths, and Nicholas felt compelled to answer him with strict accuracy.

'Are you going to manufacture your own cloth?' he asked.

Richard laughed. 'Why not?' he countered, 'Why should those rogues in Devon have all the profit from my wool? Just consider all the water sources available here. If John Berkamstede will sell me the mill at Trevigro, I think I could produce some cheerful worsted cloth for our winters — and some fine cloth too, for the ladies,' he added, beaming at the attentive Mary. 'Light as gossamer, delicate as a petal of St John's wort . . . but not white. I think a dusky pink would look well on my Mary.'

'Oh, Richard!' sighed his little wife in ecstasy.

'Yes, we shall call it Marydew cloth,' continued Richard triumphantly, as if the cloth and its colour were already achieved. His enthusiasm was infectious, and with ideas on dyes and standards of cloth bubbling out like a newly tapped spring, the discussion went on until well into the afternoon, with complete confidence in the ultimate success of this new venture of merchant Richard.

It was only when Richard's ambitious ideas turned to altar vestments that Nicholas suddenly remembered the plans for the new church. Calling Ellin to clear all vestiges of their meal from the table, he brought out the rolled parchments and spread them on the table, pegging them down with heavy pewter tankards which he fetched from the cupboard. Then he stood back to await reactions from his guests.

Richard looked 'mazed', for his thoughts were still on cloth, and the colourful design of stone and glass meant nothing to him. But, Mary, who had to climb on to a stool to examine the parchments, exclaimed at once at the beautiful church. Her shyness now evaporated, she beamed at Nicholas and asked eagerly: 'You will build this church?'

He nodded, pleased at her interest. Then she spotted the out-line of an old chapel incorporated in the plan, and in the corner another outline labelled 'Chyket', and the full impact of the plan struck her. She jumped down from the stool and ran to Nicholas, clapping her hands in excitement.

'Of course, I know,' she called triumphantly, 'You are going to build us a beautiful new church in Calyngton. Oh, but the Lord will bless you, it is wonderful, wonderful.'

His heart melted in pure happiness at the praise of this simple and natural country girl. He took both her hands in his and smiled down at the diminutive figure.

'Yes,' he said, 'we are going to build you a new church for Calyngton. You are the first to have seen it, and as it pleases you so well, perhaps we will ask the bishop to dedicate it to the Virgin Mary, for whom you are named.'

Mary's simple nature was not equal to this, and she melted into tears in Nicholas's arms until firmly rescued by her husband. Whether the tears were in protest or approval was never known, and no more was said about the dedication. But Richard, roused from his own dreams by his wife's excitement, now turned his enthusiasm to the topic of the new church, and before they left to return home it had been agreed to call a meeting of householders to enlist support.

'We have, after all,' said Richard, 'not only your father's plans to work from, but also a fine team of stonemasons who owe their skill to his training and inspiration. We should build well.'

The meeting was held two weeks later. The guildhall was packed, for everyone wanted to see the young gentleman who used to be the bastard upstart but was now aspiring to be a benefactor to the town. Nicholas answered all their questions patiently, even while seething inwardly at some of the ill-informed comments on the design. He knew he needed the support of the town, so he said nothing when Nat Bullen com-plained that such a large building would block the light from the tavern windows, and just dug his hands more deeply into his sleeve pockets when Martha Crago declared; 'What was good enough for my mam and my grandmam is good enough for we! Us need no change of praying place at all.' But the enthusiasm of Richard Chyket carried all before it.

'See,' he cried, 'I have builders here,' indicating his team of stonemasons ranged in solid support behind him. 'We have good quarries for moorstone and granite nearby, and with the help of those with strong arms and stout carrying carts we could make a start before the winter. It is only for the windows that we will need to bring in other skills which will need paying for. Let us see what we can do for ourselves and for our town!'

After the crowd had dispersed Richard turned to Nicholas, and was surprised to see him looking far from happy.

'Are you not satisfied with our work this day?' he asked in hurt surprise.

Nicholas pulled himself together and smiled gratefully at his friend.

'Oh, yes,' he replied, 'you have achieved wonders, and I am well pleased.' He hesitated, then added: 'I was just disappointed that no one thought of my father.'

Not much of a start was in fact achieved that autumn. The stonemasons opened up a quarry high on the slope of the hill, and cut cornerstones and enough squared granite to start the foundations. But then, with November, steady drenching rain took over the scene and the track down the brea became impassable for heavy carts loaded with blocks of stone. Meanwhile Richard had embroiled himself in a dispute with the manor steward over his plans to open up a fulling mill and produce his own dyed cloth — they could not agree the amount of the fine payable for such an enterprise — and Nicholas had gone back to Devon to arbitrate in the dispute over Plymstok chapel. Faced with appalling working conditions and lacking the guidance of a leader, most of the masons lost interest and dispersed to other work, leaving only three of their band to build the church. Masses continued to be celebrated in the little Norman chapel, and the idea of a grand new church faded into a laughable myth.

9

Over at Fursdon the still expanding flock of sheep, now one of the largest in Cornwall, occupied all John's time and thoughts, and he paid scant regard to messages from his sister in Calyngton. He smiled with placid pleasure when his mother told him one evening: 'Meg sent word by the tinker who called today that Richard is at last setting his mill to work, and, better still, she is now with child!' Mary sat back in her high-backed chair by the fire with obvious satisfaction, and was displeased when her news drew no comment from her son.

'Why, you dolt!' she declared indignantly. 'Are you not pleased for your sister?'

'Yes indeed, good mother,' he corrected himself hastily. 'I am pleased for Meg, and for you. Your first grandchild.' He nodded rather absent-minded approval, his mind still more than half on the problem of which pasture would be best in the early spring for the first batch of lambing ewes.

'It is time you married, son,' said Mary sharply. The tone of her voice roused John to the topic of conversation. Gently he shook his head.

'The flock is my life, mother. Soon Elizabeth will be marrying — if John Jope has a say in the matter, I warrant. Willie can work with me at Fursdon, and when he grows old enough to take a fancy to the maids he can pick himself a wife and bring her here to live with us.'

'John, my son, that is not sufficient care for the future of Fursdon.' Mary leaned forward in her urgency. 'You too must marry and have sons. Now, Meg in her letter writes of a young maid newly of her acquaintance in Calyngton,' — here she pulled a folded scrap of parchment from her apron pocket and referred to it — 'Betsy Bould, her name, and Meg writes that she is sweet and kind and much interested in all that Meg tells her of us, the family at Fursdon. Why not ride over to Calyngton, my son, and visit your sister?'

John, the worker in the family from an early age, had never learned to read more than was sufficient for the buying and selling of sheep and corn, and so he relied on his mother for excerpts from his sister's occasional letters. He felt mildly interested in her new friend, but the mention of Calyngton reminded him of earlier news, that Nicholas Ayssheton was back home and planning to build a new church. After all these years any mention of Nicholas still brought tension and a slight ache to his heart as he remembered yet again that wonderful time in Calyngton with the magnificent boy who had never bothered since to visit him. That the same Nicholas had succeeded him as a parliamentary representative for Liskerret and still never sent word that he remembered him did nothing to heal the childish hurt which still lay dormant in his simple soul.

Mary repeated her question, and added, 'I have some little garments put by from Willie's babyhood. You should take them to Meg, she will be needing to prepare for the child. You could go next week?'

The last was put as a question, for Mary knew that she could no longer dictate to her son, a successful sheep farmer and a respected member of the Liskerret community.

But John shook his head. 'No, mother, next week I must go to Lanteglos fair. I have business there with Henry Weekes. Perhaps after that I will take your gifts over to Meg and see how she fares.'

It was not a good day for the fair. A strong southwesterly swept along the lines of market stalls and whipped round corners, catching the unwary, blowing off the men's hats and ballooning the women's skirts. Some of the stall-holders put up screens to try and protect their goods from the wind and the frequent downpours of rain borne on it, but by eleven in the forenoon it was evident that the market would close early for lack of both buyer and seller. The roads leading from Lanteglos to Looe and Bodmyn were already thronged with lines of carts heading homeward.

John had concluded his business with Henry Weekes and walked back to the sheep fair where he had left William in charge of a ram and two ewes he had thought to sell. To his surprise the pen was empty, and William reported, with pride, a good sale.

'It was a stranger who purchased them. He was accompanied by a very elegant and beautiful lady, for whom he was acting. He said she had recently come to live at Polcarowe and wished to build up the farm with good stock. He had been recommended to look for Fursdon sheep and so he bought these at your price with enthusiasm. I wish it was always so easy to make a sale!'

'What was his name, Willie?'

William scratched his head ruefully. 'I — I don't recall. The lady's name was Brook, Mistress Brook he called her, but no, he didn't give me his own name. But he was treated with great respect by the folk standing by — and he did say I was to tell you that if you wished to sell any more of the flock you should call on him at Polcarowe within the next week.'

John's eyes widened and he nodded with satisfaction. 'That is good news, Willie. It means that now the Fursdon reputation for sheep is so good we can breed for sale as stock rather than solely as sheep-meat or fleece. As specialists we can command higher prices. Well done, Willie, that was a good day's work!'

William looked relieved. He had expected to be berated for not having ascertained the purchaser's name. He ran to collect the cart and the brothers rode home merrily, the southwesterly on their backs rattling the tailboard of the cart and sweeping them along like a sailing craft before the wind.

Four days later John rode down again to Lanteglos and found his way to Polcarowe. It lay in a grove of elm trees, from which the steady rain dripped mournfully on the thatched roof and ran down off the eaves into a muddy forecourt. He looked around for signs of a prosperous estate, but could see only dilapidated empty barns, from beyond which came the sound of torrents of storm water tumbling down a valley stream. He was about to turn away in the belief that he had been directed to the wrong property when a voice hailed him and he saw a stout middle-aged man emerging from the stable end of the house, leading a horse. Both man and beast looked many thousands of marks more prosperous than the house, and John recognised him immediately as John Cork of Paderda, his one-time fellow burgess for Liskerret in the parliament.

'Why, good day to you, John Cork,' he called across the yard. 'What business has brought you to this dripping mudhole?'

The older man waved in reply, showing no surprise at the arrival of his parliamentary colleague. Grinning broadly as he approached he called back, in mild reproach, 'I have awaited your arrival these three days.'

They greeted each other warmly, and Cork went on to explain that he was assisting Mistress Brook as legal and financial adviser in establishing her household at Polcarowe. He invited John indoors, and after stabling both the horses he swung open the battered house door and ushered his visitor inside. Then he stood back and chuckled from the very depths of his rotund belly as he watched John gazing in amazement at the luxurious appointments of the weather-beaten old house.

'There, you see, my lady has brought the richness of her life at court into the humble scene of Cornwall. Think you not, friend, that this is all much lovelier and more comforting to the body than our sparse and practical Cornish furnishings?'

He swept a hand around the great hall, which should have been dark and filled with smoke from a central reredos but was instead filled with sombre light from a massive window let into the south wall, alongside which a cheerful fire blazed in a new chimneyed hearth. The walls were hung with colourful tapestries, their gold thread twinkling in the warm firelight.

It took John some time to recover from the shock of finding such loveliness in the drab old building. At last he turned to Master Cork and said simply: 'It is indeed very beautiful,' shaking his head as if he could not credit his own words.

They sat down together on a settle near the fire, from which they could look out through the great window at the grey wet day and the dripping trees marching down the valley along the course of the stream.

'My lady, the Mistress Margaret,' said Master Cork, pressing his fingertips together before his nose and half closing his eyes, 'like all women, has strange fancies; but unlike any other woman I have ever known, she is of a very adventurous disposition. When she came into this inheritance she decided, against all prudent advice for a lady of her class, to take ship to Fowy with all her household staff and goods and establish her home at Polcarowe. Why she wished to leave her life at court, I know not — perhaps it was a disappointing love affair.' Here he winked knowingly at John. 'She obtained leave to relinquish her duties as mistress of the bed-chamber to the duchess. The regent's wife is not a happy woman, and I believe there was no love lost between the two — although of one thing I am certain, the cause was in no way due to any liaison between the duke and Mistress Margaret. She dislikes him intensely.'

'How will she survive here in Cornwall?' queried John, then answered his own question. 'After life at court she will surely be bored to distraction. There are at present no ladies in the Trelawne household to keep her company, and the roads from here to Bodmyn are not fit for a carriage. What could she do here?'

'As I said, Mistress Margaret is one for excitement and adventure. Quite unsuitably for a lady of quality, she delights in the challenge of trying her hand at what is properly man's work. She wishes to redesign Polcarowe as a fine country *gentleman*'s residence, with pleasure gardens and a park stocked with deer; worse, she plans to go in for *farming*! She has commissioned me to make this estate once more self-sufficient in crops and livestock, just as it was in her great-grandfather's day. I bought your sheep for her, Master Fursdon, on the recommendation of Squire Trelawny — I am a lawyer, myself, I know little about animals.'

John smiled at his fat companion's protests, not a bit offended at the disparaging tone of his comments on farming. 'As you know, I am a farmer, how can I help you?'

'Oh, good sir, for that I would be most deeply grateful!' declared Master Cork, bubbling with relief. 'Your advice in the purchasing of further stock — oxen, milch cows, hens, ducks, geese; a smith and a carpenter to make us new ploughs and carts — this is all so much out of my province that I hardly know where to start. What I need most of all now is an honest, hardworking and knowledgeable reeve to whom I can delegate the work when all is set up to my lady's satisfaction. I have already purchased for her two excellent horses — that I *do* know something about!' He finished his disjointed ramble on a note of triumph, bringing another sympathetic smile to John's lips.

'A reeve?' he said, stroking his chin thoughtfully. 'I know one man who might suit your purpose well, and I will send him to you in a day or two. I am a busy farmer myself, but if I can assist in the planning of your enterprise I will be happy to do so. A challenge such as this appeals to me also.' He laughed then at himself, the inveterate worker and man of ideas.

At that moment a door behind them opened and the mistress of the house entered the hall. The two men rose to their feet. John Cork bid her good morning and bowed briefly; John Fursdon hastily followed suit, uncomfortably aware that he had been standing agape in a shamefully uncouth manner. His eyes were dazzled by the vision in gold and blue damask as rich in colour as the tapestries which she had hung on the walls. As he straightened again he found the vision was completed by a pair of twinkling blue eyes and an impish smile under a rich blue velvet turban studded with pearls.

John Cork made the introductions and Margaret Brook held out her hand to bid the visitor welcome. John bowed once more, his lips trembling as they brushed her hand, while the stout little man beside him beamed paternally at both of them.

Margaret sat herself down on the fireside settle and beckoned to John to sit beside her. The lawyer perched his rotund form on a low stool opposite, looking for all the world like an overgrown toadstool; Margaret caught John's eye and they laughed silently together, a couple of conspirators already.

Blissfully unaware that he made a comic spectacle, John Cork reported the discussion and asked for Mistress Margaret's approval. She turned to the young farmer beside her.

'I am very content that Master Fursdon will give us the benefit of his considerable experience and expert knowledge,' she replied, another impish smile lighting up her small oval face and wrinkling her little snub nose. Then, speaking directly to John she asked him earnestly, the smile now melted away, 'Would you be prepared, as well as finding us a good reeve, Master Fursdon, to design for me the best modern farm and supervise its building?'

Such a task was a tall order for John, already stretched to his full limit working his own estate, and a near-illiterate, if practical, man. But, without a second's hesitation, he accepted, and within a few moments the two were deep in ideas, proposals, counter-proposals and alterations, oblivious to the lawyer still perched on his stool and now thoroughly bemused by the discussion. It was a marriage of minds, and Margaret warmed to the serious young farmer. She was used to the admiration of men, for her lack of classic beauty was more than compensated for by her vitality and colour, but here was an admirer who, for all his shyness, spoke with courage and authority on his own subject — farming — and drew her attention and respect. She was not used to playing the subordinate role, and her interest in the young Cornishman grew.

At last John rose and begged leave to go, explaining the many duties awaiting him at Fursdon before dusk. Reluctantly he declined a goblet of mead. Once more his lips touched the hand of his lovely hostess — a goddess to his enchanted heart — and then he was out again in the dripping rain, mounting his horse and taking leave of John Cork. He promised to send Ned Palmer as soon as possible, for possible employment as the Polcarowe reeve.

'And the buildings?' queried Master Cork.

'That will take a little longer,' John admitted, 'But rest assured that I will give the matter thought and study during the dark evenings, and when I have produced a worthwhile plan I will bring it here for Mistress Brook's approval.'

His horse took him safely home, but John was so wrapped in happy thoughts that he scarcely noticed the road or the misty drizzle.

10

Mary Fursdon was at first puzzled and then increasingly alarmed when night after night John sat until the candle was guttering, long past his accustomed bedtime, drawing with charcoal on an old piece of white linen gummed to a board. When she asked was he planning new farm buildings for Fursdon he merely shook his head and gave no explanation; when she reminded him of the proposed visit to his sister at Calyngton he replied, 'Not yet,' in a preoccupied way, and carried on with his drawing.

'The boy is mazed,' muttered Mary angrily, after her third

attempt to persuade him of his duty to his sister, and she swept out of the room, tripping over the threshold because she did not have the candle with her.

A few days later William drove his mother to Liskerret market. There she heard from Ned Palmer's wife all about the rich and flamboyant 'critter' now installed at Polcarowe. This then was the answer to John's present behaviour; he was obviously bewitched by a beautiful and wicked paramour, who was using his love and his talents for her own purposes and would discard him like an old rag after use. She felt hot with anger and embarrassment as she pictured this wicked woman – for wicked she must surely be – teasing her John and laughing at his simple honesty.

That evening, from the vantage point of her fireside chair she studied her son closely as he pored over the linen board, taking measurements and altering lines in deep concentration as he visualised the scene he hoped to create. There was nothing she could do at the present time to break the spell. She must bide her time.

Eventually the lines and the figures on the linen board were completed to John's satisfaction, and the next evening Mary found fourteen-year-old William at the table with ink-horn and pen, carefully copying on to parchment his brother's rough drawings and calculations. Mary had taught William herself, and in spite of her misgivings over the whole project she could not resist a certain satisfaction when she saw how he had transformed the rough work with the tidy pen of a scholar.

At the end of the week, on a blustery March day when both John and William had spent most of the night with the ewes in the lambing pasture, John left the morning's work for his brother to complete and disappeared on his horse, the rolled parchment secured with ribbon and tucked inside his leather tunic. He did not return until just before dusk, and his mother noted with inward dismay his general air of happy contentment and satisfaction. Things had gone well for the wicked enchantress, that was clear, and still poor Mary could not find the opportunity to disillusion her son.

Clutching at straws, she enquired where he had been, expecting evasion or even silence. But John beamed at her happily and told her: 'I have taken a complete set of plans for the new farm at Polcarowe for the owner, Mistress Brook's approval,' — here he did have the grace to blush, and stooped to examine his horse's fetlock, avoiding his mother's questioning look — 'and she approves of them. I have been asked to go again after Easter-tide to check the work and its progress.'

'Who is this Mistress Brook?' His mother could not keep the disapproval out of her voice.

'Oh, an acquaintance of Master John Cork of Paderda — you know, mother, over at Linkinhorne — he told me he had done business with my father some years ago.'

'Ah, yes, the lawyer.' The name was familiar and she searched her memory, but John was keen to close the subject and interposed quickly, 'Now I will really make that visit to little Meg at Calyngton and take her those articles you have put aside for her.'

The following morning Mary packed the bundle of shawls, dresses, tiny caps and yards of banding into John's saddlebag, and waved him goodbye, with many loving messages for her daughter and admonitions to take care of himself.

He took the same route by which he had gone to Calyngton thirteen years earlier. The memory of that adventure of boyhood returned to him once more, as vividly as ever, but now there was no hurt in his soul, for he had found a deeper happiness elsewhere.

There was an air of subdued activity that morning in the little market town. As John rode in past the strip fields the last of the stored crops were being lifted and carried away by the smallholders and their families in round wicker baskets. Passing by the larger houses he caught a glimpse of handcarts standing in archways or in the courtyards behind, being scrubbed down by young servants. Some handcarts were already set up in the market place, in prime positions close to the old Celtic cross. It was the eve of the annual three-day fair, which John also remembered as the most important time in his boyhood.

Full of now gentle memories he walked his horse carefully round the corner past the church, then drew up suddenly, shocked at the scene of dereliction before his eyes. The little Norman church, seeming to him smaller and infinitely shabbier than in his boyhood, was now surrounded by a new low wall of moorstone blocks, half hidden behind several piles of roughly hewn stone and a scattering of timber and miscellaneous rubbish. A wooden hoist raised its head at the far end of the wall, but its ropes hung slack. Not a soul was to be seen, all was silent and still. John moved on, thinking to himself that new church would be a long time a-building.

Then he caught sight of the new house just below the church, and just as Nicholas Ayssheton had done the previous year, he stopped before it and studied its every detail with increasing admiration. At length he realised that he was delaying too long, and moved on into the wool-merchant's yard behind.

Immediately, before he had had time to dismount, two doors opened simultaneously. His brother-in-law stood beaming from the store-room entrance, while from the house his sister Mary skipped down the short flight of steps and ran across the yard, her arms outstretched in welcome.

'Oh John, dear brother John, you have come at last!' she cried, and as John slipped from the saddle she flung herself into his arms and reached up to kiss him. John hugged her silently, tears welling in his eyes as he realised how much his neglect had meant to her. Ashamed, he felt he did not deserve such a tumultuous welcome.

Gently he took Mary's arms and eased her from her bear hug. 'Let me look at you, little Meg,' he begged, using the family diminutive of her second name which was always used at home to distinguish her from her mother. 'Let me see what married life has done to my beloved little sister. My goodness me, it fits you well! Not even a wrinkle do I see on that pretty face!' He kissed her tenderly on the forehead, then turned to Richard who had joined them.

'Brother-in-law, you have done well, to have trained a wife who still stays as pretty as a peach!' They laughed amicably and clasped hands. Before more could be said Mary tugged at John's hand and pulled him towards the house. 'Come and see what Richard has done,' she demanded.

As she led the way up the steps he could see that her trim little figure had not coarsened in the slightest because of her pregnancy. The evidence was neatly concealed under her voluminous petticoats and worsted skirt, over which she wore a starched white apron, and the ankles glimpsed under their hems were as neat and shapely as ever.

'Bearing children seems to suit you,' he remarked with brotherly candour.

Mary blushed prettily as she opened the door and led the way into the house. Richard laughed and answered for her.

'She is wonderful — wonderful at all times. If our children are as happy and contented as we two, life in the Chyket family will be a bed of roses!'

'Get away with you!' Mary remonstrated, laughing with pleasure and beaming with happy love at her husband. He put his one arm round her shoulder and together they took John on a tour of their home, from the warm and well lighted kitchen and its buttery and pantry, to Mary's favourite room, the solar. There by the big window her spinning wheel stood, and her loom nearby. While working there she could look out over the roof tops and the orchard to the fields and the moors beyond, near her old home.

Many of the chambers at the head of the fine oak staircase stood empty or served as storerooms for the timber and glass which Richard was still working on to complete the house. Their own bedchamber boasted only a simple bed, made by Richard, and a small closet. In a corner stood Richard's latest handiwork, an oak rocking cradle.

They returned down the stairs into the kitchen, and then Richard opened large double doors and ushered John through. 'This is my dream, now almost achieved,' he announced proudly. John stepped into a vast banqueting hall, full of light from the morning sun streaming in through two rows of mullioned windows. Looking up he saw the queen posts and rafters of the main roof, while halfway down the end wall he noticed a small round peep-hole, and he remembered seeing this in the solar and wondering what it viewed. In the opposite end wall was a cavernous hearth in the modern chimney style, big enough for the roasting of an ox. A long trestle table ran almost the full length of the hall, lined with an assortment of stools and benches, while at each end was an elaborately carved highbacked armchair.

'You made those?' queried John, turning to Richard and indicating the two chairs.

'Yes, they are part of my dream, a dream of a banqueting hall fit for the entertainment of judges and bishops, and — who knows? — perhaps one day the king himself, or the regent, may come this way, and we cannot entertain royalty in the street!' Then he added, laughing, 'One day my family may be grand enough for those chairs, so I am working on more of them — one for each member of my future family!'

'I admire your tenacity as well as your skill,' said John, 'You deserve to succeed, and I am sure you will. Your hall is truly magnificent!' He looked round again, impressed by the size and spaciousness of what he had expected to be merely part of a merchant's house. This grand hall would not have been out of place at Polcarowe, he realised, only falling short by its bare walls and its unlighted fire.

'Come, let us eat,' said Mary, and led the way back to the kitchen. A pot of chicken and vegetables bubbled on the fire, and Mary brought from the buttery a new crusty loaf as good as any her mother made, and a great mound of dewy butter. They took their seats on the rough stools at the scrubbed board and exchanged family news over several bowls of chicken stew.

After the meal Richard took John out to the yard, and showed him Mary's brewhouse and bakehouse before they adjourned to the woolstore for a happy hour in their own specialist field, discussing quality and prices.

As the sun began to sink towards Carnedon John decided reluctantly it was time to leave. Only then did he remember the saddlebag packed with baby clothes and hastily carried them into the house. Richard pressed him to stay until the morrow, for the sheep fair, but John declined.

'I am tempted to stay, but there is too much to be done at Fursdon, and we have no animals prepared for sale, even if there were time for Willie to bring them over. Perhaps another year we will bring our sheep to Calyngton instead of Liskerret.'

Mary gave him a long hug and tearful kiss, with many murmured messages through gentle sobs for her mother and her sister and brother. As he rode out of the gate John turned in his saddle to look back. The little figure at the top of the steps looked small and forlorn, one hand waving and the other covering her mouth. He blew her a kiss and rode quickly away.

Mary's baby was born safely at full term late in June. A blue-eyed boy, he was baptised in the little Norman church and given the name John after his uncle, to whom he was said to bear a remarkable resemblance.

11

Richard's fine new banqueting hall saw its first event that same summer, but it was not yet the scene for the grand entertainment of bishops, judges and the nobility, nor did Mary preside at the long table as Richard had envisaged. This was a more homely affair, ostensibly a celebration of the birth of the Chyket son and heir, but in reality a gathering together of all the town's more prosperous tradesmen, craftsmen and farmers, men who were beginning to show a pride in their town and might be expected to help provide it with a church worthy of its future.

For Richard was worried. The building of the church had almost ground to a halt. Hewing the moorstone from the quarry high on the slope of the hill was slow and arduous work for the three stonemasons, who also had to bring the loaded cart down the long haul to the town and off-load the blocks themselves before being able to start any building work. Then the long dry summer brought a cessation of work when there was hay to be saved and sheep to be sheared. Meanwhile the lack of visible progress at the church site had brought the usual caustic comments from the doubting Thomases in the population who now said they always knew the church 'would never happen'.

A boost was needed to the scheme, an influx of enthusiasm and financial backing. Hearing that Nicholas Ayssheton was briefly home at Theupath while being elected to the parliament for Dunheved − after several years as one of the members for Helston − Richard took a chance that his lawyer friend might be just the boost required. The invitations went out, and the prospect of being among the first to banquet in the new hall ensured a full company, everyone keen to drink to the baby's future and take a good look at the Chyket home. Baby John of course, was not present at this celebration in his honour — he was represented by his uncle, John Fursdon.

The banquet was provided by Mary, who had worked for two days with Betsy Bould in the bakehouse, concocting sweet and savoury pies, plucking and drawing ducks and partridges, and preparing for the spit the fine yearling ram which John had contributed. Betsy's two young brothers were brought in to serve at table, and when all was carried in and the guests assembled, Mary and Betsy left the two scullery maids to clear the kitchen and tripped quietly up the stairs to the solar, where they took turns, with much giggling, at spying through the peep-hole at the diners in the hall below.

From their vantage point the long laden table made a pretty picture, with pride of place going to Mary's prize possession, a shiny pewter charger on which Billy Bould had arranged slices of juicy mutton skilfully sliced from the carcase sizzling in the great hearth. No one had yet cut into the pies set along the table; a star-gazy pie, two partridge pies, a duck pie flavoured with mushrooms and sliced apple, and several sweet custard pies each decorated with a cherry. In between were crusty loaves and huge mounds of golden yellow butter, and cheeses as colourful as the bowls of freshly picked strawberries sitting between them.

Mary sighed with satisfaction. 'Don't it look magnificent?' she murmured, lost in admiration and quite oblivious to her own prime part in producing it.

But down below one at least among the laughing, chattering men already quaffing their first tankard of ale had not forgotten. From his position near the head of the table her brother John glimpsed a movement behind the peep-hole high in the wall. He smiled at it and raised his tankard in salute, then on a sudden impulse rose to his feet and in a stentorian voice quite unlike his normal quiet tone demanded attention.

'Friends, on this memorable occasion, let us not fall to on these delicious meats without first expressing our thanks to the provider of our feast.' All eyes turned to look at Richard. 'But no, 'tis not my brother-in-law I would have you toast, but the mistress of the house. Masters, I give you — Mistress Mary!' and John swung his tankard up to indicate the tiny window high up on the wall.

Mary blushed in confusion as a sea of faces gazed up at her, twenty-two tankards were raised and a growling shout proclaimed, 'Mistress Mary!' For a moment she remained rooted to the spot, framed in the round opening like a portrait on the wall, then she sank down on her stool, happy tears running unchecked down her rosy cheeks.

Betsy chuckled. 'That was your fine brother, was it not? Let me take a peek,' and she stopped rocking the baby's cradle to take her turn at the window. But she was too late to catch John's eye. All she saw were platters piled with a glutinous mixture of hot mutton, cold duck pie and pilchards from the star-gazy pie. Some of the diners in their eagerness were already reaching out to the strawberries with one hand as the other stuffed hot mutton into their mouths. As she watched, the laden board began to resemble a battlefield, littered with strawberry hulls, splashes of gravy and crumbled pastry, as the worthy townsmen tucked into the banquet. The noise of talk and laughter rose up to the little peephole in a crescendo, and after a short while the two women retired with the baby to a quieter part of the house.

Down in the banqueting hall the baby's uncle relaxed into his normal shy reticence, quietly observing his fellow diners as Mary's ale induced a general air of bonhomie. Opposite him the rector, Thomas Baron — who had considered the occasion sufficiently important to warrant one of his rare appearances in Calyngton — was in earnest conversation with Robert Manaton on the profitability of turning further glebe land to sheep and growing less corn. John's neighbour, Robert Heye, nudged him rather violently so that his ale slopped down over his sleeve, and in a hoarse undertone already overlaid with the fumes of alcohol, said, 'They wax and grow fat over at Southill, do they not, that fine pair? Just look at poor old Keryet down yonder.'

John followed his glance to the far end of the table, where the curate sat with the lower orders, the stonemasons and the lesser officials of the manor market. Old Nicholas Keryet was lean and gaunt, his bearded face deeply lined and his watery eyes barely open under straggly brows.

'He fell asleep half-way through the mass last Sunday,' chuckled Heye. 'He will struggle on there until they force him out in his coffin. Perhaps it would be best to build the new church round him, with no doors and windows, and make that his tomb!'

John smiled politely, his serious nature not taking to this irreverent young farmer who appeared to have respect for neither the church nor the dignity of old age. Then, glancing back along the table he suddenly found himself caught by a pair of twinkling brown eyes.

John had been observing Nicholas Ayssheton, but the lawyer's severe demeanour had discouraged any approach on the lines of boyhood memories and he could only admire the elegant attire and air of authority which marked him out as a superior being in this simple rural setting. Now, astonishingly, that severe face had melted into a boyish grin, and an elegant ringed hand reached across the table, its silk sleeve slipping, disregarded, into the splashed gravy and strawberry juice.

'Remember me? We have met before, you and I. We were boys together, here, and since then I have followed you into parliament, and wondered if I would ever see you again!'

Remember him? How could he ever forget him? John gripped the proffered hand, and they laughed together in warm renewal of that boyhood friendship.

At the head of the table Richard rose to his feet and called for silence. Judging to a nicety that all were now well fed but still sufficiently alert to give full attention to his words, he set out to enlist their support for a renewal of the church building work. He described the current stagnant situation, and then continued, 'We started well, my good friends, but in our ignorance we did not fully realise the magnitude of the task on which we had embarked. You cannot erect a fine stone church of proper magnificence in a matter of months, it is unkind of our critics to demand a miracle. It could be a lifetime's work. We need time, patience and skill, and we need more hands to haul, to lift and to carry.' Indicating the three stonemasons at the far end of the table he said, 'My friends there, Warne Pengelly, Thomas Benet and Ben Drewe, are fine craftsmen in stone, but they need assistance to enable the work to go ahead at a reasonable pace. Master Pengelly asks for four men to work with him at the quarry. We have a stout cart specially strengthened to carry six blocks at a time, and my strongest oxen are reserved for this work along with my wagonmaster.

Another four men are needed at the site, for the hoisting of the blocks into position.'

He paused expectantly. Immediately offers of extra hands came from those with labour to spare, among them Robert Heye, who promised the assistance of two of his fieldhands, 'Until next plough time.'

Then Richard continued, outlining with clarity and enthusiasm the need for funds to pay for experts in glazing, woodcarving and painting to be brought in. Now he looked at the merchants among his guests, and after some hesitation several spoke up for a hundred marks or so, upon which the rector and Robert Manaton put their heads together and then came out with an offer of two hundred each. Richard almost purred with pleasure.

John looked across at Nicholas and saw him watching Richard intently, apparently waiting for a signal; Richard nodded towards him and he rose to his feet.

'Gentlemen of Calyngton,' he began, and every man in the hall sat up straight in pleasure at being thus addressed by the distinguished lawyer, 'My father designed that church, for the realisation of my dream that our town should have a church worthy of it. There must be no cheese-paring, no cutting out the beauty to save the cost. I give here my note of hand to our host, promising to pay all wages, and the cost of all materials, incurred by the employment of glaziers, carpenters and painters, providing only that these must be men approved by our lord bishop of Exeter, who has experience of the fine craftsmen who worked on my father's designs there.' He passed a rolled parchment to Richard, who waved it aloft in delight as the audience sat stunned momentarily before bursting into spontaneous applause.

'There, my friends, see the munificence of one son of Calyngton!' cried Richard, grinning from ear to ear. 'We others now only need to provide for the stonework and the roof. Surely we can accomplish that with ease?'

The reply was a babble of shouted offers from all around the long table, even the curate offering a small portion of his minute income. Richard made out a list, which Billy Bould then carried round for each man to sign or make his mark.

'We will start work again on the first day of the month,'

Richard announced, nodding to Warne at the foot of the table. Then he signalled to Billy's brother, and in a moment every guest had before him a pewter goblet of mead in which to drink to the success of the project, and to the health of the infant Chyket — who would never know that the party in his honour had been put to other uses.

Nicholas and John left together. 'Will you ride over to Theupath with me?' suggested Nicholas, 'we have much old ground to recover and new ideas to exchange.'

John was about to refuse, knowing that he was awaited at home, but as in the old days, he was caught in the spell of Nicholas's commanding charm and accepted the invitation.

The two men rode out through the north gate and up the lane to Pengelly, just as they had done on their first meeting. This time, however, they did not pull up at the farm, now in the hands of John's cousin Henry Hicks, but trotted on over the common and down the hill to Theupath.

Theupath was just the same as John remembered it, although it did seem to have shrunk a little in size. Thomas Hicks led their horses away, with only a curt nod to his cousin. Taken aback, John called after him, 'Good day to you, cousin Thomas, I hope I see you well, and your kith and kin also.'

A surprised Thomas stepped back out of the stable, still holding the rein of one of the horses. His swarthy face lost its habitual scowl as he recognised John, and he grinned, showing a mouthful of blackened teeth.

'Why, if it isn't little John from over on the moor!'

He disappeared back into the stable, and John followed Nicholas into the house, wondering why his Calyngton cousins remained so rough and uncaring.

In an upper chamber where Nicholas spent much of his time during his rare visits home, they sat together on a wide bench seat before a window from which they could look down on the bell-cote of the little chapel. The afternoon sun lit up the gold and brown slopes of Hingston Down beyond the trees, and above it the sky was sapphire blue.

But to two practical men, still replete with good food and drink and with plenty to talk about, the country scene outside meant nothing. They sat with their backs to the window and were immediately engrossed in conversation. Nicholas asked many searching questions about John's methods of sheep farming, of which he said he had heard interesting reports, and he listened attentively, almost as if he intended abandoning his lucrative law career to take up farming instead. Then they exchanged views on their parliamentary experiences, agreeing that there was little a yeoman delegate could do but concede to the royal demands. Nicholas now had considerable experience in parliament, and he explained to John that with the advantage of his legal training and growing importance — all of which he stated as a simple fact without any show of self-aggrandisement — he was now able, by devious means with pressure groups and by consorting with the influential and high-born, to obtain small measures of relief and benefit for his borough. His reputation had thus grown, and this was how he was now able to abandon Helston and choose instead election for Dunheved, so much nearer home.

'I did hear tell that you served as a squire to the late king during the war in France,' said John. 'Is the tale true that you were present at his tragic death?'

Nicholas answered briefly in the affirmative, but on this one subject he refused to elaborate. It was as though the memory was too painful and he wished not to revive it. Instead he described his brush with the pirates and the decision to make law his life so that he might ultimately bring greater security to the people of his native Cornwall.

'It is richly rewarding work, too,' he acknowledged, laughing. 'I am well paid by those for whom I act in the "Common Place" at Westminster. In a few years' time I shall become a reader and eligible for election as a full serjeant-at-law — a *serviens ad legem*. Then the rewards will be greatly higher, but even now as an apprentice, riches come rolling in as one's reputation grows. My master, Serjeant John Fortescue, is now a justice of the Common Pleas, and that brings even more reward to all his assistants. That is how I can without difficulty further my ambition to build my father's church.'

'May Calyngton become renowned through you!' said John admiringly, adding, almost under his breath, 'And may her people always give you due reward.'

Nicholas laughed, much as his father had before him, not

really believing that any credit would be given him by the town of his birth. That old antipathy against his father and himself would take a long time a-dying.

'You, as a breeder of sheep, will be far more famous in the area than a lawyer who comes and goes without ever putting down roots! Marry well, and your success will be assured!'

Marriage? It was the signal for John to unburden himself of his personal problem, that of his love for Margaret Brook and his lack of confidence that prevented him from asking for her hand. Nicholas listened quietly to his story, until John, covered in confusion at his own temerity, trailed off inconclusively, shrugging his shoulders and grinning foolishly at his friend.

Nicholas did not laugh. He studied the embarrassed young man thoughtfully, then patted him on the back and recommended him to press his suit. 'You have much to offer this lady, who has presumed to take to a rural life without knowledge of how to succeed therein. Do not underrate yourself, my friend. Your reputation, as far away as Exeter, marks you as a man of vision and skill – one who will succeed. Mistress Hicks, your aunt, was always very proud of your ancient lineage, and would surely applaud your alliance with one of the newer gentry.'

He leaned back against the corner of the window embrasure, his face as solemn as if he was working on a law-suit, but his eyes twinkled. 'Marry the wench, marry her, I say!'

John shook his head, then looked again at Nicholas, questioningly. Finding there the encouragement he needed, he took a deep breath and said at last, with a weak smile, 'Thank you, that I will!'

12

The building of the church did go ahead, and the stone walls rose gradually to show the shape the finished building would take. Openings were left for doorways and windows, and Warne Pengelly scoured the district searching for the right quality granite for carved frames, sills and mullions. Triumphantly he carried back in the now much battered ox-cart a sample load from Calestok, and for several months the churchyard rang to the sound of hammer and chisel as the three stonemasons worked on the windows.

Richard Chyket paused each day, on his way down to his fulling mill at Trevigro, to check the work done and smooth over the small problems and disputes which inevitably arose. In the eyes of the town he was the leader and the inspiration for the project and little thought was given to the man who had promised to bear a large portion of the cost, or to his father whose design was being carefully followed. Only the three stonemasons still remembered with some gratitude the man who had taught them their craft and died because of it.

Nicholas was not seen again in Calyngton for three years. He had been appointed to serve on the commissions of peace, most of which were held at Westminster. Twice he made the tedious journey down to the south-west, but the rapidly expanding amount of legal business in which he was now involved required him, each time, to hurry back to London without even a brief detour to his Calyngton home.

The first occasion was in August, when a commission of assize took him to Helston to investigate the complaint of the king's tenants that they had been evicted from their holdings by the manor reeves, who were selling off the crops to their friends, cutting down acres of trees and even burning the cottages to prevent the lawful tenants from returning. Nicholas rode down to Helston with John Cork, the stout lawyer from Linkinhorne, who joined him at Dunheved where he spent one night of his journey conferring with the burgesses and the constable of the castle, John Frensshe. At Helston they joined the local squires appointed to serve on the commission, among them Sir John Arundell and his son Thomas, with whom Nicholas had gone to the French wars in 1420.

Nicholas's relationship to the Arundells, although acknowledged, was now largely forgotten, and so it came as a pleasant surprise to Nicholas when the old knight drew him aside.

'I hear excellent reports of your work,' he wheezed. 'Sir John Fortescue has recommended you as a legal executor of my will, for the proper disposal of my affairs.'

Nicholas thanked him with due gravity. The old man prattled on, 'Master Copleston will assist you, and the lord bishop will also serve. It is important that my son is not allowed to slide aside from his obligations to maintain my five chaplains and a clerk at the church of St Columb, to pray for our souls and say all the masses, just as I have instructed. It is also most necessary that all my properties are clearly and irrevocably willed to my sons, and a proper share to my daughter. Renfrey, of course, is to have Lanherne, but Thomas must have Respery and St Neot, and I have bequeathed St Udy to my daughter.'

He paused for breath, and Nicholas intervened gently, 'Good Sir John, it shall be done just as you desire.' He went on to suggest that after the commission had concluded its inquest he might be permitted to study the documents from a legal angle, and advise. Sir John was happy to have his complicated estates examined by yet another expert, and so it was arranged.

The commission spent two weeks on its inquiries at Helston, but then in the absence of one of the accused men the case had to be adjourned. Richard Penpons had conveniently taken himself off fishing, and failed to return in time to appear before the commission. His fellow reeve, Robert Treage, did present himself at the assize, and pleaded throughout that he was only trying to modernise and streamline the king's property, not to exploit its resources as claimed by his accusers. Nicholas, observing him closely from his position at the end of the bench, decided that he was an honest, if misguided, servant, and so advised his fellow commissioners. But as the evidence of the missing man could not be taken, the commission reluctantly dispersed without making any award, and Nicholas was able to spend two days at Lanherne with Sir John before setting off again on the long ride back to Westminster.

A few months later he came again within a few miles of his home, without being able to visit it. Again John Cork was his travelling companion, but with the highways of midwinter turned to ice in Hampshire and bog in Devon they decided a sea passage would be safer, their destination being Plymouth.

As the little merchantman which had brought them from the Medway glided into the sheltered waters of Plymouth Sound, Nicholas pointed out to John Cork the lonely little hill away to the north, capped by a wintery mist. Cork nodded. 'Yes, that is how I often see it from Paderda, too!'

That glimpse of their local landmark was to be the nearest they got to their homes. After three weeks at the castle, investigating a complaint of piracy, the weather was suddenly favourable for an eastbound passage, and with a ship preparing to sail for Dover they abandoned any ideas of loitering at home.

'At least it is more restful to the legs and buttocks, if not to the stomach,' commented Cork, blenching somewhat as the ship emerged into open water and began to roll heavily. With a last lingering look at the receding green hills of Cornwall, Nicholas followed him down into the cabin and they began to gather their report together.

After a few moments he put down his pen, struck by a sudden memory.

''Tis strange, John, I first thought to become a lawyer after a brush with pirates in these very waters. I thought to make life safer for the people of Cornwall, especially those living close to the river highway of the Tamar. But I never thought to find my neighbours from Devon as the first pirates I would judge – and moreover, carry them back with me to await the king's justice at Westminster.'

'I hope our friends Colyville and Rygelyn are better sailors than I, for they will have very little comfort clamped in the hold,' murmured Cork, holding himself very still as his complexion began to turn grey-green.

'Hold on until we round Bolt Head and the movement will ease comfortably,' Nicholas assured him. To demonstrate his own ease he leaned back against the bulkhead with his hands clasped behind his head.

'Pity those poor devils in the hold! Poor wretches, did they really believe it was a French ship they had seized?'

'All foreigners are Frenchies to a simple sailor! If the ship was not carrying the ensign of the Doge of Venice, as they declared on oath to be the case, then all the jabbering of the Italian and Spanish crew would have seemed no different to them than the chatter of Frenchmen; and they had seen the vessel set sail from Brittany.'

'Their error could have been made good when they brought the ship into Plymouth and Master Chudleigh spoke with the Venetian captain in Italian. It was their refusal to return the stolen goods which was their undoing. Ignorance is no excuse for robbing our friends; retribution must be made.'

Perhaps it was his sea-sickness which made Cork feel sympathy for the Plymouth pirates. At the assize he had agreed wholeheartedly with the other commissioners, especially as international relations could be affected by their decision. Now however he found himself viewing the affair as a local man with local sympathies.

'There was little they could in fact do by then,' he countered. 'The barrels of salt had all been sold, and also most of the bales of silk. As for the brandy — well, brandy shipping from France to Ireland is surely fair contraband for any honest English sailor! Anyway by the time Master Chudleigh reached the scene every seafaring family in the port would have had its share already hidden at home.'

'No, the real reason they persisted in their sale of these ill-gotten goods was the general belief down here that the power of government is too far away to bring any effective punishment. We were correct in judging against them, we must bring the strength of the king's law down to the furthest reaches of Devon — and Cornwall.'

Nicholas spoke severely, his face as stern as if he were then sitting on the judgement seat rather than in a stuffy cabin rolling at sea. Cork recognised his mood of strict justice and said no more.

13

The very afternoon that the two lawyers sailed out of Plymouth Sound on their way back to London, John Fursdon left Polcarowe on his way home to St Cleer in a mood of excitement and elation. He had at last, that morning, asked the hand of Margaret Brook in marriage — and she had accepted him.

As his horse trotted along the muddy rutted track leading inland from the coast towards Liskerret, John burst into song. It might be winter, but to him the whole world was warm and rosy; even the bare landscape seemed full of green spring promise as in his newfound confidence he surveyed it from the saddle, singing as he went, and swaying rhythmically to the horse's pace.

Was it, could it be true? Yes, it was not a dream, he was betrothed, and the lady who had accepted his ring was the most fabulous creature in the whole wide world. It had taken him two years of patient and devoted service to persuade himself that he was in any way valued by Margaret as more than a farm adviser; even now, after she had smiled warmly at his halting proposal, clasped both his hands in hers and replied sweetly, 'I will be happy to become your wife, dearest, honest John Fursdon' — half his mind still told him it could not be true.

He laughed aloud, suddenly — startling his horse so that it shied, almost throwing him into the water-logged ditch. But even that narrow escape from uncomfortable disaster could not dash his spirits, and he laughed again as he remembered her next words, whispered modestly as he kissed her forehead, 'I had come to believe that you did not consider me worthy of you!' — when all the time he had been her humble admirer. Even in the plain country garments and pattens which she wore as working garb, to John she shone as a queen, a goddess, a being superior to his humble status.

Now she was his! They had gone straight to the priest for the ceremony of espousal in the church, when the ring carried for months in John's pocket had been placed tenderly on Margaret's finger. While they would continue to live in their separate homes until the marriage contract was complete, no one could now take his goddess from him. Again he startled his horse, this time with the joyful shout of the successful conqueror, as he set the horse to canter down the hill towards Trewoodloe.

Even as the horse raced along, so John's mind raced ahead with his marriage and plans for the future; before he reached home the Fursdon estate was divided so that he could keep control of his breeding flock while handing over the general farming to William, and he was picturing his mother spending many happy weeks at her daughter-in-law's much grander home. In his euphoria he did not even countenance the thought that his mother might not admire this grander home, and he still sang happily to himself as he rode down the farm lane to break the joyful news to his family.

At Polcarowe Margaret too was singing, but then she habitually did so at the close of day, before adjourning to the little chapel for vespers.

None of her household remarked any difference in her manner, and had they known of the afternoon's betrothal, would merely have commented, 'Well, why not, the poor lady is lonely and bored with this desolate country – Master Fursdon is almost the only man with whom she keeps company.'

Margaret was pleased, however, although not in the same sphere of heady courtship as John. Her quick brain matched his deep and sober mentality like a delicate violet on a spring hedge. From John she had learned not only the business of successful farming, but also the key to a happy life far from London and the king's court. He had taught her much about Cornwall, with the true devotion of a man who had no ambition to venture away from home. His ignorance of the courtly world had made it easier for him to accept her, not just as a figure-head, but as a person of sensibility with whom he could talk on equal terms. Their marriage, she hoped, would be a partner-ship of ideas and not just the satisfying of a man's physical needs and the bearing of children.

She prayed deeply that evening in her chapel, and retired to bed with plans already forming in her mind of the next stage of improvement at Polcarowe. Relaxing under her down quilt she pictured, not her future life as the wife of John Fursdon, but the colourful garden and extensive park stocked with deer which she would make at Polcarowe.

Mary Fursdon was deeply concerned when John bounced home with his joyful news. She had always remained suspicious of this up-country lady who was enticing her John away from his duties at Fursdon. Faced however with his ecstatic happiness, her fears were lulled into a mood of reluctant congratulation, and she joined in with her children in the excitement of planning the future.

Elizabeth was already betrothed, and her marriage to John Jope arranged for the spring. Dancing round her brother in delirious delight, she begged that his marriage to Mistress Brook should take place before hers, so that she could attend on the bride. John caught her up in his arms and kissed her tenderly.

'I fear not, little sister,' he said, a little wistfully, 'My betrothed has many important matters she wishes to complete before we are wed. I too, must work hard to arrange our affairs here so that Willie can run the farm, with our good mother's help.'

'Then we must make haste to find a good wife for Willie, for your good mother is not as active or as willing as she used to be,' interposed Mary from her place by the fire. The winter damp was seeping into her bones making her hips ache. She stretched out her rheumaticky hands to the warm flames, wishing once again that her beloved son had allied himself to an honest Cornish wench, who would have lived at Fursdon and cared for an ageing mother-in-law. But she listened attentively as John described for his sister his dreams for the future of Fursdon and Polcarowe as a rich estate bringing fame and fortune to the Fursdon family.

'Remember, it is not I who will be leaving you, but my beloved who is coming into our family.' In the chimney corner his mother prayed that the alliance would indeed be a good thing for all the family.

It was early March before the euphoria began to give way to

little niggling worries in John's mind. It was not that his devotion had in any way lessened; he loved Margaret with the humble tenderness of a simple man, and Margaret was deeply touched by his selfless devotion, of a quality she had never before encountered. What troubled John was Margaret's determination to carry out her grand design for the Polcarowe estate before the marriage took place. It was as if she felt obliged to complete one phase of her life before embarking on a new and different one. The subconscious feeling that his love was not her first priority created a small ache of unease in his mind. There was no one to whom he could confide his worries, for he sensed his mother's disapproval of Margaret.

Mary's disapproval was only partly justified. Margaret was no wicked schemer, only an intelligent opportunist. She had accepted John for his tenderness and companionship, but equally valued his skills. At each visit of her devoted and urgent lover she side-stepped the issue of marriage and pressed him to assist further with her plans for Polcarowe. At length John accepted that he must let her have her way.

It was not as simple as he had hoped. Prepared as he was to spend all available time at Polcarowe, he now found that Margaret's dream was going to need not only a considerable workforce but also materials not available in Cornwall. Somehow he found that he had engaged eight labourers to work at Polcarowe at his own expense. Margaret smiled sweetly when he told her what he had done, and she chuckled like a boy who has successfully stolen the marchpane sweetmeats from his mother's store.

'Dearest heart, all that I have will soon be yours!'

'And our children's,' added John, pressing his lips to her hand — for he still hardly dared to touch her body.

They walked together out of the house, and John allowed himself to slip an arm loosely round the brown worsted hooded cloak which Margaret had adopted for the country life. Her wooden pattens clinked daintily on the flagstone path, and John matched his big-booted strides to hers as they passed together round to the western front of the house.

'Can you not see it, dear husband?' asked Margaret, teasing him gently with the title he did not yet possess. 'If we were to remove all those trees on this side of the stream, and that distant clump of untidy rowans also, we would have a magnificent vista right down to the little cove where the stream falls out into the river. Then we will build a quay there of Cornish granite, so that my Spanish marble can be brought up river to our own estate.'

'Spanish marble? Do I hear aright?' John released his hold and stood back, amazed and horrified. 'And if we build our own port, where will such a commodity be obtained?'

'Why, my lord, where else but from Spain! I would have preferred the beautiful pink Italian marble, but now I am told there is a quarry not far removed from Bilbao in northern Spain where the marble is of passable quality, and fast becoming fashionable in the new houses. I shall make my pilgrimage to the shrine of St John de Compostela, and when I return we will bring the marble to our own quayside.' She flung her arms round John and gave him a rare kiss, then smiled so sweetly that his heart was in a turmoil. 'And while I am away, you, dearest husband — you will have the quay built to be ready for my return.'

John remained speechless, his mind befuddled with marbles, pilgrimages and ocean voyages, all far beyond his normal experience. Margaret nestled into the curve of his shoulder in a provocative way as she continued coolly to assess what needed to be done.

'There must be a firm trackway above the bank of the stream, but not directly in front of the house, where it might mar the outlook. You will need to design a strong cart to carry the marble. Perhaps I may be able to bring some of them home already shaped for the columns.'

John at last found his voice. 'What shall we build with the marble?'

'Why a colonnade, of course, just as my Greek dancing master told me they still have in his country. A parade with marble, here, across the front of the house, where we may walk among the columns and admire the new gardens below us.'

There was a touch of scorn in John's voice, as well as incredulity, as he said, 'The Cornish climate will grow a fine garden of moss on your marble parade and colonnade.' She did not seem to have heard him; he took her by the shoulders and looked earnestly into her blue eyes, now serious and intent.

'It is a wild dream, which could never be realized here. Do not make this dangerous pilgrimage, I beg of you. Stay here with me, be content with your fine estate and do not squander your resources in a useless attempt to plant Greece in Cornwall.'

The gamin face looked solemnly up at him; there was no laughter in the eyes. 'I must go,' she said. 'You will build the quay and I will bring the marble by the summer's end.' She smiled. 'Then we may have our marriage.'

The decision made, Margaret pursued her plans with her customary verve and enthusiasm. The prior of Tywardreath was impressed by her pilgrimage and sent three of his monks to accompany her, and also persuaded the master of the Fowy brig *Isabella* to take the party.

John felt sadly excluded from all these arrangements; he had never thought to go on a pilgrimage, his simple faith was satisfied by regular service at his church and by seasonal visits to Cornish shrines, but he would have gone to the ends of the earth to protect his beloved Margaret from the dangers she would surely face, if only she had wished him to go. Margaret did not wish it; when he remonstrated, she told him it was far more important that he should devote his time to the building of the quay against her return.

Six weeks later he stood, alone and forlorn, on the quayside at Polruan as the *Isabella* slipped out to sea on the outgoing tide. As she came abreast the headland a gentle offshore breeze filled her sails and in moments she had disappeared from view. John gripped his horse's reins so tightly that the animal shook its head in protest; quietening it, he buried his face in its shaggy mane to hide his tears. Bystanders watched in silent sympathy from a discreet distance, until John mounted and rode off up the hill.

He did not go along by the coast to see if the brig was still in sight. Margaret had gone, nothing was to be gained by a remote view of her further departure. He turned inland, passing the turning to Lanteglos and Polcarowe, and rode home to Fursdon. The lambing season was not yet finished, and he had a great deal of other seasonal work to put behind him if he was to spend the greater part of the summer building a road and a harbour.

14

Later that summer Calyngton had its first glimpse of lawyer Ayssheton for several years, when he was on his way down to Lanherne after the death of Sir John Arundell. Heads were turned, caps doffed in respect and forelocks pulled as the stern man in black rode through the town to the church. There he met Richard Chyket and they walked together round the new building, followed by an inquisitive murmuring crowd of onlookers.

The new church now stood like a covering shell over the Norman chapel. It had battlemented walls and a fine Dalabole roof, but as yet there was no glass in the mullioned windows and the porch doorway stood as an entrance arch to the existing church door. At the western end a square tower was just beginning to emerge above the roof level.

'By Christmastide that tower will be roofed, but we have no bells to hang there for a proper celebration of our Lord's birth,' said Richard. 'The bells must wait, I dare not ask my trader friends for further money until I can show them a building fit for the mass to be said, with the whole town inside, out of the weather.'

'I go down to Lanherne only to fetch documents for the proving of Sir John's will,' said Nicholas. 'When I return to Exeter I will send the glaziers, with their materials, which are all prepared. When think you that I should entreat the bishop to make a visitation here for the consecration?'

'Oh, not this year, most certainly. When the windows are complete we must start inside to take down the north and west walls of the old church, before your carpenters come to make the screen and embellish the chancel. There is still so much to be done, and it is slow work, with the planting, the harvesting and the shearing all to be taken care of as well. Perhaps three years more? We can, after all, continue to use the chapel when it is incorporated in the new church.'

Nicholas agreed, and they stood for a few moments watching a roughly carved angle stone being hoisted to its position on the corner of the tower. Several moorstone blocks lying on the ground looked remarkably like gravestones, reminding Richard of the gruelling walk to St Sampson's with his father's coffin.

He touched Nicholas on the arm. 'We should now also have our own burial ground, when the new church is consecrated,' he said. 'Will you put our request to the bishop?'

'Yes, I will do so. Such a request has to go through many channels, and it may take a year or more to obtain a papal bull from Rome. But Bishop Lacy is impressed by your work and will, I know, do everything he can to help.'

They went out into the street, where Nicholas's horse stood shaking its bridle impatiently as a young boy struggled to keep control of it. Richard pressed Nicholas to take refreshment with him at Chykets, but the busy lawyer declined. His stern face warmed into a smile as he sent his regards to Mistress Mary, then he mounted his horse, tossed a groat to the eager boy, and called back as he moved away, 'I shall return in September, to see the glaziers' work.'

15

By the end of August John had completed the task of supplying Polcarowe with its own harbour. He had used oxen to pull out protruding rocks from the river bed to provide a safe deep-water berth alongside the quay at high tide, and his men had shovelled a vast quantity of shingle from the harbour bottom and spilled it out on the roadway, firming it down to provide a hard-packed surface for the haulage of heavy loads. He had re-opened the small quarry above the stream which had provided the stone for the building of Polcarowe, and which now supplied further blocks for the construction of the quay. As he stood watching his men trimming the last bollard down to size, he could not resist a surge of satisfaction, weary as he was from months of hard construction work.

We are ready for you now, *Isabella*, he thought, a smile touching his lined and weary face. Instinctively his eyes scanned the lower reaches of the river, looking for the brig's return; but the river mocked him, winding its glossy grey path through acres of low-tide mud flats. Not even a coracle could berth at Polcarowe until the tide came in.

He turned away from the river and looked up towards the house, through the gap where he had dutifully, but with deep regret, uprooted the rowan trees in high summer. He had jibbed however at taking down the elms on the bank of Polcarowe stream and had cleverly routed the roadway through the trees to emerge into the stableyard without at any point being visible from the house. Although Margaret might not approve of this change in her design, John was pleased that he had been able to avoid destroying more trees in their growing season, and at the same time had achieved shade and shelter for the road.

The men finished their work, and tossing their tools on to the ox-cart began to trudge up the new road to the stableyard, where John had promised them a firkin of cider in celebration. He followed them slowly, a little distance behind, heavy with weariness and worry. The work had kept him so busy, with a target to achieve, that the heartache had subsided, and even his mother had ceased to be anxious for him; but now all was set for Margaret's return, and each day – and every minute of each day – would be aeons long for him in endless waiting, watching and longing. He decided to go home to Fursdon and help William with the wheat harvest, relying on Ned Palmer to send him instant word of news if *Isabella*'s sighting came through from Fowy.

As the little cortège approached the stableyard he saw Palmer run out excitedly, speak to the men and then come on down the road towards him at top speed. His heart leaped in anticipation – *Isabella* had been sighted!

'Quick, master, come quickly,' the reeve called as he ran.

John dashed up to him, panting. 'What is it, Ned? News of the *Isabella*?

'Aye, master, bad news. A messenger has just ridden over from Looe, where the *Marianna* berthed this morning. The *Isabella* has been seized by pirates!'

'Lord preserve them!' cried John. Without waiting to hear

any more he took to his heels and ran to the house as fast as his legs would carry him, half deafened by the thumping of his heart.

In the kitchen he found Josh Williams, whom he knew well as an unofficial harbour officer for the fishing boats and coasters plying from Looe. Josh was enjoying a tankard of ale, watched over by Margaret's elderly housekeeper, who stood beside him dabbing at her tearful eyes with her apron. He put down his tankard and stood up, his face assuming an air of mourning almost as doleful as the weeping Eliza.

'Sir, I beg leave to bring you news from the master of the Looe brig *Marianna*.'

'What is it, man? Tell me, tell me what has happened to Mistress Brook? Are they all dead?'

Josh cleared his throat and launched into his message.

'I am to tell you, sir, that the *Marianna* and the *Isabella* were in company off the coast of Finistere, lying becalmed and await-ing the sou'westerlies, when two skiffs, each carrying ten oars, surprised them at dead of night.'

He paused, shuffling his feet and twisting his cap in his hands as he made a visible effort to remember the next part of his message. John, normally one of the most patient men in Corn-wall, shook him roughly by the arm.

'So what has happened? Hurry, man, what is the message?'

'Sir, the master of the *Marianna* — that is James Jenkin, sir, and he has sailed the seas between Cornwall and Britanny these many years without let or hindrance—' John shook him again, in frustration — 'nay, let me be sir, you will have it all.'

Bit by bit the story came out. It appeared that after searching both ships the pirates released the *Marianna* and told the captain to find a ransom of five thousand marks for the *Isabella*, her crew, passengers and cargo of Spanish marble. They had towed their capture away in the dark, leaving the *Marianna* helpless until the breeze freshened and she was able to set her sails and escape northwards. Master Jenkin was to deliver the ransom money at a rendezvous off Brest at Michaelmas.

Five thousand marks! Where could he find such a sum? John felt a leaden weight of despair bearing down on him, pinning him to the spot so that he could neither move nor think, and squeezing his heart so that he almost cried out in physical pain.

Desperately he forced his paralysed mind to think again, and began to pace up and down the big kitchen, watched anxiously by Josh and the tearful Eliza. Gradually his thoughts cleared, and he began to list the assets of both Polcarowe and Fursdon estates in a desperate bid to find five thousand marks.

It was not a good time of the year to sell his sheep, which had not yet grown their new coats after the shearing, while the flock at Polcarowe was still much too small and too young and unproven to be of much value. Horses, cows, oxen? Nowhere could he visualise the realisation of even one thousand marks.

Up and down the kitchen he paced, cursing himself for all the money he had laid out on the building of the harbour. What use was a quay with no ship to berth there?

John was a careful, prudent man, and never in his life had he borrowed either goods or money; now, as his mind went round in circles searching for an answer, he came at last to the conclusion that he must seek help with a loan. He stopped pacing the floor and spoke sharply to Josh.

'Ride back immediately to Looe and tell Master Jenkin that I will find the ransom money. Then meet me at Calyngton, at Master Chyket's house, by midday tomorrow.'

Eliza burst into floods of relieved tears as Josh hurried out. Angrily John bade her be quiet and busy herself instead preparing for her mistress's return, then hurried out himself to the yard where Ned and all the hands stood silently waiting, and called for his horse.

'I shall be back from Calyngton by sundown tomorrow,' he called to Ned, as he set the horse to an immediate canter into the lane.

The twenty-mile ride to Calyngton seemed to John the longest journey he had ever made, and his horse sluggish and unwilling. It was a hot summer's day after the early autumn mists of the morning; the roads were hard-baked and the horse stumbled at times in the deep ruts left by the winter's cartwheels. Panting up the steep hills and slipping and sliding down into the valleys, the poor animal was still urged on by John to greater speeds on every stretch of flatter road. At last they came to the ford below Cadsonbury, and as he felt the cool water round his fetlocks the horse reached for a drink. Reluctantly John slackened the reins for a few moments before pressing up through the woods. Here he dismounted and led the exhausted animal up the steepest part of the track, his mind going back, as he trudged along, to the first time he had come that way, a shy starry-eyed boy following his handsome new-found leader.

Lawyer Ayssheton, where would he be now, he wondered? From all accounts there was a man who had grown immensely rich, indeed, he had himself told John how his work as a pleader in the Court of Common Pleas was bringing him in rich rewards. Nicholas would be sympathetic to his distress, for he had encouraged the betrothal. But, no, it would take too long to travel to London and look for him at the Inns of Court; he must pin his hopes on his brother-in-law Richard and his prosperous commerce.

When he entered the town he was surprised to see how neat and tidy it had become, with the stone house fronts all scrubbed clean and the older cottages pristine under a fresh coat of white-wash. The inn on the corner had been enlarged; in place of the low cottage with its ragged weed-strewn thatch there stood a large hostelry with an archway leading to stable accommo-dation, and an upper storey, topped by a shiny new roof of Delabole stone. He was so busy looking at it as he turned the corner by the church that he did not observe the crowd gathered at the church door, or the tall turreted tower above them. He had forgotten all about the new church – he had more urgent personal matters on his mind as he pressed on down towards Chykets and rode into the yard.

Mary appeared at the house door, a small baby in her arms and a toddler clinging to her skirts. 'Why, John!' she cried, in startled amazement. Hampered by her children she could not run to greet him, but instead beckoned him in welcome.

'Mary, love, good-day to you, where is Richard?' John called urgently as he slid down from his horse. He looked across to the woolstore, but the door was closed and the usual cluster of bales and barrels had been tidied away.

'Why, John he is here, he goes now up to the church.'

At that moment Richard appeared behind Mary, adjusting his hat and settling himself comfortably in a short brown worsted houppeland over his best scarlet doublet.

'Richard, I need your help' cried John, leaping up the steps two at a time.

'Oh, not now, brother-in-law, we have a ceremony at the church which the prior of St Germans is attending. Stay with us until the evening and then I will be free to discuss with you any business you desire.'

'I cannot wait,' cried John, and blurted out his news. His sister gave a distressed cry and gathered little John to her as if he too were in imminent danger of being captured by pirates.

'How much did you say?' asked Richard, his commercially tuned mind grasping most readily the financial aspect of the disaster.

'Five thousand marks.'

A low whistle came from Richard. He shook his head. 'I could not find such a sum, John, not until I had spent months travelling to collect all that is owed to me. The mill is doing well, but there is much chicanery in this trade, and to succeed one has to let the cloth go out and await payment, sometimes for more than a year. I have a warehouse full of wool, but if it is all sold hurriedly the price will not be worth the having.'

He put his hand on John's shoulder and gave it a brotherly squeeze.

'This mistress of yours, brother, has been, it seems to me, as fiery as a hornet's nest. If you cannot help her, leave her to the troubles she has willed on herself. Take yourself a sensible Cornish-woman — like our Betsy here — who would make you a homely, happy wife.'

John shook himself free. 'You cannot say such things,' he blazed. 'I love her. I suffer agonies, imagining the tortures, the — the humiliations she may be going through. I could not live without her, I could not live with the knowledge that I had abandoned her.'

There was a clatter of hooves in the yard. 'That will be Nicholas,' said Mary. 'Richard, you must go. We will consider John's problems while you are away.'

'Nicholas? — Nicholas Ayssheton? Perhaps he could help me!' cried John, and rushed out again into the yard.

Nicholas had pulled up at the stables and was about to dismount when he was startled to find an excited, incoherent John

Fursdon tugging at his stirrup. His habitual frown deepened, and the severity in his voice silenced John.

'Wait,' he said, slipping out of the saddle and handing the reins to the waiting Diggory. He adjusted his well-cut black clothes with methodical care and brushed down his hose before turning again to a now frantic John.

He listened quietly to John's story, a look of gentle concern softening his severe features as his legal mind sifted the facts from the confused account John poured out in his distress. At the mention of five thousand marks his eyebrows shot up in surprise, but at the end he said quietly and reassuringly, 'We can help you. Rest here until we return from the church.'

John sank down on the house step, shivering with relief. He was not aware of the two men talking together and then walking out into the street on their way up to the church. When, a few moments later Mary came to sit beside him and took him to her like a small child to be comforted, he laid his head on her breast and wept unashamedly.

The ceremony at the church was a simple one. The prior of St Germans had come to see the beautiful coloured glass now installed in the new windows. At each one he related for the benefit of the audience the biblical story illustrated, from Adam and Eve with the serpent, to Noah with a bright yellow ark on a rich blue sea, Jonah emerging from the whale, the annunciation by the Archangel Gabriel to Mary, and Lazarus rising from the dead. For a little local touch the glaziers had given a window to St Neot and his endless supply of fish, and even showed the local legend of Colan and Gottlieb, who were said to have fought to the death at the holy well at Theupath. The prior was nonplussed by these illustrations, unable to place them in a biblical context, so Richard described them, acutely conscious as he spoke of Nicholas Ayssheton's simmering wrath at the totally untrue Gottlieb legend about his father's chapel being given a place of honour in his father's church.

Nicholas bowed to the prior, accepting in icy silence his praise for the provision of such magnificent windows, and told him that during the winter a team of woodcarvers and carpenters would be busy on the rood screen and choir stalls. The prior then celebrated the mass at the Norman altar in the chapel within the incomplete church. A sumptuous feast followed, not this time at Chykets but at the new inn directly opposite the church, where the prior was so copiously wined and dined that he agreed very readily to apply to Rome on the town's behalf for a papal bull to license their own burial ground.

How he came to help John so readily Nicholas could not really explain, even to himself. A man of clear-cut decision, used to command and being deferred to, he had ordinarily little patience for timid followers. If he had met John in a law court, he would have demolished his case with ease and scorn, in a matter of minutes. How was it then, that he had now agreed so readily to find five thousand marks for this man he had always known as timid and shy — even if the salt of the earth? He could find no answer to it as they sat together with Richard in the cramped little office among bales of combed wool and the hanging samples of coloured worsted, and John told the whole story again.

He was, Nicholas decided, as he studied him quietly, the sort of man born to be put upon by others, always at the mercy of unscrupulous schemers. Not for a moment did he doubt that Mistress Brook was an arch-schemer, who had used this simple countryman to her own purpose and deserved the trouble which had now befallen her. But he had found a magic in the boy when they first met, and he still felt an unreasoning fondness for him as for the younger brother he had never had.

John started, and flushed with embarrassment, when he saw a smile flicker on the lawyer's lips. But Nicholas had not been giving close attention to the account of John's troubles — his smile had been for past happy memories. Now he cleared his throat, assumed his normal stern expression, and took command of the situation.

He drew up a list of debts owing to him in the neighbourhood, of merchants and landowners who would be ready to lend him money against his personal note of hand, and with the contents of his wallet added to a purse which Richard and Mary had produced they finally reached the sum required.

'I must give surety for any sum which I borrow to make up this loan for you,' explained Nicholas, 'And so in my turn I must have surety from you. One cannot make a gift of such a large sum.'

John, tired and bemused after a long and wearying day, could only bow his head in sleepy agreement. Nicholas looked at him sharply, and shook his head. 'Take a grip on your senses, my good friend. You could be cheated out of your inheritance by such insouciance. What security can you offer me for five thousand marks? It would be fair, would it not, to pledge Polcarowe as surety for its wayward mistress?'

John roused himself. 'I will pledge you both Polcarowe and Fursdon, in recognition of your fine friendship in this crisis,' he said gratefully, and went on to give details of acreage and stock of both estates, all of which Nicholas noted down on his tablet. Finally it was settled that the deed should be drawn up transferring both estates to Nicholas if the debt were not repaid during the lifetime of John and Margaret.

'There, brother-in-law,' chipped in Richard cheerfully. 'You will have a whole lifetime to find your five thousand marks!'

John nodded agreement. 'And the interest?' he enquired.

'Well now, let me see.' Nicholas sat back, thoughtfully twisting a large ring on the middle finger of his left hand, then tapped his white teeth with it. 'Yes, I have it. I am very partial to roses; every year in June, at the feast of the nativity of St John the Baptist I will have one pure white rose in payment of interest on this loan. As we ride over to Lanherne to collect from Renfrey Arundell we will attend on my good friend John Cork at Paderda. He will lend us a good sum, and he will also draw up the deed of fine, to make the transaction fully legal.'

Such was now the reputation of lawyer Ayssheton in Cornwall that all went without a hitch and within three days more than enough had been gathered in. It still wanted two and a half weeks to Michaelmas when John set off for Looe with Josh Williams and Diggory Allin, their saddlebags heavy with silver coins and each armed with a stout stave to ward off intending robbers. John had recovered his spirits and was once again in charge of the situation, although he could not fully relax until the *Isabella* reached England and he knew that all her passengers were safe. But thanks to Nicholas they had achieved the impossible, and now there was hope.

He did not know how to express his gratitude adequately to Nicholas, and merely gripped his hands in a warm farewell.

Nicholas patted him on the shoulder as he would a younger brother, and called after him as the party set off, 'You will have her home by Candlemas. I must come and visit you before long, to inspect this mysterious enchantress who has cost us all so much time and trouble!'

'That would give me the deepest pleasure!' John called back, little dreaming how Nicholas's first visit to him, longed for over so many years, would so drastically change his whole life.

16

Nicholas did not return to Westminster that autumn. He was summoned from Theupath to sit on a commission of peace at Wookey, along with his mentor and friend Bishop Edmund Lacy and others. There followed a commission to trace a cargo of oil snatched by pirates on its way from Fowy to Sandwich, and then a general commission of enquiry to check that Cornwall was paying the crown all rightful dues. This general enquiry would take months to complete, comprising as it did, not only custom duties and trade taxes, but also knights' fees and advowsons returnable to the king, estates due to him through death by suicide or the marriage of a ward without royal consent, the fines payable by his manor tenants and whether such land was being well maintained, and checks on the honesty and attention to duty of all the king's customs officers and tax collectors. It was all part of a countrywide survey initiated by the king's council in an attempt to tighten the financial strings and bring more money to the royal coffers.

Where Cornwall was concerned the demands of the crown had often been successfully evaded, for in this remote countryside no one would rush to London to inform the council that his neighbour had chopped down and sold some trees, or to verify that a young heiress had the royal consent to her marriage. In the ports along the Cornish rivers it was a recognised practice to bribe the officials for a lower import duty on the wines and silks brought in, while to the officers concerned this was part of their livelihood.

The commission assembled at Bodmyn, and with an army of scribes and messengers started on its huge task, sending out officials to all parts of the county to collect the evidence.

It was the eve of the feast of St Luke when Nicholas finished a two-day enquiry into the work and charges of the king's customs officials at the port of Lostwithiell. The warm autumn sunshine filtering through the misty windows of the guildhall gave him the sudden inspiration to take the opportunity, while in the neighbourhood, of visiting Polcarowe. He had heard that the *Isabella* had returned safely with her full complement of passengers and crew, but without her cargo. Since then no further news had filtered through to Calyngton of the expected marriage between John Fursdon and Margaret Brook. He had promised a visit, so why not make that visit and satisfy his curiosity? Although he would not have admitted it, at the back of his mind was also the thought that his protection might be needed for that hapless yet endearing young man for whom he felt the warm affection of an elder brother.

He dismissed his officials, to return to Bodmyn, but kept with him his manservant, a taciturn Welshman named Gwyllym, whose beetling brows and ferocious face would intimidate any highway robber. Sadly, Nicholas could no longer travel alone in his own county; as his reputation increased, so there built up the number of resentful Cornishmen who wished him out of the way.

They followed the eastern river bank towards the sea, following a maze of twisting lanes until eventually, more by good luck than by good management, they came upon the stone posts marking the entrance to an estate. Here Nicholas left Gwyllym to make further enquiries of any passing travellers, while he himself rode up the estate road to enquire at the house. As he drew up in a paved courtyard a young boy came out of a smart new farm building, and stopped at the sight of the visitor. He was clad in a long brown riding cloak, beneath which leather boots were just visible. The hood of the cloak was drawn tightly round his face, and he carried a short whip in one gloved hand. He approached Nicholas as if to ask the stranger's business, but when only a few feet away stood stock still and stared as if he had seen a ghost.

'Is this Polcarowe?' asked Nicholas curtly.

The boy nodded. Nicholas slid down from his horse and in his usual harsh voice of authority sent the boy to inform his mistress that Master Nicholas Ayssheton begged audience with her. At first the boy seemed not to have heard; then suddenly, without a word, he crossed to the house and disappeared inside.

Nicholas tethered his horse to a post and walked over to the house door, uncertain as to whether he should knock for attention or wait like a petitioner outside in the hope that the boy had delivered his message. Something about the boy's face bothered him; had he seen him before somewhere? Perhaps the lad was one of those concerned in the Fowy piracy case, or perhaps a witness at the inquest into the suicide of Edward Burneby in his well at Bodmalgan; both decisions had been unpopular with the local inhabitants, which would explain the boy's unfriendly behaviour. No, it was those penetrating blue eyes which had fixed on him, somewhere he had seen them before, and not in a court of law. A tightness clutched at his chest, and he shook himself mentally; come now, man, you do not love young boys, leave that to my Lord Deddon and his friends! But, he admitted to himself, it was an attractive face, with an upturned cheeky little nose bearing no sign of freckles, and a wide Cupid's bow of a mouth just made for kissing.

The tightness clutched him now in his loins and he stamped his foot in rage at his wayward feelings.

At that moment the house door opened and a maidservant invited him inside, bobbing a discreet curtsey as he stepped over the threshold.

'Mistress Brook bids you welcome, sir. She sends her apologies that you have had to wait outside, and asks your forbearance. She will attend on you in a trice.' She ushered him into the great hall, warm with light from the setting sun and rich in colour from its tapestried walls. A fire glowed in the hearth, and Nicholas stood with his back to it as he took in the comfort and richness of the furnishings.

He had moved over to inspect more closely a richly coloured oil painting hanging beside the window when a movement behind him made him swing round. In the middle of the huge room stood the London beauty whom he had thought never to see again, since the night of the Midsummer Marching Watch.

It must be a dream, he thought as his pulse quickened. During his first years in London he had searched arduously for her, but not even his enquiries to minor court officials had brought any inkling of her identity or whereabouts, and he had come to look on her as a dream, designed to keep him celibate for the better progress of his law career. Now, here she was, not four feet away from him, standing like a goddess, her gown of blue and gold brocade setting off the long auburn hair hanging about her shoulders down to her waist.

He took a step forward, then halted abruptly. The face, of course! It was the face of the 'boy' in the courtyard.

He took another step forward, his heart hammering against his ribs and his whole body tense with emotion. His mouth opened to make some formal greeting, but all he achieved was a wordless stammer.

Margaret rescued him. Laughing lightly at his stupefaction she advanced and took both his hands in hers.

'I have waited a long time to see you again,' she stated simply, gazing wide-eyed up into his face. The severe lines which normally chiselled his features melted away as if by magic; his face was young again, eager with love, the lips already trembling into a kiss and the deep brown eyes searching into her very soul with their message of the oldest instinct known to man. Violently he seized her and pressed her body hard against his own. She yielded eagerly, and his mouth sought hers triumphantly, locking them in a tight embrace.

Minutes later a log fell in the hearth, breaking the silence. The tension eased. Smoothing one hand down the shape of her back, Nicholas lifted his face from hers and with his other hand tilted up her chin and kissed her very tenderly on the eyelids and the tip of her nose; then he ran his fingers through her long auburn hair, and resting her cheek against his pressed her once more tightly to him, and sighed deeply.

'This is my dream brought at last to reality. My love.'

Another moment passed; then at last they returned simultaneously to the reality of the situation.

'You are the wife of John Fursdon?' murmured Nicholas into Margaret's hair.

'We are betrothed, and have the blessing of mother church on our union, but the marriage contract is not yet complete. I have delayed it.' She was silent, then added, 'Perhaps in my bones I knew that the grand passion of my life would come to me one day, and John — dear to me as he is — is not that.'

'You cannot marry him.'

'Dear heart, I must. He returns tomorrow and I have promised him that we would then set the day for the marriage ceremony.'

'You cannot marry him.'

She clung to him desperately. 'What shall I do? I wish you had not come!'

Nicholas drew away and looked at her questioningly, in hurt surprise.

'No, no, don't go! I love you so! Why does love hurt like this?'

She drew him gently to the settle by the fire, where they sat together like any pair of young lovers, her head on his shoulder and their fingers intertwined. Nicholas could feel her heart throbbing against him, and his own drumming its own urgent reply. For a moment he felt almost as if he would choke, and then let his hand feel the shape of her thighs through the bro-cade gown.

'You cannot marry John, you are mine,' he whispered at last, his voice husky with emotion.

'Oh, what should I do? I have plighted him my troth!'

'Mine, mine!' The husky whisper through her hair made her whole body tremble its acceptance. He drew her to her feet and slipping the brocade gown off her shoulders began to kiss her passionately on the throat and shoulders and between the breasts. Margaret gave a low moan as her body tensed and arched to meet his touch.

The brown eyes again searched hers, and their message coursed through her limbs. 'Now?' he whispered softly, his voice no longer husky but clear and confident.

For answer she took hold of his hand and led him from the hall to the seclusion of her own chamber.

17

The news of the elopement was something of a nine days' wonder in Cornwall, a cause of shocked disapproval or ribald comment as the story rippled round the countryside. It lost nothing in the telling, and those who had suffered from lawyer Ayssheton's severe justice were quick to blacken his character and represent him as a wicked ogre who had abducted the innocent wife of a gallant Cornish farmer. Only in the neighbourhood of Polcarowe were excuses made for Master Ayssheton on the grounds that the marriage between Mistress Brook and Master Fursdon would never have taken place — 'She kept him dancing on a string awhiles too long,' declared Josh Williams — while Margaret's housekeeper, Eliza, excused her mistress on the grounds that she had arrived home both physically and mentally exhausted from her experience as a captive of the pirates and could not be considered responsible for her actions.

Reports of the couple's whereabouts were numerous and conflicting; they had been seen taking ship to France; they were hiding at Theupath, where Dan Jewell and his daughter Mattie remained unusually tight-lipped and silent on the subject; while a merchant visiting Richard Chyket vowed he had seen them at an inn near Reading and had watched them ride off towards London in the morning.

Mary Chyket was heartbroken and would talk to no one, not even the well-meaning friends who called to commiserate as for a family bereavement. She wept silently as she tended her three children, smothering little John with tearful kisses as she thought of his dear uncle. Margaret had been his whole life, and see how much trouble and anguish she had brought him, even to the extent of mortgaging the home which had belonged to his forefathers since Saxon times — and sold it, moreover, with little hope of ever buying it back, to the very man who had now robbed him of his mistress, herself the very cause of the transaction. Life was cruel, and Mary wept again as she thought of Nicholas and how much she and Richard had admired and loved him. She felt that her simple world was breaking up, and she clutched baby Richard tightly to her, thankful that after all they had decided against giving him the name of Nicholas.

It was two weeks before news came from her mother at Fursdon. The message was terse, merely reporting that John was home again and busy on the farm. That was all, and Mary wept again in sorrow for the whole family.

While Cornwall bubbled with scandalised excitement, the ripples did not spread very far. His fellow commissioners were concerned at Nicholas's absence, but when Gwyllym appeared with a message that his master would return to his duties within the week, some coarse comments were made at that night's *cena* concerning the needs of the male animal, and there the matter rested. When Nicholas did return to the castle again, alone, to take up his duties, everyone assumed that the affair was now over and could be forgotten − apart from a few knowing nudges and winks.

Nicholas behaved as if nothing had happened, but there was a noticeable change in his appearance which worried John Fortescue. The severity had gone from his manner and there was a warmth in his eyes and in his voice which the judge saw as a softness likely to be a threat to a promising legal career. He had looked on Nicholas as one of his most successful apprentices at law and one likely to be soon elected serjeant and destined to join him on the judges' bench − but who had ever seen a smiling gentle judge?

But as the work of the commission proceeded and he observed how efficiently Nicholas still performed his office, his fears were lulled and the whole episode forgotten. If anyone had thought to query the fate of the woman in the affair, Justice Fortescue would have said, like anyone else, that she had presumably returned to her home.

When Nicholas returned to Bodmyn he had not in any way abandoned Margaret, but had left her in the care of the nuns at Exeter.

They had left Polcarowe at daybreak, attended only by

Gwyllym and by Margaret's maidservant. Nicholas confided to Margaret that with his legal knowledge and the help of Bishop Lacy he hoped to free her from her legal ties so that they could marry. So, starry-eyed and blissful in their happiness together, they had ridden by the less frequented hilly bridleways to Exeter and sought audience of the bishop.

Edmond Lacy's smile of welcome changed to a deep frown of disapproval when he heard the details of the couple's predicament. But he was predisposed to favour the son of Reginald Ayssheton, however badly he might have sinned, and he was very much aware of the man's lonely childhood — which he felt could account for a special need for a deep and possessive love. And when he learned how Margaret had constantly delayed the marriage his disapproval began to soften. Their deep attachment was very evident, and reluctantly he agreed to help them.

'I will obtain for you the annulment of the espousal,' he said at last, and held up his hand to stop them as they began to pour out their thanks. 'I will also, in memory of my good servant and friend Reginald Ayssheton, marry you myself — but only after a period of retreat and penance. Mistress Margaret will perform daily four hours of penitential prayer under the guidance of my sister abbess at the convent, where she shall remain in retreat until the feast of the Purification. Master Nicholas must continue with his legal duties, and he will therefore do his penance daily, on rising from his bed and before retiring at night, wherever his work may have taken him.'

Margaret made to protest, but Nicholas's gentle pressure on her arm restrained her. Together they knelt before the bishop in obedience and to ask his forgiveness and blessing.

However, on leaving the bishop's palace, they did not go immediately to the convent as the good bishop had intended. Instead they lay together that night at lodgings reserved for them by Gwyllym in a quiet part of the city. There they made love with all the desperation of prisoners condemned to die on the morrow, oblivious to the rough straw palliasse beneath them.

At last Margaret cried out in anguish, 'How can I remain immured in a nunnery for half a year? Let us escape — take ship for France or Spain. We could live happily there together and never need to leave each other's sight.'

Nicholas rolled away from her on his back, still holding her hand. 'That is no real answer to our problem, dear heart. Just a little patience and then we will have our whole lives before us, to walk together honourably and with pride. I love you; I long to show you to all the world as my love and my wife, not to hide you and pretend to my friends that you do not exist.'

'I would gladly undertake another pilgrimage as part of my penance,' said Margaret, and Nicholas nodded in the dark, acknowledging the independent adventurous spirit of this unusual woman, 'but to be inactive, just waiting − without the comfort of your presence − oh, *caro*, how can you abandon me thus?'

She took his hand and laid it over her heart, and at the feel of her pulsing body he turned to her as passionately as before.

At last Margaret fell asleep, nestling beside him, and in the quiet hour before dawn the unthinking joy of requited love gave way to the thoughts of his troubled conscience. Vividly in the dark he saw the friendly trusting face of John Fursdon, smiling his gratitude and his admiration. How that expression must now have changed! And he had done this to a man he had wished to protect, not to plot against and trick! He groaned inwardly, knowing that he would always carry a secret sense of guilt.

But was it not sheer misfortune that had allied John to the goddess of Nicholas's dreams? And was it not significant that she had delayed the marriage because at heart she searched for a greater love − his?

It was done. The bishop would marry them, and Nicholas would make every effort to recompense John for the great wrong done to him. He sighed, and drew his arm more protectively round his sleeping companion.

The following morning he delivered her to the convent and hastened back to his duties at Bodmyn, feeling that he had left half of himself behind at Exeter.

The commission's work in Cornwall was finally concluded, and its lay members dispersed to their homes. The lawyers were to return to Westminster, both to present the findings of the commission and to convey a considerable quantity of monies recovered in overlooked or avoided fines. They were to travel together in a party, for safety and company. Master Ayssheton however, pleaded family affairs and rode off alone, with his servant, after arranging to join the cortège at Exeter.

Nicholas did not go home but rode direct to Exeter, to make a last sad visit to Margaret, knowing full well that it could be several months before he might be able to return to the west country.

She seemed even more bewitching than ever, and there was a serene beauty in her gamin features that he had never seen before. As they sat together in the visitor's parlour and talked of his return at the end of Margaret's retreat there was none of the grief and anguish of previous visits. Nicholas marvelled at the skill and influence of the abbess in bringing about this calm acceptance of her situation. The thought made him feel calm and rested himself, but his sense of peace was shattered when Margaret told him serenely, 'I bear your child, *carissimo*. We await your return in happy contentment.'

Somehow the news stunned Nicholas, he had not thought beyond his passionate need for her; that the fruit of her womb should be his put their relationship into an entirely new concept. Then, as the idea sank in he was overwhelmed with joy. He took her fine white hands in his and caressed them tenderly, as if he dared not touch her body because of its delicate condition.

'*Our* child,' he corrected her gently.

He leaped to his feet. 'I will ask the bishop to marry us without any further delay,' he declared.

Bishop Lacy conceded that the needs of the unborn child superseded the requirements for abstinence and penance. He was also familiar with the sad story of Reginald's mother and, being a kindly and compassionate man, he was determined that such a tragedy should not be re-enacted. So the marriage was arranged, and at a nuptial mass in the convent the following morning he pronounced them man and wife and prayed for God's blessing on their progeny. Then, breaking from Latin into English he addressed them soberly, as a father two wayward children.

'You have much need of prayer, my children. I will pray for you, and the good nuns here will also remember you in their prayers. But you will spend much time travelling from one part of the king's realm to another as Master Nicholas's work decrees, and may have little time to attend the mass in church; I will therefore grant you a licence that wherever you may be in my diocese of Exeter, divine service may be celebrated for you and your children at the house where you rest at that time. God go with you, my children.'

Humbly they kissed his hand, vowing that they would make full use of his special gift.

The horses and servants awaited them, and an hour later they had slipped in behind the cortège of lawyers and officials on the road to Honiton.

PART THREE

Justice for the Justice

1

Susannah Ayssheton was born at Theupath at the height of a long hot summer which had driven her mother from the heat and smells of London city to the sanctuary of Cornwall with its sea-stung breezes and sweet-scented hedges. The long and weary ride in a litter which bumped and swayed with the stumbling tread of the mule over the hard-packed ridges of the summer highway had made poor Margaret desperately sick and increasingly fearful of losing her precious burden. Each night she carefully laid her aching, awkward body on the straw palliasse of a roadside inn, gently stretching her muscles and easing the unborn child into a more restful posture, and each time she longed to be back in the two dusty chambers which were their home in Chichester Inn, with all the sickness and squalor of the city around them.

But she endured the anguish and discomfort of her journey with grim determination to survive and bear her child, and it was only when they had crossed into Cornwall that she relaxed a little — and the pains began.

Nicholas had ridden ahead, just to have first glimpse of his home from the brow of Hingston Down. He came cantering back, the anxieties of the journey forgotten in the joy of being at last almost home. He reined in to tell Margaret that he had spotted Dan and Thomas saving hay in the meadow below Balston, but the sight of her ashen face and clenched fists froze the words on his lips.

It was much too soon for the baby to come, but this was no

time for counting dates, they must hurry the last two miles to Theupath. As he urged the pack driver to hasten his beasts, a gasp of pain from Margaret added urgency to his order. Nicholas slipped from his horse and led the litter mule himself down the hill, sending Gwyllym on ahead to alert all at Theupath.

Fortunately there was little earth or mud on the Hingston road and the mule trotted smoothly on the stone-packed surface, with only an occasional slither as a hoof skidded on worn rock. Margaret hid her face and her moans in a large kerchief which had served her as a fly swot and sunshade, praying desperately to the Blessed Virgin that they might reach their destination without mishap.

Her prayers were answered and the pains subsided. When at last they arrived at Theupath there was Mattie waiting for them, flanked by both Dan and Thomas ready to bear the mistress into the house, and watched from the corner of the barn by three inquisitive little girls.

Mattie proved to be an excellent mid-wife, although this was her first case — apart from her experiences in bearing her own, the three little girls. She took charge with quiet competence, and Nicholas was happy to be relieved of any further responsibility. He remained outside, and was discussing estate matters with Dan when two hours later Mattie announced from the house door that his wife was delivered of a fine daughter.

Susannah was in fact a pathetic little baby, her six-weeks' prematurity giving her the appearance of a wizened and aged dwarf. But she had a lusty cry and a good appetite and was soon suckling to her mother, who nursed her with tender reverence and beamed proudly over her head at her father.

Nicholas stroked the infant's smooth dark hair, noting privately a marked similarity to a skinned coney and wondering what compliment he could pay this strange creature who had grown from his seed. Then, as Margaret reached out and took his hand, the baby relaxed from feeding and turned a sleepy face towards her father. The conquest was made, Nicholas the ardent lover yielded first place to Nicholas the proud father and the little group of three remained, just as they were, for some time, still and happy together.

First thing the following morning Nicholas sent Gwyllym to

Southill with a message to the rector to come and arrange the baby's baptism. The message was acknowledged, but Thomas Baron did not arrive at Theupath that day or the next. Apprentice-at-law Nicholas Ayssheton was not to be insulted in this manner; Gwyllym was despatched again, with a demand for immediate attendance at Theupath, but the only reply was, 'He will come when he can.'

Margaret had never seen Nicholas so enraged. As he paced the chamber in frustrated anger, spitting out vituperative comments on the wretched rector and his ancestors, even the baby turned disturbed towards the noise of anger, and Margaret begged him, 'Be at peace'. But he could not unwind so instantly, and as his rage rumbled on she thought to herself for the first time what a formidable opponent he must be in the Court of Common Pleas.

At last she pleaded, 'Dear heart, let us rather invite the rector of St Dominica to attend and baptise the infant here in your chapel, where you yourself were baptised.'

Again Gwyllym was despatched with a message. The reply came immediately; Sir William Whytyng regretted he was too infirm to attend on such a matter. This time Margaret wept. Her tiny child was without the protection of the church, and she herself would in a few days be strong enough to attend at church to be cleansed of the impurities of child-bearing; without holy blessing, both of them were outcasts condemned to eternal fire.

It was Mattie who discovered her new mistress sobbing in her bed; when she learned the reason for Margaret's unhappiness she was able to explain the reason for the ostracism. The whole community of Calyngton, she told her, was bitterly against its benefactor because of his elopement with the espoused wife of his friend.

'Folk jump very readily to speak ill of other folks' private affairs,' she said scornfully. 'The very ones who exchanged wives after high goings-on last Shrove Tuesday now lead the condemnation of your marriage. They paid scant service to Master Fursdon when he was merely another farmer, but now they have made of him a veritable martyr — and blame you and my master for his sorrow.'

'Indeed we are to blame, Mattie,' said Margaret, stifling a sob. 'How fares my dear John? Do you know? Have you seen him?'

'Nay, mistress, he sees no one, and goes nowhere. Mistress Chyket his sister tells me that he works all day with his sheep on the moors, and speaks to no one of his feelings. She says he loved you dearly, mistress.' Mattie's voice was gently reproachful, and Margaret turned her head away as fresh tears welled in her eyes.

'His love was far better than I deserved,' she murmured, 'and I loved him too, in a fashion — but not as I now love my lord,' and she snatched up the baby in tight embrace, as if finding strength in this physical evidence of their relationship.

Mattie slipped quietly from the chamber, latching the door behind her. As she left the house and crossed the yard, her three little daughters ran out excitedly from the cottage door. She gathered them round her, and gave each a kiss on the cheek and a slap on the behind as they went indoors together, a happy family group, free of cares.

Nicholas had ridden over to Southill, and he returned shortly afterwards in chastened mood. Still bitterly angry at the insult to his wife and child he recognised the logic of local opinion against himself. Resourceful as ever, he was determined that his daughter should not be denied her entry into Heaven, and that his wife should be restored to her state of grace without delay, and so Gwyllym was despatched to Exeter with a supplication to the bishop for the baptism and churching to be held there.

'If Calyngton does not want us, then we will shake off the dust of this miserable town and take ourselves elsewhere,' he said lightly, with just the faintest catch in his voice.

They set off into the morning sun two days later, and neither gave a backward glance to the familar Cornish countryside now being left behind.

2

Memories stirred for Richard Chyket as he journeyed along the London road on a cold spring day. It was the first time since his return from France that he had ventured out of the west country, but he still had vivid recollections of many of the hills up which he had trudged thirteen years ago, and he spotted several of the huts and hovels in which he had begged a night's rest. Now, as he rode comfortably along on a good horse, he remembered with gratitude the toothpuller who had found him sheltering in a cave near Shaftesbury, who had tended his arm stump with a herbal distillation which had ended months of pain, and then carried him right through to Cornwall, squeezed in the family cart with his children, animals and the tools of his trade. And the destitute Richard had run off without even thanking the man, he remembered with a touch of shame; if he could meet him again, now, on the same road, he would reward him handsomely.

This journey to London was not of Richard's choice, for Mary had only recently been brought to bed of her fifth child and she was taking a long time to recover her strength. But she had insisted that Richard should go to London and see Nicholas Ayssheton and beg of him the release of the mortgage on her brother's farm. When Richard had demurred at leaving her she had protested, 'If you value my happiness and peace of mind, you will carry out this commission to help my unhappy brother. I fret over him and my mother, but rest assured I will soon be strong and well again if this worry is removed. You are the only one who can ask this favour of Nicholas and make him understand the great harm he is causing to one who was once his friend.'

Richard sighed, thinking of the difficult task ahead, and wishing he were back at home to care for his ailing wife instead of riding the rough highway all the way to London, to demand a favour of the lawyer friend who had apparently left his home town for ever, and in anger.

It had been an unhappy time at Calyngton, from the day when the scandal broke until tempers had cooled down, months after the angry departure of Nicholas Ayssheton and his family. There had been denunciations from the pulpit and excited meetings in the guildhall − where, in spite of Richard's reminders of all that was owed to their benefactor, enthusiastic declarations were made banning lawyer Ayssheton from the enjoyment of local respect and services. Poor Richard was torn between his friendship for Nicholas and his concern for his brother-in-law's distress, and so while the storm raged around him he took no part and buried himself in his work. But all the time he was acutely aware that he was the one person, being a close friend to both Nicholas and John, who might heal the hurt and bring about a reconciliation.

Now he was on his way to London, and fearful of what lay before him.

He rested the last night at Brentford, and then pressed on to the capital in the morning. As he rode eastward along the river − which he knew must eventually lead him to the courts of law at the palace of Westminster − a strengthening east wind blew in his face at each bend of the highway, and by the time he reached the little village of Chelsea the gale was so strong that flurries of apple and cherry blossom were blowing into his path. The biting cold caught his breath, and the horse slowed down almost to a halt, but Richard bent his head to the wind and urged his horse on; he was determined to find Nicholas and fulfil his mission before the day began to wane, for he did not like the idea of having to spend a night in a bustling overcrowded city.

It wanted a few minutes to noon by the time he had reached Westminster and found the entrance to the law courts in the palace. There he was stopped by a surly doorkeeper who demanded his business, and seemed surprised that he sought lawyer Ayssheton.

'You will not find him here at this time of day,' he scoffed. 'The courts concluded the day's business a full hour ago, and the lawyers have long since gone back to their inns to dine and wine with their ladies.'

'They have finished their work for the day?' Richard asked incredulously. His work-day ran from dawn to dusk, and to finish at mid-day seemed to him an amazing waste of God's time. But the doorkeeper answered grudgingly, 'They do other work during the rest of the day, especially those who are readers to the mootmen. They also attend at the parvis at Paul's for consultation by those wishing to plead a case before the king's court. But it is an easy life, my friend, and well-lined, to boot!'

He looked expectantly at Richard, who reluctantly extracted a florin from his purse and paid the man for his meagre information.

'Where will I find lawyer Ayssheton then?' he asked. 'I pray you, direct me to Chichester Inn, where I understand his family resides.'

The doorkeeper bit the silver coin and tucked it carefully into the inner reaches of his tunic before replying, but his face changed to a friendly curiosity when he observed the skill with which Richard swung himself into the saddle, his one hand holding the reins while his whole body leapt gracefully in an arc on to the horse's back.

'That is cleverly done, master,' he commented admiringly.

'Oh, years of practice,' replied Richard nonchalantly, as he settled himself in the saddle.

The doorkeeper became immediately friendly and eager to please, and he gave Richard very careful instructions on how to find the Chancellor's Lane, a short distance before the entrance to the city at Ludgate. 'That will take you to Chichester Inn, and tell the gatekeeper I sent you; he will look after you and see that you find lawyer Ayssheton without delay. He will know whether he is at Paul's or in hall.'

Well, that was after all a florin well spent, thought Richard as he rode away, his instructions carefully memorised.

And so it proved. In less than half an hour his horse was being led away to the stables of Chichester Inn, while he himself followed his guide along dim stone passages and up dusky creaking stairways, a flutter in the pit of his stomach and an increasing weakness in his legs as he approached the confrontation with Nicholas and his 'woman'. He had rehearsed many times the interview as he would like it to go, but as his guide stopped and knocked on a door he realised that all coherent thought had fled from his brain.

A woman's voice called, 'Enter', and the gatekeeper opened the door and pushed Richard inside, latching the door noisily behind him.

'Who is it?' the same female voice inquired from somewhere in the shadows. It was a young and musical voice, with the timbre of a well-tuned bell and the ring of commanding self-assurance, and it spoke carelessly, as if it did not really matter who had entered the chamber.

Richard announced himself nervously. There was an answering gasp of astonishment: 'Oh! Please to enter, Master Chyket.'

As he stepped forward uncertainly, she rose from the stool where she had been perched screening the fire, and in the firelight aided by the dusty light filtering through a small window, he was caught immediately by the magic of the vitality that was Margaret Brook, now wife of Nicholas Ayssheton. His nervousness vanished, he stepped forward towards the fire, and she held out both hands to welcome him.

'Oh for a breath of Cornish air,' she laughed, apologising for the stuffy chamber, 'How I wish you could have brought some with you! Sit you down by the fire and give me news of Calyngton.'

Her continued self-assurance amazed Richard, who had expected either guilty apologies or a harsh dismissal, and had certainly not expected such a warm welcome. But then he recollected that it was nearly two years since she and Nicholas had left Calyngton, and the events of their new life together in London would have blunted their memories of abuse and guilt. Could it be possible, he wondered, that they had both actually forgotten the great hurt they had done to John Fursdon?

Margaret plied him with questions, and he answered frankly and effortlessly, charmed by her natural manner into the illusion that they were old friends of many years' standing. Only when he described the loneliness and unhappiness of John at Fursdon did her eager questioning cease, and she sat silent awhile, gazing pensively into the fire.

At last she said: 'Poor John, what great harm I did him,' and turning to Richard she asked him earnestly: 'Is there aught we can do to help him?'

'Yes, there is one great favour you could do which we think, my Mary and I, would do much to ease his mind and help him back to normal life. Mistress, it is the loan which refuses to let him shake off the past, for he finds himself working a farm which is no longer his — so what call to improve and prosper and even find himself a wife?' Richard braced himself to speak the brutal truth: 'Nicholas — a much loved friend — took his wife and took also his inheritance. Now he has nothing to live for.'

'Fursdon? Indeed, I had forgotten. What troubles my foolishness brought! It was a wonderful adventure for me, and I am thankful to the good Lord for sending me to Santiago de Compostela to the shrine of the blessed saint, but after all that — well, we lost the marble, and now I think we may have parted with Polcarowe also.'

The sudden wailing of a small child in an adjoining room cut short the discussion. It was joined by the distinctive cry of a baby just awakened, and Margaret hurried away. In a short while she emerged with a tiny baby in her arms, followed by a little girl staggering on uncertain legs which had evidently only recently learned to walk. Shielding her toddler from the fire, Margaret introduced the children to Richard, who was delighted to discover that the baby Edward was only weeks older than his own boy, Ralph. Inevitably the conversation turned to small children and their miraculous doings, and the two doting parents were still thus engaged when an hour later Nicholas returned from the parvis.

He did not at first notice the visitor, and Richard was able to observe him quietly from his corner as the lawyer flung his rolled parchments on to a cluttered table by the small window, then snatched up Susannah from the floor and danced round the room with her to the accompaniment of her gurgles of delight.

This little routine over, he put her gently to the floor and held her hand while she walked the few paces back to her mother, only then becoming aware of the visitor. He peered at him in the dim light and asked crossly, 'Where is the nurse?'

'I have sent her out to the country to seek some good cows' milk from farmer Jasper at Hoxton,' replied Margaret serenely. 'We have an old friend here, dear heart, come all the way from Cornwall to see us — and to ask a favour of you.'

Richard stood up and held out his hand in greeting. What he

had planned to say to Nicholas was quite forgotten; instead he said, as he would have greeted his friend in the old days, 'It is good to see you again, Nicholas.'

'Richard, Richard! — My friend! What a happy surprise to find you here! Almost the last person I would expect to find closeted in this dusty chamber, but indeed the most welcome!'

Nicholas sat himself down on the floor beside his little daughter, who then scrambled on to his lap amongst the folds of his crumpled gown. He looked up quizzically at Richard, and after a brief moment's hesitation enquired: 'Is the church completed? Or have they knocked it down so as to remove all remembrance of me?'

Richard laughed. 'No, it still stands!' he reassured his friend. 'It now boasts a finely carved chancel screen, and the carpenters — your carpenters, Nicholas — started work just recently on the creation of your father's design for the Great Rood.'

Nicholas's face was a picture of bland satisfaction. 'And the consecration?'

'We still await the Holy Father's ruling on our petition. These things take time — as you yourself told me, some years since, my friend!'

''Tis so, indeed. And your sweet Mary, who is to share in the name of our new church, how goes it with her?'

Richard's face clouded. 'Unhappily, not in the best of health.' He launched into a full account of life at Chykets, their growing family and Mary's pregnancy problems, and, without really meaning to, went on to describe her worries about her brother. He stopped, embarrassed at his own clumsiness. There was an awkward silence, then Margaret came to his rescue.

'Richard has come, my dear, to ask you to release the mortgage on Fursdon.'

Nicholas looked at her, then at Richard, and slowly shook his head.

'Too late,' he said sadly. 'I have just completed the purchase of Calyngton Manor, for the lives of myself, my wife and my son Edward.'

Richard's eyes went wide with surprise and interest.

'You may wonder why,' continued Nicholas, 'and if you think it could be from a motive of pique, to obtain my revenge on those farmers and shopkeepers, and labourers, who virtually threw us out of the town — well, you would be partly right. I do indeed intend to return to Calyngton in a position of authority and high standing where none may deny me any service which I require.'

For a moment the old look of severity and bitterness returned to his features, and he drew his daughter protectively towards him, as he declared sharply, 'Never again will one of my children be denied her baptism into the kingdom of God — not if I have to buy up the advowsons of every church in the west country!'

Remembering his own lack of action at that time, Richard smiled somewhat apologetically at the little girl nestled in her father's arms.

'But it goes deeper than that,' continued Nicholas, his mood changing to that of an enthusiastic leader. 'I love our town — I want to build it up into a place of importance in the life of Cornwall and Devon. Once the church is finished we should engage on the building of a new guildhall — and why not, Richard, show the way by enrolling a guild of west country woolmen? Then we should enlarge the market place and provide a new pound on the outskirts of the town, and as the market grows in importance — as it surely will — we may beg an indulgence of the bishop for the building of a good stone bridge over our river.'

Richard slapped his hand on his knee. 'What a vision!' he cried in admiration. 'We need you in the town to lead us to it!'

'That will be difficult,' replied Nicholas, shooting an anxious glance at Margaret, who was sitting very still and quiet on her stool by the fire. 'My work holds me here in London, except when travelling on commissions or to an assize. But I have made a start for the betterment of Calyngton with the purchase of the manor, and I promise you that I will not be a harsh landlord but will reward generously all who apply their labour honestly and diligently on their holdings. Unfortunately for John the purchase has cost me all the monies that I could raise — we even sold Polcarowe — and so I could not repay to the lenders what we borrowed from them for the ransom. Without the security of Fursdon to back those debts I would face imprisonment.'

'We must do something!' pleaded Margaret in a whisper, clenching her hands so that the knuckles showed. 'You know how dear he was to me — and I am responsible for his present misery.'

Nicholas reached out and took her hand. 'It would help, maybe, if we were to send a message of assurance to John, through our good friend Richard, telling him that I will do all in my power to return his property to the Fursdon family one day.' He put his arm round the little girl on his lap and kissed her on the top of her head.

'Tell John,' he said, smiling at Richard, 'that he must marry as soon as he can and thus ensure there is a Fursdon family to whom I can return the manor. Show him the delights of fatherhood, and persuade him I would be very loath to release Fursdon to an ageing bachelor!'

Richard did not leave London that day; he was so enjoying himself that he did not even remember his original plan.

When the children's nurse returned from her foray in the country, she and her mistress busied themselves feeding the children and preparing them for bed, while Nicholas and Richard sat together on a corner bench by the fire and talked of men's affairs.

'Is it true that we have lost Paris?' asked Richard.

'Yes, it is so. It was, I think, inevitable after the death of the regent, my Lord Bedford. They say he died from exhaustion after so many years controlling that rebellious territory. These are troublous times even here in London — did you see any riotous crowds as you came from Westminster?'

'No, all was as peaceful as a Sunday in Calyngton.'

'It was early in the day, perhaps. Should you go out again now, down by the Flete, or into the city, you could well be drawn into some pitched battle between apprentices and Flemings, or find your way barred by an angry gathering protesting against the privileges of the hated Hanse.' Nicholas paused, listening to the sound of tramping feet in the street below; he drew Richard to the window and opened the pane. They peered out together, as a band of uniformed men marched by, their cressets leaving a trail of smoke which drifted up to the high window.

'There goes yet another cause of trouble in our land,' said Nicholas, as he closed the window again against the bitter night air. 'Twice when I sat in the parliament we made laws banning liveried armies, but our good king and his council do nothing to enforce them and every lord seeking power protects his interests with these bands of cut-throats sporting his colours.' He listened again as through the closed window came a distant noise of shouting. 'There,' he said; 'they have met up with my Lord Somerset's band down on the Flete! Well, it all makes for more business at the Common Place, my Lord Somerset will seek redress. But, how can a country live in peace and prosper when such lawlessness goes unchecked?' He shrugged his shoulders and spread out his hands in a gesture of despair, just as Margaret emerged from the sleeping chamber where she had left the nurse watching over the two small children.

At sight of her an invisible cloak of anxiety fell from Nicholas, and he was again the affable and urbane family man and devoted lover.

'My love!' he said, simply; he took her hand and gathered her to him, with his other hand on her hip as he looked intently into her eyes. Richard waited as one witnessing a trance; then quite suddenly Nicholas gave his wife a quick peck on the cheek and turned, still holding her hand, to address the visitor.

'Come, let us descend to the hall for the *cena*.'

They groped their way down the dark stairway lit only by occasional rush lights set in the wall. The hungry Richard sniffed appreciatively at the delicious smells of roasting pork wafting up the stair well. At the end of the building they entered a vast hall, already humming with the voices of lawyers and students, and their servants and wives. They took their places in a corner where a group of women was seated; here Margaret was soon in her element, gossiping with her friends and discussing families and servants.

Richard ate all that was put before him, and was still working on a huge cheese which had been placed at his elbow when the women all rose from their places and silently left the hall. Their departure was ignored by the rows of noisy mootmen and pleaders, and the flagons continued to pass along the tables as arguments and laughter rose to the rafters.

Nicholas rose from the bench, pressing his hand on Richard's armless shoulder and saying quietly, 'Stay here.' Slowly but purposefully he advanced up the hall, bowing occasionally to the more senior lawmen at some of the tables and followed by a wave of hushed attention. By the time he had reached the dais at the head of the hall and stepped up to the lectern the whole company was turned towards him, attentively waiting. For nearly two hours he recited, from a massive tome, the law lecture appointed for the day, and long before he had finished Richard had succumbed to the good food and wine, and the warm stuffiness of his surroundings, and was slumped fast asleep on the table.

A cold dawn was seeping through high windows when he awoke, chilled to the marrow. He found that someone had laid him near the fire, alongside other sleepers – or had he lain down here himself after further unremembered festivities with these same fellows, he wondered? He disentangled himself and his clothes from his neighbours without waking them, stretched and shook himself, and went in search of the latrine. Then, his toilet completed with a rinse under the pump, and his horse fed and watered, he climbed the stairs to bid his hosts good morning and goodbye.

Nicholas had also just risen, and as soon as Richard appeared he roused the young nurse from her bed on the fireside bench and sent her off to the pastrycook's to find them some breakfast.

Richard was now anxious to be gone, to get out of London on the road leading to the west country before the sun was above the rooftops. But then Margaret appeared, yawning the sleep from her eyes and looking just as bewitching in her morning deshabille as when elegantly dressed, and Richard forgot his urgent need to set off for home.

The nurse returned with oatcakes and buttermilk, the fire was relit and they took their breakfast sitting before it.

Nicholas said he would go with Richard as far as Charing Cross, and show him the most direct road westward, before carrying on himself to the law courts at the palace of Westminster.

Suddenly Margaret flung down her bowl of buttermilk and stood up, looking around her frantically as if in mortal danger. Nicholas also rose, moving towards her protectively. Richard was amazed to see her lovely face had changed to one of haggard misery.

'Dreary! Dreary!' she moaned in a low voice. 'Smells,

pestilence! Dust and darkness! Why do we live like this? I need room to move, and air to breathe. *I suffocate!*' She ended on a note of hysteria and broke down, sobbing. Nicholas took her in his arms and soothed her as he would have done his small daughter.

Looking over the top of her head to Richard, he explained, 'Margaret does not like living in Chichester Inn. She wants us to return to Cornwall. But my work is here — Justice Fortescue has told me I could well be appointed serjeant in a few years' time — and so we must needs put up with this meagre residence.'

Margaret eased her sobs and murmured into the folds of Nicholas's gown something which sounded to Richard like 'home'. Of course, he was going home — that had triggered off her outburst — because she too longed to get away from the dreariness of family life in the Inns of Court. Best go as soon as possible, he thought, and quickly rose to his feet.

'Stay!' said Nicholas urgently, without looking at him. Gently he seated his wife on the bench, and going on one knee before her, tilted her chin and kissed her very tenderly on the lips.

'My love, we shall go home to Cornwall.' She looked at him in tearful astonishment.

He continued, 'When the term ends we will take our little ones to Theupath for the summer months. The country air will refresh us all, and perhaps I will be able to restore good relations with our neighbours in Calyngton.'

The cure in Margaret was instant and miraculous; wiping her tearstained face with a flick of her fingers she kissed her husband and then ran across to Richard and gave him also a joyful kiss on the cheek. He grinned foolishly at her, then collected himself and looked more serious.

'It will be a delight to have you at Theupath again,' he said eagerly, as Nicholas rose to his feet and dusted down his clothes. 'I will do what I can to restore you in the community. I will tell everyone that one day you will give Fursdon back to John — that will sweeten the air amongst our townsfolk: And if you are there with us as a good landlord, who knows? — you may live to become the most popular lord of the manor ever known in Calyngton!'

Nicholas took hold of Richard's collar and made playfully as if to shake him as he used to do when they were boys together, then pressed him on the shoulder gratefully. 'I will do my best, my friend, and I will look to you for advice and guidance at all times!'

Richard looked at him speculatively. 'Perhaps another period of service in the parliament would be of use to us all.'

The suggestion was thrown out like a bait as he walked over to the door, where, as he turned to say goodbye with his hand on the latch he added, 'As lord of the manor you could be elected to represent the whole of Cornwall as a knight of the shire.'

Nicholas looked doubtful. 'Do I know enough voters of forty shillings' worth?' he asked.

'I will work on it,' replied Richard cheerfully, with a touch of the old confidence and impetuosity which had brought him success in the wool trade. 'Now I must leave at once, without you if need be, for I too have a wife to be comforted and cared for.'

It was a glorious summer. They took the children by sea from Queenhithe to the Tamar, running down the coast as on wings with a gentle following breeze in a blue sky. Their arrival at Theupath delighted Mattie and Dan, and even the taciturn Thomas, while the sun continued to smile kindly, filling the countryside with the scent of honeysuckle and new-mown hay. For Margaret it was, after London, the Elysian fields, and she dreamed away the weeks, lazing in the cool grass of the orchard with baby Edward, while Susannah became the adored baby to Mattie's little trio. Nicholas did not relax. He spent the first few weeks walking his new vast estate in company with Richard and Dan, meeting his new tenants and making his first friendly overtures, with a modicum of success. Then for two weeks he rode the length and breadth of Cornwall, guided by Richard to the landowners most likely to support his candidature for election as one of the two county members. Richard had prepared the ground with commercial thoroughness, and at the midsummer election, Nicholas once more found himself a member of the king's parliament, at a more effective level than as a burgesses' representative, and with the courtesy title of 'knight'. The reflected glory brought pleasure to his Calyngton copyholders, and men began to doff their caps to him and address him as 'Sir Nicholas'.

But time span, and not only would the new parliament meet in the early autumn, but the law courts beckoned for the Michaelmas term. Nicholas and Margaret surveyed their world and their children and agreed, with some real anguish, that the little ones should not be taken back to London to be immured in the inns of court for the winter, but would have a better chance to thrive if left in Cornwall in the care of Mattie.

The weather broke the night before their departure. Margaret felt the world was weeping for her as she bade her two children a tearful farewell and was lifted on to her horse in the pouring rain by a husband whose doleful face showed that he too was not far from tears. It was small comfort to them both when they turned at the brow of the hill to wave goodbye, only to see Susannah running after the big girls, her parents' departure already forgotten.

3

John Fursdon married Betsy Bould the following year, at a simple ceremony at St Cleer. His mother was too sick and frail to travel as far as Calyngton, so Betsy reluctantly agreed to the change; in any case, the new church at Calyngton was not yet consecrated, and its interior more like a workshop than a house of God, as joiners and plasterers finished off their work.

'I shall bring my first child home to be baptised in the new church,' Betsy declared to Mary as they drove past on their way to St Cleer, in the carriage borrowed from Squire Manaton for the occasion.

The entire Chyket family was squeezed into the carriage with her, while her dower chest was strapped to the roof behind Diggory Allin on the driver's box. The eldest little boy, seven-year-old Johnnie, was craning his head out past the carriage blinds, while his father kept a tight hold on him by his collar. Richard had braced himself in the front corner to prevent himself toppling on to the womenfolk and the other children, and he grinned happily at the spectacle of Willie and Dick bouncing on Betsy's knee, while Mimi — third generation Mary — clung to her neck. Mary caught his eye and smiled with him as she struggled to prevent the energetic baby Ralph from trampling too vigorously on her.

She turned to Betsy. 'You will make a wonderful mother, dear Betsy, you are so happy with them,' she said.

Betsy prised little Mimi's grip off her throat and grinned cheerfully. 'I love 'em all!' she chuckled exuberantly, slapping both boys on their backsides.

'We will all miss you,' added Mary, with a gentle sigh. Indeed, she dreaded the days ahead without the companionship and cheerful assistance of Betsy, who would run the home efficiently and keep the children well and happy, and under effortless control, while Mary rested during the last month of pregnancy. The next baby was already tickling her under the ribs, but this time there would be no Betsy to help. She pictured Betsy at Fursdon, nursing her own babies in Mary's childhood home, and she felt a sudden pang of jealousy and homesickness.

The carriage jolted through the ford and rocked its way up the rutted road. One by one the children grew quieter and dozed off, and Mary too closed her eyes and relaxed her bulky shape as Ralph slept on her shoulder. Richard studied her pretty little face; there was still none to compare with his lovely Meg in his mind; she was fine and delicate and made the rosy-cheeked, chubby Betsy seem clumsy and rough-hewn; but he was concerned to see dark hollows under her eyes and a delicate blue tinge under the pastel skin. Dear Meg, she looked poorly again, he must take better care of her. He would find her a new nursemaid to take the place of Betsy.

Thinking of Betsy took his thoughts to the bridegroom, John, and he congratulated himself that his journey to London last year had resulted at last in a happy outcome. John, he reckoned, had taken a very long time, even then, to 'come to the boil' — probably still day-dreaming of his beloved Margaret — but soon all would be settled, another family formed, and his mother-in-law happy in her declining years.

The carriage drew up at the lych-gate outside the church. Mary opened her eyes and cried with delight when she saw her two brothers and her mother waiting to greet them. One by one

the small Chykets awoke and stretched, and in varying degrees
of happiness and ill-humour scrambled out of the carriage to
rush at their uncles. John brushed them aside and stepped up to
the carriage to greet his bride, his lined face wreathed in smiles.
Betsy stood a moment, awkwardly shaking out her silk gown
where it had been rumpled by the children, and smoothing the
fur tippet and cuffs. John bowed over her hand.

'Welcome, Mistress Betsy,' he said. 'Shall we lead the way?'

The wedding group formed and they moved into the church,
where even the children were suddenly quietened into complete
silence by the cool dark solemnity of the place and the occasion.

It was quiet at Fursdon that evening. The Chykets had departed
back to Calyngton, and Elizabeth also had returned home to
her husband and family at St Neot, after acting as hostess for
her mother for the wedding breakfast. William had gone out
alone to deal with the milking and to pen the geese and pigs,
leaving Mary and the bridal pair at the fireside.

It was an agonising time for Betsy, for she longed to chatter,
but felt intimidated by the very stillness of John and his mother.
She also felt excluded from their thoughts, and so eventually
asked permission of her mother-in-law to prepare her a drink of
mulled ale or warm milk.

'Yes, my dear,' said Mary, startled. She had been dreaming of
the old days, and it was a shock, albeit a pleasant one, to find
that she was now to be waited on by someone else. She watched
Betsy bustling about the kitchen, and nodded in satisfaction
towards John.

'She will do very well, my son,' she said.

John's thoughts too had been elsewhere, but over at Polcarowe in those halcyon days when he and Margaret had
designed her estate together. So, now he had found himself a
housekeeper and a mother for his children. Would such a
simple remedy spell happiness? He sighed, but smiled reassur-
ance at his mother.

Mary Fursdon was in reality worn out. Having struggled for
years to keep on her feet and continue to look after the household for her two sons, she was not able to enjoy for long the care
and attention of her daughter-in-law. Once the need to be
active was no longer there she retired to her bed, where she was

found dead one morning only six weeks after the wedding day. Her final wish, to see the birth of a Fursdon grandson, was not to be realised. But her daughter, Mary Chyket, was safely delivered of a daughter the day her mother died.

4

'They are to build a bridge at Lostwithiell,' John Fursdon told his brother-in-law Richard Chyket the day they buried his mother.

'Ay, I heard,' replied Richard. 'One day we must beg an indulgence to build one over the Lynher. But after nigh on ten years of labouring to build our church, we will rest content awhile with that.'

'Is it finished now?' asked John.

Richard nodded. ''Tis the most beautiful church you could wish to see,' he said proudly, 'and the Holy Writ is illustrated on the walls as well as in the windows. It is so full of colour when the sun shines through the clerestory windows that you might well be in Heaven itself! The bishop approved it mightily, and will come in person to consecrate it when we have completed the preparation of our own burial ground. The consent of my Lord Stafford has not reached us yet, but we are assured he will approve, indeed welcome, this new and larger church.'

'But, until the bishop visits you, you have no church?'

'Oh, we manage. The altar of St Nicholas is still there, and if we cluster together on the floor which was once the old chapel we are on holy ground and may take part in the mass. The crowds who used to fill the churchyard now stand in the new church to watch the celebration. And so we get by.'

'When is the bishop to come?'

'He is growing old and does not like to travel on visitations during the bad weather. We plan for next summer. I have asked for donations of malt this harvest time which can be used for brewing the church ales for the festival — so that it can be a merry occasion.'

'And bring financial gain to your church!'

Richard nodded. 'Of course!' he said.

The one thing which Richard had not told John was the bishop's comment on admiring the church: 'You have a great benefactor in Master Nicholas Ayssheton. I trust that you give due thanks to his goodness and merit.' Any mention of Nicholas still clouded John's day, so the subject was avoided.

Richard worried in his mind whether he should send word to Nicholas to attend the consecration festivities, or whether for the peace of the community it would be wiser to ignore him, on the pretext that he was known to be too busy at Westminster. But then, in the early summer of 1438, when news of the bishop's visitation was awaited daily, Thomas Hicks brought word to Richard that the Aysshetons were home at Theupath.

'The mistress is to remain here with the children,' said Thomas. 'She expects to be delivered of her third child during the octave of St Thomas; Master Nicholas has work to do in the west country.'

'Will we see him at Calyngton, think you?' asked Richard, cursing himself for not sending the invitation. His heart quailed at the prospect of the lord of the manor, the unthanked benefactor of the church, arriving unbidden at the consecration ceremony or, worse still, when it was all over.

'I doubt we shall see him here,' said Thomas, drawing himself up with an air of due importance as the harbinger of national news. 'He will be travelling on a commission of Sir William Bonevyle, investigating with the sheriffs the desertion of ship-masters and mariners from the Earl of Warwick's forces sailing to Normandy. The rascals disappeared into the night, they say, with their ships and carvells, leaving the troops stranded at the ports. All along the coast the commission will have to go — so Master Nicholas has told me — to track down the miscreants. He thinks that more than likely they are pirates, for they took the king's wages before they disappeared.'

'So, meanwhile Mistress Margaret will be with her children at Theupath? I must pay my respects and invite her to attend our festivities.' What a relief, thought Richard to himself; he was safe to issue the invitation, for Margaret would never venture into the town on her own.

Calyngton was still awaiting the arrival of Bishop Lacy when in mid-July Margaret's second daughter, Joanne, was born. Then word came from Chudleigh that the bishop was still too ill to travel and the visitation would be postponed until August. So the plasterers continued their work on the barrel-vaulted roof of the nave, the wrestlers went on practising their skill for an even better festival in August, and Richard checked the barrels of ale in his beer-house and set more malt to brew, 'just in case'. Three troupes of travelling players arrived in the town, each hoping to strike the day of the festivities for their performance, and each disappointed with the small audiences before their cart as they performed parts of the *Ordinalia* in the market square, before moving on to another town.

It was Mattie who kept Margaret's interest alive in all that was going on in the town — a town which she had never visited and whose people had rejected her. Mattie was a born raconteuse and purveyor of local gossip, and the two women laughed together many a time over the foibles of local folk and the accidents they fell into. But one day she brought serious news.

'Mistress Chyket has not risen from her bed since the last babe was born, months ago in the spring. They say in the market place that she is like to die.'

Margaret remembered the happy family talks she had had with Richard, and was shocked into action by the thought of that lovely family being without its mother.

'I will go and visit her,' she said crisply, rising from the window bench where she had been sitting at her needlework. 'Ask your father to harness the small cart, and bring me that basket of strawberries that Ellin gathered this morning.'

'May I go with you, to drive the cart?' asked Mattie anxiously.

'No, you watch over the children and baby Joanne, I will go alone. Just give me clear instructions how to find the Chyket home.'

Mattie knew it was useless to argue the point, so she shrugged her shoulders and went off to do as she was bidden. A short while later the cart rattled off up the lane with Margaret, the lady of Calyngton manor, dressed in a simple homespun country gown and with a kerchief over her lovely auburn hair, handling the reins like an experienced farmhand.

It was a sweltering hot day, but she looked cool and poised as she drove through the town, causing heads to turn and figures to pop out of doorways, inquisitive to have a good look at the stranger.

Word soon got round; this then was '*her*', and now she was the new lady of the manor. A little crowd trailed after her down the street and gathered at Chykets gate after she had gone in, patiently awaiting her departure – when they might either drop her a curtsey or throw a turd or two at her, as the spirit of the moment took them.

Oblivious to the stir caused by her passage through the town, Margaret was shown up to Mary's bedchamber by a startled little maidservant, whose mistress was equally startled by the appearance at her bedside of this stranger of ill-repute. But it took Margaret only a few moments to reassure Mary by her natural charm and ease of manner, and they were soon talking together like old friends, the past forgotten.

Mary's long illness was the exhausation to her frail body brought on by too-frequent pregnancies, coupled with a lack of mental stimulus now she no longer had the company of Betsy. By the time Margaret Ayssheton rose to take her leave, after spending the afternoon gently gossiping, nursing the baby, playing with the infant daughter – her namesake Margaret – smoothing the bed and bringing cooling drinks to the invalid with as much finesse and competence as ever Betsy had done, Mary's spirits had already begun to revive, like a young seedling refreshed by a shower of rain after a drought.

'Must you go?' she pleaded, sinking back against the pillow as if to emphasise her helplessness.

Margaret took her hand. 'I will return on the morrow,' she said.

She was as good as her word. She returned the following morning, bringing Mattie with her, who supervised the little maidservant in preparing the solar with a day bed for her mistress, and there Margaret and Mary spent long hours together each day, while Mattie took the five older children in the cart to Theupath, to play there with her own and the Ayssheton children. The invalid began to make a marked recovery. It was only then that she confessed to Margaret that baby Robert had not yet been baptised.

'Richard has been too much engaged with church affairs to

think about his own son's baptism,' she said, wiping a small tear from her eye. 'Poor mite, with a sick mother, both of us likely to die without the protection of Mother Church.'

Margaret protested vigorously. 'You speak as if the matter were of no significance. I too have yet to have baby Joanne baptised, and myself received back into the church. I planned to await my lord's return from the commission, but shall we rather go together with our babes to the church, without delay?'

Mary shook her head. 'I could not walk there, I am still too weak — although now for the first time I long to be about again.'

'Diggory will carry you there,' declared Margaret. 'Richard will arrange for the double ceremony with the rector, and we will go together.'

It was a strange little procession which wound its way up the street three days later. Diggory led the way, carrying his pale little mistress in his arms, and closely followed by an anxious Richard awkwardly burdened with his youngest offspring. Behind him Margaret was a picture of graceful beauty as she walked slowly along, the baby Joanne cradled in one arm while the other lifted the hem of her rich blue silk gown clear of the dirt. After her came a meandering trail of small Chykets and Aysshetons, all marshalled from the rear by Mattie.

The Norman chapel was still in use, although surrounded by delicately carved screens, beyond which plasterers and painters were still working. The baby Robert bawled lustily when he was dipped in the font, but Joanne Ayssheton seemed unperturbed by the cold water. An unhappy omen, said some, when the news flashed around the town — the devil had not been expelled from her by the holy water.

For her mother, however, it was a happy day. As she left the church surrounded by the gaggle of chattering children from both families she was greeted with smiles and curtseys by the women gathered outside, while a group of men outside the inn on the other side of the street waved their caps in the air with a cheer as the baptism party passed by.

The lady of the manor had come into her own.

5

August 31st was the day set for the consecration of the church and its burial ground. Excitement mounted as the day approached, and the portreeve had no difficulty enrolling a working party to assist the town scavenger in cleaning up the streets. Out in the fields whole families, down to urchins smaller than the sheaves they staggered under, worked from dawn to dusk to complete the corn harvest and earn themselves a holiday for the festival.

Outside Chykets Richard was supervising final cleaning work in readiness for the bishop's arrival the following day, when a horse came cantering up the hill from the north gate and with a clatter of hooves on the cobbles was drawn up alongside him. Before Richard could greet the rider, whom he recognised by his livery as one of the bishop's retinue, the man called out, without dismounting, 'My lord bishop is ill and cannot visit you. He is sending instead the bishop of Enachdun.'

Richard's world fell from him. 'The bishop of Enachdun? Who is he?' he asked aghast.

'I know not, master. He is an Irishman, and he has been assisting my lord bishop — since the bishop collapsed after the lengthy proceedings concerning Abbot Mede of Tavistok. He brings the bishop's ordinance with him, which he will deliver to you.'

He made to move off again, but Richard caught at the horse's bridle.

'Hold! Tell me, before you go, when may we expect this Irish bishop? We thought to have Bishop Lacy with us at mid-day tomorrow.'

'He lies at Launceston tonight, master, at St Thomas's priory, and will be with you before noon tomorrow. He then goes on to the bishop's manor at Cuddenbeake to rest that night, and on the morrow proceeds to Menheniott. I go now to the manor and to Menheniott to advise them.'

Richard released the bridle and the messenger set spurs to his horse and cantered off up the street towards St Germans, watched by a despondent Richard.

After all these years of devoted work, the final touches were to be put, not by their beloved Bishop Lacy, but by a stranger and an Irishman. It seemed as if their wonderful new church were not rated very highly at Exeter; but then, he reminded himself, the bishop had been full of praise when he visited only last year. It would be only his age and infirmity which prevented him from making this promised visitation, and the town would honour him better by giving due respect to his appointed suffragan. He went in to saddle his horse and ride over to Southill to take the news to the rector.

John Bower, bishop of Enachdun, threw up his hands in wonder when he stepped inside Calyngton church.

'Sure, and 'tis a miracle indeed!' he exclaimed.

The crowd pressed in behind him, and he moved forward into the centre of the nave, where he pivoted himself slowly on his heels to take in the full effect.

Two lines of clustered granite pillars supporting the roof led as an avenue to a delicately carved rood screen through which he could just glimpse a chancel lined with carved stalls. On all sides he saw bright and cheerful colours, from the painted tympanum glittering with silver stars to the walls gay with biblical pictures between the sunlit stained glass windows. Even the carved screens glowed richly where the sunbeams caught them.

'My, my!' murmured the bishop, studying the white arch of the barrel-vaulted roof with its carved bands and rosettes rich in green and red. 'Like the rambling roses of Killarney!'

Thomas Baron nudged him and they moved forward to the chancel steps, where the bishop dropped to his knees, paying homage to the Crucifixion portrayed in lifelike details on the great rood above. The rector and the bishop's retinue knelt behind him, while the crowd squeezed itself quietly into every corner of the nave and tower.

The people stood shoulder to shoulder and waited patiently when the priests moved into the chancel for the consecration of the altar, the dedication to St Mary, and the ritual of the first mass, but as they could see little and hear nothing, a gentle susurration of whispers gradually expanded into excited chatter, which was halted eventually when the new curate, William Mensham, hurried out of the chancel and stood waving his arms in urgent protest. The bishop then moved slowly round the church, preceded by his official and the curate clearing a way for him, and followed by his holywater clerk. The prayers of consecration and the sprinkling of holy water completed, he returned to the chancel steps and addressed the crowd.

'Your bishop sends you greetings,' he said quietly, his soft Irish lilt giving the statement a musical cadence. 'When he has fully recovered from his present infirmity he will visit you again. But now I am to declare to you his ordinance, made by his lordship on the fourth day of this month at his manor of Chudleigh, and accepted on your behalf by the following: Robert Clay, John Burneby and William Mensham for your rector Thomas Baron; Thomas Wasek and John Forde for the parishioners of Southill and John Crabbe and Benedict Drewe for the parishioners of Calyngton. Hear ye now the rules laid down by your lord bishop.'

It was a long document, and there were to be many questions posed to the literate members of the community later by those unable to read the record for themselves. But they nodded in acceptance that they were to be responsible for the maintenance of their new church and its furnishings, and that the rector would continue to supervise their religious life and to supply them with a resident chaplain. There were smiles of pleasure at the prospect of an annual procession with Southill parishioners from Hece Cross to St Sampson's church, but one or two whispered objections to the requirement for the provision of such expensive items as two two-pound candles stuck with pennies, and many later declared that two shillings was much too high a charge for their annual payment to the mother church, to be paid according to the ordinance each year on the festival of St Sampson.

But while the ceremony went on, in the colourful sunlit church, the mood of euphoria persisted, with everyone happy to be part of this wonderful occasion. For many, the words of the bishop, given to them in a soft Irish brogue, merely floated over their heads and they were only roused to full attention when he put away the document and gave them his benediction.

Up in the choir loft a trumpet sounded, quavering at first as old Tom Benet, the sexton, fought his nervousness, but gradually gaining in strength and confidence. It was the signal for everyone to kiss and clap each other, to laugh and cheer in festive mood. In vain the curate struggled to maintain some semblance of order; the crowd jostled and pressed in all directions, some to peep into the chancel at the altar newly dedicated to St Mary, some struggling to get out of the church to follow the bishop as he moved with the holywater clerk up and down the newly prepared burial ground.

It was just as well that the consecration of the small burial ground only took a few moments, for at this point Diggory Allin and two of the stonemasons drew up in the market place with a cart loaded with the church ales. Like bees round a honeypot the entire population swarmed round the cart, the church and the Irish bishop quite forgotten. Soon the market place was filled with groups of dancers, swaying and singing in happy abandonment. At the far side a small area had been taken over by a more stationary crowd, who were shouting encouragement to their favourite wrestling champions.

John Burneby, the bishop's official, stood at the church door, looking down his long nose at the happy, noisy crowd in disdainful disapproval.

'My lord bishop will not like what I shall have to tell him of Calyngton,' he declared.

'There now, no cause to fret, Master Burneby,' replied Bishop Bower, soothingly. ''Tis only natural that folks should celebrate this happy occasion in a happy manner. They have been good, and they understand not, as we do, the needs of Mother Church. This beautiful new church will draw them back to the Lord, come the Sabbath — you mark my words.'

He moved off down the street to where, at a discreet distance, his mule-drawn wagon and the accompanying horses waited. The rest of his party hurried after him, leaving Calyngton to its worldly celebrations.

*

Nicholas was at Aveton Gifford on August 31st, near enough in distance but too busy on the commission's work to reach home in time for the church consecration. He had sent Gwyllym home when the commission had moved on down the coast from

Noss the previous week, with gifts and a long letter for his wife, and he now sat reading her reply for the twentieth time, his eyes misted with tears and his whole body aching for her.

So, the baby was baptised, and Margaret had made friends with John Fursdon's sister. That was good, and he could rejoice with her for her success; but he missed her all the more, and felt wholly miserable whenever he thought of her. Try as he would to control his desire, it was as strong now for his wife as it had been when he had wilfully seduced her five years ago — there were times when he would gladly have thrown up his important legal appointments so that he could remain in Cornwall with his wife and family. But service to the young and ailing king was now ingrained in his character, and he knew that his personal affairs must give priority to the king's law.

He would send word to Margaret to join him in Exeter. The decision made, he returned to his work in a more relaxed mood.

But the commission did not reach Exeter until early October, after investigating every little harbour of the South Devon coast-line, and there Nicholas found a sad little letter from Margaret awaiting him.

'Dear Heart, I cannot come,' she wrote, 'Both Sue and the baby have the fever, and I could not bear to be parted from them in their sickness. Mary and her baby are also both afflicted, and I must help care for them. Pray for them, and for us all, that the fever be not too severe. Your ever dutiful and loving wife, Margrit.'

The commission pressed on to London, pleased that they had discovered and fined all miscreants who had abandoned the king's service after accepting his wages. One of them however, turned his back on the west country very reluctantly, filled with a desperate longing to turn back to Cornwall to find his family, and picturing in his tortured mind his lovely wife surely dead and all his children stricken.

But there was work to be done. The report had to be pre-pared, and this the commissioners did each night at their lodg-ing place. It would, as Sir William Bonevyle explained, save much valuable time when they arrived at Westminster as the Michaelmas term in the courts of law had already begun. In addition Nicholas was now a justice of the peace and was called to the commission of assize opening in October. So, however much his heart longed to be home with his family, his duty took him inexorably further away.

The party split up at Charing Cross, and Nicholas rode on alone with Gwyllym towards the inns of court. Everywhere seemed strangely quiet, and as they turned into Chancellor's Lane he noticed that the entrance to Serjeants' Inn was closed and boarded up from within. Much to his consternation, when they reached Chichester Inn, its big studded doors were also firmly shut against all comers.

Nicholas hammered on the metal with his crop so sharply that his horse shied. He swore at it and pulled it round again close to the door, hammered again and shouted, 'Open up, open up, you villainous bastard! — Noah, do you hear me? This is lawyer Ayssheton, come home. Open the door to me or I will see that you are drowned in the river in penance to your namesake! Open up, I say!'

A tiny window was opened immediately above the archway.

'Go away, Master Ayssheton, I beseech you,' cried the doorkeeper from beyond the window. ''Tis the plague!'

Nicholas backed his horse away into the middle of the narrow street. From there he could just discern the outline of a man's face in the window.

'The plague is here — in the inn?'

'No, master, but everyone has gone from here and that is why the gates are shut, to keep out the plague carriers. There are many dead down at Ludgate, and more falling ill every day out at Shoreditch. The king has closed the courts of law until the Hilary term and has retired to Wallingford.'

'Has everyone gone away until the spring, then?' called Nicholas, a ridiculous tremor of joy stirring in his mind, even while physically he shrank away from the buildings of the plague-infested town.

'All gone, master, all gone. Get you away also,' replied the doorkeeper, and slammed the window shut.

'Come, Gwyllym, we must get well on our way out of this pestilential town before we touch ground again,' said Nicholas and set spurs to his horse.

They reached Cornwall in five days, sleeping in the open and only stopping at the remotest farms to buy food. As they neared home Nicholas wondered with increasing anxiety if the same sickness had caught his family and they were perhaps all now lying dead at Theupath, as his father had before them.

All the more joy then, when the two horsemen rode in to Theupath to be greeted by a bevy of happy, chattering children all now fully recovered from a mild local sickness which had killed no one. Margaret ran out when she heard the children's excitement, and was promptly gathered into her husband's arms for a passionate embrace tinged with relief.

'How long, dear heart?' she whispered.

'Until next year, my love! It will be a wonderful winter!'

6

The reputation of lawyer Ayssheton continued to grow in the west country year by year. He had become one of the symbols of the king's justice, liable to appear unexpectedly in the most remote places in quest of the truth of some reported crime or misdemeanour.

As Ted Serle confided to Betsy Fursdon one day at Liskerret market, after he had given evidence on finding the drowned corpse of Edward Burneby in his own well:

'He treats you like you was a man, one worthy to be listened to. 'Tis easy to speak the truth, and the whole truth of the story, to one such. Indeed, 'twould be nigh impossible to fabricate a falsehood, for you sense he knows what is true and what is a lie.'

Betsy went home that day deep in thought, turning over in her mind all that she had recently heard about this popular figure, a man who was still a villain to the Fursdon household. It had even been said that he had deliberately avoided appointment to the rank of serjeant at law because he wished to continue in Cornwall, dealing with the increasing scourge of piracy.

Why should he hate pirates so? she wondered. Without them and their capture of Margaret Brook's ship on its return from Spain, she would not now be lawyer Ayssheton's wife – and Betsy Fursdon would likely be a maid still! She shifted impatiently on the hard wooden seat of the cart, and poked her stick at the lumbering ox. How she longed to give John sons and daughters, to fill the little manor house with children. But the good Lord had decreed otherwise, and she had only two grown men, both of bachelor habits, for whom to cook and sew. She sighed with envy as she thought of the four Ayssheton children at Theupath — and another on the way, so she heard.

As she drove into the Fursdon yard John waved a greeting from the rickyard and came over to help her dismount. With the detached friendly air to which she was now well accustomed, he examined her market purchases and lifted them from the cart.

On an impulse Betsy blurted, 'Husband, I believe it is time you made your peace with Nicholas Ayssheton.'

She saw the muscles in his neck tauten. He said nothing. She laid her hand on his arm, pleading gently.

'So many years have slipped by, it will soon be a full decade since he wronged you so wickedly. However great the sin, it is surely time now to forgive with Christian charity.' She paused, sensing a frozen stillness in her husband, then hurried on, panic-stricken at what she had said, 'You are a good man, John. It is my grief that I have not given you the comfort of a family.'

John turned to face her and said, in a voice warm with compassion which belied the bitterness in his face, 'Betsy, you have been a good wife to me, no man could have a better one. But leave me be, where Nicholas Ayssheton is concerned — although I know what you say is right. Perhaps, in time. . . .' He humped a heavy sack on to his shoulders and walked away without completing the sentence.

It was a gang of pirates operating from the Fowy and the Fal estuaries which had caused most trouble over a number of years. It was common knowledge that local gentry and merchants were all involved in a lucrative campaign of seizing ships plying between Brittany and Ireland, which of necessity passed close to the Cornish coast, and which usually carried letters of safe conduct from the king's council. By the time complaints from the continental owners had reached the council and a commission of inquiry been appointed, all the wines and silks, salt and even coal and household furnishings, had vanished in private sales, while the ships were sailing under other colours.

Only one ship's master had so far been identified, along with one or two of the Penryn merchants who had bought from him. But in the absence of tangible proof the Cornishmen were blandly ignoring demands for restitution and saying, in effect, 'Just prove it!'

It was in pursuit of proof of the whereabouts of forty tuns of stolen wine and two shiploads of salt that Nicholas Ayssheton had spent several months exploring the whole southern coastline of Cornwall, interrogating seamen and their families, and inspecting boathouses, sail lofts, cellars and stores of every kind. Gradually, with consummate patience, he had built up the evidence, and had now decided to spend a week or two watching the boats which worked from the little fishing port of Falmouth.

Margaret had accompanied Nicholas on his travels, enjoying to the full being alone with him and his work to the exclusion of all other concerns and people. They had grown even closer together and were both supremely happy, and it was with a sense of deep contentment that they took comfortable quarters in a waterside inn and settled down to wait and watch.

Below their window the rippling tide sparkled in the afternoon sunshine of a brilliant spring day. Across the creek, banks of stately beech trees shone like silver, with just a delicate blush in their upper branches where the leaf buds were swelling. Above them the arch of heaven shone richly blue, unmarred by a single cloud, while the smoke drifting from the huddle of fishermen's cottages behind the quay soon lost itself among the trees. Even the seagulls bobbing on the tide looked unusually serene and quiet.

Nicholas caressed the soft auburn hair nestling against his shoulder, lulled by his contentment into momentary oblivion of the task in hand. Suddenly all the seagulls took to the air and disappeared down river towards the open sea. He rose and opened the casement; the distant mewing of the gulls filtered clearly into the room, and he leaned out of the window, searching the wooded headland for the first sign of sails or masts. Margaret sat quietly waiting, listening to the peaceful sea sounds of water and birds and accepting without rancour the memories they stirred of that other harbour across the sea where she had been held as a pirate's hostage.

Nicholas was the only person who had heard the full account

of that adventure. The monks accompanying her had told a reassuring story to John and all inquisitive friends who wondered aloud how she had fared in the hands of the lawless Bretons, and it was generally accepted that the whole affair had been solely a financial matter without any overtones of violence. Only Nicholas knew about the nightly siege waged on Margaret and her maid and the trick by which two unscrupulous seamen had eventually forced their way secretly into the women's room. Margaret shuddered now as she remembered that night of terror, and she could still see vividly the possessive leer on the face of the sailor who had raped her, when the following day he handed her on to the ship to sail to the ransom rendezvous.

The experience had tainted her return to John, but with the passionate love of Nicholas all things had been possible and she had expunged the sense of ruination and guilt by a full confession both to him and in church. Soon the memory no longer hurt.

Nicholas withdrew from the window. 'Here they come. I wonder what they are carrying in their holds apart from mackerel. Come, see, my love. The last two balingers, just rounding the headland at the tail of the fleet of smaller boats, are the *Jesus* and the *Fleur de la Mere*. Ah, and here comes another; it could be, yes, I do declare it is — 'tis the *Mary* from Fowy. All three coming in together into Falmouth, under cover of the fishing fleet! I wonder what their cargo could be!'

There was an urgent knock at the door, making them both jump, so intent were they on scrutinising the boats tacking into the harbour across the creek. Gwyllym entered.

'The king's messenger for you, master,' he announced, in a tone of disdainful disapproval, and standing back ushered in the messenger as he might have done a barnyard fowl. The messenger scowled back at him, then bowed ceremoniously to Nicholas and handed over his document. Nicholas broke the seal, glanced at its contents, and swore vigorously.

''Tis as I feared. It has come at last, my love — and could not have been more inopportune.' He glanced over his shoulder at the boats now slipping into harbour, then turned to Gwyllym.

'Ride round quickly to yonder quay — do not let them see you, but watch what comes off those three balingers and where they take it. This will be our last opportunity, for we must return to London.'

Gwyllym sprang to the door, then looked back. 'Who will tend to this wretch?' he asked scornfully, indicating the messenger.

'Go, lad, I will see to him. He only does his duty; if he offended you 'twas no doubt because he imagines that no countryman has any brains.'

'Ay, you see to him!' said Gwyllym, and slammed the door behind him.

The messenger looked after him. 'What an uncouth fellow!' he said, his sense of affront making his voice rise to a squeak.

Nicholas quelled him with a glance. 'To each the dignity of his calling,' he said icily. 'Get you down to the landlord; tell him I order you food and bed. We leave at dawn.'

Margaret waited until they were alone again, then asked quietly, 'Why must we leave? What is the message, dear heart?'

'I am appointed serjeant, my love — that is why we must leave. I have avoided it long enough, for I like my work and we live well by it, while as a serjeant I will be more a tool of the king's council.'

He unrolled the parchment and read aloud, 'Under pain of one thousand pounds to make ready at the octaves of St John the Baptist next to take upon him the estate and degree of a serjeant-at-law as by advice of the council the king has appointed him to do.'

'One thousand pounds! That is a heavy fine!' said Margaret.

Nicholas did not answer. He was perusing another smaller parchment which had been rolled inside the official document.

'There is a letter here from Sir John Fortescue,' he said, as he read it. 'He says I am to be made a judge, as soon as next year, so that it is necessary I be formally enrolled as a serjeant this summer.'

He put the documents down and came to stand behind his wife, laying his hands on her shoulders as they both gazed out of the window at the now empty waterway.

'It is of course promotion, and success — we should be glad. But the initial expense of the serjeants' feast is enormous, and at least sixty gold rings will have to be presented. And it will mean a change in our life style, with less opportunity to escape from London. Let us hope that the accommodation at Serjeants' Inn will be an improvement on our dusty chambers at Chichester!'

'We will go together where you must,' Margaret assured him, taking one of his hands where it rested on her shoulder and covering it with kisses.

John Fursdon did take to heart what his wife had said about the need for Christian forgiveness. It never left his mind as he walked the moor checking his sheep, or herding the huge flock down to the farm at shearing time, and in the autumn when he spent the shortening days walking behind the ox and plough in the fallow field, preparing it for the next year's corn crop. At last, in the spring, when all work stopped for the May Day celebrations in the village, he saddled his cob and rode over to Calyngton to seek his sister's opinion.

He found Mary, peeked and thin, and aged far beyond her thirty years, dozing in a high-backed chair in her solar. He stood, silent and in a state of shock, hardly recognising her for the lively and beautiful little sister whose boundless energy had seemed inexhaustible. How she had danced down the steps to welcome him on his first visit here thirteen years ago!

He caught his breath in a sob. Mary opened her eyes listlessly; but at the sight of her brother her tired grey face warmed into a smile and she stretched out her arms to him.

'Brother John! Welcome to Chykets!'

Her voice was thin and weak. John knelt before her and pressed her two hands to his lips while tears coursed unheeded down his face.

'Little Meg! Dear little Meg! What ails you?'

He fought back his tears and wiped his eyes with the loose end of his sleeve.

'Tell me, was it the fever?'

'No, dear John, only weariness. I exhaust myself so quickly that I like to sit here and rest, with the warm spring sunshine on my face. It lulls me to sleep, and when I awake I can look over the orchard and the fields to the moor above Fursdon. Sometimes I pretend I can see you and Willie up there with the sheep. How fares Willie, John? It is so long since I saw you.'

John drew up a stool and sat beside her, full of remorse for his neglect of her. Quietly he gave her a full account of life at Fursdon, of how efficiently Betsy ran the house — 'We live in such comfort that Willie has no desire to marry and set up his own home!' — and how the marketing of his pure-bred flock still prospered sufficiently to keep them all in comfort, if not in riches.

'I miss Betsy,' said Mary, so quietly that John could hardly catch her words. 'I am happy to know she does well for Fursdon, but she should be mother to a large family. You still have no children?'

She had turned to face John; he averted his head and replied, woodenly, 'No, no children.' The words reminded him of the reason for his visit, and he hurried on to tell Mary of Betsy's wish that he should make his peace with Nicholas Ayssheton.

Mary nodded. 'Yes, indeed,' she murmured, 'Betsy always speaks good sense. Life is too short, dear brother, to allow past wrongs to sour the present.'

John could not speak for the lump in his throat and the tears again welling in his eyes at the poignancy of her last comment. When at last he felt able to control his voice, he deliberately changed the subject and asked, 'Where are all the children, Meg? The house is strangely silent.'

'Gone to the maypole dancing,' replied Mary. 'Nan is with the little ones.'

'And Richard too?' asked John.

'No,' she replied, her thin voice sounding even more tired and dispirited; 'He is away in Devon, talking wool with his merchants. He has taken Johnnie with him — to teach him the trade, so he says.'

There was a heavy pause, then she continued, 'My Richard does not take kindly to sickness of any kind. My weariness bothers him, so he spends much time travelling.' She sighed. 'I am very much alone, John.'

She closed her eyes. They sat silently for a while, brother and sister hand in hand, until John fancied she had fallen asleep and rose to leave. Immediately her grip on his hand tightened and she opened her eyes.

'Must you go so soon?'

'Yes, sweet sister, if I am to go to Theupath and see Nicholas Ayssheton and still reach home before dusk.'

'But, John, they are not there, they left for London a moon since. Nicholas has been appointed serjeant and they are gone to prepare for the installation and the great feast.'

'So — then I too must go to London.' He spoke with such unusual firmness that Mary's eyes widened in surprise.

'Every year,' he continued, 'I have sent my mortgage payment — the white rose — remember, little Meg? — to Theupath. Come the feast of the Nativity of St John this year, I will deliver it myself to Nicholas in London. Betsy was right. You are right, Meg; life is too short to allow past wrongs to mar the present.'

7

The dry heat of midsummer shimmered in the narrow confines of Chancellor's Lane; even in the small patch of shade under the overhang of the upper storeys the atmosphere was more that of a bakehouse than of the open air. A blind beggar sat slumped against the gateway of Serjeants' Inn, his little acolyte — a ragged barefoot girl not more than six years old — sitting cross-legged beside him, nursing the wooden begging bowl as if it was a poppet; she made no attempt to look for custom from passersby, for the street was deserted except for the occasional servant hurrying by. The faintest draught of air now and then drifted through the archway on to the blind man's cheek, and he turned his sightless eyes towards the courtyard and garden which he could only imagine.

There was a sound of voices — the chatter of children and some women scolding — and the little girl stopped nursing the begging bowl and jumped to her feet to peer into the inn for possible patrons. But all she saw was an elegant lady walking away among the trees of the garden, her pale cream gown and the fine veil anchored to her tall headdress both rippling behind her. She slumped down disappointed beside her master, as Margaret Ayssheton joined her children in the garden of Serjeants' Inn.

Margaret sat down on a bench under a shady mulberry tree and closed her eyes, enjoying the scented air of the garden after the confines of their airless chambers. She could hear Edward and Joanne playing *tag*, and little Roger calling, 'Wait for me!' as he toddled after them, and she knew that at the far end of the garden under the oak trees the nursemaid was rocking the new baby, while nine-year-old Susannah clung to her arm, begging to nurse the youngest of the family. The hot sun filtering through the mulberry leaves kissed her eyelids much as Nicholas had done that morning before leaving for the feast with the other new serjeants. Margaret smiled to herself as she thought of the effect of his new attire, the white silk coif fitting so closely over his thick greying hair that she could hardly recognise him; it had changed him, as if by magic, into a venerable older man, the lines on his temples and down his cheeks accentuated by the lack of visible hair. She had gazed at him in solemn awe as at a stranger — until his face lit with the boyish grin that she knew and loved, and they embraced with as much ardour as ever.

Now, as a distant blare of trumpets reminded her, the feast provided by the new serjeants was over, and the whole company was processing in solemn state to St Thomas of Acons in the Chepe.

She opened her eyes momentarily as she felt a child nestle against her on the bench. It was Susannah. Margaret put her arm round the little girl's shoulders and kissed her on the top of her head, where the sleek auburn hair was hidden under her white cap.

In the warmth and peace of the garden she must have dozed, for she was startled to hear a man's voice close by and opened her eyes to see the doorkeeper standing before her.

'If it please you, my lady — a gentleman here desires speech with you.'

Margaret sat upright and looked to see who her visitor might be. Her heart thumped suddenly against her ribs and she felt her cheeks redden as she recognised John Fursdon. It was small consolation that he too appeared embarrassed, but the head which he bowed over her hand was unromantically grey and thinly covered, and she had time to remind herself that this was an old love, long since discarded for a deeper one, so that when John stood up again she was once more calm and self-possessed.

John hesitated, his hand trembling slightly as he relinquished hers. Then a curious sensation of relief came over him as he realised how the years had changed her; he had grieved for ten years over a dream of youth, but here was just a matron, like any other, with faded hair and wrinkled chin, a mother of five children.

'Mistress Margaret, I am pleased to find you in good health. I come to pay my annual due to your—' here he hesitated again, confused by the painful memory of that summer — 'to Master Nicholas, your husband. I come also to assure him that I wish once more to be counted among his friends.'

'John, you are the kind, good man you always were!' Margaret's voice rang with warmth and compassion, and John's heart did a little skip for old times' sake. Then he noticed, for the first time, the little girl curled up on the bench, and his heart did another skip — for here in miniature, was the dream of his youth repeated.

Margaret turned to Susannah. 'Sweet child, slip down and make way for Master Fursdon to sit awhile and talk with me.'

The child uncurled herself and slid to the ground, then dropped a pretty little curtsey before running off to play with the other children. John watched her go, a look of dreamy fascination on his face.

'How she resembles her mother!' he said, in a strange soft voice which Margaret had not heard since the early days of their romance. The memory made her look sharply at him, but he smiled at her somewhat ruefully and sat down on the bench.

'Our days of young romance are over, are they not? Now we can have true friendship, without hurt or hindrance.'

Half regretting it, Margaret knew that he was right; the past was dead, and after that moment of confrontation, neither of them felt any depth of emotion towards the other.

Peacefully, like old friends, they exchanged family news to fill in the missing years, and Margaret outlined for John the great day now going forward for the new serjeants-at-law.

'They have been feasting at Ely House since eleven of the forenoon. All London Town is there, and Westminster too, dining on beefs and muttons, porks and veals, capon, pigeons, swans and larks! There are six new serjeants — Walter Moyle and John Prisot among them — to share the expense of giving this feast on their promotion, and each of them also presented gold fidelity rings to the Duke of York, the Earl of Exeter, the lord chancellor, the mayor and aldermen, the bishop, and all the justices, serjeants and other dignitaries of the court of Common Pleas. I assure you, John, we are near to penury because of the cost of this legal promotion!'

'You complain,' remarked John, 'but you are very proud of Nicholas, and rightly so.'

'Indeed, yes. This was an honour he did not seek, but I am happy that he has it. I was present in the hall, here in the Serjeants' Inn, yesterday, when the lord chief justice put the white coif on his head, tied it under his chin, and laid the scarlet hood on his shoulder. I felt like to burst with pride!'

She laughed apologetically, but it was a happy confident laugh, and John smiled at her happiness, feeling light-hearted himself in his release from the bitterness of the past.

He drew a small package very carefully from a pouch hanging on his belt.

'Here is this year's white rose for payment this day.'

He unwrapped a fold of soft leather and lifted a clump of moss, revealing three white rose-buds nestling in the sphagnum below.

'They have borne the journey well,' said Margaret — 'only one has bruised petals. Take them to the fountain yonder and refresh them.'

John rose to do as he was bid. As he walked over to the fountain he called back over his shoulder, 'They may not survive till the morrow. That is one reason why I should speak with Nicholas this day. Where might I find him now?'

Margaret waited until John had returned with his dampened offering and sat down again beside her.

'Walk into town,' she said, 'and up the hill to Paul's. There the crowds will tell you if the procession has passed. They offer at St Thomas of Acons, then again at the shrine of St Erkenwald at the north door of Paul's. If they are all departed inside the church you must seek him there at the parvis. You may have trouble finding him, for the serjeants are dressed alike in black and murry gowns and their heads covered in the white coif.' She laughed, 'This day I did not know my Nicholas in his white coif, until he smiled at me!'

The nursemaid approached with the children. 'May we go in now, my lady?' she asked. The children stood in a row before their mother, Susannah smiling mischievously at John while

Edward, Joanne and Roger studied him solemnly with the disconcerting stare of small children. Taking the baby from the nursemaid, Margaret showed him to John, a tiny bundle of lawn surrounding a sleeping pink face.

'This one is so young we have yet to name him,' said Margaret. 'Now methinks I would give him the name of John, so that we shall remember always this day, when you came to be our friend again.'

John bowed his acknowledgement of the compliment. But as he took his leave, it was the eldest child, Susannah, to whom he paid most attention.

The noisy bustle outside London's great steepled church on the hill was in sharp contrast to the deserted inns of court. John squeezed his way through the jostling crowd until he could see the churchyard and the entrance beyond it.

Someone near him shouted: 'Here they come!' A roll of drums and a fanfare of trumpets confirmed the approach of the procession, and all heads turned to look down the Chepe. A great cheer went up as the lord mayor rode by, resplendent in red and ermine and surrounded by his retinue. The liveried band of drummers and trumpeters followed, then at a discreet distance a long rustling ribbon of silk-gowned lawmen, their white coifs bobbing up the street like a stream of white tennis balls.

The crowd watched them pass in respectful silence, and John searched in vain for the familiar face of his old friend. Disappointed, he waited as the crowd dispersed, and then made his way to the church and pushed his way through the crowd in the entrance.

For a moment he thought he had strayed into a market hall, for the groups of laughing, chattering merchants reminded him of market days at Liskerret. Then he realised that they were not buying and selling goods, but gathered round lawyers stationed by the base of the pillars which supported the roof of the church.

Again he had to squeeze through the crowds, and he worked his way from group to group, searching for the new serjeant-at-law, Nicholas Ayssheton, newly appointed to his allotted place at the parvis.

Margaret was right, he realised, the white coif concealing all of a man's head but his face, gave him a sort of disguise, for without its surrounding hair and the shape of the ears the picture was half gone. None of the faces he studied anxiously seemed at all familiar, and he was about to give up in despair when a serjeant near the west door, whom he had just passed, called after him, over the heads of the crowd surrounding his post: 'John Fursdon! A fellow Cornishman! Come, may I be of service to you?'

The crowd turned to see whom the new serjeant was addressing in such friendly terms and made way for John to come through to the front. He knew the voice, but the lined and solemn face was, he thought, that of a stranger. His confidence deserted him, and he could not remember a word of the message of reconciliation which he had rehearsed on the way from Cornwall. Desperately he thrust his hand into his pouch and drew out a damp white rose bud, half covered in moss.

'This is for you.'

Nicholas took the rose, bowed his thanks, and laid it aside. Then he stepped down from the small tub which was his stand, laid both hands on John's shoulders and looking him squarely in the face said:

'Welcome, my friend.'

As he spoke his serious face melted into the boyish grin of the Nicholas John remembered, and in the twinkling brown eyes John saw understanding and friendship. He smiled back and in a voice quivering with emotion replied:

'I bring you also my friendship.'

8

It wanted but a few days to Susannah's sixteenth birthday when
the Ayssheton family slipped quietly away from London in the
wake of the justices' procession bound for Dartmouth. Susannah
and Edward peeped out through the hole in the canvas wall of
their covered wagon as they rattled along the cobbles of the
Flete, but no one was paying any attention to the baggage train;
up ahead they could hear the crowd cheering as the richly robed
judges and their liveried retainers rode by. Susannah sat back in
the musty darkness and whispered excitedly to her twelve-year-
old sister Joanne, 'Soon we will be in Cornwall, Joany.' But it was
to take longer than she imagined.

The procession had passed Maidenhead before Nicholas felt
safe, and began to relax. In the increasing political unrest in the
capital, which had even invaded the sanctuary of the Serjeants'
Inn, he knew that when he rode the circuit of the southern
assizes his wife and family were regarded by the queen's men as
hostages to his good behaviour. A loyal liege of his king, Nicholas
Ayssheton was no supporter of his monarch's French queen and
her party, and he had thankfully seized on this opportunity to
take his household safely away into the remoteness of the west
country. It was a commission of enquiry, on which he had been
appointed to serve with the lord chief justice, Sir John Fortescue; as they rode on together across the Berkshire downs with
their army of retainers and the long train of carriages and
wagons he blessed his own foresight which had reckoned that
the presence of the lord chief justice would protect him from
attack and arrest.

They had passed the border into Devon before Sir John
broached the subject of the commission.

'This is not an isolated case of family feuding breaking into
open warfare,' he said. 'It is symptomatic of the state of the
country — a general unease, a sense of insecurity causing

persons with a grievance to take the law into their own hands. Walter Reynolds was attacked and imprisoned much as happened to John Beauchamp at Falmouth two years ago. In both cases the attackers claim they had a grievance, money being owed or land stolen, or a person illegally imprisoned and held to ransom. No matter that legal redress could have been sought at Westminster. Their excuse is time and distance and − which grieves me − the uncertainty of a fair hearing in the capital.

'Now we are taking the law to them. But the scent is cold. Master Reynolds' attackers will need a determined ferreting out. A fair judgement will be difficult, and I fear will do little to reassure the populace that the law can protect them.'

'And assuredly more complaints of assault and battery will be awaiting our attention when we return to Westminster,' added Nicholas.

Sir John shot a quizzical glance at his junior judge.

'But I fancy you will not be there?' he asked quietly.

'Aye, my lord, you are right,' replied Nicholas. 'The children thrive in the rich air of Cornwall, and I have a mind to build myself a new house. I acquired a small estate recently which lies close to the river Lynher, not far from the ancient fortress hill of Cadsonbury where I often played as a boy. Just riverside meadows and a stretch of woodland; it once belonged to my old friend John Berkamstede who helped me with the new church, but lacks a house.'

Sir John reined in his horse as they came to the crest of the hill and saw the city of Exeter in the valley before them. The great towers of the cathedral shone warmly red in the afternoon sun over the huddled rooftops; behind them the wooded hills on the far side of the valley warned the traveller of the wildness of Dartmoor awaiting them. To the two judges, however, this was home territory, a country that they both loved and where they felt secure.

Sir John sniffed the air in deep satisfaction, then said as he scanned the view before him, 'The Trinity term is over; you have until Michaelmas to build your house. I may need to call on you for further commissions during the summer, but so far as is possible I will leave you in peace in your Cornish seclusion.'

'I am indeed indebted to your friendship and understanding, my lord, and I thank you humbly,' replied Nicholas.

*

The commission was over and the lord chief justice had left Dartmouth with his retinue on his way back to London when a great storm swept the area.

That rare event, a summer storm of winter dimensions, it was remembered and talked of for years to come by those who experienced the chaos and damage it caused. Hurricane force winds swept without warning up the southern valleys and over the hills, flattening acres of woodland as corn before the reaper's scythe, scattering haystacks and ripping the thatch from cottage roofs. A deluge of rain turned all roads into muddy torrents and flooded whole villages, while the combination of wind and tide wrecked dozens of fishing boats in their own harbours.

The storm was at its height when Nicholas and Gwyllym stood watching helplessly from a sheltered spot high above the Dart near the river's mouth, as four carvells laden with fish capsized in the maelstrom of flooding river and storm-driven incoming tide. There was no way to reach and help the drowning fishermen, and after a moment's silent prayer they turned away and walked their horses slowly back to the hostelry, heads down against the rain and swirling wind which whipped around every corner, even in the lee of the combe.

'We must rest here a while longer until the storm abates,' Nicholas told his family. 'Beyond the shelter of this combe the wind is vile and the roads are impassable. It would be foolhardy to attempt the journey across the moor in these conditions.'

Margaret sighed; she was tired and uncomfortable in her latest pregnancy. The smoke-filled room with its shutters closed against the streaming rain made her think of purgatory, and she fingered the rosary at her belt. The smaller children broke into tears, finding this elusive Cornwall as far away as ever, so Susannah took four-year-old Stephen on her knee, and with the others clustered round her began to weave for them romantic stories of remembered Theupath.

Nicholas sat down on the bench beside Margaret and took her hand.

'At least we are all alive, thank the good Lord,' he said, and told her about the drowning fishermen.

While at Dartmouth the Aysshetons remained safely in shelter, across the moor and the Tamar at Calyngton, tragedy struck.

Unaware that such a storm was brewing, Betsy Fursdon had walked over from St Cleer to visit her sister-in-law Mary Chyket. She was delighted to find her old friend looking much more cheerful, although noticeably frail, and she spent two whole days with her before deciding reluctantly that she must return to Fursdon.

It was then that Mary pleaded, 'Take me with you, please, dear Betsy, I do so long to see Fursdon again.'

'But, sweet soul,' protested Betsy, ''tis a long walk! I took all of a day to cover the distance. You would get no further than the town gates on those delicate legs!'

Mary flushed, and with her thin veined hands drew her skirts more closely to conceal the sticks of her once shapely legs.

'We could take the cart,' she suggested. Betsy looked doubtful, but did not answer. Mary brightened and pushed herself out of her chair with determination.

'I will instruct Diggory to harness the mule to the light cart — you can drive that, can you not, Betsy? Please, dearest Betsy!'

'I can drive it,' Betsy agreed reluctantly. She did not relish the responsibility of taking her sick friend on such a rough journey, and instinctively she feared complications. But at the sight of Mary's happy eagerness her doubts melted away and she agreed to the venture, insisting only that they take with them a plentiful supply of clothes and blankets, and a chair for the invalid's better comfort.

Diggory lashed Mary's high-backed chair to the centre of the high wheeled cart, and with Betsy's help settled his mistress in it. Then he handed Betsy a long handled corded whip, and bade her use it liberally on the mule — 'a stupid, ill-tempered beast.' Betsy was well used to handling mules and oxen; she climbed on to the box, gathered the reins, and with a flourish of the whip over the mule's long ears urged him forward out of the yard.

So intent had they all been building this chariot that no heed had been paid to the increasing wind and the thickening storm clouds. As they left the town for the open common the cart caught the full force of the gale and began to yaw perilously on its high wheels. Betsy made for the trees at the crest of the river valley and halted the cart in the lee of a hedgebank, topped by hawthorn and alder, which bounded the wood.

''Tis not safe, we must go back,' she called to Mary above the howl of the wind in the trees. To her amazement, when she turned round to look at her, Mary's face peeping from her shawl and blankets was a picture of ecstatic exhilaration, and the colour in her cheeks almost as pink and rosy as it had been in her youth.

''Tis wonderful, wonderful!' she called back, her voice singing its excitement. 'I had forgotten how real the world is!'

Betsy made to turn the mule and return home, but Mary stopped her.

'Stay,' she begged, 'Let us watch and feel the storm! 'Tis beautiful, so alive, so real!'

Poor soul, thought Betsy, all those years captive in her room have turned her brain, best to humour her; so she sat dutifully still, hunched on the driving box and keeping a tight rein on the mule, which merely twitched its long ears at the feel of the wind but made no attempt to move.

It began to rain, first as a heavy patter on the summer leaves, but almost immediately as sheets of soaking wet. Betsy turned to Mary. 'We must return to Chykets, dear Mary, now — before the storm drenches us. It could be the death of you; John would never forgive me if I let you fall ill again.' She did not mention Richard, for to all the family his virtual abandonment of his ailing wife was scandalous.

She flicked the mule's ears with her whip and attempted to turn it back towards the town. Its only response was to shake its head vigorously then hang it as low as the reins would permit; its hooves remained firmly planted where it stood under the shelter of the hedge bank. Betsy stepped down off the box to pull the mule by its bridle out on to the road. Several blankets slid down on to her feet and she looked up in surprise; Mary had risen to her feet and was standing with arms outstretched as a heathen priestess invoking the gods, the rain streaming down her upturned face doing nothing to mar its expression of sublime ecstasy.

'Sit down!' Betsy called urgently, her voice almost drowned in the howl of the storm, the shattering rain and the crashing of flailing boughs and branches. She stooped to pick up two of the blankets; perhaps if she could wrap Mary up in them, wet as they were, she could get her safely home to Chykets before the fever took them both.

To Betsy's relief, Mary sat down, silently and sedately. The look of ecstasy had gone, in its place was a distant, vacant expression, as if she had been emptied of all joys and all hopes and passed the gate of final experience. That she was desperately ill in both body and mind was all too evident to Betsy as she stood there by the cart, two sodden blankets clutched in her arms.

There was a sudden flash of lightning, and a deafening clap of thunder immediately overhead. The mule reared up in terror, then bolted away down the hill, with the cart swaying and bumping madly behind it.

For a moment Betsy stood transfixed, the leap of her heart almost choking her. Dear God — Mary would be killed for sure! Pulling herself together mentally and picking up her skirts for speed, she ran after the cart as fast as she could go. Twice she stumbled, where rocks protruded from the muddy, rutted track, but she picked herself up and plunged on. Desperately she sought to catch up with the cart before it reached a sharp bend where a solid stone hedge bounded the track, and where she knew an upset would almost certainly be fatal.

Gasping and panting, her skirt torn by brambles and her eyes blinded by rain and splashing mud, her third stumble was over a tree root which caught her toe and threw her face down in the thorny undergrowth. Her weary body would have remained there, defeated, but she forced herself up again, tearing her petticoats and stockings and leaving both her pattens and her cap where they had fallen.

The cart had disappeared. Betsy ran on desperately. To her relief, when she rounded the corner there was no battered body against the stone hedge, no overturned cart and no mule. Only a muddy blanket at the foot of the hedge gave proof that the cart had passed that way.

Betsy slithered and jumped down the steep hill which gave on to the river bank by the ford. She emerged from the trees and there right before her eyes, stood the cart, still upright, and still carrying its passenger. Betsy gasped with relief and cried out, 'Mary!', but her voice produced no sound beyond a feeble squeak.

The cart was standing in the river, just downstream from the ford, the flood waters lapping half-way up its wheels and the mule standing motionless in the shafts as the water cooled its limbs and eddied against its heaving flanks. The chair had slipped sideways but was still upright. On it sat Mary, a queen on her throne, still and expressionless as a statue of stone.

Betsy ran to the river bank and waded in, the strong current tugging at her tattered skirts and causing her legs to sway uncertainly as she sought a balanced footing for her stockinged feet on the rocky bed of the stream. Reaching the downstream side of the cart she clung to the edge and called urgently to Mary.

'Mary, climb down to me, quickly! Sweet Mary! Mary, my love, can you hear me?'

There was no response. Betsy climbed on to the cart wheel and reached out to grasp her friend; as she did so the wheel sank under her weight and the cart heeled over towards her, tipping the chair and its occupant crashing over her head.

As Mary tumbled head-first past her, Betsy managed to catch hold of her skirts; she hung on desperately until the tug of the current pulled her feet from under her and the skirt slipped from her grasp as she struggled to regain her foothold.

Overcome with exhaustion, she could no longer make the smallest effort even to save herself, and her weary arms floated helplessly as both women bobbed a hapless *pas de deux* in the swirling water, their full skirts ballooning round them. Then the flood burst round the obstructing cart, the shafts snapped, and Betsy had a fleeting impression of the mule's hooves thrashing towards her as the current swept the remnants of her skirts over her face and floated her away downstream in suffocating oblivion.

9

They said in Calyngton that Richard Chyket's hair turned white overnight when the news of his wife's death reached him at Bydeford. As he was seldom seen at home it might have been happening gradually, but the sight of his anguished face under the thick mane of pure white hair when he entered Calyngton church for the requiem mass brought murmurs of genuine sympathy and even tears from the crowd gathered in the church. Flanked by his sons John and Richard – both towering above their stocky little father – he looked old and shrunken, with none of the old defiance and challenge which had once marked him out as a man of enterprise. Hands reached out to press his one arm in sympathy as the three men followed the curate into the chancel. Betsy's body had been given a Christian burial at St Cleer, but Mary had floated out to sea to meet her Maker and was never found.

A latecomer entered the church. Heads turned, and an audible gasp rippled down the nave, bringing the curate hurrying back to the chancel steps.

Resplendent in ermine-trimmed scarlet travelling robes, his round white coifed head topped by a black tricorne hat, Justice Ayssheton swept as a creature from another planet through the sea of drab homespun and leather. Behind him marched six halberdiers in black and gold livery emblazoned with a golden ash tree sprouting from a cask. The judge was ushered into the chancel by the flustered curate, while his retinue took up their station at the foot of the steps facing the crowd. The effect of their scowling faces and gleaming halberds was to ensure a mesmerised silence among the usually talkative crowd, so that not even a whisper or a rustle disturbed those following the mass on the other side of the richly carved rood screen.

When the mourners emerged, a noticeable change had taken place. It was not only that the two young men were now in second place behind their father while the judge in all his stately magnificence walked beside him, but that Richard himself seemed to have recovered some of his old spirit and determination. He was no longer bowed and shrunken, but stood erect at the top of the steps and bowed briefly to the assembled company.

The judge stood motionless beside him, an expressionless statue in all but his lively eyes, which scanned the crowd with merciless penetration.

To Diggory Allin they seemed full of condemnation, and he hung his head in shame as he thought again of the carelessness with which he had sent those two women to their death. Behind him Warne Pengelly straightened his aching back and met the judge's gaze with pride, sensing there a recognition of his work on the creation of the splendid church around them.

'I give you thanks, my friends.' Richard's voice, strong and clear, broke the silence. He bowed again, then led the little funeral party out of the church.

Back at the house which he had built for Mary, Richard's new-found self-assurance deserted him. As if by habit he and Nicholas had climbed the stairs to the solar, and it was a shock to find the room just as Mary must have left it the day she went off in the cart with Betsy. Richard picked up a light woollen shawl which was lying in a heap where the high-backed chair used to stand facing the big window. He sat down wearily on a stool and laying the shawl across his knees smoothed it tenderly with his fingers.

'This was her favourite shawl,' he said, a sob catching at his throat. 'So soft and light, and yet so warm, just like Mary herself. And I killed her — just as surely as if I had come home and strangled her with it.'

His voice trailed off into silence. Nicholas was standing at the window, gazing out over the rooftops to the moors edged in black against a vivid russet sky. His scarlet houppeland and tricorne hat had been left below with Gwyllym; his black doublet and hose and long pointed leather shoes were those of a man of fashion and suited his long lean figure superbly; only the white coif, fastened under his chin and completely covering his head of curly hair, marked him out still as a person of special status.

Presently he asked, without turning from the window, 'Why are you so seldom at home?'

'Because I loved her so!' cried Richard, almost with relief. Nicholas spun round in surprise.

'She was not strong enough to bear more children,' continued Richard, 'and I thought to keep her in better health by staying out of her bed. Loving her as I did, this was impossible unless we were far away from each other; and so I travelled, and worked, and stayed away for long periods in a vain effort to forget my need of her.' He laid the shawl very tenderly against his cheek. 'I killed her, just as surely by staying away from her as I would have done had I stayed at home and shared her bed as I longed to do. I killed her!'

'And Betsy too,' the man at the window added in an undertone as he turned back to look out of the window again at the moors, below which the Fursdon home now lay in the shadow of dusk. Poor John, he thought, we have both brought you such sadness, we two who claimed to be your friends. How can we ever recompense you for two wives lost?

The thought took his mind to Margaret, and he turned back to face Richard.

'You have good cause for your unhappiness, but you have work to do and a family to comfort and nurture. Mimi especially, who has cared for her mother so tenderly these past five years — she will need your love to smooth away the shock. Who else is at home?'

'Only little Peg. Mimi has no patience with her, poor soul. Peg sits out in the orchard all day, painting flowers and butterflies, even spiders, if you please!'

In spite of himself, Richard smiled as he thought of his two so different daughters. 'They should have been named *Martha* and Mary, not *Margaret* and Mary!'

'Then, if you please, my Margaret will be happy to have her namesake at Theupath for a while. There Peg can paint as much as she pleases, none will gainsay her.'

Richard nodded agreement without enthusiasm; he had already sunk back into his misery. 'You rest awhile at Theupath?' he asked.

Nicholas nodded, and went on to explain his plans for building a new house at Neweland. Too late he realised that

Neweland was close to the same river which had drowned Richard's wife; he stopped short, biting his lip in annoyance at himself.

There seemed nothing more to be said. Richard still sat with Mary's shawl clutched in his hands, his face crumpled in sorrow. Nicholas squeezed his shoulder in sympathy, and as he moved towards the door, said: 'You learned from my father how to build this house. I would value your advice and help with mine.'

There was no reply.

'Tell Peg that Edward will fetch her in the morning,' he continued, and left his friend alone with his grief.

The leaves were beginning to change colour when on a soft and sunny afternoon in late September, Margaret went down to see the new house nearing completion at Neweland. Nat Bullen was passing the time of day with Diggory outside the inn when the cart passed through the town, driven by fourteen-year-old Edward Ayssheton at a very sedate pace. Nat could not straighten himself for the rheumatism in his back, but he peered up at the disappearing cart through the tangled mat of his long greasy hair, then chuckled and poked Diggory with his stick.

'See there, she be well nigh her time again. She be holding to the seat as if any moment she be brought to bed! Who be that waving to us?'

'Ah, that be my little Mistress Peg,' Diggory replied, as he waved back to the passenger in the back of the cart; 'A lovely one she be, my Peg! As like as not she'll marry young Master Edward, my Margery says the Mistress Chyket always wanted it. There she be now, riding behind him, and with the little Ayssheton infant in her care.'

Edward was driving very carefully, and keeping a tight rein on the pony, avoiding every stone and rut which might jolt the cart and distress his mother. The calls from his four-year-old brother Stephen in the back of the cart to, 'go faster! go faster!' he was happy to ignore, but his young man's dignity was sorely tried when thirteen-year-old Peg joined in. He could hardly resist the urge to whip the pony to a mad gallop, just to show her what he could do; but a glance at his mother's tense and anxious face brought him back to the reality of the situation, and he stuck manfully to his task of conveying his mother, in her delicate health, safely to the new house site in the river valley. He realised too that the visit was not merely to see the house; the river must be visited again, and the ghosts of Mary Chyket and Betsy Fursdon laid, so that the family could take up residence in the riverside home with equanimity.

The lane ran steeply down under arching elm trees, emerging at the bottom on to the riverside plain, where the shelter of the trees gave way to hedgebanks smothered with brambles and a tangle of red berried honeysuckle. From the back of the cart little Stephen tried to pluck some of the tempting red berries; just in time Peg prevented him, and turned his attention instead to the luscious ripe blackberries which they could also reach, and which they could eat and enjoy. With much squealing and scuffling they succeeded in picking several handfuls as the cart moved very slowly along the narrow lane.

Not a breath of wind stirred between the tall hedgebanks. It was very hot, and Margaret began to feel faint, wishing she had stayed at home. All she wanted now was to get down from the hard, bouncing board on which she was perched, and ease the weight in her body to a soft resting place.

At last they reached the turning into Nicholas's newest property. Margaret sighed with relief as the cart moved in under an avenue of beeches. A carpet of beech husks crunched under the cart's wheels, and a soft breeze from the river ahead wafted in their faces and rustled the high leaves now turning to yellow and copper.

They came out into a meadow, bounded in a great arc by the broad river, now the merest trickle over stones and gravel banks in the shade of the trees on its opposite bank. To their right, set in a bay of beech trees, stood a long low building with a partly thatched roof. A man working on the thatch waved to them and announced their arrival to invisible companions, and in a moment Nicholas came striding across to meet them. There was now no sign of the judge in his appearance or his demeanour; he was a country workman, picking straws from his close-cropped curly iron-grey hair and shaking dust from his drab homespun shirt and breeches as he came. He grinned in boyish delight at the sight of his wife, and called out as he came:

'Welcome, my love, to your new home!'

Edward jumped down and with great care helped his mother

to alight, just in time to be tenderly gathered into her husband's arms and carried away to some sort of comfort in the house.

'Help me down!' called little Stephen standing poised on the tailgate with his arms outstretched. What a miniature of our father he is, thought Edward, as the dark haired bundle leapt into his arms, slithered down and made off across the meadow on his stubby little legs.

His thoughts were broken by a softly whispered 'Edward' and he turned to lift the rosy-cheeked Peg from the cart. As their hands touched, her wide-set grey eyes flashed him a shy smile even while her face remained solemn. Edward squeezed her hand and held it very tightly as they walked together towards the new house.

The sun was sinking behind the trees on the other side of the river when Margaret roused herself from the couch of grass and bracken which the men had made for her in a shady spot near the house. She could hear hammering still going on, and men's voices calling and swearing. She knew they would work on until the light entirely failed, but also realised that Edward must take her home in daylight while they could still pick their way smoothly on the road. Her lower abdomen felt as heavy as lead, and although the baby was lying quietly and not kicking her, she dreaded the return journey. But she had done what she had set out to do: she had seen the river and prayed for the souls of her lost friends, and she had seen the house, where she could imagine many happy years. But it was not *home* yet, and she must return to Theupath.

She stood up, staggering under her own weight. I grow too old for child bearing, she told herself — none of the others felt like this.

'Edward, are you there?' she called uncertainly.

She heard a soft feminine giggle from behind some bushes. Edward emerged picking pieces of grass and burrs from his shirt, and leading Peg by the hand. His fair hair was tousled and his face pink with embarrassment, Margaret frowned; nothing had been arranged yet about their alliance, there was still plenty of time.

'Where is Stephen?' she asked, her tired voice sounding more severe than she intended.

Edward looked at Peg, and Peg looked at Edward. The little boy had obviously been left out of their activities and forgotten. They hurried off together to look for him in the house.

Margaret sat down again on her bracken couch and waited. She heard Edward and Peg calling for Stephen in the beech wood behind the house. The evening shadows lengthened and the breeze from the river grew cool. Nicholas came from the house, wiping cow dung from his hands.

'We have just finished the plastering, my love,' he announced with pride, dropping down on the couch beside her. 'Within the month we will have the roof on, the floor laid and the windows ready for the glaziers. Then you will say where the dairy is to go and where we should have the brew house and the ice house.'

Margaret interrupted him. 'Dear heart, I know it will be a wonderful house and I shall love living here. But now it is imperative that I return to Theupath before dark, and Stephen has run off and cannot be found.'

'The varmint, he shall be chastised. Send him to me when he is found.'

It was the voice of the stern judge; Margaret in her weariness trembled for her small son, and the tears welled in her eyes as she watched Nicholas stroll off towards the river to wash himself clean of dung and dust.

Edward and Peg came back, having found no trace of Stephen. In the desperate hope that he might have started to walk home they ran off across the meadow towards the lane. As she watched their figures fading into the twilight, a cold clammy horror suddenly seized Margaret's mind; hurriedly she turned towards the river, only to see Nicholas standing a few paces away, tears streaming down his grimy face and the dripping body of his son in his arms.

'He was lying face down in the water, in the only pool in the river deep enough for him to lose his footing,' he croaked, laying the little boy on the couch beside his mother. Margaret took him in her arms, kissing him, smoothing his wet head against her cheek and calling his name.

'He is dead, my love,' said Nicholas quietly. 'Drowned. Come, there is nothing you can do.'

The reply was a piercing scream from his wife as she fell inert beside the dead body of her youngest child.

*

An hour later there were two more Aysshetons awaiting burial. Without fully recovering her senses Margaret had gone into labour and produced two baby girls – tiny, premature creatures, and both dead. Then she had drifted again into unconsciousness, her hand slipping nervelessly from her husband's as if she too were dead.

Hastily Nicholas wrapped her in the blankets for which Edward had dashed two miles in the dark to the neighbouring farm, and together they lifted her gently into the pony cart. Then, pausing only to murmur a soft '*Requiescant in pacem*' over his dead children, Nicholas made a shroud for them of his cloak and laid the bundle in the cart at Margaret's side. Wearily he clambered in himself and sat beside her, cushioning her head on his lap, as Edward and Peg in heavy silence climbed up in front and Edward grimly set the pony to a canter towards the lane.

None of them ever saw Neweland again.

10

A frosty autumn which merged imperceptibly into a damp and cheerless winter of mist and rain did nothing to aid Margaret's recovery, and it was early December before she felt strong enough to tread carefully down the stairs, with Susannah's help, and ensconce herself in a deep chair by the fire in the Theupath great hall.

She was dozing by the fire, on her second day's descent from the sick room, when Susannah rushed in in great agitation to report that there was mould creeping up the walls of the dairy.

'There, my child, don't fret yourself,' Margaret reassured her, 'it will dry up when the weather improves.'

'Oh, dear, this everlasting rain!' sighed Susannah, sinking to her knees before the fire and stretching out her hands to the glowing logs. Margaret caressed the rich red-gold tresses cascading down her daughter's back, and noted the dimpled chin and the classical nose which made her want to forget her own up-turned urchin's one. She is more beautiful than I ever was, she thought, with motherly pride. She deserves a handsome and loving husband – like mine, her father.

'Susie, it is time you were wed,' she said, speaking her thoughts aloud. 'We must seek a good match for you. Is that not so, husband?' she added, looking across the hall to where Nicholas stood motionless, apparently absorbed in a study of the soft grey rain shrouding the world outside.

He did not answer her, and Susannah hung her head as the colour in her cheeks mounted – whether from embarrassment or the heat of the fire would never be known.

Margaret studied her husband more closely, and noted with concern that he was absently twisting the serjeant's ring on his middle finger, his thoughts far away. It could only mean one thing; he was feeling the need to return once more to the world of lawsuits and commissions of enquiry, to the life of riding the circuit or sitting in judgement at the Court of Common Pleas.

Well, he had tended her devotedly for several months, and she must not begrudge him the wish to be out again in the world of affairs; but still, a lump formed in her throat at the thought that she was no longer fit enough to travel with him. With all her family around her she would still feel desperately lonely.

There was a clatter of hooves in the courtyard, and a glimpse of someone running across from the byre to meet the new arrival. Then footsteps, and the two women looked expectantly toward the door. Into the hall came two figures, shaking the wet from their clothes.

Edward's fair hair was plastered in wet streaks down his long thin face, and his leather boots squelched as he walked, making his companion seem only slightly moist in comparison. It was John Fursdon, now a regular caller at Theupath.

The tragedies of the summer had tended to bind the three families together in mutual sorrow. Strangely though, while Richard Chyket and the Aysshetons had been devastated by their loss, John had shown an unexpected resilience – as if his earlier misfortunes had inured him to further tragedies and bred in him a philosophical acceptance of all that unkind Fate could heap upon him. He loved to visit Theupath, where he was a great favourite with all the children and a welcome visitor for the invalid.

At the sight of him Susannah ran across the hall, made to hug him as a child would, but recollected herself and instead dropped him a bashful curtsey, then skipped out of the room to tell Joanne, Roger, John and William that 'Uncle Fursdon' was come. Edward was dispatched, protesting, to find dry clothes, and the two men joined Margaret at the hearthside.

As John kissed her hand and said gently, 'I am pleased to find you so much improved in health, Mistress Margaret,' Margaret's thoughts strayed once again to the romance of their youth and the wild adventure which had brought it to an end. What would her life have been like, had she married John? A quietly peaceful but dull life at Polcarowe, perhaps mercifully without the tragedies which had hit them all? Life might have been easier, she reflected. Then a glance across the wide fireplace at Nicholas brought the old familiar longing to be wrapped in his embrace, and she hastily lowered her eyes lest they give away such lustful thoughts, but smiled secretly to herself in satisfaction that a lifetime's passion had not yet deserted her.

The men were discussing matters of more public importance.

'I have a message for you from your rector,' said John. Nicholas's eyebrows shot up.

'What does Thomas Baron want with me? Has he been counting my absences from the church? Maybe he has forgotten that while Margaret has been ill the rector of St Dominica has attended here at my father's chapel to celebrate the mass on all stipulated occasions.'

'No, both he and I are only messengers from a higher source,' said John. 'He has been instructed by the lord bishop to advise you that the lord chief justice enquired privately for you when he passed through Exeter at Martinmas. Sir John intimated that if you do not return to your duties you will run a grave risk of imprisonment. Up to recently he was able to conceal the fact that one of his judges was *in absentia*, but then my Lord Beaufort demanded the list of dignitaries and has marked down those who do not appear regularly at Westminster. All such are immediately suspected of plotting with my Lord York,'

Nicholas put his hand up to the mantelshelf, the firelight

catching his serjeant's ring so that it glowed and twinkled. He thought for a moment, before speaking with slow deliberation.

'I will celebrate the Nativity of our Lord here, with my wife,' he said. 'But after the Feast of the Epiphany I will go to Exeter. If I find there instructions from the lord chief justice I can carry on my work before returning to London. I will be better protected if I go armed with a report for the council!'

'You know my Lord of York is returned from Ireland? They say troops are being gathered and he aims to seize control of the government.'

'My Lord of York is a fine man, he could give our monarch much valued advice were he allowed. I will serve the king faithfully always — as I have vowed on oath — but I like not these Beauforts, nor this French queen.'

Nicholas rubbed his ring finger against his cheek, and added softly, 'My allegiance is to the king and the law. I will take no part in machinations by Beauforts or Yorkists.'

'It would be safer not to write direct to the lord chief justice,' suggested John. 'Shall I send your reply by the same circuitous route?'

Nicholas laughed in mockery at such a conspiracy, but John's sober face stopped him.

'Take care, my friend,' warned John, 'this is no laughing matter. The situation is fraught with explosive dangers.'

Over the next two years Nicholas Ayssheton was seldom seen at Theupath. He did not suffer imprisonment, nor a fine; it was a period of increasing unrest throughout the country, and the serjeants-at-law were kept at full stretch in the council's struggle to maintain control. In normal times Justice Ayssheton would officiate at assizes in all the south coast counties from Kent to Cornwall, but now he was also ranging widely over the west country on commissions investigating disturbances and riots, acts of sabotage against the king's troops and against foreign ships, and even complaints of trading with the enemy. From Plymouth to Bristol, from Dartmouth to Fowy and Penzance, everywhere was increasing evidence that the poorer classes cared nothing for the rights of Lancaster or York or the English possession of Aquitaine and Normandy. No longer serfs, they would sell their service or their goods to the highest bidder, whether a French captain, a trader of the Hanseatic league, or a local 'gentilman' looking for strong-arm support in a private feud with his neighbour. Many of them were surprised and even offended when the law caught up with them in the form of the lord chief justice or one of his judges or serjeants.

Justices Ayssheton and Prisot were amongst the busiest, and when news filtered back to Calyngton of their activities a contented Margaret reflected that her husband was safely busy, away from the clutches of the queen's ministers. So it was a shattering blow when word came in the early summer that the justices had returned to Westminster to present their report to the king's council. For two weeks Margaret could neither sleep nor eat; she imagined her husband stripped of his authority and flung into the Flete prison, and her night-time dreams were a wild extension of her worries.

At last, on a sunny day in early June, Gwyllym rode in with a letter. Nicholas was not in prison; he and John Prisot had been commended for their work in the west country, and he was now so much in the royal favour that he had been appointed to the commission going to Wales to investigate the reports of a treasonable plot to capture the king and put the Duke of York on the throne.

Margaret relaxed; she cared nothing for the rebellious Welsh and did not fear for her husband's safety in Wales; Nicholas was free and in favour, that was all that mattered.

When John Fursdon paid his customary visit that same afternoon, he found Margaret seated before the open window, through which the scent of late gillieflowers drifted in from Susannah's flower garden under the south wall of the house. She gave him the good news, smiling apologetically and excusing herself.

'I have had bad dreams this fortnight past,' she explained.

'You had no real cause for concern,' said John. 'It was clear when Nicholas and Judge Prisot, with the help of Serjeant Moyle, dealt so efficiently with the discharged soldiers in Plymouth that the king's council would wish to make full use of his legal expertise. The only unhappy one in that case was Sir Thomas Hoo, faced with a judgement forcing him to pay the soldiers from his own private estate! Then there was the case of the ship's masters and crews who tried to escape from being detained as troop carriers; only judges of Nicholas's local knowledge could have dealt so firmly and yet so fairly with those disgruntled men. His judgements in all these local affairs have greatly enhanced his reputation as a fair-minded man of law.'

Margaret nodded, smiling with pleasure. Then her brow clouded and she commented thoughtfully, 'There are so many soldiers these days in Plymouth, and in Fowy too. So unlike the old peaceful times.'

'We are in the forefront of war these days,' said John. 'It is the west-country men who are now being pressed into the service of the king to fight his battles in Aquitaine and Normandy. However unwilling, they must fight well, or we shall soon face invasion of our coast by the Frenchmen.'

'War! always there is war! I wonder, when he judged those soldiers and those mariners, did my husband remember the senseless horrors he saw when he fought in France for the last king?'

'Fighting is in man's nature, Mistress Margaret,' said John quietly. Margaret opened her eyes wide at such words from a man so unaggressive by nature.

John guessed her thoughts and turned away to lean out of the window. After a moment's silence she heard him talking and laughing with Susannah, whom he had discovered working in her knot garden outside. Margaret closed her eyes and slipped into a peaceful doze.

Looking around at her children as they gathered for the *cena* that afternoon brought Margaret's mind back to the problem of marriage. Some family alliance for the two eldest was long overdue, she realised; they had been remiss in not arranging this while they were still in London and in touch with suitable families. When she had reminded Nicholas last autumn of their parental duty to find a match for both Edward and Susannah he had brushed off the urgency with the plea that the children's marriages might be needed in negotiations if his legal career stumbled in the feud between the houses of Lancaster and York.

She turned to John for advice, thinking as she did so how good it was to have this friend on whom she could lean. The family sat attentively round the table as their futures were discussed — all except six-year-old William, who continued to gnaw at his chicken bone as if his life depended on it. Roger and John dissolved into giggles and poked their sister Joanne painfully in the ribs; seated between them she had no defence and squealed in protest. At the head of the table, where he sat in his father's seat, Edward glowered angrily as he heard his mother suggesting suitable families to which they might be allied through the marriage of their eldest son. His face grew longer and the frown on his forehead deepened as the names of Radford, Manaton, Trevinour, Edgcumbe, Rous and Trelawny came tripping off her tongue.

John Fursdon listened quietly, but there was a certain tautness in his body and the jaw was set in his normally soft features.

'What know you of these families, John?' asked Margaret finally. 'From your position as an influential burgess of Liskerret you must know something of their circumstances, and whether they would welcome a judge's daughter into their family or be happy to give their daughter to a judge's family. I believe Master William Trevinour is a fine lad and as yet not spoken for; it is whispered that his family favour the Yorkists, so if Susie were betrothed to him we would need to find a bride of the other persuasion for Edward so that Justice Ayssheton's impartiality could not be impugned.'

There was a deadly silence. Edward at the far end of the table looked as if he would explode. Susannah, seated at Margaret's left and directly opposite to John Fursdon, had hung her head so that her fine long hair concealed her face as the boughs of a weeping willow tree hid its secrets, but a slight movement of her shoulders showed that she too, like the willow, was weeping.

When John spoke, it was with a great effort, as if his voice were choking him.

'I am but a simple Cornish farmer, Mistress Margaret,' he said. 'I recognise that you desire to ensure a safe future for all your children, and also that Nicholas expects some measure of security from the marriages contracted; but do you not think that the children themselves should be consulted in the matter — especially Susie and Edward, who are now quite old enough to have—' here he faltered, then hurried on: '—have established preferences of their own?'

At this Edward banged his fist on the table, and shouted: 'I wish to marry Peg Chyket, and you always told me I should!' He burst into tears and ran from the room.

'Would it not be advisable to await their father's return before taking any irretrievable step?' suggested John.

Margaret ignored him; turning to Susannah she asked, 'Susie, dear, would you like to be wedded to William Trevinour?'

Susannah shook her head, without looking up.

'Come now, dear child, it would be a fine match for you. They are people of consequence; you would have your own estate, and a fine new mansion — no damp dairies and muddy farmyards as at Theupath!'

As she gazed in puzzlement at her weeping daughter she became aware that John had risen from his seat. He walked round to stand behind Susannah, and put his hands gently on her shoulders. The girl's sobbing ceased and she raised her tear-stained face to acknowledge 'Uncle Fursdon's' support. They smiled understandingly at each other.

Margaret averted her eyes, overcome for the first time in her life by a sudden pang of jealousy.

11

It was a shock for Nicholas, when he arrived home later that summer, to find his normally contented household in a state of strained and unhappy confusion. He was not in the sunniest of moods himself, having been attacked in the Theupath lane by two boys armed with catapults and stones, one of the shots bruising him on the jaw. His fury at the indignity of this attack knew no bounds when his halberdiers dragged his assailants from their hiding place in a hedge and he recognised the two dirty unkempt lads as his own sons.

Gwyllym had ridden ahead to advise of the master's arrival, and when the cortège clattered into the yard Margaret and the other children were gathered at the house door to greet him. Nicholas pulled up his horse sharply, almost running his family down.

'Woman!' he demanded, in a voice of thunder not often heard outside the courts, 'what means this?'

He waved his whip towards the two ragged bundles hanging over the halberdiers' saddles. Margaret looked bewildered, but then recognised the dark curly heads of Roger and John and ran towards them, crying distractedly, 'Let them down! What have you done to them?'

Nicholas dismounted from his horse and went into the house without a word, while the two boys were released by the halberdiers and ran to their mother for comfort.

'Mother, it was a game . . . we meant no harm,' sobbed eight-year-old John, as Margaret ushered them into the hall, her arms still protectively around their shoulders.

Nicholas was standing by the fireplace, where, although it was high summer, a low fire burned. His travelling clothes were grey with dust and lay in a heap at his feet. As the family trooped into the room behind their mother he unfastened the coif, its whiteness sullied by sweat and dust, and dropped it on to the other garments as he shook out his thick greying hair and ran his fingers through it in a mixed gesture of relief and impatience.

Margaret and the children stood in silence, then Susannah, at the end of the row furthest from her mother, said, in a small timid voice, 'Welcome home, father.'

Nicholas turned at the sound of his favourite child's voice, just in time to catch a gesture of impatient annoyance from Margaret directed at her daughter. It was so out of character for his kind and loving Margaret to behave in this way towards her children that he was jolted out of his own indignation and looked more closely at his family.

There was no doubt about it, something was wrong. Margaret's thin pale face was piqued and petulant, while behind her stood Edward, stiffly erect, his lower jaw thrust out as if in defiance at the whole world. The two miscreants, Roger and John, hung their heads in anticipation of punishment; next to them little William shuffled his feet so that the pointed toes of his shoes almost tied themselves in a knot, and he gazed up at his father, round-eyed, like any baby tawny owl caught out by a sudden light. He was holding tightly to the hand of his sister Joanne — ah, here was one in his family who looked serene and unruffled, Nicholas noted with some relief, while feeling at the same time uneasy under her cool disinterested gaze. He moved on hurriedly to study Susannah, and with a sense of outrage realised that here was something very wrong indeed.

Normally neat and tidy, Susannah was carelessly dressed in a faded brown gown trimmed with badly torn lace; she wore no kerchief over her hair, which hung in a tight plait down her back. Next to the cool elegance of her younger sister she looked more like a gypsy maid, and he almost looked at her feet to see if she had bothered to put on her pattens.

But her face! Ah, there was surely sadness, what could have been happening while he was in Wales?

Mattie came into the hall with goblets and a flagon of wine. Nicholas poured out two, and beckoned to his wife to take her accustomed seat in the big chair by the fire. Margaret slid forward anxiously and sat down, only then realising that it was a clever tactical move by Nicholas to separate her from the boys whom she was seeking to protect. He drained his goblet and then pointed an accusing finger at Roger.

'You, boy, are a disgrace to the Aysshetons. Filthy, unruly, it is time you learned the manners and customs of a gentleman. You will go tomorrow to Master William Venour at Lyston Overhalle in the county of Essex. I have an interest in the estate, he will not deny me, he will take you as his valet until such time as he deems you are fit to go out into the world as a gentleman.'

Eleven-year-old Roger straightened up and looked at his father, astonishment and pleasure written all over his face; he had expected the birch and instead was being sent out into the world where there was adventure and real life!

Nicholas frowned at the smaller John, now anxiously peering up at him through a tangle of black unruly curls. It occurred to Nicholas that his family was strangely assorted, in that apart from the sandy-haired Edward all the boys took after their father while the two girls were both faithful copies of their mother in her dazzling youth. He glanced at the faded Margaret, querulously upright in her chair, and at the same time his mind flashed back to that other curly-haired son whom they had lost a year ago. He smiled reassuringly at his wife; John was her favourite son, he must not deprive her even more.

'You too are a disgrace,' he said to John, 'but we will not send

you two away together. You will go to Liskerret to learn your
Latin and the grammars. It will be time enough to send you
to service when you are one or two years older and have the
backing of logic and rhetoric and can speak in Latin as you
should.'

John was crestfallen, he would have preferred to continue his
catapult hunting; he cared not for education.

The children were dismissed and filed out of the hall in the
same silence as when they had entered, Edward stiffly bringing
up the rear and closing the door noisily behind him.

Nicholas went down on one knee beside Margaret. He took
her thin white hand in his, kissed it gently, and said, 'Now, dear
heart, tell me all.'

The flood gates were opened, and it was some minutes before
Margaret could speak coherently. At last she managed to say,
gulping back her sobs, ''Tis Susie, she wants to marry John
Fursdon.'

Nicholas reeled backwards as if he had been physically
struck, his jaw dropped and he stared disbelievingly at his wife.

'Wants to marry *John*?' Margaret nodded her head and
sobbed, 'And he loves her!'

Nicholas rose to his feet, swearing softly under his breath,
and gripped the high mantelshelf with both hands as he gazed
sightlessly into the small summer fire. After a few moments
Margaret ceased her crying and in a broken voice began to pour
out vituperative comments against the man who should have
been her husband. The vehemence of her accusations brought
Nicholas swinging round to stop her, with a stinging slap of his
hand across her face.

They gazed at each other for a moment in a state of shock,
then his face softened and he drew her up into his arms. They
stood together a long while before the fireplace as he smoothed
her faded hair, whispered endearments in her ear, and kissed
away the tears on her face. And when at last he spoke again
about the problem of the moment Margaret nodded her head
and nestled more securely in his arms.

'My sweet love,' murmured Nicholas, gazing over the top of
her head towards the great window standing open on to the
garden, 'you are my wife, and we have had a love together which
could not be surpassed. I cry mercy that I have neglected you

too long this time, so that you have consoled yourself with dreams of your old love.'

He tilted her face up towards him and said gently, 'You cannot keep John for yourself; we have done him harm enough. Have you given thought to why he would wish to marry your daughter?'

The look in her eyes told him that she had only now begun to realise the truth. He laughed.

'Susannah is Margaret, young and lovely again as she was when she captivated his heart. He could not have you, so he would have your daughter! And so he shall, by my troth; if Susannah wishes it we will join them together as man and wife — and may the devil take both royal houses and their political fighting which blurs a man's vision of the worth of true love!'

He paused, then in a complete change of mood said very softly, 'It is the real Margaret whom I love, with all my heart and for always,' and pressing her body close to his he kissed her long and passionately, as he had in the young days of their love.

The celebrations of the betrothal were short and simple, but before he left Theupath again at the end of the week Nicholas could see a happy transformation in the appearance of Susannah. Like a young plant refreshed by rain after a long drought she burgeoned into curves and colours and the graceful beauty of a happy, loving woman.

'We did you much harm in years gone by,' said Nicholas to John, 'but now in giving you our beloved daughter — who might have been your own child, had the good Lord ordained it — we hope to make amends for the wrongs of the past; and we look to you to care for her as a father as well as a husband.'

They clasped hands in silence, for John was choking on tears of happiness and could not speak.

Beside them Edward, who had been called in to witness the terms of the marriage contract, stood in glowering disapproval of the satisfaction displayed by his elders. He had been told by his father that he must be patient for a year or two in case a political alliance became necessary. This infuriated him, for he was impatient to lead his own life — in which Peg Chyket would play a leading part. To mollify him Nicholas had undertaken to discuss the affair with Peg's father at his next visit; nothing

could be done this time for Richard was away from home, the
rumour being that he had gone to Chudleigh to seek from the
bishop an indulgence for the people of Calyngton for the building of a bridge across the river Lynher at the spot where his wife
had drowned.

'Take heart, my son, you may yet have your way too,' said
Nicholas, slapping Edward so hard on the shoulder that he
winced. 'If William Trevinour's parents consent to an alliance
of their son with our beautiful Joanne — though I would that she
was some years older before we lost her — and Roger is accept-
able to a family supporting my Lord Somerset, then the way will
be clear for another marriage of true hearts!'

'Linking our three families most admirably,' added John
Fursdon.

12

There was no happier man in Cornwall than Richard Chyket as
he set his men to work building the new bridge. They had found
good granite in the hill near to the river bank and the sound of
chisel on stone rang cheerfully in the warm spring air. No long
haul here, from quarry to site, thought Richard, each stone
could be barrowed or hauled as it was cut and shaped. He
smiled in satisfaction as he remembered the problems of carting
the stone down to Calyngton for the building of the church.

It had been a dry spring too, after a mild winter, and the
water level in the river was quite low, so there should be no
problems making firm foundations for the bridge piers.

Someone hailed him from the other side of the river, and he
turned to see his brother-in-law John Fursdon splashing across
on his horse.

'Good morrow, John. Is the wedding day settled now?' he
asked, noting that John must be returning home from Theupath.

John shook his head.

'Nicholas is in Southamptonshire, and he writes that there is again some uprising in Kent — not just a mad captain this time, like Jack Cade, but the Duke of York himself, who is seeking to have the Duke of Somerset dismissed from the king's council. Nicholas will stay within reach of London while this crisis continues; he admires my Lord York, perhaps he hopes that the government will pass into his control. So, meanwhile,' John smiled ruefully as he continued, 'Susannah and I await patiently the return of her father for our nuptials.'

Richard looked away; he could not meet his friend's gaze for he had been forcibly reminded of that other long and patient wait of John's, and he could only pray for him that this time there would be a happier outcome.

With great pride he showed John the plans for the bridge, and took him along to the quarry where the first foundation stones were being laid on sledges harnessed to a pair of oxen.

'You may cross the river dry-shod come the Nativity of the Blessed Mary,' he called after John as the latter set off up the steep hill towards Liskerret.

'Make sure that Somerset's men, or Yorkists, for that matter, do not set gunpowder to it before I return!' was the laughing yet apprehensive reply from the retreating horseman.

It was high summer before Justice Ayssheton completed the many commissions and assizes which marked a year of increasing unrest. The Duke of York's foray into Kent had come to nothing; the Duke of Somerset was still in government and York had retired to his Welsh castle. While he escaped indictment there were many charges of treason against lesser persons in the southern counties to be heard, all cases which sorely tried the judge's admiration for York and desire to be fair to lesser conspirators.

Finally, in July he accompanied the lord chief justice to Bristol, to investigate a complaint by the abbot of St Augustine's monastery against thirty local men who, the abbot claimed, had broken into the monastery, attacked and beaten him and locked him in the monastery cellar.

Sir John Fortescue tended to treat the whole affair as something of a joke after the cases of treason which the judges had been hearing. He knew Abbot Thomas and called him a thieving old prelate.

'I warrant you, my friend,' he said, 'he had been squeezing them of tithes and fines and more service than was his due. I know many of the good folk of Bedminster, Burton and Naylsy, and they would not break into any man's home, without they felt that right was on their side but the law had failed them. We must do them fair justice this time.'

He was exactly right. The story which emerged at the hearing was of exorbitant fines being demanded of the villagers, and their goods being seized by the abbot's bailiffs. Finally one of the bailiffs had overstepped the mark and taken a pretty young girl from the household of the Burton tanner; her forcible detention had sparked off an explosion of anger which carried the men from the three villages in a successful assault on the monastery. The indignant abbot denied all knowledge of his bailiffs' action, but the judges were not impressed. They imposed fines on all the parties to the dispute and ordered an impartial reassessment of the tithes payable by the three villages.

'No man may break his neighbour's close,' declared the lord chief justice in pronouncing sentence on the thirty men, 'nor may any man take away another man's child or servant without his permission. In this realm we would have law and order, in the king's name.'

As the two justices left the courthouse together the crowd gathered outside cheered enthusiastically. They proceeded on their way with the straight-faced severity of law men, but Nicholas heard his chief murmur under his breath, 'How I would have enjoyed seeing Abbot Thomas all trussed up like a Somerset chicken and laid among his own wines!'

They parted company at Crediton, for here was a chance for Nicholas to travel on to Cornwall and pay a brief visit to his home. He had not yet seen the baby born to Margaret in April, and there was the matter of his eldest daughter's marriage to be seen to.

He sighed, wondering if the baby Elizabeth could ever be as dear to him as Susannah had always been.

Nicholas did not go straight home. When they came to the spot where he liked to catch his first view of Theupath, he sent

Gwyllym ahead to advise the household, and with his retainers rode on into the town to the home of Richard Chyket. He found Richard grading and marking the season's fleeces, with the help of his teen-age sons Ralph and Robert. At the sight of his friend Richard leapt up from his stool and signalled to the boys to stop work.

'Welcome back to Calyngton, Sir Nicholas! We have awaited your return with impatience.'

'Indeed, and I have been anxious to arrive!' replied the judge, grasping his friend's one hand in both his own. 'I weary of the travel and the judges' lodgings, and many times long to be back in my own home with my family.'

He fell silent as he heard footsteps in the yard, and he glanced at the two boys sitting in the shadows of the storeroom on a bale of fleeces.

Almost in an undertone, he asked Richard quickly, 'Have you completed my commission?'

Richard nodded. 'All is prepared. We did it quietly and at night, not a soul in the town knows what is afoot. When shall we declare it?'

The door opened and the two daughters of the house came in. Mimi, the mistress of the house, with her chatelaine tinkling softly at her waist over a sober gown of dull green holland cloth and her hair concealed under a countrywoman's kerchief of the same material, was followed by her younger sister, Peg, now fifteen and as sparkling in colour and vivacity as her sister was drab.

Mimi bobbed a neat curtsey to the judge. 'May we offer refreshment to you, sir, and to your bodyguard outside?'

She looked so like her mother and namesake that Nicholas felt a lump form in his throat. He coughed, then stepped forward and bent over her hand with an air of gallantry which brought a soft blush to her cheeks and a frightened look to her eyes.

'Thank you for your kindness, little Mimi, but no, I speak only briefly with your father and then I must hasten on to Theupath where I am awaited.'

He turned to Peg, whose rosy face wore a happy smile, so confident was she that Edward's father could only be here to discuss her marriage. Richard scowled at her and broke in, before

Nicholas could say anything, 'Get you hence, back to the house, all of you — yes, you two boys also. Sir Nicholas and I have business which concerns none of you.'

The children trooped out despondently.

'So that is little Peg — grown into a handsome young willow of a woman!' commented Nicholas, as the door closed behind them. He stroked his chin thoughtfully. 'Small wonder that Edward is anxious to marry her, before another comes to pick such luscious fruit! What say you, Richard, shall we arrange a betrothal between your Peg and my Edward? I doubt that Edward will ever be persuaded to take another for his bride.'

'It would indeed be a great joy to me as well as to my daughter — if, my friend, you do not jeopardise your career too far with a second marriage offering no political security?'

Nicholas shrugged his shoulders.

'I find I no longer care,' he said. 'I stand high in the profession, and none can impugn my integrity. If neither the king's party nor the Yorkists feel they have me safely in their pocket they may not then prevent my early retirement to my Cornish estate. In any case, Roger does well at Lyston Overhalle, and negotiations for the alliance of Joanne to William Trevinour proceed satisfactorily, so perhaps the younger ones can give us the protection we would have.'

As Nicholas turned to go, Richard checked him.

'And the other matter? When do we proclaim it abroad?'

'What better time than on the day when my daughter marries a Fursdon and my son is betrothed to a Chyket? Let it all happen together!'

The nuptial mass was over and the bridal party stepped out from the cool shadows of the church into the hot and dusty market square of Calyngton. A crowd had gathered, to watch the splendid judge and his retinue as much as to see the young bride who was marrying her father's friend, but there were smiles and exclamations of pleasure when the bride appeared.

She was dressed in a gown of the palest ivory silk under a full-length houppeland of Honiton lace with trumpet shaped sleeves drooping almost to the ground. Her rich gold hair had not been entirely confined, but lay cleverly entwined around the horned head-dress so that it glinted richly through the lace wimple which completely encircled her head. Framed in this gold and ivory setting, Susannah's face shone with such radiant happiness that the onlookers burst into cheers, and some of the men pressed forward to congratulate the bridegroom with a hearty slap on the shoulder.

As he handed Susannah into the Ayssheton carriage, John reflected to himself how short was the public memory; less than twenty years ago the Aysshetons had been banned from the town, now they owned it and much of the land round about, and so proud was Calyngton of its famous judge that the sorry past had been conveniently forgotten.

But he, John, had no need to forget the past, for now, in Susannah, he had recovered the prize which he had formerly lost; the thought brought a deep happiness to his patient soul; he forgot his faded greying hair, his wrinkled tanned face and gnarled hands, and grinned like a boy at his well-wishers.

Suddenly a great crash of sound brought the entire crowd to an instant silence; John, about to climb into the carriage, whirled around in confusion as some put their hands to their ears and others looked round the square in puzzled fright. The noise reverberated between the tall house fronts, then faded away into heavy silence. Everyone remained still, stunned, and there were cries of fright as the discordant noise crashed forth again.

This time John noted that it came from the church, and when he looked towards his new father-in-law he saw that Nicholas and Richard Chyket were laughing together and looking pleased with themselves.

Of course, it was bells! — several bells, all being rung at the same time to make such a cacophony of noise! He turned to reassure Susannah, just as the bells rang out again, but this time in some ragged sort of order which declared their true identity and brought relief and laughter to the crowd.

Within minutes everyone in the square knew that the bells were a gift from Justice Ayssheton to the church to which he had already given so much; when he mounted his horse and followed the carriage, protected by his escort on either side, caps were doffed and thrown in the air, amid cheering so sustained that the sound of the bells became quite muted. The judge continued on his way, the expression on his face as severe as ever, but at the town gate he stopped, turned to look back at the church tower still crashing with joyous sound, and raised his black tricorne hat in salute. The crowd cheered again ecstatically, and there were those standing near to the gate who afterwards maintained that as he replaced his hat on his white coif Justice Ayssheton actually smiled with pleasure.

The banquet at Theupath went on all day. The rafters of the great hall hummed with conversation and laughter, the occasional shouts of well-wishers drinking to the bride and her groom, and snatches of song as the good wine took effect. Only at the head of the table was there an oasis of relative quiet as the principals of the day talked together in subdued tones, sipping only lightly from their goblets.

At last Mattie and her daughters silently removed the remains of the feast and left the board swept clear except for several flagons of wine.

Nicholas stood up and knocked loudly on the table with the base of his goblet.

'Friends,' he declared, in his stentorian voice of the courthouse, bringing all conversation to an abrupt close, 'I crave your attention while I speak briefly on two matters touching my family and this happy day.'

He paused, almost hesitated, as every goblet was placed on the board and every face turned towards him. He glanced down at Margaret sitting pale and silent beside him, and pressed her hand reassuringly before continuing.

'First, I would say that on this happy day I am humbly aware of the great harm which I once did my good friend Master Fursdon.'

Several throats were cleared as the older guests remembered that tragic time in John's life and looked with some embarrassment at the two offenders at the head of the table. Susannah turned towards her husband with a puzzled air, but he merely smiled his gentle smile and raised his goblet to salute his host.

Nicholas picked up his own goblet and continued quietly, 'My wife and I hope that with the marriage of our daughter to him we are forgiven our past misdeeds. As evidence of our goodwill a portion of her marriage dowry is the mortgage of Fursdon, which I have held these twenty years. John and Susannah, we drink to your love, happiness and prosperity, and may the Lord bless all your progeny.'

As he spoke, Nicholas had gently drawn Margaret up to stand beside him, and now they drank a toast together, Margaret smiling through free-running tears at her daughter and the man who should have been her husband.

Someone called out, 'The bride and groom!'; all the guests rose from their seats and toasted the happy pair.

'You may remain on your feet, my friends,' called Nicholas, as the benches were being shuffled and scraped to accommodate their occupants once more, 'I have more news to give you, which I trust will merit another hearty toast. Many years ago there were three boys in this town who were good friends. Today two of them are united by marriage; today with a betrothal our triangle is complete. My good friend Master Chyket has consented to the marriage of his daughter Margaret to our eldest son Edward, and their betrothal will be celebrated in our chapel on the morrow.'

As he finished Nicholas indicated Edward and Peg, standing among the guests lower down the table and now both blushing in happy confusion. Peg dropped to her seat and hid her face in the folds of her sister Mimi's gown, while Edward disappeared under an avalanche of back-slapping good wishes.

The party had broken up into small groups at the table and by the fireside when Nicholas noticed a dark figure standing in the doorway. He advanced across the hall towards the uninvited guest.

'Welcome, stranger,' he said. 'You come to Theupath on a happy occasion.'

The stranger bowed. He did not have the appearance of a wedding guest, and his leather travelling clothes smelled of horse and human sweat, while his boots and spurs were deep in mud as if never cleaned.

'Your name, sir?' asked Nicholas, his voice a shade less hospitable than before. Instinctively he distrusted the swarthy bearded face and the cold green eyes which gazed unblinking into his.

'The same as yours, my lord,' replied the man in mocking tones, pulling off his greasy hat to reveal a head of tangled black hair very similar to the dark curls of Nicholas and his sons.

'Your name is Ayssheton?' asked Nicholas, 'I know no others of my name.'

'*Asshton*, my lord.' He laid great emphasis on the short *a*. 'I am your sole surviving cousin, Denis Asshton — the legitimate family from the manor over the hill.'

'Denis? My uncle Philip died many years ago — alone and unloved, so I am told. He had no family, and was the last of the Aysshetons of Aiston.'

The chill in Nicholas's voice would have deterred most intruders from venturing further. But Denis Asshton was different. He leered at Nicholas as though they were conspirators together.

'What would you expect, when an old man weds an innocent, ripe young girl? My mother left him when he fell ill. I was born in Bristol, where she was taken in by the nuns of St Augustine's.'

Nicholas's head jerked at the mention of the monastery where he had recently performed his legal duty, and he listened more intently as the man continued.

'I have worked for the nuns and the monks there all my life — and would have been there still if the law had not intervened in the abbot's affairs.'

He thrust his face nearer to Nicholas, who with difficulty prevented himself from stepping back in self defence. He stood his ground, however, not even flinching at the stench of the man.

'When I heard that one of the judges was called *Ayssheton* and came from Calyngton, I said to myself I must visit this cousin — and claim my inheritance. But when I reach Calyngton I find the manor house of Aiston in ruins and the land in other hands — some in that of Nicholas Ayssheton. And while the legitimate family is impoverished, the *bastard* branch flourishes over here at Theupath.'

He lowered his voice and continued in a near-whisper, 'They tell me you are one of the richest men in Cornwall; you own land in many places, including Dorset and Essex, and property in London too, and have the livings of many parish priests in your pocket.'

Nicholas inclined his head and said coldly, 'I am now a rich man, but none of my riches came from your father — if indeed he was your father.'

Denis laughed, and there was evil menace in his voice as he

said loudly, 'As a rich man you will not deny hospitality to a poor cousin. I intend to rebuild the manor house and win back some of the land, but presently have no shelter over my head.'

There was no escaping the man, Nicholas knew. The rules of hospitality forbade him to turn away anyone who asked for shelter, and until he could prove this man's claim of kinship as false he must treat him as a cousin. In his coldest voice he said, 'You are of course welcome to stay here at Theupath while you rebuild your home. As you are badly stained by travel I will instruct my housekeeper to prepare you a chamber and find you more suitable clothes. Tomorrow we will talk more.'

He had just handed over the intruder to Mattie's unwelcoming care when a second caller brought the wedding festivities very definitely to a close. It was Sir John Fortescue's messenger, bearing the king's commission to several of his judges to proceed to Lostwithiell to investigate an insurrection there by twenty-two of the town's leading inhabitants.

'The whole of the west country is in turmoil,' wrote the lord chief justice, 'and it is imperative that the king's law officers attend speedily to settle all disputes and restore calm, before our enemies across the Channel take advantage of our internal troubles and invade our shores.'

13

The recall to legal duties prevented Justice Ayssheton from attending the betrothal of his son to Margaret Chyket in the little Theupath chapel. However, his wife, free now from the emotional strain brought on by John Fursdon's love for her daughter Susannah, prayed happily for the couple, and kissed them both when the service was over and everyone trooped out into the grove.

As they led the little procession into Theupath courtyard a dark figure stepped out from the house and stood watching them approach. Edward stopped and turned to his mother.

'Who is this man? He has an air of insolence, and moreover shows no appreciation of our hospitality.'

'He says he is your father's cousin, my son,' replied Margaret, repressing an involuntary shudder as the man swept her an ostentatious bow. 'He intends to rebuild the family home at Aiston. We must be kind to him; your father tells me he has had a hard life.'

The little group of Aysshetons and Chykets acknowledged the visitor and passed on into the great hall. Denis Asshton followed, and stood silently observing the happy family gathering with the detachment of a bored spectator at a marionette show. Richard Chyket, entering the hall alone a little while after the main party, came up behind him and was disturbed to see him clenching and unclenching his fists as if possessed by some suppressed fury. He took him by the elbow and invited him in his friendliest tones to join in the simple festivities, then, suiting the action to the word, guided him across the room and presented him to the mistress of the house.

Margaret felt cornered and was forced to offer her hand. At the touch of the man's cool lips a strange tremor ran through her. Terrified, she pulled her hand free, only to find the man's eyes boring into her as if he could read her very soul, while a mocking smile played on his lips. Margaret leaped to her feet and with only a cursory apology to the assembled company, retired to her chamber, calling to Mattie to send water for her to wash.

Nicholas was back at his chambers in Serjeants' Inn, after weeks of travel and court hearings in Wales, Buckinghamshire and Kent, before any news reached him from Cornwall. On a gusty day in October he sat at the window looking out on to the garden of bare trees and drifts of dead leaves, which every now and then whirled up into a dance of frenzy as the wind caught them and the suddenly darkening sky pelted them with noisy, heavy rain.

He fingered the letter on his lap, and sighed. What could he do? Here was a plea from his wife to have the family guest removed from Theupath.

'He is a mischievous person, who wishes us all harm,' wrote Margaret. 'He has made no move at all to start work on his ruined home. Instead he goes fishing with William, and fills him with wild stories which no one but a small boy would believe. He wishes to ingratiate himself with me, but failing in this — and husband, I find it most difficult to speak civilly to him — he has now commenced most ostentatiously to win the attentions of Joanne. She evidently finds entertainment in his evil character, and they are much in company together. Master Trevinour has not visited at Theupath for some time, and I fear the outcome. We must hasten and conclude the alliance before it is too late. To this end I have dispatched this day an invitation to Master Trevinour for the festival of All Saints. Hasten, dearest, beloved husband, to our succour, I fear we are in mortal peril.'

Nicholas read and re-read the final sentence many times, deeply disturbed by his wife's obvious fear of some real danger threatened by Denis Asshton. He sighed again, and absently watched some clouds scudding across a blue sky. Eventually he moved over to his table, took up a quill and a small parchment and carefully penned some brief words of comfort and encouragement to his wife.

'God willing, I will be with you by All Saints,' he concluded.

But the festival passed, with Nicholas still held in London by his duties in the Court of Common Pleas. He had sent Gwyllym down to Cornwall with news of the delay and instructions to await his return before proceeding with the betrothal of Joanne.

'If she be wayward, lock her in her chamber until I come,' he wrote. 'And ask my friend Richard to provide tools and men to start on the work at Aiston and so occupy Master Denis. I will hope to find him removed from Theupath when I return.'

Gwyllym was back at Serjeants' Inn twelve days later. The letter which he brought was much briefer than the previous one. Margaret wrote merely to inform her husband that the baby Elizabeth had died of the croup.

Nicholas sat back in shock. Automatically he crossed himself and prayed for the dead child — another child whom he had never known as a personality — but his thoughts were with his wife. The baldness of her statement, and the brevity of the letter, spoke volumes in telling him that the woman whom he loved so dearly was in some dire trouble.

He must return home. By mid-day the following day he had

arranged matters with the lord chief justice and with his escort was riding at full gallop over the Berkshire downs westward towards Cornwall.

Everything seemed normal when four days later the travel-stained party reached Theupath. Edward and his mother stood at the door to welcome the master of the house, and by the time he had dismounted Joanne and William had joined them. Everyone looked relaxed and contented, and for a moment Nicholas wondered if he had imagined trouble where there was none.

Of Denis there was no sign, and no mention was made of him as the family gathered at the warm fireside in the November dusk.

'I can remain a few days only,' Nicholas told Margaret. 'Sir John has asked me to take him a report on the disorders rumoured from various parts of the county. But while I am here let us proceed with the arrangements for Joanne's betrothal. I will ride over to Sir William on the morrow.'

He was relieved to see his daughter looked quietly pleased. She was a sensible girl, not given to romantic adventures, and, thank the Lord, she must have found the measure of this fellow Denis and discarded him.

Margaret too looked pleased, but he was worried to see her looking drawn and pale again, no better than during her illness two years ago. But she kissed him warmly, clung to his arm, and joined in with the light-hearted family chatter at the hearth-side, apparently secure in her family happiness.

It was only when they lay together in bed, and he felt her shrink away from his touch as if trying to refuse his love-making, that Nicholas knew his instinct had been right, something was grieviously wrong.

Was she grieving over the lost baby? Was she attempting to deny another pregnancy to avoid such another tragedy?

'My love,' he murmured softly in her ear, and covered her with caresses.

The following morning Nicholas sought out Edward, whom he found preparing to ride into Calyngton to visit Peg. He asked what had happened to Denis Asshton.

'He left four days ago — taking my best horse and a chest full of clothes. He told Thomas we would hear from him soon, and gave Thomas covert hints that he should be prepared to abandon his work at Theupath "for better things". There are rumours in the town of a revolt being planned, a widespread uprising covering the whole of East Cornwall under the leadership of William Avery of Wolston.'

'Is Denis Asshton involved in this plot?'

Edward shrugged his shoulders, and flung the reins over his horse's head. As he mounted he said, 'Three men from Wolston have been working for Asshton on his manor house. You may deduce from that what you will.'

Nicholas sent Gwyllym to call out his escort from their quarters and set off to visit Sir William Trevinour and finalise the marriage alliance between his son William and Joanne. Making discreet calls of enquiry on the way he returned to Theupath well furnished with material for his report to the lord chief justice.

There was no doubt about it, a large-scale insurrection was in the making. It was being whispered about in St Ive, Linkinhorne, Launceston, Altarnon, St Kew, St Bruard and Boscastle — a great sweep of Cornwall right up to the north coast. What he could not be sure about was the purpose of the revolt; it did not have a definite political angle which would suggest a treasonable uprising against the king in favour of Richard of York; it could be a plot among farmers and tradesmen, with the connivance of the priests of Trebeigh, to seize for themselves the land they tenanted. Such an enterprise would undoubtedly appeal to Denis Asshton.

Theupath could well be in danger if this were the case. Which should he do, stay at home to defend his family and property, or ride at all speed to London with his report in the hope that the uprising might be nipped in the bud? If Denis Asshton seized the estate he might even imprison Margaret and the children, holding them to ransom until Nicholas quitclaimed in his favour.

But his years of service *pro rege et lege* had imbued Nicholas with a firm idea of his duties, and he realised that he must report immediately to the lord chief justice as instructed. So he decided to take Margaret, Joanne and William with him, leaving Edward to defend Theupath with the help of Thomas and some of his loyal Calyngton tenants.

William protested that he should stay to help his brother at Theupath, but no one took any notice of him; with four children lost, he was still at seven years old the baby of the family, and treated as such.

It was with mixed feelings that the four set off the following morning, Nicholas on his horse behind the carriage carrying his wife and children. There was a sense of dread that they might never see Edward again, and they pictured an army of cut-throats streaming down the lane towards the house. But by the end of the first day's journey, with the danger far behind them and therefore less acute, William was bouncing with excitement at the prospect of going to London, while his mother was notice-ably relaxed, as if a great load had been lifted from her shoulders. Each day found her rosier and more cheerful, and not in any way wearied by long hours being constantly jolted and bounced in the carriage. Thrilled with her recovery, Nicholas produced a horse for her to ride on the final day, and they rode together into London side by side, just as they had done when starting their life together.

The winter passed peacefully at Serjeants' Inn. The judge and his wife were welcomed back into the social life of the inn, where his high standing among his fellow serjeants-at-law was immediately apparent. In the season of banqueting which marked the festivals of St Thomas the Apostle, Christmas, St Stephen, St John the Evangelist and Holy Innocents, it was easy to put aside their concern for Edward's fate at Theupath while they enjoyed good company and entertainment.

Even Joanne lost her air of cool detachment and began to look as if life could, after all, be fun. Overnight she blossomed into an elegant lady of fashion, surrounded by admirers, her calm self-assurance softened by just an occasional teasing trace of a dimpled smile. There was no doubt about it, she was the aristo-crat in the family.

Nicholas had hoped to return to duty on the bench of the Court of Common Pleas, but a few days before the Hilary term began in January he was ordered to Kent and Essex to investi-gate disturbances there.

'If you thought to sit comfortably at Westminster, you ought not to have been so successful on the circuit,' Sir John Fortescue commented, when he observed the judge's disappointment. Nicholas nodded ruefully.

'You see, even now, your work in Cornwall has borne good fruit. That little plot you uncovered was dealt with by William Bourchier and his men before any real harm was done – only one farmhouse burned down, its owner assaulted and made prisoner. All thirty-two miscreants were captured, and after examination, clapped into Bodmyn gaol.'

'Edward Ayssheton, my son, is he mentioned? Was he the one who was assaulted?' asked Nicholas urgently.

The lord chief justice studied the document lying on the desk before him, carefully perusing all the names. Nicholas waited, in an agony of suppressed impatience. At last Sir John looked up at him with a puzzled frown.

'No,' he replied, and Nicholas sighed with relief, 'there is no Edward Ayssheton here, but I am disturbed to find another of your name among the conspirators. A Denis Ayssheton, gentilman, is listed as being one of the leaders.'

'And he is now in prison?'

'Indeed yes, and will be for the next five years. It will not look good in Cornwall for Justice Ayssheton to have a kinsman in gaol as a common criminal.'

Nicholas laughed, and explained why he felt happy to have Denis shut away for five years. The good news so cheered him that he set off for Kent in a much more willing frame of mind.

He returned to London four weeks later to find further commissions awaiting him, three of them concerning Cornwall, where the state of lawlessness had so increased that the upper classes were now engaging in wholesale piracy.

Names he knew well stared up at him from the parchments – Penpons, Treynwith, Arundell, Vivyan and Treworgy – all apparently conspiring in various ways to capture Italian, Portuguese and Irish ships and seize their cargo. Sadly Nicholas reflected that all his years of labour to bring law and security to his native county had been far from successful. But what could he hope to achieve, when all through the length and breadth of England fighting and factions had taken over?

However, at Calyngton life should be safe and peaceful now, with Denis removed from the scene. He decided they should all return together to take up their country life again at Theupath. He found Margaret strangely reluctant, she had always loved Theupath so, but now she made various excuses, pleading for a longer stay in London so that William could be put to school at St Thomas of Acon's hospital.

'He may go to Liskerret with his brother John,' Nicholas rejoined peremptorily. 'Or, if you prefer, we will send him to Lyston Overhalle to learn with Roger how to be a gentilman.'

William did not relish the studious life of a scholar, and begged to be a valet. Watching him depart, riding pillion behind Gwyllym, with his little legs sticking out from the horse's sides and his small box of clothes strapped to the saddle behind him, Margaret felt tears welling in her eyes and a weight of deep sadness pressing on her breast. It would be years before she saw him again, not until he was a young man and a stranger; another child lost to her, and with Joanne to marry they would soon all be gone.

She winced with pain as the foetus in her womb moved. It gave her no joy.

The baby was born a few weeks prematurely in July. She was a beautiful child, perfectly formed, and the first of the five daughters to favour her father in appearance. When Nicholas returned to Theupath from Exeter, where he had been summoned to hear of the bad state of the war in France and the growing need for coastal defences and volunteers for Devon and Cornwall, he was entranced by the little bundle crowned by a head of silky black curls.

Elizabeth he had hardly known, and the twins had never lived, while the older girls he no longer thought of as daughters who had once been babies; they were young women, each in her own way a copy of their mother.

But here, being rocked in her hooded cradle by Beatty, Mattie's eldest grandchild, was a little creature whom he felt he could take for his very own. She was already a week old, her peach-like skin soft and unblemished and her tiny fingers so elegant it was difficult to imagine them ever being exposed to work of any kind. She waved two little fists towards her father, and opened her eyes to gaze vacantly in his direction, before settling to sleep again. He was captivated, and spent several minutes watching her every sleeping movement, before finally going up to the chamber where Margaret still lay in her bed.

'She is a beautiful child,' he said as he perched on the edge of the bed and took her hand in his.

'Is it so?' she replied, her eyes wandering from his face to focus blankly on the arras on the wall behind him.

Nicholas was deeply hurt. He withdrew his hand and went to stand by the window, quite oblivious to the magnificent picture view it gave of the evening sun gilding the rocky slopes of Hingston Down.

Something had gone badly wrong in their relationship. He realised now that Margaret had never wanted to have this baby; it had been foolish to imagine that his love-making would ease her mind of the worries and problems which beset her last autumn. It seemed that those problems still occupied her mind, and the baby meant nothing to her. For the first time in his married life Nicholas felt a stab of dislike poison his love for his wife. He shook it away, and told himself that she would grow to love this child as she fed it, and would soon love it just as deeply as she had loved and cared for the others.

Comforted by this elementary thought he was about to return to the bedside when there came a knock at the door. Beatty entered.

'The wet nurse is here, mistress.'

'Take the baby to her, and look after it when she has finished.'

The girl hesitated, then pleaded, 'Do you not wish to see the baby, to check how she grows and thrives?'

'No.'

The answer was emphatic. Beatty bobbed, and scuttled from the room, pursued by an indignant Nicholas determined to inspect this wet nurse and make certain she would not be harmful for his daughter.

Margaret kept to her bed until the dog days were over and the autumn settled on Cornwall. Because of her disregard for the child Nicholas put all other matters aside and gave his undivided attention to his baby daughter. She was baptised in the little chapel, sponsored only by Joanne, Mattie and her father, who gave her the name of her predecessor Elizabeth. Something triggered in his mind as he handed her to Beatty to carry back to the house after the baptism; as if a window had been opened he remembered the French peasant girl with whom a young soldier had lost his virginity. He turned to Joanne and Mattie.

'We will call her Lisette in the family,' he said.

Three times Nicholas changed the wet nurse, until finally Susannah sent a woman from St Cleer whom he could not fault, and at last the baby enjoyed a settled daily routine.

When Margaret finally emerged from her chamber she found the domestic affairs of the house and the baby running smoothly without her. Attempts to draw her into the care of Lisette completely failed, and eventually the household divided itself into two – one for the mistress and one for the baby, with Nicholas and Joanne sharing their time with both in a strange dichotomy. In their separate establishments both Lisette and her mother grew healthy and contented, each seemingly unaware that the other existed.

The Michaelmas term had begun, and Nicholas knew that he could not much longer delay his return to Westminster. It was time to finalise Joanne's betrothal with the church's blessing.

Joanne, now fifteen years old, looked every inch the self-possessed lady of high society as she walked on her father's arm to the chapel. Her turban was several inches taller than any her mother had ever worn, and the shot silk material flashed in the sun so that she might almost have been wearing a crown. William Trevinour was a tall lanky young man, nearly twenty years of age but gauche and childish in comparison with his betrothed. He was clearly overcome by her elegance and cool charm, but he grinned with pride when complimented on her appearance.

Susannah and John had come over from Fursdon, and had brought with them her brother John, who was now living with them while continuing his studies at Liskerret.

'We have renamed him "Jack", to prevent confusion at home,' Susannah told her mother laughingly. Margaret took her son in her arms and kissed him warmly.

'To me he will always be John.' She looked at John Fursdon and smiled. 'Do you remember, "Uncle Fursdon", I named him John for you, for your faithful friendship?'

'Yes, mistress, I remember,' was the quiet reply. Susannah

looked from one to the other and wondered again what this old secret could be between her mother and her husband. Somehow she felt inhibited from telling her mother the exciting news that she would be presenting John with his first child early in the new year. She turned away and caught her father looking at her; he knew, and understood, and they smiled at each other. They had their secrets too.

Nicholas for his part was overjoyed to see Margaret kissing her son, for it meant that there was still some love in her soul, even if she had none for her baby or her husband.

It was only a small family party which gathered that evening in the great hall at Theupath to celebrate the betrothal with wine and music and some of Mattie's best partridge pies.

What was it, Nicholas wondered, as he stood by the fireside and listened to the flute piping delicately a sad little air — what was it which made him feel threatened as well as sad? For an instant he imagined he saw a dark figure standing in the doorway, just as he had at the last family celebration.

But no, Denis was in prison, he was being over-imaginative. He turned to watch the dancers, wondering if he should go and check baby Lisette.

A hand touched him on the shoulder, and Gwyllym spoke quietly behind him in his sing-song Welsh voice.

'My lord, there is a messenger awaiting you. He brings you instructions from Sir John Fortescue.' He coughed and continued, 'He also brings news that the king has been struck down by a mysterious illness, and lies speechless and incapable.'

It was indeed momentous news, when Nicholas opened the letter in the seclusion of his private chamber — the same room where many years ago his father had first shown him the plans for the church.

The lord chief justice ordered him to return to London immediately. The king's mind had completely deserted him, he could not think or speak, and recognised no one. A council would have to be appointed, and it was imperative that every one of the king's judges be present to ensure a fair and equitable selection. Pressure would be needed to prevent the queen taking the whole government of the country into her own hands, and there was a possibility that the Duke of York would now press his claim.

Nicholas read through the letter a second time, then sat in thought. Finally he went to the door and told the waiting Gwyllym to make all preparations for their departure within the hour.

The news had filtered through the family by the time he returned to the hall; the celebrations had ceased, William and his retinue had left, and the others were gathered at the hearthside discussing in low tones what the news could portend.

Nicholas went to Margaret and took both her hands in his. Looking earnestly into her eyes he said, 'Dear heart, I love you as I have always loved you, and I have rejoiced today to find you once more happy and loving as you used to be; my Margaret has been gone from me this past year.'

Tears swam in her eyes as she smiled rather mistily up at him, and there was a catch in her voice as she cried out, 'I have loved none but you, my lord — and none shall take your place in my heart.'

'Then for my sake, please care for our daughter Lisette while I am gone.'

The expression on her face changed to one of horror; she seemed about to say something, but instead burst into tears and buried her face against her husband's shoulder. He fondled her faded hair with affection, and waited for her sobbing to ease before guiding her to her chamber. A few moments later the clatter of hooves in the courtyard announced the presence of his bodyguard, and Justice Ayssheton was soon gone from Theupath on his way to Westminster.

14

Nicholas remained in London for over a year, working in support of the new protector's government. Each month Gwyllym rode down to Cornwall with long letters from his master describing with great enthusiasm the progress being made towards a peaceful and stabilised country now that the duke of York was at last in control. Reading between the lines Margaret could see that he was in his element, with little time to miss his family.

For his sake she had forced herself to take an interest in Lisette, and as the months slipped by her maternal instinct responded to the charms of a healthy and attractive child. With her dark curls concealed in a white baby cap buttoned under the chin she looked for all the world like a miniature Nicholas Ayssheton, serjeant-at-law, in his white coif, and Margaret would nurse her fondly as she day-dreamed about the past. It was only when the cap was removed that the glossy black curls reminded her forcibly of a nightmare horror, and she would abruptly have the baby taken away.

Early in January 1455 a letter from Nicholas brought the news that the king had recovered from his illness.

'We should rejoice, and thank the Lord who has restored him to normal life,' wrote Nicholas. 'Indeed, I am even now lately returned from Paul's where we held a service of thanksgiving. But, dearest wife, I fear that the old order will now return and we will lose all that has been so hardly gained this past year. My Lord York has resigned his office as protector and retired to Sandal, and the queen is now ordering the release of Somerset − with whom she will doubtless scheme once more, and bring confusion and enmity back to our land.'

From a purely personal point of view Margaret was not sorry at the political change in London, for almost immediately Nicholas was once more riding the circuit, and there was always a good chance then that he would come to Cornwall. Her hope was justified, for in the spring he was appointed to a commission carrying out a survey of all the royal property in the county.

Such a lengthy task should have left plenty of opportunities for the commissioners to take a break and visit their estates, but none of them did, for they had barely started when they were recalled urgently to Westminster. A battle had taken place at St Albans between the queen's supporters and those of Richard of York; the king was a prisoner of the Yorkists and the queen had fled. Chaos reigned in the capital, and the lord chief justice deemed it vital to hold conference with his fellow judges to decide where their allegiance now lay.

For many months the news was sparse, and as rumours of the king's death, countered by rumours of the execution of the Duke of York, spread around the west country, in Cornwall piracy increased even more and private feuds flared into open warfare. It was one of these which eventually brought Justice Ayssheton back to Cornwall the following year.

He rode across the bridge and up the long steep climb past Kyrrybullok park to the ridge of Hingston on a hot and dusty August day. Walter Moyle rode with him, and both men were so eager to look again at their Cornish homeland that they left their escorts well behind and breasted the ridge side by side on exhausted horses. They drew rein and scanned the view southward in deep satisfaction.

Below them lay a rolling countryside of stone-hedged cornfields round small clusters of farmsteads, all neatly sheltered on the lower slopes and close to a spring or streamside. Above the fields stretched the unfenced common pastureland, dotted with sheep and outcrops of rock, the grass pale and dusty after the scorching summer. Beyond the furthest ridge a pearly glimmer of reflected sunlight on the sea stretched right across the horizon until it joined with the wide estuary, where the winding river which they had crossed flowed into it.

They sat in silence until the escorts joined them, then rode on down the hill towards their homes. They parted company where the lane turned off to Theupath, for Walter had still six miles to go to St Germans, and there was no time to waste as the commission was due at Bodmyn the following day.

Nicholas now rode more slowly, sniffing contentedly at the heavy scent of honeysuckle from the hedges, and allowing plenty of time for Gwyllym to reach Theupath ahead of him and prepare the household for his arrival.

At last, there were the tall chimneys, and the blue stone roof, then the dip in the road beneath his horse's hooves which told him, as it always did, that in precisely six more steps he would be at the courtyard gate with the house before him.

She was there at the door, as he had known she would be but feared she might not, for it was almost three years since he had left her in a state of deep distress. She stood erect, but relaxed, in a gown of pale gold silk which brought richness to the faded hair braided on the top of her head with a simple comb. On her arm sat a diminutive creature in white, the little face under the white baby cap observing the strange arrival with anxious interest. Nicholas slid from his saddle like a young man half his years, and took both of them into his arms.

In a strange way that briefest of all his visits home was the most wonderful, and one which he was able to look back on later with a true happiness, untinged by regret. They walked until sundown in the meadows, picking here and there a handful of blackberries which they shared with Lisette. The little girl scampered around, tripping over tussocks of grass or her own feet, and bringing tributes to her mother of buttercup and daisy heads. The setting sun was filtering through the branches as they returned to the house by way of the orchard, bobbing under the rosy ripening apples and picking some small ones from the grass for Lisette to carry home in her skirt. As she walked carefully ahead, her eyes on her precious load lest she let any drop, Nicholas put his arm round his wife's shoulder and they stood together, watching the little girl and laughing at her natural clowning. He picked up the hand resting idly on the silk gown, and pressed it gently to his lips.

'This is all that a man should require of life,' he murmured.

They sat late that evening by the open window, with the smell of the lavender from Susannah's garden giving an added dimension to a golden evening. Joanne was presently visiting Susannah, to discuss her future needs as the mistress of Trevinour, and Edward was at Chykets, for years now his second home.

'Two marriages still to be arranged,' said Nicholas thoughtfully, 'and in the present unsettled state of our country only the good Lord Himself knows when I may next return to Cornwall. It would be good if arrangements were made for both nuptials to be celebrated soon.'

'Will you be many days at Bodmyn?'

'It is a troublesome affair we are to investigate, and there are eight commissioners appointed to hear the case and give sentence. Yes, it will be many days before all is settled. But with three other judges and four lay magistrates all sitting on the case, my absence for a day may not be of consequence.'

'Rumours have reached Calyngton of grave disturbances at Bodmyn; they say that the priory has been robbed of all its precious silver, even that the prior himself has been murdered and the priory utterly demolished by vandals.'

Nicholas smiled.

'We shall see,' he replied. 'Trust not in rumours, they can fancifully embroider the truth. The prior has not been murdered, he is very much alive, and full of complaint against the behaviour of the townspeople these past three years. There has been much dispute over the ownership of the fish ponds in the area, which the prior claims all belong to St Petrock's. But the people deny this, and in their anger at the confiscation of fish and the damming of the river they finally followed the leadership of hotheads and on three occasions broke into the church. How far the prior's complaint is true we have yet to judge, he claims no less than one thousand pounds in compensation for damage, loss of goods and the assault on himself and his servants. What is sadly certain is that while the people's grievance may have been a just one, being denied their right to take fish, in attacking the priory they have put themselves heinously at fault.'

'The prior is a man of God. They are evildoers who assault him, and surely condemned to everlasting torment for despoiling the holy place,' said Margaret, shuddering at the thought of such sacrilege.

At that moment Gwyllym reported at the door that all was ready for the judge's departure. As Nicholas rose to go, he replied, 'Nothing is certain until a full inquiry has been held. Some priors, my love, are more men of the world than of God, and very acquisitive of worldly goods. Like the good Abbot Thomas of St Augustine's!'

He kissed her tenderly on the brow, and added with a laugh, 'And that brings to mind that my unwelcome kinsman who came from St Augustine's is now a prisoner at Bodmyn, methinks I should enquire after his welfare!'

He had turned to leave and did not see the look of horror on Margaret's face or hear her whispered 'Oh no!'

The two marriages duly took place when the Bodmyn commissioners went into recess for Lammastide. Master William Trevinour's importance as a kinsman to the Bodrugan family dictated that his marriage to Joanne take precedence, so she was no longer with the family when two days later the Chykets and Aysshetons were united with the marriage of Peg and Edward. This second, purely local, wedding was celebrated with enthusiasm by all the townsfolk as well as both families; there was roast ox provided by the lord of the manor in honour of his son's marriage, while a copious supply of ale from the bride's father was dispensed at the church door. The market square rang until early dawn with the shouts and laughter of the festive dancers.

The following day Nicholas left to return to his duties at Bodmyn.

There was an air of excitement in the crowd clustered at the priory gates when the escort swung in, the blazoned badges on their livery declaring to all bystanders that here was Justice Ayssheton arriving for the inquiry. Nicholas did not normally take much note of crowds, which always seemed to him to be composed entirely of stupid minds too easily swayed by a clever rogue, but he could not ignore the way in which people were pointing at his retainers and then at himself, and he wondered idly what might have caused this sudden interest.

As he dismounted and Gwyllym came to take his serjeant's travelling coat and shake out his hood and mantle, a beadle appeared at his elbow.

'My lord, good Sir Nicholas, the captain of the gaol has grave news for you.'

'The gaol? What news of the gaol could have interest for me?' The judge's voice rang with scorn, although he knew in his inmost heart that it could only be news of Denis Asshton, and a sudden sense of foreboding weighed him down.

The beadle smirked, uncertain whether to treat this eminent man as king's justice or prisoner's friend.

'The prisoner Asshton, my lord — your cousin, as he told us, many times these past four years.'

'What of him?'

'He has escaped, my lord. He broke out two nights ago, and has not been recovered.'

Nicholas stood silent, his face stony and expressionless, but his mind in a whirl of doubt and worry. If Denis escaped, where would he go? Would he leave Cornwall and head back to Bristol, or London, maybe? Or would he brazen it out and return to

Aiston — or even to Theupath to do what damage he could before disappearing?

As if in answer to his thoughts, the beadle continued his message.

'I was to tell you, my lord, that the prisoner spoke often of you and your family, swearing to take vengeance and claim his own.' He coughed apologetically. 'The captain begs you to make provision to protect your household, he fears evil may soon befall them.'

The judge nodded curt acknowledgement of this advice and gave instructions for his absence from the court to be explained. Within two minutes of their arrival the livery tunics of Ayssheton could be seen disappearing up the hill at a full gallop, eastward towards Calyngton.

Denis Asshton did not make his appearance at Theupath. There were rumours that he had been seen at Calestok, but news of his threats against the Aysshetons had brought a ready support for Nicholas when he convened a court leet and demanded that a protective defence force be raised, and this would have been adequate warning to Denis that an attack would not be successful.

By Christmastide the threat was all but forgotten, and early in the new year Nicholas left for Westminster again. But he paid his retainers well, and before he left he made sure that an adequate force would continue to protect Theupath.

As he said goodbye to his wife and small daughter he felt for the first time a deep longing to be able to give up all official duties and remain quietly at home for good. Margaret's eyes were moist, but she was now used to his departures and accepted them as a matter of course. Lisette was playing with her hobby-horse and did not pay much attention; looking back from the lane he saw Margaret standing motionless at the door and Lisette cantering across the courtyard, her father already forgotten.

15

When Thomas saw Denis Asshton six months later he did not report the fact to Edward, nor did he talk about it to his wife. It simply did not occur to him; he merely observed, in his taciturn way, and then got on with his work.

Edward had gone with Peg to visit her brother Ralph Chyket at Ashburton. Thomas had sent his grandson Robert to bring in the cows while he himself finished carting the second cut of hay from the bottom meadow. His wain was trundling up the field track, with Thomas lying outstretched at his ease on the top of the load, when he noticed a man slip out of the house across the farmyard. He had only a fleeting glimpse as the man disappeared into the lane, but he recognised him immediately as the one-time guest of the house, and a man who had once invited him, Thomas, to join a conspiracy of discontented tenant farmers.

Thomas had no ambitions. He had a good wife, who kept a warm and cheerful home and brought up his children to give due respect and obedience to their father; meals were wholesome and satisfying — far better than the fare of some of his yeomen friends — while gleanings from the Ayssheton household kept his family well clothed and still left an ample surplus for lucrative trading with his neighbours. It mattered nothing to him that the land he worked and the animals he tended were the property of another. The invitation from Denis had therefore fallen on stony ground and been promptly forgotten.

Idly now Thomas wondered what business Master Asshton would have at Theupath, seeing that he had escaped from prison last year and been the subject of a hue and cry for several months.

The ox halted by habit below the hayloft door; Thomas picked up his fork and set to work pitching up the load, his nose sniffing appreciatively at the sweet-smelling grasses and his mind a blank. He had almost finished when he heard Mattie calling.

'Mistress needs you.'

Dutifully he left his pitchfork stabbed into the remaining hay, brushed himself down, then lurched across the farmyard towards the kitchen court at the side of the house.

Margaret stood waiting. She seemed impatient, and even Thomas could not help but notice that she was pale and trembling.

'We need horses on the morrow, at first light. Also a mule and a pair of panniers. We ride to St Cleer.'

'How many, mistress?'

'Lisette and Beatty will come, they can both ride pillion, with you and with me.'

The thought of having sole care of three defenceless females startled Thomas out of his lethargy. At the back of his mind, too, there lurked the submerged idea of Denis Asshton lying in wait on the moorland road.

''Twill not be safe,' he muttered. 'That man—'

His words had the surprising effect of calming Margaret. Her trembling stopped and she drew herself up erect and calm, every inch of her the dignified mistress of the house. All she said was, 'Then muster an escort to ensure our safety,' as she turned away into the entry passage.

By dawn the next morning the travellers were on their way. Thomas headed the little procession, with his granddaughter Beatty clinging to his waist from the pillion. Margaret followed, but she had Lisette astride in front of her on the same saddle. Four tenant farmers on Theupath ponies made up the escort, one of them leading the pack mule and all armed with stout staves for beating off footpads.

They descended the hill to Richard's bridge over the Lynher, and were half-way up the steep road flanking Cadsonbury when the rising sun burst over the wooded slopes behind them, warming their backs and chasing the mists away into the valley bottoms. The horses' hooves wrung a soft cadence from the hard ground, and the leaves of high summer rustled in the hedge-banks as birds and mice scuttled about their morning affairs. On the open downland contented sheep hardly gave them a glance as they trotted by, and as they dropped down into the next valley towards Trebeigh only the distant tinkle of a wandering goat's bell broke the still and comforting silence.

Nothing dreadful could happen in such a world. The tension in Margaret's mind eased, she relaxed in the saddle and squeezed her small daughter lovingly into the curve of her body. John Fursdon would protect them, all would be well.

They turned off the main highway towards St Cleer, then down the rough track to Fursdon at the foot of the moor. The clatter of the hooves at the approach to the farm gate brought a man to the door of the byre.

William Fursdon, still unmarried and now in his middle age, had over the years acquired a marked resemblance to the animals in his care. Although the morning sun was hot he wore a sheepskin vest over his homespun smock, and his bare feet were thrust into ill-fitting leather sandles. He peered at the visitors through long, unkempt hair, and made no attempt to approach them or learn their business.

Margaret had never met the man who would have been her brother-in-law, had she married John. She sniffed audibly, as if from her distance outside the farm gate she could detect the animal smell of this herdsman.

'Open the gate!' she commanded peremptorily. 'Then run and tell your mistress we are here.'

William remained where he was, and his attitude was sufficiently threatening to deter Margaret's escort from opening the gate themselves. To add to their discomfiture two huge hounds, as long-haired and dishevelled as their master, cantered into the yard from the orchard and stationed themselves on either side of him, their hackles raised and their heads swaying warily.

William measured the size of the intruders, and noted the two children. Then, turning on his heel to go back to his work in the byre he shouted, 'Bain't no one 'ome. Gone to Lanson.'

Margaret's heart plummeted; she had brought Lisette, and two panniers of personal belongings, with the intention of taking refuge at Fursdon with her daughter and son-in-law. Then she thought of her own son, John, who would either be here or near at hand, and her spirits revived.

'But Master Ayssheton, my son, is he here?'

William turned in the doorway.

'H'm, so you be Mistress Margaret?' He looked her up and down for a moment in insolent silence, then shrugged his shoulders and turned away again.

'Naw, he be gone too.'

He disappeared into the byre, slamming both upper and lower doors behind him.

Thomas slid off his horse and went to Margaret.

'Best be going home, mistress,' he said, a touch of sympathy colouring his normally toneless voice.

Margaret shook her head as she turned her horse away from Fursdon.

'No,' she declared, 'We ride on to Liskerret to find my son.'

The escorting farmers grumbled at this between themselves, for they were anxious to get back to their own work. Lisette begged to dismount from the hard saddle, while Beatty whispered a similar request to her grandfather, but Margaret ignored them all and put her horse to a steady trot westward towards Liskerret. Dutifully Thomas rode after her, Beatty almost reduced to tears as she bounced behind him. They had almost reached the town when they discovered that the escort had deserted, taking the pack mule with them.

Again Thomas's pleas that they give up and return to Calyngton fell on deaf ears. Margaret pressed on into the town and Thomas had perforce to follow her closely for fear of losing her too.

The market square was thronged, and a large crowd was gathered round the fountain, where a man in a tall hat was waving his arms and gesticulating excitedly. Finding her way blocked, Margaret called for passage, and as a man in the listening crowd moved reluctantly aside she enquired, 'What goes on?'

He looked at her in surprise.

'Have you not heard, mistress? The French have taken Fowy. The town is quite destroyed, not a house or a warehouse left standing.'

'Nay, that be not right,' a fat woman with a baby on her hip contradicted. 'They say that Mistress Treffry be beseiged in her house, that she has killed many Frenchies with boiling oil poured from her gate tower.'

'The second I could believe, but not the first!' said Margaret
scornfully. 'I have known Mistress Treffry; she is a brave woman
and a better soldier than many men. But indeed no marauding
band of Frenchmen could win their way into Fowy harbour to
reach her gate tower! Fowy is impregnable.'

Signalling to Thomas to follow her she pushed on through the
crowd, almost disappearing from sight as she headed down the
narrow street towards the western gate, laden mules and
donkeys eddying round her as their excited owners struggled
into the town.

What could she be thinking of? In his desperation Thomas
managed to get quite close behind her.

'Mistress, we go the wrong way,' he shouted. 'We must now
make a wide sweep southward to Menheniott to get to Calyngton.'

Margaret merely nodded in reply, then touched her horse to a
quicker trot as they left the town behind them. The road led
down a steep hill, and the crowd of travellers coming up to
Liskerret thinned gradually to a trickle.

At the bottom of the hill Margaret drew rein where a stretch
of common bordered a stream. She slipped to the ground and
lifted Lisette down, rubbing and cuddling her to reassure the
tired and tearful little girl. Thomas and Beatty dismounted
also, and Thomas led both horses to the stream in his usual
silence. Then he turned to face his mistress.

'What is this dance you are leading us?' he demanded angrily.
'We have lost our escort, we have lost your goods. We are far
from home, my girl and the infant are both tired and hungry,
and still you persist in travelling even further away from Theupath. If the French are at Fowy it is madness to be going this way
when all the world is fleeing inland.'

It was a rare outburst for Thomas, and Margaret looked at
him with interest. Then she said, smiling as if to reassure him,
'Let us find a cart for the children to ride in, it is not far now to
Polcarowe.'

Thomas's jaw dropped.

'Polcarowe? Where would that be?' he asked curtly. He had
never heard of the place.

'It was my home once, before – before I married Sir Nicholas.
It is now the property of Justice Prisot, who works with my

husband and knows us well. We will be welcome at Polcarowe
— and safe.'

'Safe from what, mistress?'

She did not answer. Instead she pointed down the valley at a
mill half hidden among the trees shrouding the river bank.

'They will have a cart there, and will be glad to hire it to us.'

The little party remounted — although Lisette could only be
persuaded to put her little legs over the harsh saddle by being
assured that this would be only a short ride. As they followed the
track down the valley Margaret explained to Thomas why
Polcarowe would be safe.

She was not at all frightened by the tale of the French invasion, for there had been many similar alarms in the past, and
all unwarranted because, as she laughingly explained, 'No
foreigner could force an entry into the harbour by reason of the
chain stretching from bank to bank between the blockhouses.'
If there had been some small skirmish or disturbance, as happened from time to time, it would not affect them at Polcarowe,
because it lay at some distance upstream and on the eastern
bank. The whole story, she declared, was just another wild
rumour which had upset the good burgesses of Liskerret.

Encouraged by her confident mood, Thomas asked again
what was the danger at home?

Margaret sagged visibly in her saddle, then with a great effort
said wearily, 'I am seeking refuge from the threats of Denis
Asshton.'

It was no more than he had expected. He nodded, and waited
for more, but at that moment they rounded the corner and
found themselves at the mill. No one was about, and there were
no replies to calls and knocks, even the miller's family was
obviously, and very unusually, away from home. There was a
strange air of silence about the place. Even more strange was the
sight of a cart in the yard, already part-loaded with sacks of
grain and with a mule standing sleepily in the shafts, as if abandoned at the point of departure.

Thomas scowled as he looked about him.

'There must be danger, folk have run away from here in
haste.'

'They will return before nightfall. Put my horse in the stable,
as a pledge, while we borrow this cart. Hurry, man!'

Still scowling, Thomas did as he was bid, then remounted his own horse and followed the cart as it rattled away down the rough track with Margaret at the reins and the two children nestled among the grain sacks. Further talk was impossible, all he could do was keep a wary eye open for signs of footpads – or perhaps of Frenchmen, although he was miserably aware that he was completely unequipped to defend the party against any sort of attack.

Apart from sheep and goats nibbling peacefully at the close cropped turf on the upland commons the whole countryside seemed deserted. Although it was still only mid-afternoon, stooks stood in half harvested fields of oats, and several haystacks were still without their protective cover of thatch. The farmsteads lay silent in the hollows, crouched low and still, as if huddling from an impending storm.

Thomas had just caught sight of a patch of blue sea in a cleft of the distant downs when the cart ahead of him suddenly swung to the right and disappeared down a narrow track between high hedgebanks. Anxiously he followed, and after many twists and turns in the road found the cart drawn up at a wide gateway flanked by ornamental granite posts.

'This is Polcarowe,' Margaret called cheerily to him, as she set off again, down a long straight avenue of elm trees. Thankfully Thomas observed buildings in the distance among the elms; here at last was food and shelter, and the chance for him to relax from his irksome stewardship of this madcap lady.

The cart rattled into the courtyard with Thomas close behind. Both came to an abrupt halt before a scene of devastation.

The house had been gutted by fire. It stood, gaunt and roofless, its windows blind holes in the smoke-blackened stonework, its great oak door charred and part burned, and hanging listlessly on its strap hinges.

Margaret sat motionless, stunned and beaten.

Beatty peeped up from her couch of grain.

'Where be this, granfer?'

A sudden buzz of sound startled Thomas, and he swung round in time to see a swarm of men burst from the stable on the far side of the yard. In less than a minute the little party was surrounded by the gang, all shouting threateningly and brandishing staves and pitchforks.

Thomas shouted back and swore at them, for he could make no sense of their threats. Surely they could not be fearing attack from one man, a woman and two children?

A crowd of women clustered at the open door of the stable, small children peeping from between their skirts. Thomas looked again at the men around him; they were obviously fishermen, some were farm hands, and these would be their families. Why had they taken refuge here, and who had set fire to the house? He shuddered with fright; the French must have reached Polcarowe after all. There was no safety here.

The noise quietened as another voice called for silence. A man came running from beyond the house, and as he called again Margaret suddenly lifted her head and came alive again. He pushed his way through to the centre of the group.

'Oh, Ned, Ned Palmer!' Margaret cried out in tremulous relief. 'What have they done to my house?'

'Why, Mistress Margaret! What unlikely cause has brought you to Polcarowe, and at this sad time?'

Making a great effort to speak calmly, for she could not weep before her old reeve and all these uncouth rustics, Margaret explained to Ned that they had hoped to find shelter at the home of Justice Prisot.

''Tis well you did not come yesternight, you would have been burned in your bed! Mercifully too, the judge is in London, and his household with him.'

'Then these blackguards—?' Margaret glanced angrily at the men, who had now dropped back to a respectful distance.

'Oh, no, mistress, 'twas the French invaders. These fishermen escaped up river when the French attacked the town — they say they came secretly over the headland at dead of night when all were abed, and the cries were terrible to hear as folk were slaughtered and their homes burned down.'

'But why, here?'

'They burned most of the boats, but a group of the villains saved one and came upstream in her. They found our quay — the one you built, mistress — the one,' he corrected himself hastily, 'Master Fursdon built — they were crazed with the excitement of making fire and destruction, they piled brushwood against the fine big window and set it alight, the thatch caught too, it was bone dry in this summer heat. We hid in the woods until they had gone, but it was too late to save the house. If the falling tide had not sent them scurrying back to the boat the stables and barns would have been destroyed too.'

Margaret sighed, and looked about her, at the ruin of her old home, a place which she had beautified, and loved; then she gazed at the range of farm buildings which John had designed for her and helped to build. But her thoughts were interrupted by a wail from Lisette, who had just awoken, hungry and aching and frightened at the strangeness of her surroundings. Beatty tried to hush her but the child only wailed more loudly and insistently. Her mother turned to Ned.

'Ned, we need shelter for the night, and food – if you have it.'

'Yes, mistress, there is food enough for all. But the only shelter not already occupied by these men and their families is a corner of the hayloft over the oxen.'

Wearily Margaret thanked him.

'We will go home on the morrow. There is nought else I can do.'

16

The moorland heights were lost in mist on a cheerless day in the late spring of 1458 when fifteen-year-old John Ayssheton walked from Liskerret to Calyngton to visit his mother.

The purpose of his visit was two-fold. Since Susannah's marriage he had spent much of his time at Fursdon with his namesake's family, and now he had been asked to bear the news to his mother that Susannah had at last given birth to a son. The story of the old romance and elopement was now common knowledge in the family, and John – the gentle, contemplative student, already aiming to take holy orders – was reckoned by the Fursdons to be the happiest messenger for this delicate mission.

But he also had news of his own for his mother. Through the good offices of his teacher, Master Knoll, the vicar of Liskerret, he was to go to the university at Oxford just as soon as his father's consent had been obtained. He knew that Nicholas had not been home for months, and he needed to find out where he could be found.

Deep in thought he ambled past Cadsonbury without noticing it, and was down the hill and over the new bridge before he realised how near he was to Theupath. So he sat himself down on the riverbank and contentedly watched the grey water rippling over the stones, crossing himself and saying a prayer for the souls of the two women who had perished near that spot eight years ago. As he moved on up the hill towards the town he thought to himself how fortunate his mother was, the only one of the three still alive and blessed with a husband, hearth and home.

He had turned into the lane running down to Theupath when he heard a horse approaching from the direction of the house. He stepped into a gateway to let it pass. It cantered by without slackening speed, and he caught only a glimpse of its rider. As he watched horse and rider disappear over the brow he wondered who the man could be and what there was about his receding figure which seemed somehow strangely familiar.

Theupath courtyard lay quiet and deserted, its cobbles shining as though polished by the damp air. By a sudden impulse John turned from the house door and crossed over to Mattie's cottage, flinging open the door as he had always done as a small boy with the expectant shout, 'Here I am, Mattie!'

Mattie was sitting before the fire with Lisette, roasting chestnuts.

'Oh, my Johnnie lad!' she cried, upsetting her stool as she scrambled to her feet, and holding out her arms to embrace him. They hugged and laughed as if John were still the little boy whom she had mothered in his childhood.

Lisette, on the other hand, saw a tall and dusty stranger in this brother whom she hardly remembered, and she studied him in grave silence from her stool at the far side of the hearth. At last she melted, and held out a blackened chestnut in her grubby hand. John took it, gravely thanking her.

''Tis the last of last winter's store,' she explained. 'The trees are even now in bloom again. Soon we will have more.'

'Sit you here awhile, Johnnie lad, while I go tell the mistress,' said Mattie, and slipped out of the door before he could protest that he would go with her. So he sat quietly by the fire for some little while, sharing Lisette's chestnuts and telling her in simple terms where he had been and what he had been doing.

At last Mattie returned.

'She was resting in her chamber — so overjoyed at my Johnnie's return that it took her some time to compose herself. But now, come quickly, she is impatient to embrace you.'

'Is my sister-in-law not in the house?' asked John as they left the cottage.

'Oh, that one!' replied Mattie scornfully. 'We see precious little of her! She spends all day walking the fields, or crouched in the little attic over her chamber, where she draws and paints. Beautiful pictures, they are, and most elegant lettering, but it is not seemly for one who should be mistress of the house to be thus occupied.'

They entered the hall just as Margaret came down the stairs from the gallery. There was a hesitation in her manner as she welcomed him home and sat with him on the settle by the window that made John feel awkwardly ill at ease in his own home. He had always been her favourite child, now he felt like a stranger who was intruding on her private affairs.

He felt suddenly acutely unhappy, and in his confusion blurted out his two items of news at once and without the gentle tact and preparation which he had planned. To his surprise Margaret merely nodded politely, as if neither the news of Susannah's baby nor John's departure for Oxford concerned her in the very least.

How his mother had changed! Did she not love them any more? Did she not feel any concern at all for their wellbeing?

Awkwardly he asked for news of his father. Margaret's face brightened momentarily as she drew from her pocket a crumpled piece of parchment. She smoothed it out on her knee, then handed it to John.

'It was written on the eve of the feast of St Mark, from his chambers at Serjeants' Inn. Read it, you will see that he writes that life in London is now more secure, and he hopes that he may return home during the dog days. Perhaps when he does I may be able to accompany him back to London for the Michaelmas term.' She dropped her voice almost to a whisper, 'I will feel safer there.'

John nodded in sympathy. Of course, his mother's odd behaviour was due to the wide-spread rumours of invasion by the French. It was less than a year since they had landed in Plymouth and Fowy and plundered both ports, burning houses, warehouses and ships and blowing up ammunition stores. But at that time there had also been riots in London against the authority of the inns of court, with chains across the streets and armed protesters everywhere. He had heard that even the river above London bridge had been full of barges carrying armed men. It sounded like revolution in the capital — but now his father was writing that life there was safe? He turned to the letter.

'Dearest heart, you are ever in my thoughts and my prayers. I long to be with you once more, and if my prayer is answered this may be now not so long distant. For, dear wife, *mirabile dictu*, there is now peace between our warring houses of Lancaster and York. My lord the archbishop of Canterbury has brought them together, and to demonstrate his success led them all in procession through the city. We gathered at St Thomas of Acons, and made obeisance as they passed along Chepe. The queen bowed haughtily, but my Lord of York who walked beside her raised his hat in smiling friendship. After them came Warwick and Exeter and the other nobles of both houses, two by two, as if old friends rather than old enemies. There is still no love there, but all are anxious that peace shall return to our land. So I pray to the Almighty that this may be achieved, so that you, my beloved one, may again rest always in my arms.'

'How deeply he still loves you!' commented John as he folded the parchment and handed it back to his mother. She nodded, and began to dab at her eyes with a small pocket handkerchief. John laid a comforting hand on her bowed shoulder as he continued, 'I must go to London to obtain father's consent for my studentship at Oxford. Come with me, mother, I will protect you on the journey and see you safely to my father.'

Margaret looked up at him in delight, but then suddenly turned away shaking her head.

'I am not yet strong enough for such a journey, my son. Go you alone, give my salutations to your father and tell him I long for his return to Theupath. Then I will go with him happily, where he will, even to the ends of the earth.'

He kissed her hand, secretly relieved at her decision. He was not at all sure of his ability to take himself to London in safety, even without the responsibility of a woman to protect.

He left the house and went over to the stables to find a horse for the journey. Thomas had just ridden in, and the sight of him astride the horse reminded John of the stranger he had seen in the lane.

'Was there another visitor this day?' he enquired. Thomas scowled at him, and nodded. 'A very elegant gentleman?' Another nod. 'He seemed familiar to me, who was he?' Thomas remained silent, but glanced uneasily at John.

John shrugged and went into the stable to find his favourite old mare to take him unspectacularly but safely on his journey, for he was not a good horseman. He was leading her out into the yard when Thomas suddenly spoke.

'The master should come home.'

'Oh?' asked John, surprised by this unexpected outburst. 'Why?'

'Denis Asshton is why,' replied Thomas. He spat in contempt on the cobbles, then added, 'And blackmail. He is blackmailing the mistress.'

Nicholas was in his chambers when John arrived, breathless and anxious, on a horse dripping with exhaustion. The judge was delighted to see his student son. The little boy of memory was now a fine young man as tall and as slim as he himself had been when he had ridden off to the French wars at much the same age.

But this young man was not light-hearted and adventurous as Nicholas had been, he seemed to have all the cares of the world on his shoulders. He barely allowed the minimal civilities of greetings before launching into a full account of his visit to Theupath.

Nicholas listened attentively. But at the mention of Denis Asshton he jumped to his feet with an oath and stood drumming his fingers angrily on the table behind him as John completed the sorry tale.

'I pressed Thomas and Mattie for all they could tell me,' said John, 'but all they know is that he has some hold over my mother, something which dates from the days when he was a guest in our house.'

'The devil! The devil incarnate! May the Lord rot his soul!'

John remained silent, a little eased in his mind now that he had passed this terrible problem to more experienced hands. His father would have the answer, and very probably have the wicked Denis clapped into gaol before more harm could be done.

Nicholas sat down by the window, and for a long while sat staring into the garden below, the garden where his wife years ago spent happy summer days with her children. John sat waiting, only dimly conscious of the London street noises stirring in his memory.

Away across the gardens and beyond the rooftops London life was rattling by on horses' hooves and iron-shod wheels. The melancholy cry of the chimney sweep was echoed and imitated by some jackdaws in the trees at the far end of the garden; then the sweeter, higher tones of a woman calling her wares reminded him sharply of the old days, when the call of the sweetmeats seller or the woman with a basket of poppets on her head would have the children begging excitedly for permission to go out into the street with a groat to buy sweets or toys.

His father's voice, stern and decisive, roused him.

'I will return to Cornwall immediately. Now, this very day. There is no time to waste. Pray God it be not already too late.'

'Shall I go with you?'

'No, my son. You have served me well, but your own future must be attended to as well. You will proceed to Oxford, as Master Knoll has requested. I will send him word from Theupath. Gwyllym will accompany you to Oxford and remain there with you until he has found and trained a younger man to be your personal servant. I will send him now to find a fresh horse for you, and muster my escort. We will ride together as far as Maidenhead.'

Nicholas made even better time on the westward journey than his son had done coming up to London. As a result, it was less than a week since Thomas's revelations to John when his master did just what he had asked by coming home.

Edward and Peg were seated at table when the clatter of nine horses trotting into the courtyard took Edward at a run to the house door to find out if the intruders were friend or foe. Used as he was to having his father's arrival announced by Gwyllym he was completely taken aback to find Nicholas already dismounted and approaching him.

'Your mother, where is she?' Nicholas demanded.

'She rests in her chamber, father. She prefers to take her meals there.' Edward shrugged his thin shoulders. 'Now that I am running the manor on your behalf she takes no interest in anyone. Sometimes I wonder if her mind has become unhinged.'

Nicholas brushed him aside and strode into the hall, where Peg hurriedly slipped from her stool and stood, awkwardly awaiting his orders.

Nicholas pushed aside the platters and manchets, propped himself, dusty and dishevelled as he was, on the edge of the table, and demanded of his son and daughter-in-law a full account of Margaret's behaviour and well-being. He found that they knew very little, and castigated them for paying so little attention to the true mistress of the house.

'Go send Thomas and Mattie to me, they have given more notice to their mistress's distress than her own kith and kin,' he said, striding over to the hearth and giving a small dead log an impatient kick with his boot.

Thomas and Mattie duly appeared and recounted all they knew about Denis Asshton's visits to Theupath. Edward was appalled when he discovered what had been going on under his very nose, but his complaints against Thomas for not reporting his suspicions were cut short by his father.

'I have sent word to the high sheriff that the escaped prisoner Denis Asshton is at large in this district. He will be mustering a force to seek this man out and recapture him. You, Edward, have been severely remiss in allowing the protective force to disperse. Send word to your portreeve for the court leet to be convened immediately and a strong body mustered to aid in the hunt.'

Edward shot out of the door like a hunted hare. Nicholas cast a brief disdainful glance at his daughter-in-law standing by the table, her gown stained with ochre, fruit juices and oils, then turned on his heels and climbed the stairs towards his wife's chamber.

Left alone, Peg fidgeted a few moments, then silently slipped away to the garret where she kept her paints and boards.

Upstairs, Margaret had been so taken by surprise by her husband's sudden arrival that she had no time to dissemble the joy and relief it brought, and she was soon in his arms, responding to his fondling caresses as a hungry child.

At last he put her from him and, holding her at arm's length, demanded, 'Can it be true that my wife is being blackmailed, and by Denis Asshton?'

He watched in consternation as her face crumpled from happiness to stark misery, she sank down on the edge of the feather bed and buried her face in the folds of her gown.

'Wife, what have you done? How could a scoundrel like Asshton find anything with which to blackmail you − you, my beloved wife of blameless character?'

He waited. Margaret sobbed quietly into her skirts.

'Come, tell me,' he said at last, very gently. 'You will find I can understand and help.'

She lifted her tear-stained face and peered up at him.

''Tis Lisette,' she whispered.

He thought he could not have heard aright. 'Lisette?' he repeated.

She nodded.

'What of Lisette?' Nicholas's tone had become impatient, almost rough.

'She is his child!'

He reeled back against the doorpost. For a while there was no sound in the room except for Margaret's sobbing, muffled by the gown which was again pressed against her face. Then the sound of deep, heavy breathing began, a slow, intermittent rhythm which grew in volume and frequency until suddenly Nicholas strode across to the bed, seized his wife by the shoulders and pulled her roughly to her feet.

'His child? His child?' he thundered. 'How? How? Tell me, you whore!'

A sudden change came over Margaret. She dashed her skirt across her face to dry her eyes, then drew herself up to her full height and stared coldly into her husband's outraged choleric face.

'You are no better than he!' she declared with biting scorn.

Nicholas blinked, let his hands fall to his side, and stepped back abashed.

'I will tell you how it happened,' she said in a small clear voice. 'It was after my Elizabeth died, Elizabeth the daughter whom you hardly acknowledged to exist. You were so taken up with affairs of the king's law that this new small person in your family meant nothing to you.'

He hung his head, remembering with shame that he had taken very little note of the child.

'When she died, he came to comfort me. I feared him, but he was very clever, and I was lulled into trusting him by his gentle solicitude and understanding. It was such a comfort to be no longer alone in my misery, and when he suggested that my husband did not care for me, while he did, it was a kind sort of oblivion to take solace in his arms.'

'How many times?' His voice croaked and he did not even raise his head.

'Once, my lord — at that time. Afterwards I hated it all, the memory of it haunted me, and when you came home and into my bed I could only think of him and that horrible time.'

'And since?'

She hesitated, and when she spoke again her voice was barely more than a whisper.

'Three times. This is his blackmail; I must submit to him, or my husband will be told that the little daughter he loves so well is a bastard and the child of his deadliest enemy.'

An anguished sigh told how this blow would always have struck home. They stood in silence, facing each other at a little distance, unable any longer to make physical contact to comfort each other.

There was a tap at the door, the latch lifted and a child's voice piped, 'Is my father there?'

Nicholas turned and charged through the partly open doorway, almost knocking Lisette off her feet.

How he got there he could never explain, even to himself. Afterwards he remembered blundering out of the house and over the cobbles to the lane, and he had dim memories of opening gates and of wandering aimlessly in the fields.

Then he was standing on the cliff edge looking down into the depths of the quarry on Balston down, pondering childishly what those stone age quarrymen had looked like who worked there aeons before his own father had taken stone for the building of Theupath. The greeny black water in the pit reminded him of the pit into which his own soul had dropped, and the impulse seized him to lose his miserable identity in that yawning blackness. Somehow he did not jump, but instead must have stumbled on down the slope of the grassy common, for when he came to in cold possession of all his faculties he found himself sitting on the grassy bank of the old henge at Castelwich.

He looked about him. What had brought him here? He had lost his wife, he had lost his child; what comfort could he expect from the spirits of past ages?

Lower down on the common a buzzard took to its wings, and he watched it emptily as it climbed circling to its hunting height. Then a familiar flat round place just peeping above the sloping downs caught his eye. He had not realised that Cadsonbury was visible from here; viewed from down in the river valley it was a majestic mountain, from Castelwich it looked more like a flat dish.

Another ancient habitation of past ages — Balston, Castelwich, Cadsonbury, what could it mean that at such a time of stress he had come here?

Exhausted from travel and emotional strain he laid his head on the soft smooth turf and drifted into sleep. Men in weird costumes danced around him — hunters, priests, farmers wrapped in sheepskin and others stark naked brandishing little stone axes, followed by French soldiers, Cornish sailors, serjeants-at-law, all prancing and dancing, and each in turn bending close to him and leering knowingly into his face. They began to chant some devilish incantation which he could not follow, until one of the lawmen stooped over him to enunciate in the crystal tones of Sir John Fortescue, 'We are all the same, you know, from the beginning of time.' There was a great roar of laughter, then they all turned round to applaud noisily a new arrival at their dance. Nicholas strained to see who it could be, as the chanting grew louder and the dancing wilder. Suddenly there swam into his view a man who looked just like himself, except that he did not wear the coif and his dark curls had no touch of age in them. He could not see the man's face but he knew who it was; the man danced and twirled, and as the

refrain came again — 'We are all the same' — turned and
grinned wickedly at him. It was Denis Asshton.

He awoke, cold and shivering, his body aching with fatigue
and his shirt wringing wet with perspiration. But in a strange
way he felt mentally refreshed. The mists of misery and uncertainty had cleared from his mind and he knew exactly what
he was to do.

He got to his feet, slipped off his gown to let the sun dry his
shirt, then unbuttoning the coif, mopped his face with it and
ran his fingers through his iron-grey curls.

The breeze had dropped and the air was very still and warm,
lightly scented with furze blossom. He heard the distant cry of
the curlew, and then saw a blackbird eyeing him inquisitively
from the top of a hedgebank. His ghosts had all disappeared.

He breathed in deeply, and stretched expansively, then
laughed to see the blackbird flutter away in panic. It was good
to be alive, he must return instantly and share this wonderful
sense of well-being with his wife.

What right had he to demand the utmost excellence and
purity from his wife, when it was he himself who had first
seduced her from the path of honour? He would beg her forgiveness now. The thought warmed his heart.

And Lisette? He was gathering up his discarded garments
when the thought of her made him pause, momentarily; then he
slung the gown over his shoulder, stuffed the soiled coif inside
his shirt and began to trudge up the steep slope of Balston
down. She was his daughter, whether or not she was his by birth.
He could have sired her; perhaps Margaret was mistaken and he
was indeed her father? In any case, doubt as to her parentage
must not cloud his deep and caring love for her, and he would
challenge Denis Asshton in the courts if necessary. The thought
of Denis brought back to his mind the strange dream, and in
spite of himself he glanced around nervously, half expecting to
see that hated face leering at him from a furze bush.

He had almost reached the brow of the hill when the sound of
distant voices broke the silence. He stopped to listen. They were
cries of alarm and they came from the direction of Theupath.
Taking to his heels he dashed up the hill, noticing as he ran that
a thin wisp of smoke had appeared above the horizon, spiralling
into the air and thickening rapidly. There were more shouts,

and then the scream of a frightened woman. He ran on desperately, only pausing an instant at the crest of the hill to confirm what he had already guessed: it was a fire, Theupath itself was ablaze.

So Denis had been not just a ghost; he had been here in person, seen Nicholas asleep and slipped off to Theupath to destroy his home and abduct his wife and child! Or perhaps he had murdered them? A sob caught at Nicholas's throat as he raced on down the hill, scrambling over hedges and hurdles and mindless of his judge's gown left festooned on a furze bush where it had caught in passing.

He reached the lane at last, almost falling in his haste and the heavy weariness of his legs, and gasping for breath as his lungs sent a warning taste of blood into the back of his throat. Bitterly he regretted the loss of physique which forty years ago would have carried him swiftly and effortlessly over far greater distances than this.

He paused to catch his breath, gazing in horrified fascination at the thick clouds of brown, grey and black smoke jostling and fussing their way into the sky from the house roof, just visible now where the lane dipped ahead of him. As he staggered on, a series of rapid explosions stopped him in his tracks, and he stood, rooted to the spot, as the lovely Delabole roof slates burst apart, their fragments flying in all directions and leaving a great gaping hole in the roof through which hell's inferno came belching forth. Blindly he ran on, sobbing and gasping as he thought of Margaret trapped in her chamber in that blazing furnace.

At last he came through the gateway into the courtyard, where men were dashing to and fro with buckets and ladders in a confused attempt to stem the blaze. No one noticed Nicholas as he clung for a moment, exhausted, to the open doorway of the linhay, searching for his wife, his son, or some member of his household.

Richard Chyket came running from the chapel path, trying to move smoothly so that the water in his bucket would not slop out. He handed it to one of the men tackling the fire and picked up another bucket. How futile, thought Nicholas as he watched; a one-armed man having to carry water a furlong or more from the spring, one bucket at a time! What chance was there of saving the house or the folk inside it?

He made a great effort and shouted. Richard turned, startled
at the sound of his name, then ran towards him, calling to the
others, 'He's safe, the judge is here!'

Nicholas was still supporting himself against the doorpost,
panting heavily and wincing with pain as sharp needles stabbed
him behind the ribs. He gulped some air and managed to say,
'Margaret?', before doubling up with pain.

'She's safe, my friend, and the little one too – and even that
wretch my daughter Peg. They are all with Mattie in the cottage, and we have soaked the roof with water to prevent the fire
spreading. But we were worried about you – where have you
been?'

He whistled in surprise at the judge's strange appearance, but
seeing his friend's extreme exhaustion moved to his assistance.

'You have hurried faster than is good for you at your age.
Come, let me help you to the cottage.'

Taking him gently by the arm he steered him past the confusion of firefighters to the little cottage on the far side of the
yard.

'All's well, sweet Margaret,' he called, pushing open the door
and assisting Nicholas into the dim interior. 'Not a soul lost in
this disaster. Even the master of the household safe – although
the good Lord alone knows what he has been doing!'

Nicholas stood, panting, and struggling to adjust his eyes to
the dark little room. Another needle of pain shot through him
and he gasped. Over by the window someone was sobbing and
moaning.

'Quiet, you slut!' commanded Richard sternly.

Nicholas felt he was drowning in weariness. But he must
make a final effort to find Margaret, make sure she was indeed
safe as incredibly seemed to be the case, beg her forgiveness and
tell her how much he still loved her.

'Margaret, my love?' he whispered hoarsely. There was a
rustle by the unlighted hearth, and her soft voice answered
timidly, 'Here, my lord.'

Another stab of pain struck him in the chest as he took the
two steps to reach his wife. He stooped to kiss her hand but
instead crumpled into a heap unconscious at her feet.

It was several days before Nicholas awoke from what his family had feared might be a death trance. He had been carried carefully to Chykets and laid in the big feather bed which had been Richard and Mary's pride and joy when they were first married. There he had been tended and watched over anxiously by his wife and Richard's elder daughter Mimi, with Lisette skipping in with her favourite poppet from time to time to see if her father had 'waked yet'. And it was Lisette whom he first saw when he opened his eyes and tried to identify the strange but vaguely familiar surroundings.

She was sitting on the edge of the bed, talking earnestly to her poppet and jumping it up and down in a form of dance. Sensing she was being watched, she looked up, her little face under its round white cap breaking into a beam of delight when she found him at last awake.

'Daughter!' Nicholas whispered, making an effort to reach out towards her with the arm which lay on the coverlet. It lay helplessly still, and the effort left him exhausted.

Lisette slipped off the bed and ran to the door. His mind swam in a sea of confusion, in which the sound of a woman's scream and the shouts of men mingled with the little girl's excited call: 'He's waked, he's waked!' He closed his eyes and drifted away again.

A gentle hand caressed his brow. He opened his eyes to see, not Lisette, but Margaret bending over him. He managed to smile with his eyes, but half his mouth refused, like his arm, to move. Margaret lifted the useless hand and cosseted it in both hers, her eyes brimming with tenderness as they scanned every feature of the face on the feather pillow. A wave of contentment washed over him and through his whole being, thoughts fighting for recognition in his awakening brain melted like snow in summer, leaving only the deep sense of security of a baby in its mother's arms. He slept peacefully.

It was dark when he awoke again, and the room was warm with firelight and candle shadows. This time he was fully himself, even if weak and helpless; he looked around as far as he could turn his head, and recognised the room. A few days ago — or was it a lifetime since? — he had talked in this room with Richard after the requiem mass for Mary. God rest her soul, this was Mary's bed, and here was Richard, still sitting on the little stool with her shawl across his knees!

'Richard?'

The man on the stool started when he heard the familiar voice, weak but recognisably that of Justice Ayssheton. He had been indulging in some nostalgic thoughts about Mary and their happy early days together, but the sound of his name broke the dream. Quickly he crossed to the bed to attend to the invalid.

'Richard, why am I here?'

'Well — of course, you remember? The house was totally destroyed in the fire.'

'Ah, the fire. . . . My wife and daughter are both safe, I have seen them.'

'Yes, they are well.'

'Was no one hurt?'

'Only your goodself. You exhausted yourself running from some great distance, forgetful that you are an old man of sixty summers and no longer a spry young boy!'

'Ah yes, I remember.' The afternoon's events came flooding back to him, his sense of security slipped away and he was once more pounding up Balston Down as a woman screamed and smoke belched from Theupath roof.

Richard noticed his agitation. Laying a comforting hand on his shoulder he said quietly, 'All is now well, my friend, do not upset yourself.'

'Denis Asshton? Have they caught the scoundrel and punished him for — for burning my house?'

'Well, that is two stories, in reply to your one question.' Richard seated himself on the bed and considered his reply, plucking at some flowers embroidered on the bed cover.

'Richard! Is he taken yet?'

Richard looked up at his friend in obvious relief.

'Oh no,' he replied, 'but I had word this day that he had been seen boarding a Genoese carrack in Plymouth harbour. The vessel was bound for Lisbon and Venice, and sailed two days since on the morning tide. He will not be back to trouble you for many moons — perhaps never, if he has sense, for the Bodmyn beadle still seeks him.'

'I would see him hang for harming my family—' Nicholas paused, wondering how much Richard knew, then '—and for burning down my house,' he finished lamely.

'Well, that is the other story.' Richard again plucked at the coverlet as he plucked up the courage to confess. At last he said, ruefully, 'It was not Denis Asshton who set fire to Theupath. Would that it had been him! No, it was my foolish, useless daughter, your Edward's wife, Peg. The stupid wench was so careless with her oils and colours that when she spilled some oil on the floor she merely trod it in with more rushes, then was so absorbed with her painting that she did not even notice a candle which fell from its sconce on to the floor.'

So it was not Denis! The relief was so tremendous that Nicholas wanted to laugh. He could only manage a croaking chuckle, but he smiled crookedly as he whispered, 'Silly wench!'

'Aye, silly wench,' agreed Richard. 'The guilt of it will stay with her for years, and I doubt she will ever paint another picture. She did have the sense to cry out a warning when she discovered the fire, and she tells me she ran from room to room to ensure that everyone had escaped before she herself left the house. Now she mopes in a corner of the big barn, where Edward has made space for them to sleep. They are both distraught, for they feared Peg had caused your death.'

The door opened and Margaret entered quietly. As Richard rose to go Nicholas spoke clearly in his normal rich tone.

'Tell them both that I will soon be well — for I have the love and care of my beloved wife to give me strength.'

Making a great effort he reached out towards Margaret with both arms, and both arms responded to his determination. Margaret ran to him.

Epilogue

On a summer's day in the sixth year of the reign of the fourth Edward 'after the conquest', two old men stood admiring a fine tomb in the chancel floor of the church at Calyngton. Both related by marriage to the occupants of the tomb, they also had a lifetime of friendship, tragedy and happiness to reflect on. It was in a sense their personal leavetaking of Nicholas and Margaret Ayssheton, and they had paid their respects by providing a magnificent brass memorial set into the top of the tomb.

''Tis a fair likeness,' said John Fursdon, moving to the foot of the tomb to look at the engraved brass figures in better perspective.

'I hope you approve of the tribute I composed. Let me translate it for you.'

John nodded, for he knew no Latin. He stood back and listened as Richard Chyket recited from memory the poem which he had composed in English and given to the rector for translation into Latin. At the end he commented quietly, 'You have him well described. I like best the line about the common people.'

'"The common people deemed him just, compassionate and kind",' quoted Richard. 'Especially in his last years, when he lived with us and among us, and every tenant knew that he would have a fair hearing from the lord of the manor, and likely as not help with goods and money as well.'

'Amazing how long he survived after that illness.'

'That was Margaret's devoted nursing of him. You might say that the tables were turned, when for two years he was entirely dependent on her. I believe that they learned to know each other then with a deeper understanding than they ever had time to do before — with all that coming and going on the king's business.'

'And his illness kept him safe, and his estates too. Just think,

Richard, what a parlous state he would have found himself in when Edward of York took the throne, if he had been fit enough to serve at the inquisition the previous year. Remember? "The goods and chattels Richard Duke of York and other rebels had in Cornwall on Friday the eve of St Edward the King and Confessor".'

Richard laughed. 'What a memory you have, John, for detail! Yes, the good Lord protected him from certain attainder by keeping him weak and ill at home at a time when his oath of allegiance to King Henry would have surely ruined him.'

They were silent for a few moments, each man thinking his own thoughts, then as by mutual consent turned away and stepped down into the nave.

Glancing back over his shoulder Richard commented, "Twas sad that Margaret took ill and died before Nicholas.'

'It was to him the end of his own life. He was heartbroken, and lost, without her. Even his beloved and devoted Lisette could not keep him from simply fading away. I believe that Margaret was to him the sole reason for his own existence, from the time when he stole her from me. Even the king's law was less important.'

They had emerged from the cool shadows of the church into the porch. John sat himself down on the coffin ledge and looked out into the busy market square.

'Let us wait here,' he suggested.

'I heard rumours of Denis Asshton when I last travelled over to Dartmouth,' said Richard, taking his seat beside him. John shot him an angry glance, for his loyalty allowed no mention of this scoundrel who had done such harm to his dearest friends.

Unabashed, Richard prattled on.

'I talked with a sailor in the tavern who told me a man calling himself Sir Denis Ayssheton took ship in his carrack from Plymouth seven years ago, on the very day that my stupid Peg set fire to the house with her paints. The man claimed to be a captain in the Duke of York's army escaping from certain death at the hands of my Lord Somerset. They thought it odd that he did not ask to be landed in Brittany, but stayed aboard until the vessel reached Genoa; then slipped ashore at night without leaving any payment for his passage. The carrack did not have more cargo for Genoa until last year, when the captain made determined inquiries for his defaulting passenger — only to find that he had been impressed for service in the fleet, and his ship had been taken by the Barbary pirates.' He threw back his head and laughed heartily. 'What say you, John, to such just tribulation?'

John made no reply, although he relaxed in noticeable relief. Richard shuffled his feet in irritation at the lack of response to his news, and stood up to survey the market scene.

'Here they come, at last!' he cried, and John jumped to his feet and stood beside him. 'How like women! They loiter to gossip with all and sundry, leaving the old men to await their pleasure!'

Then he lowered his voice and said, in a confidential tone, 'But see, John, how like their parents they both are! Your Susannah, with that lovely smile, and the auburn hair peeping from her hat − she even moves just as her mother did. And as for that dark beauty, the Mistress Lisette—' he broke off, sighing as one appreciating a splendid portrait, and the two men watched in silence as a woman and a tall young girl came slowly along the street.

'How like her father she is,' Richard continued at last, almost under his breath. 'That splendid lissom figure, those dark aristocratic features, that smile of fun and understanding − how it takes me back to the days of our youth! If you dressed her in boy's clothes you would swear she was the boy Nicholas − she could be no other man's daughter.'

'You speak truly,' John agreed.

'So we have bade our farewells to Nicholas and Margaret, may the Lord bless them for evermore. But in their daughters they live with us still. Come, John, let us join them.'

The two men left the shelter of the church and walked slowly in the baking sunshine across the market square towards Susannah and Lisette.